monsoonbooks

CHASING THE DRAG

John D. Greenwood was bo⋯ ⋯and educated at the Universities of Edinburgh and Oxford. He is currently a professor at the City University of New York Graduate Center, where he specializes in the history of psychology. He is the author of seven books and numerous academic papers.

He was a lecturer in the department of philosophy at the National University of Singapore from 1983-1986, when he first fell in love with Singapore, her people and her history. He returned as senior visiting scholar in 1999-2000 and as visiting professor in 2008-2009. He considers NUS to be his second academic home. He also returns regularly to Singapore to visit old friends and old haunts, and considers a trip to Pulau Ubin followed by chilli or pepper crab in the evening at Changi Village to be a perfect day.

He lives in Richmond, Virginia, USA.

'Brimming with memorable characters, this colourful reimagining of the early history of Singapore ... brings the intrigues, personality clashes and violence of the era vividly to life.'

Tim Hannigan (author of *Raffles and the British Invasion of Java*) on *Forbidden Hill* (Singapore Saga, Vol. 1)

CHASING THE DRAGON

SINGAPORE SAGA, VOL. 2

JOHN D. GREENWOOD

monsoon

monsoonbooks

First published in 2019
by Monsoon Books Ltd
www.monsoonbooks.co.uk

No.1 Duke of Windsor Suite, Burrough Court,
Burrough on the Hill, Leicestershire LE14 2QS, UK

ISBN (paperback): 9781912049202
ISBN (ebook): 9781912049219

Cover design by Cover Kitchen.

A Cataloguing-in-Publication data record is available from the British
Library.

Printed and bound in Great Britain by Clays Ltd, Elcograf S.p.A.
21 20 19   1 2 3 4

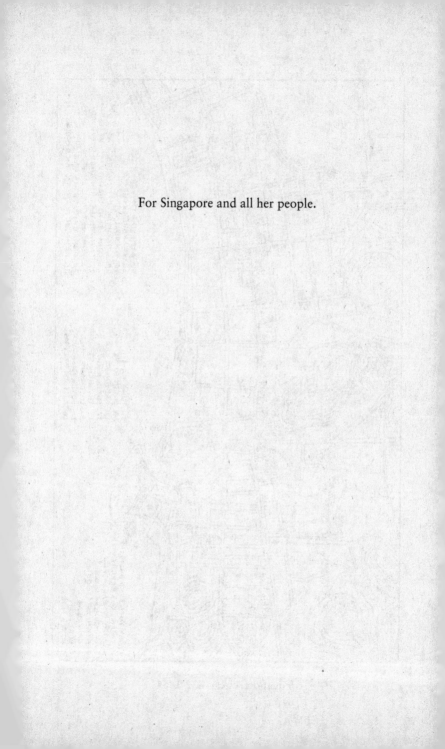

For Singapore and all her people.

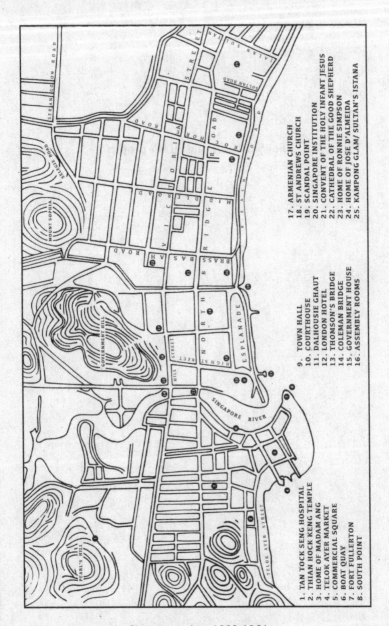

1. TAN TOCK SENG HOSPITAL
2. THIAN HOCK KENG TEMPLE
3. HOME OF MADAM ANG
4. TELOK AYER MARKET
5. COMMERCIAL SQUARE
6. BOAT QUAY
7. FORT FULLERTON
8. SOUTH POINT

9. TOWN HALL
10. COURTHOUSE
11. DALHOUSIE GHAUT
12. LONDON HOTEL
13. THOMSON'S BRIDGE
14. COLEMAN BRIDGE
15. GOVERNMENT HOUSE
16. ASSEMBLY ROOMS

17. ARMENIAN CHURCH
18. ST ANDREWS CHURCH
19. SCANDAL POINT
20. SINGAPORE INSTITUTION
21. CONVENT OF THE HOLY INFANT JESUS
22. CATHEDRAL OF THE GOOD SHEPHERD
23. HOME OF RONNIE SIMPSON
24. HOME OF JOSE D'ALMEIDA
25. KAMPONG GLAM/ SULTAN'S ISTANA

Singapore, circa 1832-1854

Acknowledgements

Chasing the Dragon is the second volume of Singapore Saga, a series of historical fiction about the early development of Singapore. Once again, I am indebted to a number of people and institutions for their help and support in producing this work.

Thanks again to Donald McDermid for giving me the original idea for a historical novel about early Singapore; to my wife Shelagh for supporting my year-long sojourn to Singapore to complete the original manuscript; to Arne Adland and Stella Fogg for critiquing the original very long manuscript; to the late Beverly Swerling for persuading me to reduce that manuscript to three shorter novels, of which *Chasing the Dragon* is the second (and *Forbidden Hill* the first); to the National University of Singapore for providing me with the opportunity to spend 2008-2009 as visiting professor in Singapore, enabling me to complete most of my research for the book; and to the staff at the circulation desk of the NUS library for tracking down microfiche copies of the early Singapore newspapers, such as the *Singapore Chronicle*, the *Singapore Free Press*, and *The Straits Times* and *Singapore Journal of Commerce*. Thanks also to Arnie Adland (again), my wife Shelagh, Sai Ying Ng and Alex Mendez for proofreading *Chasing the Dragon*, and to my daughter Holly for creating the map of Singapore.

Like the early newspapers, many of the books that I read while researching the novel provided the germ of plotlines that found their way into *Forbidden Hill* and *Chasing the Dragon*. For *Chasing the Dragon*, a number of these deserve special mention. Charles Burton Buckley's *An Anecdotal History of Old Times* in Singapore

(Fraser and Neave, 1902) and Walter Makepeace, Gilbert E. Brooke and Roland St John Braddell's *One Hundred Years of Singapore* (John Murray, 1921) suggested some plotlines while also providing invaluable checks on my historical time line. The narrative of Duncan Simpson's expeditions with James Brooke against the Borneo pirates (and the story of James Brooke himself) owes a great deal to Henry Keppel's *The Expedition to Borneo of HMS Dido for the Suppression of Piracy*, with extracts from the *Journal of James Brooke, Esq.* (Harper and Brothers, 1846) and Nigel Barley's *White Rajah: A Biography of Sir James Brooke* (Little, Brown, 2002). The historical background to the story of Hong Xiuquan, the Taiping Rebellion and the first Opium War is based upon Jonathan Spence's *God's Chinese Son: The Taiping Heavenly Kingdom of Hong Xiuquan* (Norton, 1996), Rayne Kruger's *All Under Heaven: A Complete History of China* (John Wiley, 2003), Hunt Janin's *The India-China Opium Trade in the Nineteenth Century* (McFarland & Co, 1999) and Saul David's *Victoria's Wars: The Rise of Empire* (Viking, 2006). Background material for the tale of the were-tiger is drawn from Hugh Charles Clifford's *In Court and Kampung* (Grant Richards, 1897); for the tale of the bomoh from R. O. Winstedt's *Shaman, Saiva, and Sufi: A Study of the Evolution of Malay Magic* (Constable & Co, 1925); for the story of Mother Mathilde and the Convent of the Holy Infant Jesus from Lily Kong, Low Soon Ai, and Jacqueline Yip's *Convent Chronicles: History of a Pioneer Mission School for Girls in Singapore* (Armour, 1994). For explication of the intricacies of the relations between the Chinese secret societies at the time of the novel I am indebted to Lee Poh Ping and Wan Ping's *Chinese Society in Nineteenth Century Singapore* (Oxford University Press, 1978).

I have, once again, done my best to maintain historical accuracy with respect to the real characters and episodes, to the best of my knowledge and ability, with only a few minor exceptions concerning a couple of dates to facilitate the continuity of plotlines. Some of the readers of *Forbidden Hill* told me they had difficulty distinguishing the real characters from the fictional, which I take as a compliment of sorts. I hope readers of *Chasing the Dragon* find them all engaging.

John D Greenwood

PROLOGUE

1834

Tan Poh Neo sat by the upper window of her parents' shophouse at Telok Ayer, looking out at the people going about their business below. A Chinese merchant on his way to work; a hawker carrying his pots and pans on a pole across his shoulders, looking for a place to set up a temporary stall; a tall Kling [i] woman in a red sari, moving with quiet grace across the road, weaving between the puddles left behind by the rain. Poh Neo's grandmother was playing cherki [ii] with her Bibik [iii] friends downstairs in the front room, the sound of their laughter and the clacking of the cherki cards drifting upstairs. Poh Neo was excited and sad. Tomorrow was her twelfth birthday, when she would enter the world of womanhood. She would learn how to cook, sew and embroider, to conduct herself like a lady and to manage a household in preparation for her future role as wife and mother. Unusually for a Peranakan Chinese,[1] Poh Neo's father had also arranged to have his daughter tutored in arithmetic and English, since he thought these would be useful skills for a wife to have, assuming her husband would be a merchant or clerk working for a British company in Singapore. She was excited about the forthcoming elevation of her social status, which marked the beginning of the long prelude to her own marriage.

---

i Indian.
ii Peranakan card game.
iii Elderly Peranakan woman.

Yet she was also sad, because after the day was ended she could no longer play with her friends in the garden or travel in an open carriage in the streets. There would be no more games of catch or hide and seek, of marbles, congkak,[iv] or masak-masak,[v] no more days of flying kites with other boys and girls along the seafront. From tomorrow, she would be confined to the house and would only be allowed to speak to the members of her own household. If for any reason she had to venture out of the house, she would be transported on a redi, [vi] hidden beneath a heavy sackcloth suspended from the wooden poles borne by two attendants.

She heard her mother calling and went below to help her prepare the feast for her birthday celebration. The next day I get to see the whole world again will be my wedding day, she thought to herself. Already she longed for the freedom it would bring.

* * *

Alexander Guthrie and Tan Hong Chuan had tiffin together at John Francis' Refreshment Room and Billiard Hall in Commercial Square.[vii] After they had dined and discussed their business, Guthrie returned to his office, where he read the shipping reports and had a cup of tea. Tan Hong Chuan returned to his office, where he read the shipping reports and smoked an opium pipe. Tea and opium – the godowns [viii] along Boat Quay were full of tea and opium. It was the foundation of the China trade and the commercial success of Singapore.

---

iv A mancala board game.
v A child's game of cooking using miniature kitchen utensils. 'Masak-masak' means 'cook-cook' in Malay.
vi 'Modesty board'.
vii Open space of land behind the godowns on Boat Quay. Present day Raffles Place.
viii Warehouse or other storage space, usually on a dockside.

The East India Company's trade with China was originally based upon the export of British woollen goods and the import of Chinese silk, but all that had changed when the British acquired their habit of drinking tea. Chinese green tea had been imported as a medicine and *digestif* since the seventeenth century, and became fashionable among the gentry when Samuel Pepys, the famous diarist, gave his stamp of approval. It had remained an expensive indulgence of the upper classes until the early eighteenth century, when demand was stimulated by the importation of cheap sugar from the West Indies. When the Company began to import cheaper Chinese Bohea tea, [ix] stimulating demand further, the British collectively embraced tea drinking as the most pleasing means of imbibing sugar, and never looked back. They also developed a taste for Chinese porcelain, which conveniently provided the necessary ballast for the Company ships, as well as aesthetically pleasing crockery in which to brew and dispense the rich brown liquid.

The tea trade increased almost fifty-fold between 1720 and 1770, from the importation of around two hundred thousand pounds per annum to close to nine million pounds per annum, providing windfall profits to the British Treasury, which shrewdly put a tax on it. By the 1820s, imports had reached thirty million pounds per annum, with taxes on tea making up ten percent of British government revenues. Yet there was also a major downside to the tea trade. The Chinese had very little interest in exported British woollen goods, which became uncompetitive with local products after China imposed trade restrictions in the eighteenth century, or European goods in general, with the exception of mechanical curios, such as automata in animal or human form. The increasing British demand for tea had to be met with increasingly large shipments of silver, which put a huge drain on the financial reserves of the Company and the British treasury.

---

ix Black tea.

Then in the early eighteenth century the Company found a commodity that enabled them to reverse the flow of silver. This was Indian opium, which was produced under a British monopoly in Bengal and Malwa. British exportation of opium to China had gradually risen throughout the eighteenth century, from about two hundred chests in 1730 to around four thousand chests in 1790. Then it expanded rapidly at the beginning of the nineteenth century, rising from around ten thousand chests in the 1820s to over thirty thousand in the 1830s.

In a series of Imperial edicts dating from the early eighteenth century, the Chinese had declared the use, cultivation and importation of opium illegal and subject to prosecution, but European, American, Parsee and Jewish merchants, who bribed the customs officials and merchants at Canton, continued the trade illegally. By the early nineteenth century, they had introduced a 'corruption fund', with a levy of forty dollars on each chest of opium to maintain their elaborate network of 'blind-eye' officials. Their fast clippers and small craft, known as sandhoppers and crawling dragons, ferried the opium up and down the Chinese coast and inland along the minor rivers. European and American merchants such as Jardine, Matheson and Co, Dent and Co, and Russell and Co reaped huge profits, as did the British government, which – notwithstanding an anti-opium lobby and a parliamentary inquiry – was only too aware that it depended on the tax revenue from the opium trade to cover its tea imports and Indian deficits.

Then the river of silver that had flowed eastward to China began to flow westward to Great Britain. China went from a twenty-six-million-dollar surplus in her trade with Britain in 1810 to a thirty-six-million-dollar deficit in 1830. This greatly alarmed the Emperor Tao Kwang, for it created such a drain on the economy that one of his advisors presciently predicted that 'if we continue to allow this trade to flourish, in a few dozen years, we will find ourselves not only with no soldiers to resist the enemy, but also with no money to equip the army.' At the same time, many of his traditional Confucian mandarins condemned the immorality of opium smoking and warned the Emperor of the need to address the growing problem of opium addiction, which was said to afflict some ten million Chinese, from the lowliest labourers to the highest scholars and ministers.

In the 1830s foreign trade with China was confined to the mouth of the Pearl River. Trading vessels were detained at Macau, the Portuguese occupied island at the mouth of the river, while contracts were negotiated with the foreign merchants, who occupied assigned factories on the Canton waterfront, outside of the city wall. When contracts were agreed, the European or American ships were first measured and taxed by the custom officials, then allowed to proceed to the main port of Whampoa to unload their goods. The conditions of trade and factory occupation were rigidly regulated. The foreigners were only allowed to occupy the factories during the trading season, which ran from October to May, and could not communicate directly with the Hoppo, the Superintendent of Maritime Customs: all business had to be conducted though the licensed Chinese merchants or Hongs, known collectively as the Cohong. No women or firearms were allowed in the factories; warships were not allowed to enter the Bogue, the narrow strait leading to the harbour approaches to Canton; and all trading ships were searched while they were detained at Macau. The representatives of the trading houses were confined to an area within one hundred yards of the gates of their factories; except that on the eighth, eighteenth and twenty-eighth days of the moon the 'foreign barbarians' were allowed out to visit the Flower Gardens and the Honam joss-house, so long as their parties were confined to less than ten members.

Prostitutes plied their trade to sailors of all nationalities from the gaily painted junks anchored along the length and breadth of the river. Meanwhile, the British, American, Dutch, French, Spanish, Austrian, Danish, Swedish and Greek merchants lived in the lap of luxury in their gated brick houses and godowns, with their Chinese cooks and servants, their fine porcelain and silver, and their well-stocked wine cellars and stores of cheese, ham and fine French brandy and malt whisky. Their wives and families lived in luxurious homes on the shorefront of Macau, where the merchants retired to join them during the summer months when trade was suspended. They were making undreamt of sums of money, but they were also champing at the bit, for they knew that they had scarcely begun to tap the trading potential of the Celestial Kingdom. With the support of their governments, they wrote memorials petitioning the Emperor Tao Kwang to open more ports to European trade. As did the manufacturers and merchants of Manchester and Liverpool, who were desperate to extend the products of the industrial revolution to world markets.

PART ONE

'WHIT WE NEED
IS A WAR'

1834 – 1842

1

1834

When the East India Company lost its monopoly on the China trade in 1833, the British government sent out Lord John William Napier as Chief Superintendent of the British merchants in Canton. Napier's primary mission was to supervise the Canton trade, but it was also hoped that through careful negotiation he might in due course be able to establish diplomatic relations with China, which the British government had been trying to achieve for the last century. Napier, a former Royal Navy captain who had served with Nelson at Trafalgar, saw no reason for delay. After depositing his wife and children at Macau in July 1834, he promptly sailed up the River Pearl in the cutter *Louisa*. When he reached Canton, he dispatched a letter requesting an audience with the Viceroy Lu Kun.

Napier was a proud Scot, but he was no diplomat. He badly misjudged the Chinese, who barely tolerated the European trade, and did so only because of the extensive bribery and corruption that sustained the opium trade and permeated every layer of government administration. The Chinese believed that their Heavenly Middle Kingdom was located under the shadow of the circular Heaven, at the centre of the square Earth, with the Emperor at the centre of the Heavenly Middle Kingdom – the Lord of All Under Heaven. The Emperor and his mandarins were on a higher level than the 'foreign barbarians' who dwelt outside the circular shadow of Heaven, at the outer corners of the Earth, and who were dependent upon them. They believed that the barbarians of Great Britain depended on Chinese tea and rhubarb to keep them alive, to alleviate their chronic constipation brought on by their indulgent use of milk and cream. Given their self-sufficient economy and sense of their own superiority, the Chinese had no interest in developing diplomatic relations with the British government, and for the Viceroy Lu Kun to meet with a representative of the barbarian traders would be a serious breach of protocol. It had long been established that all communications from the foreign Canton traders and their representatives had to be delivered through the Cohong merchants, who were the only Chinese who were allowed by law to talk with the barbarians.

The viceroy refused Napier's request for a meeting and returned his letter. Lu Kun then ordered the Cohong merchants to suspend trade with the European and American merchants, and to instruct Napier to return to Macao, where he was to seek formal permission to enter the Pearl River before conducting negotiations through the Cohong merchants. Napier was affronted by this action. He responded by bringing up the armed frigates HMS *Andromache* and HMS *Imogene* from Macao to force the viceroy's hand, but soon found his ships blockaded by the Qing navy. Before he could send another letter to the viceroy demanding an audience, he developed malarial fever and was forced to ask the European merchants to negotiate the lifting of the blockade through the Cohong merchants, so that he could return to Macao to receive medical attention. Viceroy Lu Kun agreed to lift the blockade and rescind the suspension of trading, leaving Napier to slink back with his frigates to Macao, where he died on October of that year.

* * *

William Jardine [2] sat in his office in Canton, cursing Viceroy Lu Kun. He had just heard the news about the death of Lord Napier.

He muttered something about them a' bein' under hell and stormed off to consult with his partner James Matheson. [3]

The two men had formed their own company, Jardine, Matheson and Co, in 1832. They worked well together – Jardine was the tough negotiator and visionary planner, and Matheson, the master organizer in total command of finances, correspondence and contracts. When the East India Company lost its monopoly on the China trade, Jardine and Matheson had swept into the vacuum, and quickly dominated the trade in China tea and Indian opium, with a host of other businesses and financial services. Both men were widely respected in the business community for their commercial success and their honesty and integrity in their dealings with their fellow merchants. Jardine became the acknowledged leader of the business community in Canton, and became known as the Tai-pan, or 'great manager'.

Jardine was tall, lean and wiry, a proud and sometimes overbearing man, with wavy brown hair and thick sideburns, a long aquiline nose and penetrating brown eyes. He was serious and reticent outside of business and had not much time for social company or graces. He had small, pouting lips, but from these almost feminine appendages came the most fearful obscenities if he was crossed. He was known in Canton as the 'Iron Headed Old Rat.' When an irate Portuguese captain once struck him over the head with a heavy cudgel during a fight in the European club, Jardine shrugged it off and knocked the man to the ground with a powerful right hook. Jardine worked long hours, and although he amassed a vast personal fortune, his Canton office was bare except for his desk and a cabinet for his papers. There were no chairs in his office other than his own, which served to impress upon the merchants who did business with him that he had no time to sit around and chat with them about social affairs or petty politics.

Jardine operated the company's opium trade through various

Chinese middlemen, and smugglers who carried the drug inland and up and down the coast. With his undoubted gift of the gab, he managed to persuade Christian missionaries to serve as interpreters on his smuggling ships, so they would have the opportunity to make converts on their travels to the coastal towns and villages. Both Jardine and the missionaries wanted the Celestial Kingdom opened to British influence; Jardine to expand the trade in opium, the missionaries to spread the word of God.

Matheson, by contrast, was short and somewhat portly, with bushy eyebrows, full red lips, a high forehead and a receding hairline. He was suave and avuncular, jovially at ease in social gatherings, and a great lover of the arts. He was an accomplished pianist and owned the only piano in Canton. But his easy manner did not get in the way of doing business. When a ship's captain refused to unload opium in Canton on the Sabbath, Matheson had him dismissed. He explained to the man that while he had every respect for those with religious principles, they had no business in the opium trade.

When Jardine entered Matheson's office, his partner offered him a chair, with a smile. It was their private joke. Jardine refused, and stood towering over Matheson's desk.

'It's a damned disgrace,' he fumed, 'and an insult tae a' o' us. We're goin' tae have to do something aboot this, or we're goin tae lose the China trade altogether. We canna just sit here and let thae corrupt bastards dictate to us as if we were nae mair than coolies. And we're nae going to open up this country by talkin' to them, that's for sure – we'll need the big stick afore there's any talk aboot carrots.'

'What do you propose we do?' replied Matheson, urging his friend to calm down and sit down, although Jardine did neither. 'We've written to the king and the government and sent innumerable petitions. They do not seem to be very interested in China, although they're happy enough to profit from it.'

'I'll tell you whit we should do. You were thinking o' a trip hame, James, so why don't you tak' it and gang and see the foreign secretary and tell him that whit we need are men o' war and marines tae open up the place, nae sniveling superintendents.'

So, it was decided that Matheson would take their case directly to the British government.

2

1835

Tan Poh Neo could not concentrate on her studies. Normally she enjoyed doing the complicated additions and multiplications, as well as engaging in the imaginary conversations she held with herself in English. It was a form of mental exercise that made her feel alive, which she much preferred to the endless cooking, sewing and embroidery that occupied her days, and which she knew would consume much of her married life. How she envied men, who got to use their brains all day in their businesses, calculating their gains and losses, and carefully planning their investments.

But today she was too vexed to concentrate on her calculations and conversations. For today the matchmaker was coming, an elderly aunt who played cherki with her grandmother, and she was bringing Poh Neo's prospective bridegroom to visit her father and mother. He was Mr Ong Chai Tong, a rich merchant and tin miner, who her father had known in Malacca. She had heard her father talk about him with respect, but she had never met him.

She heard the doorbell jangling, and immediately motioned her maid to silence. She was forbidden to go downstairs to meet her intended, but she crept out of her small sitting room and tiptoed across the landing, until she came close to the window above the front door of the house. As in many Peranakan dwellings, there was a spy hole on the first floor just above the entrance hallway, and she bent down and peered through it.

It was as she had expected. Ong Chai Tong was an older man,

almost as old as her father, but unlike her father, who was tall and dignified, Ong was short and fat. He was neatly dressed in a baju lok chuan, a long-sleeved black silk jacket, with white trousers and a straw boater. But when he took off his hat she saw that he was completely bald and had a podgy baby face. She shivered in disgust and crept back to her room, trying to hide her tears. Later that evening her mother informed her that Mr Ong was acceptable to them, and that she should soon expect an official visit from Mr Ong's family, which would include the matchmaker and an even number of elderly female relatives. If the family approved the match, their horoscopes would be consulted and auspicious dates set for their engagement and wedding.

On the prearranged day, Mr Ong's relatives arrived, while Poh Neo's family were having their evening meal. This was considered an auspicious sign, so the visit got off to a good start. Poh Neo offered them sireh, betel nut and lime paste wrapped in betel vine leaf. Most of the Bibiks indulged themselves; the younger Nonyas and Babas merely touched the container to acknowledge the hospitality that was being offered. The relatives made small talk with her parents, who feigned surprise when the official reason for the visit was mentioned.

Poh Neo served them tea and cakes. She wore a dark blue silk baju panjang, a long tunic with tapered sleeves over a light blue sarong, secured by a set of three silver jewelled kerosang.[x] Her hair was wound in a tight sanggul chignon,[xi] which was held in place by two gold hairpins. The gold hairpins supported a bunga chot, a lower hairpiece wound with a garland of jasmine flowers. Poh Neo's clothes were neatly pressed and creased, and she wore a red handkerchief tucked under her right shoulder to match her red embroidered slippers. The visitors seemed to approve and the

---

x Pinned brooches.
xi Tight hair bun.

matchmaker gave her a secret smile. Poh Neo's stomach fluttered with anxiety. She was desperately trying to think of some way to discourage the relatives without offending her family, but her usually creative spirit failed her. They seemed to think she was an eminently suitable young lady, who could serve her husband well and manage his household.

Her mother confirmed this when the relatives left. It was agreed that the families would exchange the days and times of their lunar births, so that an astrologer could compare their horoscopes. Poh Neo's heart sank.

* * *

In February William Matheson arrived in London and arranged to meet with the Duke of Wellington, who was foreign secretary in the government of Sir Robert Peel. Wellington kept Matheson waiting outside his office for most of the day, then late in the afternoon he was admitted and allowed to present his case for expanding British trade and missionary work in China.

The duke heard him out, but then responded with barely controlled anger: 'I am appalled, sir. Are you not aware that this drug is illegal in the home country as well as in China? And are you not aware of the great immorality of your trade? Even the greatest of men succumb to your black mud. The Honourable Mr William Wilberforce and the great Lord Clive of India were hopeless addicts until the day they died. Did you know that, sir?'

Matheson was insulted, but did not show it, and replied to the duke as best he could: 'Your grace, I have been in China many years, and have never seen a native in the least bestialized by opium smoking. The Chinese upper classes smoke opium on convivial occasions, in much the same way as the English upper classes imbibe champagne, and alike in moderation. My own opinion is that the damage to health and morals wrought by gin and other spirituous liquors in England is vastly greater than anything associated with the smoking of opium.'

The Iron Duke was unmoved.

'Humbug and hypocrisy, Mr Matheson! I will not waste the resources of Great Britain in promoting such a damnable poison. We are done, sir! Good day!'

3

Tan Poh Neo scratched her ears, but they continued to itch. She knew it! It was surely a sign that she was about to receive some news. She hoped it was good news, for little that had happened in the past few weeks had brought her any pleasure. She almost wished that she could remain unmarried; she would at least have her calculations and language studies. How strange that she took so much pleasure in numbers and symbols. Her mother and sisters certainly thought it very strange, but her father did not mind; on the contrary, he did everything to encourage her. It had been his suggestion that she receive a basic education in arithmetic and English, so that she could be of some practical help to her future husband, beyond running his household. Her future husband? She sighed when she thought of Ong Chai Tong. He was pleasant and prosperous, but the bald and tubby middle-aged man was not the vision of her childhood dreams. However, she was resigned to her fate, which was not worse than death, she reflected with little comfort.

Her mother entered the room and stood before her, her face and eyes downcast.

'I have bad news, little one,' she said, trying to control her voice. 'The astrologer tells us that your horoscopes are crossed and warns of disaster if you marry. Mr Ong and his family do not wish for the wedding to go ahead, and we agree with them. I am so sorry for you. I know how much you were looking forward to the wedding, as we all were.'

Poh Neo covered her face with her hands and bent her head down to her knees. Her mother stroked her head gently, and then shaking her own, left her daughter to deal with her sorrow as best she could. But behind her hands, Poh Neo smiled a smile of wholehearted relief. Good news indeed!

* * *

When Matheson returned to Canton and told Jardine about his dressing down by the Duke of Wellington, Jardine cursed again. Then he turned thoughtful and mused aloud: 'Whit we need is an incident,' he said, 'and then whit we need is a war.' Matheson agreed.

They did not have to wait long, although Jardine was already on his way home to Scotland when it occurred.

* * *

Five years after the founding of Singapore in 1819, the British foreign secretary George Canning had proudly proclaimed to the British parliament that within six years Singapore would be able to produce sufficient spices to satisfy the needs of the mother country and all its colonies and dependencies. This confident prediction – based upon Sir Stamford Raffles' optimistic estimates – had not come to pass, but during the 1830s the Singapore merchants and traders seemed hell bent on bringing it to fruition. They planted huge acreages of nutmeg, mulberry, cocoa, cloves, cotton, tobacco, sugarcane, coconut, mango, mangosteen, durian and pineapple. On May 24, they formed the Singapore Agricultural and Horticultural Society, largely through the efforts of Dr Montgomerie and Dr Oxley [4], both of whom owned large plantations. A committee was appointed, with Governor Murchison as honorary president. The members met once a month in each other's houses, where they read papers on the cultivation of different types of crops and discussed the prospects for clearing and draining the jungle for the further development of agriculture in Singapore. Having determined to their own satisfaction that local conditions were conducive to the planting of nutmeg, pepper, gambier, cloves and other spices, the committee petitioned the governor-general in India to authorize the sale or longer lease of more land for agricultural purposes, which they believed would both bring in significant revenue and promote the general interests of the settlement.

The Chinese continued to develop their early investments in pepper and gambier, as the market for gambier expanded in the 1830s, fuelled by the British dyeing and tanning industries. The two crops were grown together, because the waste from gambier production served as a fertilizer for pepper. The most successful planter was Seah Eu Chin,[5] who had used the profits from his business to purchase a large acreage northwest of the town, near Bukit Timah.[xii] He had originally planted tea and nutmeg, with little success, but had made a huge personal fortune when he planted gambier and pepper, just at the time when the price of the crop rose internationally. He was the largest grower in Singapore and became known as the 'Gambier King.'

While the Chinese gambier and pepper plantations brought a fair return on investment, they had certain disadvantages when compared with other popular crops such as nutmeg, pineapple and coconut. The pepper quickly exhausted the soil, and large supplies of wood were required to provide fuel for the vats in which the gambier leaves had to be boiled, before they were pressed to extract their juices, which were then dried into a concentrated paste. The Chinese planters left a trail of devastation in the jungle as they kept moving their plantations further and further inland,

xii Tin hill.

and the wasteland they left behind was quickly overgrown with course lalang grass. As they moved further and further inland, they encroached more and more on the jungle ranges of the tigers, who snatched away increasing numbers of labourers, until it was said that they took at least one Chinese coolie for every day of the year.

4

1836

Hong Xiuquan stood outside the examination halls in the city of Canton in the early spring, preparing for his second Confucian state licentiate examination. He had passed the qualifying exam earlier in the year, and hoped to bring honour to his family by advancing to a successful career as a Confucian scholar and bureaucrat. Hong Xiuquan came from a poor Hakka farming family in Guanlubu, a small village in Hua county, about thirty miles north of Canton. He had two older brothers and one older sister by his father's first wife, who died some years previously; his stepmother had no children of her own. Both of Hong's elder brothers were married, and Hong had recently found himself a second wife, Lai, after the first wife his parents had chosen for him died within weeks of their marriage. The income from the family farm was scarcely enough to keep them all, so Hong had to support his academic studies by teaching at the local school.

He was twenty-two years old, keenly conscious of his responsibilities to his family and his ancestors, as he stood with thousands of his fellow students, waiting for the examination to begin. Hong blinked in the bright morning sunlight that sparkled on the snow-capped rooftops and pine trees, the product of a freak snow storm – the first snowfall in Canton in forty years. He noticed two figures who emerged from a side street and began to address the crowd of students from a small stage. One of them was a foreign barbarian, who was inexplicably dressed in the style of the old Ming dynasty ^{xiii}, and spoke Chinese very badly. The second man was Cantonese and was interpreting the garbled speech of the foreigner. Hong found what they said to be very confusing. They promised to fulfil the students' wishes – yet how could they do so if they did not know what their wishes were? Hong moved forward through the crowd to get a closer look, until he came to the edge of the stage.

The foreigner was the Reverend Edwin Stevens, a graduate of Yale college and an ordained Presbyterian minister of Yale Theological Seminary. He came to China in 1832 as chaplain to the American Seamen's Friends Society in Canton, but soon after began to try his hand at converting some of the local Chinese population. His mission had been particularly successful in recent years, when he had travelled with the American privateers that cruised the coastline north of Canton, and smuggled shipments of opium upriver with the connivance of the local authorities. Stevens had accompanied them ashore and upriver, distributing thousands of Chinese bibles and religious tracts along the way.

He had penned some of these tracts himself, although he had to admit their doubtful utility given his difficulty with Chinese; most had been written by Liang Afa, a former Buddhist monk who converted to Christianity. Stevens had met Liang Afa shortly after he arrived in Canton, and the two men quickly became close friends. Stevens was particularly impressed by a Chinese tract that Liang had written to explain the essential elements of the Christian faith to his Chinese brothers, entitled *Good words for exhorting the age*, and distributed multiple copies of Liang's tract on his missionary trips.

The Cantonese, whom Stevens had converted, was always on the outlook for other potential converts. He watched Hong

---

xiii Dynasty that ruled China for centuries prior to being displaced by the Manchu Qing dynasty in 1644.

approach the stage and saw the puzzled look on his face as he tried to follow their message of hope and love to all men. At the end of the sermon, he reached down and handed Hong a copy of Liang's. *Good words for exhorting the age.* He assured Hong that he would achieve the highest distinction in life, and that this work would guide his way. After the two preachers left, Hong glanced through the text. Flicking through the index, he noticed his own name, Hong, which means flood, in the title of the fourth tract. He read how the great God Ye-huo-hua,[xiv] who created all living things, had commanded their destruction in a great flood that covered all the earth, in punishment for the sins of men, who abandoned their creator and worshipped false gods and idols. Ye-huo-hua had only spared the righteous Noah and his family, whom he commanded to build a great ark, and to take on board a single pair of each of the animals that walked or flew or slithered across the earth. Hong read a few more stories before he and the others were called in to the examination.

A few days later Hong learned that he had failed the examination, and he walked home in dejection. As he trudged along the dirt road, he suddenly remembered Liang's tract, as he felt its weight in his pocket. He took it out intending to throw it into the ditch by the side of the road, to lighten his load. But for some strange reason, he suddenly stopped himself. He stood for a moment, puzzled by his own behaviour. Then he shrugged his shoulders and stuffed the tract back in his pocket as he set off again down the road.

---

xiv Jehovah.

5

1837

Soon it all began again. There was a new visitor to the home of Tan Poh Neo, come to seek her parents' approval. When she went to observe him through the spy hole, she was overjoyed to find that he was a handsome young man, very smartly dressed, and with a full head of rich black hair! He was Lee Seng Huat, the son of a merchant from Palembang, who owned shops and land in Chinatown. The relatives visited, and she offered them sireh. Her parents feigned surprise when the relatives raised the subject of their visit. Once again Poh Neo served them tea and cakes, while they carefully observed her dress and demeanour. The families agreed to exchange birth dates and times and to consult with an astrologer, but this time Poh Neo felt sure there would be no problem, and that all the signs would be auspicious. She was not mistaken, and the dates of her engagement and marriage to Lee Seng Huat were quickly set.

As soon as they were, Poh Neo set to work to embroider a pair of bedroom slippers for her future husband. She also began to sew her own kasut manek, a pair of patterned slippers decorated with cut beads in the shape of plants and animals, and her kebaya, a blouse-dress with elaborate designs worked in gold and silver threads interwoven with silk. Two weeks before the wedding, on Lap Chye,[xv] the family of Lee Seng Huat came to exchange gifts with the family of Tan Poh Neo. The groom's family brought wedding clothes and jewellery, a raw leg of ham, some bottles of

---

xv Engagement day.

Chinese wine and a bowl of keuh ee – red and white round balls of glutinous rice dough in a sweet syrup soup, the red and white symbolizing good luck and purity, and the roundness representing joy. The bride's family gave them oranges and a silver belt in return, along with the slippers that Poh Neo had embroidered for her future husband.

Lee Beng Swee, Seng Huat's father, presented Mr Tan with two pairs of red candles wrapped in red paper on a silver tray. Mr Tan took the candles and replaced them with two others, which Mr Lee accepted. Mr Tan lit the candles that he removed, and both families paid their respects to the gods and their ancestors. Madam Tan served refreshments, after which the groom's family returned home. Neither the bride nor groom took any part in the ceremonies.

Six days before the wedding, official invitations were sent out to friends and relatives. The male guests received a bowl of keuh ee with their invitations, the female guests sa kapor siray, slices of betel nut folded within triangles of sireh leaf, presented in a silver bowl wrapped in a silk handkerchief. This marked the beginning of the wedding preparations.

The Tan's house was cleaned from top to bottom, and then decorated for the wedding. Poh Neo's bridal chamber was prepared, and furnished with new curtains, tapestries, carpets and flowers. The women placed pisang raja bananas, serai [xvi] and yams in an earthenware pot, along with three joss sticks, to symbolize wealth, longevity and fertility. They placed bunches of bunga rampai around the room, pot-pourris of fragrant pandan leaves, jasmine and frangipani, and fresh incense. During the an chng ceremony,[xvii] a teenage boy born in the year of the dragon, from a large family with both parents living, rolled back and forth three times across the bed in his best clothes, to bless the first-born male child. When

---

xvi Lemongrass.
xvii Blessing of the bridal bed.

they had completed their preparations, the women placed sweet dishes and a spray of bunga rampai upon the bridal bed, to prevent malicious spirits from entering it, while male relatives of the bride stood guard outside the chamber to prevent the room from being defiled.

Over the next few days the women prepared the food for the wedding. Separate days were dedicated to the preparation of different ingredients and dishes, such as onions, garlic and sambal. Then came the ceremony of sang jit, when the groom's family walked in procession to the bride's house, accompanied by a serunee band, who played a lively accompaniment on their flutes, zithers, gongs and tambourines. Gifts were once again exchanged between the families to the accompaniment of music.

Two days before the wedding, an elderly Nonya aunt prepared Poh Neo's hair, in the ceremony known as the berandam. She combed and trimmed Poh Neo's hair, and tied it up with a white ribbon symbolizing purity. The aunt noted how Poh Neo's hair combed smoothly away from her hairline and did not curl back. She was pleased to confirm that Poh Neo was indeed a virgin.

The chia lang keh, the banquet for the wedding guests, was held on the day before the wedding. The house was thoroughly cleaned again, and long tables were set up for food and refreshments. The female guests were invited to lunch and the male guests to dinner. They presented Poh Neo and Seng Huat with ang pao, lucky red packets containing money, and a pair of red candles, also for good luck. When the guests had all left, the main hall of the house was prepared for the chiu thau ceremony, representing the entry of the bride to adulthood; a similar ceremony would be conducted for Seng Huat in his parents' home. Prior to the ceremony, the bride and groom bathed and dressed in the white suits that they would wear until the completion of the wedding ceremony. They would never wear these clothes again until they died, when they would be buried in them.

The chiu thau ceremony took place late in the evening and lasted until the early morning of the wedding day. In the home of Poh Neo, her father prayed and lit the candles on the special sam kai altar that had been set up to solemnize the marriage; the altar represented Heaven, Earth and Man, and was dedicated to the Jade Emperor. Poh Neo sat upon an upturned rice measure on a round bamboo tray, covered with a piece of red carpet. Her sang kheh umm, her mistress of ceremonies, the elderly hairdresser who had conducted her berandam, presented a tray of objects to the teenage boy who had conducted the an chng ceremony, who in turn presented them to Poh Neo. They included a ruler and a sharp razor, which warned her to exercise wisdom in her judgments and to be careful in her actions. The boy held a scale above her head, and then lowered it to her feet, cautioning her to weigh all her actions. Her sang kheh umm then set her hair with gold and diamond pins to form a jewelled crown. When the altar candles burned out, the ceremony was complete. Poh Neo was dressed in her wedding clothes, and final prayers were offered to the gods and ancestors.

At last she was prepared for the twelve days of her wedding! How long it took for Peranakans to get married, she thought, unlike other races or clans. She supposed it somehow represented the complexity of the web of interwoven Chinese and Malay customs. But she was happy and excited. Now she would get to see her husband up close at last, and she would finally experience the mysterious act her mother and her sister had prepared her for. She hoped she would be able to survive the ordeal without screaming!

6

On the morning of the wedding day, the family lanterns were lit outside the groom's house. Lee Seng Huat's father led him out to the waiting carriage and gave him a cup of wine before he left. Seng Huat, who was immaculately dressed in a purple and gold silk jacket and dark blue embroidered sarong, quaffed the wine and mounted the carriage with an eager step – he was looking forward to seeing his bride for the first time. In the back of the carriage his parents placed two sticks of sugarcane, symbolizing a sweet and long life, and a young cockerel and hen tied together in a rattan basket, symbolizing fertility.

Just before noon the wedding party set off, led by the groom's pak chindek, his master of ceremonies, who would direct him through the complex rituals. The groom's two best men accompanied them, along with a cymbal player, a flautist and two gong masters. As the procession wound its way to Tan Poh Neo's house, a company of serunee trumpeters played processional music. The groom's attendants held forth large brass trays on which they displayed the gifts for the bride, including jewellery from the groom's parents, while other attendants carried layers of lacquered wooden baskets on wooden poles, which contained gifts for the bride's parents – a roast piglet, chickens, ducks, fruit, wine and candles.

Firecrackers exploded overhead as the procession arrived at the bride's house, where the groom's party were showered with yellow rice and sprinkled with perfumed water. When Lee Seng Huat arrived at the door, he was received by a pageboy, who presented him with an orange on a silver platter. Seng Huat waited at the door until an elderly family member greeted him, whereupon he entered the bride's house and was served tea. The ronggeng band and dancers began their performance, while Seng Huat waited to meet his bride. As he waited, the sang kheh umm made final adjustments to Poh Neo's dress, sternly reminding her of the details of the forthcoming rituals. When she was done, Poh Neo's parents covered her head with a veil of black netting, symbolizing her sadness at leaving behind her parents and her childhood, and her apprehension about her future adult life.

Then it was time for the chim pang ceremony, the first meeting of the bridegroom and bride. Seng Huat knocked gently on the door of the bridal chamber, and invited Poh Neo to come out. Eventually her sang kheh umm led her through the doorway, and the couple bowed to each other. Then Poh Neo led Seng Huat into the bridal chamber, where he removed her veil, and the couple saw each other for the first time. Both were very pleased with what they saw. Seng Huat was as dark and handsome and clear-skinned as she remembered him, albeit from above, and he had very white teeth and a warm, almost feminine smile. To Seng Huat, Poh Neo seemed the very epitome of female beauty – she had a round face and a small red mouth, with a full lower lip. She had large brown eyes, a small nose and chin, and straight black hair. Her skin was pure and white, and as smooth as alabaster. They smiled at each other and their smiles were genuine smiles of happiness at their good fortune.

The couple were then seated on two red lacquered chairs and served a small bowl of keuh ee, which contained one red and one white dumpling, as a blessing for the sweetness of their life. Then came the makan choon tok [xviii] ceremony. The couple was presented with twelve different types of dishes, which they served each other using silver chopsticks. This was their first meal together as husband

---

xviii First meal.

and wife, demonstrating their care and commitment to each other. The two tall candles on the table represented Seng Huat and Poh Neo. Seng Huat's candle burned out first, indicating that he would be the first to die.

When the meal was completed, the couple knelt before the bride's parents to demonstrate their respect, and visited the groom's parents to perform the same ceremony. Then they visited their relatives before returning to their respective homes. Later that evening an attendant and pageboy invited Seng Huat back to Poh Neo's house. Seng Huat's friends were already gathered there, and they made jokes about the newly married couple, mainly concerning the subject of men and women and childbirth. Their goal was to make Poh Neo laugh; if she did, Seng Huat would have to buy whoever made her laugh a free dinner. Poh Neo could not suppress a smile when one of Seng Huat's friends made a risqué joke about looking for slippers in the strangest places, and Seng Huat agreed to stand the man a free dinner with good grace.

After Seng Huat's friends had left, the couple returned to the bridal chamber. Seng Huat was gentle with her, and she found that her first sexual experience was nothing like the dreadful ordeal she had been led to expect. It was a little painful to begin with, but otherwise quite pleasant. But she was a little disappointed that her dark and handsome husband was not a more passionate lover – he seemed to treat their lovemaking as little more than a bodily function, and it was all over so quickly! Perhaps things would improve, as they grew more familiar with each other, she thought and hoped to herself. After all, their wedding night would last for twelve whole days! She stretched out on the bed like a cat, contemplating with pleasure the beginning of her freedom. When the twelve wedding days were over, she would be free to go out into the world again – to visit friends, to go to the market, or just walk in the street outside her home.

She rose before dawn to prepare the water for Seng Huat's morning ablutions. He rose at the first sound of the cock crowing, and returned home shortly afterwards, leaving an ang pao red packet by the washstand to acknowledge his gratitude. He returned in the evening only after having been re-invited by Poh Neo. They repeated this ritual ceremony of departure and return until the twelfth day, which represented his privileged position as the special guest of Poh Neo.

On the twelfth day, their marriage was confirmed during the dua belas hari [xix] ceremony. In the early morning, a ceremonial silver platter of sireh was prepared, with sliced betel nut, lime and gambier. Then the Tans invited Madam Lee to inspect the bloodstained cloth that they had taken from the bridal chamber. Madam Lee picked up a piece of lime and squeezed its juice over the bloodstain. She nodded with satisfaction. The stain did not run, confirming Poh Neo's virginity. To demonstrate her approval, she sent breakfast platters of nasi lemak [xx] over to Poh Neo's house.

In the afternoon, a rooster and hen were released under the bridal bed, and bets were taken as to which would emerge first. The rooster came out first, which indicated that the firstborn would be a son, which made everyone very happy (except for the few who had bet on the hen). The wedding ceremonies ended with the chia ching kay, a huge dinner party thrown by the Lees for the Tans and all those family members who had assisted in the wedding ceremonies. Despite the auspicious appearance of the rooster, and the yams, bananas and lemongrass placed under their bed to promote their fertility, Seng Huat and Poh Neo did not try to conceive a son that evening. They were too tired and fell asleep as soon as they lay down on their bed. Married at last!

---

xix Twelfth day.
xx Fragrant rice cooked in coconut milk and pandan leaf.

7

Shortly after the Chinese New Year celebrations, Hong Xiuquan retook and passed the local qualifying examinations, then travelled to Canton to retake the state examinations. This time there were no missionaries to distract him, but he failed the examinations once again. When he heard the news, he was overcome with grief and shame. He had let himself and his family down. He was so despondent that he felt physically ill. When he arrived home, he immediately took to his bed and fell into a fitful sleep. He dreamed that a great crowd of people had gathered round his bedside, summoning him to visit Yan Luo, the King of Hell. When he woke, he knew he was dying, and he summoned his family and relatives to bid them farewell. His brothers raised him up in his bed and propped his head against a pile of pillows. Hong Xiuquan told them that his days on earth were numbered and that his life would soon come to an end. In a hoarse voice, he begged his parents' forgiveness.

'My parents, I have failed you, and have not repaid your love for me. I had dreamed to bring distinction to the family name, but now I know that will never be. Please forgive me.'

His wife Lai, pregnant with their first child, wept and begged him not to despair. But Hong Xiuquan told her all was lost, and that she should look to his brothers for support when he died. Then he slipped back into unconsciousness, and his brothers laid him down again upon the bed. His father called upon the undertaker and began to prepare for his death.

First Hong Xiuquan heard the music, the sweetest music he had ever known. Once again, a great crowd gathered round his bedside, but this time he felt no fear, for the music seemed to ease his restless soul. Young children appeared before him in yellow robes, and in their midst, he saw a cock, a tiger and a dragon – the fabled beasts that wander the spirit world. As he gazed in wonder some richly dressed attendants appeared and lifted him into a sedan chair, then carried him along a long road until they reached a great city, whose golden gates shimmered in the pure white light.

Attendants in black robes emblazoned with golden dragons lifted him from the chair. To Hong's dismay they proceeded to slice open his chest and stomach with sharp knives – they removed his heart, his liver and other internal organs. Yet he was amazed to find that he felt no pain and watched in wonder as they replaced his old organs with new ones, then sealed up his wounds with a miraculous salve. A woman of great beauty appeared before him, who called him her son, and explained that his body had been fouled by his descent to earth. She led him to the edge of a softly flowing silver stream, where she washed his naked body and dressed him in a black dragon robe of the finest silk. He suddenly thought that he must have died, and that this strange woman must be the goddess Meng, who had made him drink from the cup of forgetfulness before returning to a new cycle of earthy life. For he found he could remember nothing of his former life, whether he had been a good or an evil man, or whether he had married and had a son who would honour his memory. He could not remember drinking from the cup of forgetfulness – but that of course was to be expected.

The woman who called herself his mother then told Hong she would take him to visit his father. She led him through a many-chambered palace white as pearl, until they came upon a great hall, the dome of which stretched to the very edge of Heaven itself. Hong stood before a noble king who sat erect upon a great white throne. 'This is your father,' she said to him, and bowed out of his presence. Hong Xiuquan looked up in awe at the figure before him, who was dressed in a robe of silk as black as midnight when the moon is hidden, with long golden hair and a golden beard that hung down to his waist. Hong looked into the golden eyes of his father and was entranced. He saw the tears in his eyes. He sensed the silent depths of his father's sorrow and the thunderous roar of his anger. Hong fell down and prostrated himself before his father, who greeted him: 'So, you have returned, my son. Rise up and listen to what I have to say to you.'

Hong rose and stood before his father, who exclaimed in a loud voice that echoed through the great empty hall to the very edge of Heaven: 'Why do they not respect and fear me? Why do they ignore me, who has created them? Why do they make sacrifices to the demons that have led them astray? Do they not know the depth of my pity for them, or the extent of my anger?'

'I will return to earth and warn them, Father,' Hong offered. But his father only sighed in response, then raised his hand and pointed a long finger towards the white marble floor, which was suddenly rent asunder to reveal the corruption of men and women who had transformed their original good natures. Men and women who lied and cheated. Men who beat their wives and wives who poisoned their husbands. Men who had sex with other men and women who had sex with other women, or with women and men who were not their wives or husbands. Men and women who left their baby daughters to die and rot by the roadside. Hong's heart felt like a lead weight in his chest when he saw the depth of their depravity. He feared his father's anger but was moved to ask him:

'Father, if they are so wicked, why do you not destroy them, and create a new race of men and women, a race purged of sin and knowledge of devils?'

His father replied that the evil had spread too far, and that the devils had invaded the thirty-three levels of Heaven.

'But why did you let them come so far, Father, when you could have destroyed them?' Hong urged.

'My son, I have my reasons, and they will know my wrath at the end of days. But you may act now if it is your will to do so, and drive the devils out of Heaven.'

Hong assured his father that he most earnestly willed to do so, whereupon his father bestowed upon him two gifts – a great sword called Snow in the Clouds and a golden seal. His Heavenly father then introduced Hong to his older brother, who was tall and thin and whose sad eyes, Hong thought, seemed to reflect the constant sorrow of the earthly world. Hong and his brother set out to battle against Yan Luo, the King of Hell, and his legions of demons. While his brother held up the golden seal, whose piercing light blinded the demons, Hong wielded his great sword and drove them down through the levels of Heaven, until he drove them back down to the earth itself. Hong was intent upon the destruction of Yan Luo, but he proved difficult to kill, for he constantly changed his form. He transformed himself from a man demon to an alligator, from an alligator to a fox, from a fox to a flock of birds, and from a flock of birds to a mesmeric serpent of rainbow hue, who hid his dark evil from the light of Heaven. Hong eventually managed to capture Yan Luo, and offered him to his father as a prisoner. But his father told him to release the demon king on earth, for if he was taken back he might escape and corrupt Heaven once again, and feed on the souls of those who he bewitched with the false beauty of his serpent form.

'Then let me kill him, Father,' Hong cried out, 'and put an end to evil!' Yet his Heavenly father shook his head, and ordered that Yan Luo be released. However, he did not spare the other devils, who Hong and his elder brother destroyed in great numbers. The blood that ran from their severed heads and sliced bodies stained the earth dark with the foul juices of their evil spirits.

When the battle was finally over, his father and mother rejoiced, and introduced him to his heavenly wife, First Chief Moon. First Chief Moon cared for Hong Xiuquan while he rested and learned from his Heavenly father the eternal truths about Heaven and mankind; about what is and what ought to be; and about what would eventually come to pass, the time of Taiping – the time of Heavenly Peace on Earth. First Chief Moon bore him a son, a beautiful boy with golden hair, and Hong was content as he rested in Heaven and listened to the sweet melodies that freed his mind from all earthly cares and responsibilities.

Then one day his Heavenly father came to him and told him that he must return to earth, to bring about the Kingdom of Heavenly Peace on Earth. Hong Xiuquan bade farewell to his wife and son, his elder brother, and his Heavenly father and mother. As he prepared to return to earth, his Heavenly father said to him:

'Have courage my son, and fulfil my will. Fear not, for I am with you always, and will protect you against all evil.'

* * *

The family and relations took turns watching Hong Xiuquan. He was close to death, they were sure, but he had also turned quite mad. If he escaped, he would pose a danger to them all, for if in his madness he injured or killed some innocent person, they would all be punished according to the law. So, they kept the door bolted and watched over him. Sometimes Hong would sleep peacefully, as white faced as a cadaver, and they would wait for death to take him. But then the colour would return to his cheeks, and he would leap up and cry out, waving his hand in the air as if he was wielding a sword. At other times he would recite poetry, strange verses about a Heavenly father and Heavenly peace. When they tried to talk and reason with him, he screamed and spat at them in reply, and when they appealed to him as their beloved son, brother or husband, he denied they were his family.

Then all of a sudden it was all over, like a great storm abated. Hong Xiuquan woke one morning and recognized his wife Lai. He was greatly pleased to learn that she had given birth to a daughter. Hong Xiuquan did not die and was reconciled with his family. Things slowly began to return to normal. Hong returned to teaching and once again began to prepare himself for the local and state examinations. He remembered his dream vividly, but could make no sense of it, and thought it best not to mention it to the others. He absorbed himself in his study of the Confucian texts and came close to forgetting about it altogether.

They all thought that he had been stricken with madness or possessed by demons, and Hong himself had his own fears concerning these possibilities. But one of his relations, his cousin Hong Rengan, who lived nearby and who had taken his turn watching Hong through his confinement, thought differently. Hong Rengan knew in his heart that there was some deep meaning to Hong Xiuquan's mysterious behaviour. He hoped with all his heart that one day he would reveal it to him.

8

In March, George Bonham was appointed governor of the Straits Settlements.[6] In actuality, his appointment dated back to December 1836, when Kenneth Murchison had left for Europe. This was an easy transfer of authority since Bonham had served as acting governor for much of Murchison's term as governor. Thomas Church, the assistant resident, took over Bonham's position as resident councillor. One of Bonham's first acts as governor was to establish Singapore as the permanent residence of the governor of the Straits Settlements, institutionalizing the priority of the new port in relation to the older settlements of Penang and Malacca.

The first game of cricket was played on the Esplanade [xxi] by the crews of two British merchantmen, to the pleasure of the crowd who watched the game, but to the displeasure of those who objected to games of sport being played on the Sabbath day.

* * *

The first meeting of the Singapore Temperance Society was held on Monday, August 28, with Mr Church, the resident councillor, as president, and Lieutenant Ashley of the Bengal Artillery as secretary. Dr Oxley and members of the clergy served on the committee. When John Simpson visited his friend Captain Scott later that week, he

---

xxi An open field in the centre of Singapore, reserved for public use, lying between Esplanade Road (later St Andrew's Road) and the seafront. Later known as the Padang, from the Malay word for 'field'.

made a joke in poor taste about all them ministers dying young on account of their being teetotallers. Yet it was true that many of the ministers associated with the settlement had died young, and it was Dr Montgomerie's belief that a good dram was the best prophylactic against malaria.

On Saturday, September 16, HMS *Zebra* arrived from Penang bearing the news of the death of King William the Fourth. The following day, which was a Sunday, at one o'clock, the shore batteries and guns of the *Zebra* fired a seventy-two-gun salute, representing the age at which the old king had died. On the Monday morning at noon, the same guns fired a Royal salute to announce the accession of the Princess Victoria as Queen of the United Kingdom of Great Britain and Ireland, and of the British Territories in the East Indies. *The Singapore Free Press* ran black mourning borders for three weeks.

* * *

Arjun Nath and Naraina Pillai came down from Malacca to Singapore with Sir Stamford Raffles in 1819. Arjun originally worked with Naraina Pillai as a brickmaker and later as manager of half his brick kilns. Five years later, when he had saved up enough money, he bought himself a dairy herd, since he had always wanted to be a dairy farmer. He also wanted a wife but had despaired of ever finding one in Singapore. Then one night he had a dream of a tiger and a beautiful woman, with D – o – o – m – g – a [xxii] emblazoned upon her forehead. Shortly after, he came across the tiger and the woman in real life, by the well at Telok Ayer. They managed to avoid the tiger, and he learned that she was a convict transported from Calcutta, who had murdered her husband when she found him molesting their daughter. She had been put in service

---

xxii Murder.

with a Chinese shopkeeper, but Arjun managed to negotiate her release into his custody. Her name was Chandi,[xxiii] and he married her soon after.

On this day Arjun was taking his family to the shrine dedicated to the goddess Kali, the consort of Lord Siva and destroyer of demons, which had recently been built off Serangoon Road by Tamil labourers who worked in the limekilns at Kampong Kapor.[xxiv] Arjun Nath had prospered. His dairy herd had grown, and he did a good trade with the European merchants and Indian boatmen, whose populations continued to grow as the settlement expanded. He kept his dairy herd in an enclosure he had cleared north west of Serangoon Road, close to Balestier Plain, where he employed three former convicts as workmen to help him with the feeding and milking of the cattle. His wife had borne him two fine boys and a beautiful daughter, and they went to the shrine regularly to give thanks for their good fortune and to pray to the goddess Kali for her protection against future evil. Arjun Nath had built a small house, constructed from bricks he made for himself while working for Naraina Pillai. His former employer had tried to persuade him several times over the years to rejoin his company, saying that Arjun was the best man who ever worked for him. But Arjun was content with his life, for he had realized more than he ever dreamed possible when he had come down from Malacca with Mr Raffles and Tuan Farquhar eighteen years before.

Today they were celebrating Deepavali, the festival of lights. They had risen early and bathed in gingelly oil,[xxv] then dressed in new clothes and visited the shrine. In the evening they lit the house with clay lamps, while Arjun's wife laid out the cakes and sweetmeats she had prepared weeks before. Arjun and his children

---

xxiii Moonlight.
xxiv Lime village.
xxv Indian sesame oil.

set off the firecrackers and sparklers that he had purchased earlier from a Chinese shopkeeper. Arjun enjoyed this glittering festival and reflected on the meaning of the festival of lights, which represented the triumph of good over evil and of light over darkness.

Arjun remembered how Rama, son of King Dasaratha of Ayodhya, and one of the incarnations of the god Vishnu, was sent into exile by his father. King Dasaratha had granted his youngest wife Kaikeyi two wishes after she saved his life in battle: she demanded that her son Bharata inherit the throne when King Dasaratha died, and that his son Rama be sent into exile in the forest. King Dasaratha reluctantly agreed, and Rama accepted his father's command to dwell in the forest for the next fourteen years. His devoted wife Sita and his brother Lakshmana followed him into exile, saying that Ayodhya was wherever Rama was.

When King Dasaratha died, Bharata was summoned to the throne, but was aghast when he heard what his selfish mother had done. Bharata promised to restore Rama as king and set off to search for him in the forest, where he found Rama, Sita and Lakshmana living peacefully in a cottage they had built for themselves. Bharata begged Rama to return as king, but Rama said he could not, because he would not break his vow to his father to remain in the forest for fourteen years. However, they agreed that Bharata would take Rama's sandals back to Ayodhya to symbolically enthrone him, and that Bharata would serve as regent in his stead while Rama served out the remaining years of his exile.

Rama and Sita and Lakshmana learned to live as frugally and peaceably as the hermits and sages who dwelt with them in the forest. But Ravana, the demon-king of Lanka, was enraptured by Sita's great beauty. He tricked the brothers into leaving her alone in the forest, where he kidnapped Sita and carried her off into the air. Rama and Lakshmana set of in pursuit, and joined forces with Hanuman, the monkey-faced son of the Wind God, and his army of monkeys. For a year and a half, they fought the armies of Ravana, until finally Rama killed the demon-king in a pitched battle and destroyed his forces. He rescued Sita alive, and she walked through fire to prove that she had remained faithful during her captivity.

When the time came for them to return to Ayodhya after the fourteen years of exile were passed, Hanuman flew on ahead to announce their arrival. The people of Ayodhya rejoiced at the news of the return of Rama, but were concerned that he would be returning in the late evening of the following day. For on that night there would be no moon, because it was new moon day and the country would be blanketed in darkness. The following night they set out clay lamps in all the houses and lit up the night sky with fireworks to welcome home King Rama of Ayodhya, his wife Sita and his brother Lakshmana. This was the event that was celebrated annually during the festival of lights.

9

1838

Arjun Nath was having a simple breakfast of roti prata [xxvi] and curry when one of his men came and reported that two of his cattle were sick. There was nothing unusual about this. Cattle grew sick and died and were replaced by new calves in the natural order of things, while the general size of his herd had increased over the years. Arjun was not unduly worried.

But when he visited the herd that morning he did begin to worry. The two sick cattle were young heifers, normally the healthiest animals. And since breakfast another three animals had been taken sick; by evening one of them had died. The following morning another three were sick, and another two had died. When Arjun went to visit his friend Chetoo, another dairy farmer who kept a herd a quarter of a mile south on Serangoon Road, his worse fears were confirmed. Chetoo had already lost ten heifers, with another twenty-six sick. There was some kind of cattle disease spreading across the island, threatening to completely destroy what he had worked so hard to achieve.

* * *

Arjun Nath was devastated. The disease had taken nearly half of his herd of one hundred animals, while most of his remaining

---

xxvi Flour-based pancake cooked over a flat grill, usually served with curry.

cattle were sick or dying. Although some remained healthy and continued to give milk, few of his former customers would buy his milk for fear of contracting the disease. He had quarantined his sick animals, then slaughtered and burned their carcasses, but it made no difference. There was a rumour going around that the sickness was caused by small insects that were carried into the cow's stomach when it ate grass, and which caused great irritation and damage to the animal's digestive system. But if it was, the insects were very small, for he had inspected the grass on his pasture and found no trace of them. He had also purchased grain for his healthy animals, but still they had sickened and died, and now he no longer had any money to buy grain. In fact, he had scarcely enough money to feed himself, his family and his workmen. If the disease continued, he would have to let them go. And if the disease persisted, he would lose his livelihood. He would have to go back to work for Naraina Pillai. He knew Naraina would take him on, and would loan him money to tide him over, but it would be very hard to abandon his dream. He decided to make an offering to the goddess Kali in the early evening and pray for deliverance from his misfortune.

After he had visited the shrine on Serangoon Road, he returned home and shared a simple meal with his family. He retired early to bed, but had no prophetic dreams, because he had scarcely gone to sleep when his son shook him awake. He heard a great clamour outside. As he rose from his bed, his son told him that a tiger had crept out of the jungle and tried to take one of the cattle. Sahir, one of his cattlemen, had tried to scare it off by beating a milking pail with a stick, but the tiger had attacked him. The other two cattlemen had tried to drive the tiger away, but it had dragged Sahir to the ground and badly mauled him.

By the time Arjun reached the edge of his compound, the tiger was gone and Sahir lay dead in the shadows at the edge of the jungle, his empty eyes staring up at the stars in the pale moonlight.

This was disaster piled upon disaster. A tiger had made his destiny, he thought to himself, and now a tiger had undone it.

But in this he was wrong. For as he stood desolate in the silver moonlight, he and the two cattlemen froze in horror as they heard a faint rustling in the dark green jungle before them. The tiger was returning! However, before they were able to regain their senses enough to grab their buckets and sticks again, an eerie figure emerged from the jungle. He was a tall elderly man, with long white hair and a flowing beard, and a wrinkled, weather-beaten face. He had a gold ring threaded into his beard, which glittered in the moonlight, and made him look like some Hindu guru. He wore white ducks [xxvii] that were no longer white, but covered in dirt and grime and the green of the jungle. He carried two long black hunting rifles, one over each shoulder.

He introduced himself as Mr Jean-Pierre Carrol, a Canadian hunter and former bosun. He had jumped ship a year earlier because of a dispute with his captain over the matter of his not being paid. He had meant to sign on the next available brig, he said, but in the meantime, he had made such a good living from hunting tigers – especially given the increased amount of the government reward, which had gone up from twenty to fifty dollars a head – that he had decided to stay on. He had built himself a tree house in the jungle, and divided his time between hunting, brewing his still whisky, and learning Malay and Hindustani.

He had spent the last week chasing this one, a large male, he said. He found his tracks outside Joseph Balestier's house a few days past, and followed him here this evening, but lost him when their commotion had chased the tiger away.

'But I mean to kill him before the night is through, if you can help me out,' he said to Arjun.

'But how can we help you?' asked Arjun, alarmed at the

xxvii Overalls made from heavy cotton fabric.

prospect of having to face the tiger again.

'By helping me dig a shooting pit back from the jungle and handing me my second gun if I need it. It gets a bit hairy when you miss with the first shot, if you know what I mean.'

Arjun remembered facing the tiger at Telok Ayer, and knew what Mr Carrol meant. But he agreed to help him dig a pit and told his two remaining cattlemen to bring shovels for digging.

'But first we must remove the body of poor Sahir, so we can prepare his body for cremation.'

'Nay,' replied Jean-Pierre, giving him a grim grin in the ghostly moonlight, 'we need to leave poor Sahir for another few hours – otherwise this man-eater will not return. It's a mistake most plantation owners make when they wait to ambush a tiger after it has taken their coolie, and I'm damned if I've been able to persuade them otherwise. But I'll make a deal with you, Mr Nath. If you help me, I'll give you the tiger's body for sale. You'll make almost as much as me, especially if you sell it to the Celestials, who think that eating the meat will make them brave. Then you can give Sahir a grand leave-taking, after he has done one last good thing before he quits this earthly place.'

Arjun did not like the idea. He did not like it one little bit. But he badly needed the money, so he reluctantly agreed. His cattlemen were very unhappy, and would have no part of it, so Arjun and Mr Carrol had to dig the pit themselves. After they had dug a hole deep enough to remain hidden, but with a clear line of fire, Mr Carrol handed one of the guns to Arjun.

'It's ready to fire,' he said. 'Hold it steady here and be ready to hand it to me if I say "gun".'

Arjun took the gun. It was a long black deadly thing and it gave him the shivers just to hold it, even though the night was warm and humid. Hours passed, midnight passed, and his nerves jangled every time they heard the rustling of a pig or deer in the jungle. Then

Arjun smelt the sickly miasma in the air and his stomach retched when he realized the smell came from Sahir.

'Ye can smell it, can't ye,' Carrol whispered, 'and that's what will bring him, sure enough.'

Another hour passed, and Arjun knew he could not take it much longer. He felt faint, and the smell filled him with such horror that it threatened to suffocate him. Arjun knew that by now the ants and other insects would be swarming all over poor dead Sahir. In his imagination he could almost hear their tiny teeth feeding upon his eyes and open wounds.

Then suddenly they heard the sound of a large animal moving quickly through the jungle, and saw the yellow eyes shimmer in the deathly moonlight as the tiger emerged from the green darkness. He was a monster, much larger than the tiger Arjun had seen long ago beside the well at Telok Ayer.

The tiger bent forward and rolled Sadir's body over, then took his buttocks in its jaws. Carrol fired. The tiger reared up and fixed its hateful eyes upon them. The shot had merely grazed the tiger's shoulder, and aroused its fury. The tiger ignored Sahir and came straight at them.

'Gun!' hissed Carrol.

Arjun had frozen in terror when he saw the tiger take Sahir's buttocks in its dreadful jaws. But Carrol's command snapped him back to reality. He was terrified, but something within him forced him to act, some subterranean feeling that he must play out his destiny, whether he lived or died. As he turned to deliver the second gun to Carrol in the silvery darkness of the night, he felt as if he was moving against a great black tide of fear that threatened to overwhelm him. But he forced himself against it. He handed the gun to Carrol just as the tiger was upon them, and Carrol fired point blank into its mouth. The great cat pitched into the pit beside them, its hot dying breath misting the humid air, its bloody fangs bared in Arjun's face. Arjun trembled at the thought of what these great fangs could do to human flesh, but he felt greatly relieved as Carrol slapped him on the shoulder in congratulation. The bullet from the second rifle had gone into the tiger's brain, and the life had gone out of its cold yellow eyes.

'Well you're a cool un, Mr Nath,' said Carrol. 'I'll say that for ye. I'm sure glad I chose you on the one day I missed.'

They both climbed out of the shooting pit, and with the help of Arjun's cattlemen, who had come running back at the sound of gunfire, they managed to get the dead tiger out of the pit too. Arjun instructed the men to make a stretcher, while he and Jean-Pierre cleaned Sahir's body as best they could. Then they covered his corpse with a white cotton sheet and placed a lighted lamp next to his head. When the men returned with the stretcher, they carried his body to an abandoned gambier plantation a short distance away, with Arjun walking ahead carrying an earthen pot full of burning coals. There they built a funeral pyre, and Arjun laid fire upon Sahir's mortal body as the first golden rays of dawn crept across the course lalang grass. Sahir had no family in Singapore, since he was a convict transported from Bengal, where he had left his family some years before. Arjun had taken him on as a cattleman after Sahir had served his probationary period in the convict jail, and Arjun thought that he was a good worker. He was the closest thing that Sahir had to family in Singapore, so it was only fitting that he conducted the funeral ceremonies. They stood in silence as the flames crackled and soared against the golden light of dawn. When Sahir's body was almost completely burned, Arjun smashed his skull with a bamboo shaft, to release his soul from the body.

When they returned to Arjun's home, Carrol gave him some advice on how to get the best price for the tiger meat and organs. Then he made him a surprising offer.

'Ye know, I could do with a good gun carrier such as you. Why don't we go into partnership? Same deal as before – I'll take the reward and you can sell the body.'

Arjun explained that he could not, since he had to tend to the remains of his dairy herd, which had been ravaged by disease.

'Well, maybe we can help each other out, Mr Nath,' Carrol responded. 'I won't need you all the time, only when I'm on the track of a beast. I can send a boy for you then, and your sons and your men can take care of your cattle while we're on the hunt. As you've just told me, you've got less than half your original herd, so it should not be too much trouble. The money you make would help tide you over – but in fact I think we can do better than that.'

He paused while he searched in his ducks and produced a folded newspaper and a pair of brass eyeglasses, which he fitted to his nose. He pored over the columns of the *Singapore Free Press* and then exclaimed: 'Bien! I thought I read it. Indian fellow calls himself Tickery Banda, just arrived on the *Diana* and says he can cure sick cattle. The contact address is here, care of Sorabji and Co. Maybe he's a fake, but it's worth a try, and you'll be able to afford his services if you stick with me. You're not afraid, are you?'

Arjun admitted that he was afraid, but he agreed to be Mr Carrol's gun man, at least until he got though this difficult time and Mr Carrol found another man.

Two days later Arjun scattered Sahir's ashes from an Indian lighter that he had contracted to take him a mile out to sea. For the next eleven days he made offerings of rice balls at the temple, in the hope of easing the passage of Sahir's soul to the far shore.

10

Moon Ling had kept and maintained her joss house dedicated to the goddess Ma Cho Po [xxviii] at Telok Ayer for almost twenty years. Her children were grown now. Her daughter was married to a Hokkien[7] shopkeeper, who – along with other merchants – had contributed to the now considerably expanded joss house, where her son Bedang was employed. He had inherited his father's talent for woodcarving and had made some fine statuettes of the mother goddess, which he sold to sinkeh [xxix] grateful to have survived the passage from China.

One morning as Moon Ling was entering the joss house, she was met by three Chinese merchants, who asked if they might speak with her. She took them to a modest hut that her son had constructed beside the joss house, which she used for bookkeeping and storage. It had a simple wooden table and four chairs, which she offered to the guests, whom she recognized as Tan Tock Seng, Tan Hong Chuan and Hoo Ah Kay. They had all visited her joss house and made offerings to the goddess in the past.

Having established his shop on Boat Quay, Tan Tock Seng had gone into business with John Horrocks Whitehead of Shaw, Whitehead and Co, formerly Graham Mackenzie and Co. They exported gambier and pepper and imported construction materials. Tan Tock Seng now owned valuable tracts of land reaching from the Esplanade through the High Street to Tank Road, which ran behind Government Hill; he also owned a nutmeg plantation near

xxviii Queen of Heaven, protector of mariners and fishermen.
xxix Chinese immigrants.

Orchard Road with his brother Tan Oo Long, who had come to join him from Malacca, and an orchard at Tanjong Pagar.[xxx] Tan Hong Chuan had managed to expand his chandler's business, and now had extensive plantations of coconut, durian and pineapple. He had purchased large tracts of land beyond Telok Ayer and along the recently constructed River Valley and Serangoon Roads. Hoo Ah Kay was known affectionately as Whampoa, after the port city in Guangzhou Province where he was born in 1813. He had come to Singapore in 1830, at the age of 15, to work in his father's shop on Boat Quay, which sold beef, bread and vegetables. On his father's death, Whampoa had inherited the business, and become one the leading ships' chandlers in Singapore, being chief supplier to Her Majesty's Navy. Like Tan Tock Seng, he spoke fluent English, which was a great advantage in his dealings with European merchants and ship's captains.

They had all prospered, and they all wanted to give something back to their community, Tan Tock Seng explained to Moon Ling, as they sat together at the table while her son served them tea. Tan Tock Seng described the Cheng Hoon Teng Temple in Malacca, where he used to pray before he left nearly twenty years ago to seek his fortune in Singapore, like the multitude of his countrymen who gave thanks to Ma Cho Po for their safe passage. He told Moon Ling that they wished to raise money for the construction of a new temple to Ma Cho Po on the site of her joss house, which would of course be incorporated within the new complex. All the building materials, including the pinewood, the sculptured granite pillars, and floor tiles would be imported from China. Special craftsmen would be brought in to work on the building, and a large statue of the Queen of Heaven would be shipped from Canton the following year. Moon Ling and her son could continue as servants of the

---

xxx Cape of stakes.

temple if they so wished. Tan Tock Seng had already pledged three thousand dollars, and Tan Hong Chuan and Hoo Ah Kay had pledged similar amounts; they were also assured contributions from the captains of the junks that came down regularly from China, Siam and Cochin China. [xxxi]

Moon Ling was happy to agree to all this, and she and her son immediately set about arranging for the shipments of timber and granite, and the hire of construction workers. They planned to begin work on the Thian Hock Keng [xxxii] Temple in January 1839.

* * *

Arjun worked with Mr Carrol for the next few months, although Jean-Pierre only needed a second gun one more time, for, despite his age, he was a crack shot. The month of November was the worst month for the cattle disease, and things became so bad that many dairy farmers became destitute. A collection was taken up by the merchants and shopkeepers to help them, to which both Arjun and Jean-Pierre contributed. But December and January passed and twenty of Arjun's cattle survived and remained healthy, with two being delivered of calves, although whether it was due to the ministrations of Tickery Banda, the self-proclaimed healer of cattle, he could not say. Some of the other dairy farmers had managed to save parts of their herds, although they had not been able to afford to engage Tickery Banda. But Arjun did not grudge paying the man's fee, although he did smile to himself when he received his receipt from Mr Banda for payment of services rendered, for 'looking after Mr Nath's cattle until they died'. Arjun stayed on with Jean-Pierre until he found a new partner, and he kept the head of the last tiger that they shot, which he had stuffed and mounted

---

xxxi Present day Vietnam.
xxxii Temple of Heavenly Bliss.

above the door of his house. Once again, he thought to himself, he owed his good fortune to a tiger.

* * *

Jean-Pierre Carrol was not the only tiger hunter in Singapore, for it was a lucrative if dangerous business. The government upped the reward to one hundred dollars for a few months, and when they were forced to reduce the amount again to fifty dollars because of the usual economic necessities, the Chamber of Commerce stepped in with an additional reward of fifty dollars of its own. Neil Martin Carnie had been a municipal clerk and then municipal inspector, but found the life of an administrator dull and unrewarding. When he first heard of the reward for tigers, he walked out of his office and bought himself a hunting rifle. He teamed up with a Malay police sergeant, who thought hunting tigers was much better-paid and much less dangerous than police work. As the gambier and pepper farmers continued to clear increasing acres of the jungle and tiger attacks grew more frequent, the government used convicts to dig tiger pits and formed armed hunting parties that went deep into the jungle.

11

1839

After the Napier fiasco, the British government appointed Captain Charles Elliot as Superintendent of British Trade in Canton. Elliot had been master attendant of British shipping at Macao and Canton, and he understood that his main job was to keep the peace between the European and Cohong merchants in order to further the trading interests of Great Britain. Unlike most of the European traders, Elliot disapproved of the illicit trafficking in opium, to the extent that he felt obliged to post a notice in the Canton factories declaring that it posed a threat to trading relations with the Chinese. His warning was ignored. As Lancelot Dent of Dent and Co, the chief British rival to Jardine, Matheson and Co, remarked in derision, Elliot and the Chinese authorities might as well try to stem the flow of the mighty Yellow River.

Yet by the end of the decade the Chinese authorities had decided that the time had come to act against the opium smugglers. The anti-opium lobby at the Imperial Court finally managed to persuade the Emperor Tao Kwang of the dangers of the drug to his people and his treasury. In response, Tao Kwang appointed the Confucian scholar and minister, Lin Tse-hsü, as Imperial Commissioner to Canton, with orders to put an end to the opium trade. Before he departed, the Emperor impressed upon Commissioner Lin the importance of his mission. In a shrill voice, he exclaimed: 'How can I die and go to the shades of my Imperial father and ancestors, until these direful evils are removed!'

In the New Year's Day sports, the Malays once again won all the boat races. There were pony races on the Esplanade, although they were rather a ramshackle affair, with only a few riders and mounts reaching the finishing line. There were wrestling matches, almost exclusively between the Indian boatmen, and also various foot races, between men and between menageries of dogs, pigs, monkeys, goats, turkeys and frogs.

On February 6, the twentieth anniversary of the founding of the settlement was celebrated with a public ball and dinner at Government House. The following night, Commodore James hosted a large dinner and dance aboard his flagship the US frigate *Columbia*. Both events were well attended by the principal merchants and residents.

12

Ronnie Simpson was proud of the mark he had made in the world. He had risen from humble beginnings in the village of Ardersier in the Highlands of Scotland to become a successful businessman in the rapidly expanding port city of Singapore. He had already had a successful career in the Royal Navy and merchant marine. Shortly after he and his father John Simpson (who had been in the army) had put a deposit on their own vessel, he had come ashore with Sir Stamford Raffles and Major Farquhar when they visited the Temenggong and secured his agreement to found a commercial settlement on the island of Singapore. Since then, the business of Simpson and Co had flourished, and father and son were now wealthy men who lived with Ronnie's wife Sarah and their children in their mansion along Beach Road, which sparkled like a fairy castle with its polished Madras Chunam [xxxiii] finish. There had been some hard times. First the business with the American gunrunner Harry Purser, then the murder of Sarah's sister and her family by the Illanun pirates, and finally the bloody sea-battle in which they had taken their revenge on Sri Rahman, the pirate chief who thought himself invincible. That had been only three short years ago, but they had managed to put it behind them and get on with their lives. They counted their blessings – their second and third children enjoyed

xxxiii A plaster made of shell lime beaten with egg whites and course sugar into a thick paste, then blended with water in which the husks of coconuts had been soaked. When the plaster dried, it was polished with round stones to a smooth and shiny finish.

healthy and happy lives, after their first had joined the others lost to tropical fevers in the cemetery at the foot of Government Hill. Or Forbidden Hill [xxxiv] as Ronnie still thought of it.

He found he had a head for business, and dutifully put in the hours at the Simpson and Co's godown on Boat Quay. In its own way it was rewarding, but he badly missed his years before the mast. He loved to feel the salt sea breeze and spray on his face as he took the helm and drove his ship though the pounding waves, her timbers creaking and sails snapping in the wind. There was nothing like it on earth, he thought. So, every now and again he quit the office, leaving it in the capable hands of his father and subordinates, and captained one of his ships to Bombay or China.

This day he was on his way to Canton with a cargo of best Bihar opium. Opium was a profitable business, so profitable in fact that this voyage was a special delight for him – it was the maiden voyage of his new schooner, the *Fair Maid of Inverness*. She was a fine-lined beauty, built in Aberdeen by Alexander Hall and Sons, and sat low in the water with forward-raking bow and masts raking aft. She was faster than any of the full-rigged ships with square sails on three masts like his own *Highland Lassie*, which he suspected he would have to retire in the not too distant future. Yet the real beauty of the thing was that it could beat to windward against monsoon winds, which meant she could make more than one run to Canton during the season. She had proven this on the way up, even though the winds were less than full monsoon force.

He had no qualms about dealing in opium, even though it was technically illegal in China. The corruption of the Chinese officials who managed the trade ensured freedom from any threat of prosecution. There were some who considered the trade immoral, but they were few and far between, not even the ministers of the

---

xxxiv Bukit Larangan in Malay.

cloth, many of whom were heavily invested in the trade themselves. It was no worse than dealing in Scotch whisky, in which he was also heavily invested, and of which many of the ministers of the cloth did disapprove.

He was happy as a sand boy.[xxxv] He was doing what he loved best, and he was going to make a good profit out of it.

* * *

Ronnie arrived in Canton in March, after having had his ship searched by Chinese officials at Macau. After arranging for his cargo to be unloaded at the main port of Whampoa, he paid a visit to the factory of Jardine and Matheson, who were his agents in Canton. A right pair of rogues, he thought to himself, but damned clever rogues. He regretted the fact that he had missed William Jardine, who he learned was on his way to retirement to Scotland, but was looking forward to sharing a fine malt with James Matheson, who was by far the more sociable of the two men. However, when he went ashore to visit Matheson in his merchant house, which Ronnie always thought was more like a well-furnished country house than a place of business (Jardine's office aside), he was not in very sociable mood.

'Good to see you Ronnie, and William regrets he missed you, but I'm afraid you've arrived at a bad time.'

'How so, James?' replied Ronnie, who had always been impressed by the way business operated like clockwork at Canton.

'The Imperial Commissioner Lin Tse-hsü arrived here the other day, with explicit orders from the Emperor. He immediately began arresting opium dealers in the city and dockyards and had them publicly strangled in the city square before the assembled crowds.

---

xxxv A boy who spread sand on the floors of bars and was paid in ale (which usually made him happy).

A gruesome sight I'm told, although I was not there to see it. He's declared an amnesty for drug addicts who consent to treatment. He's even set up a rehabilitation clinic for them. Can ye imagine?'

'All well and good,' said Ronnie, 'but how does that affect us? Surely you have arranged everything with the Cohong?'

'We did until yesterday, Ronnie, but now Lin is demanding that we and the Cohong merchants surrender all the opium we have in the factories and the ships in the harbour, including, I'm afraid, your own cargo. Worse than that, in fact – he is also demanding that we sign a bond promising to cease trading in opium, on penalty of death.'

'I'm damned if I'm surrendering my cargo!' Ronnie exclaimed. 'I'll just turn around and try to unload it up the coast.'

'That might be the best idea, Ronnie, if you can pull it off. But I counsel against any hasty action. I have spoken to Captain Elliot, and I'm hoping he can arrange a meeting with Commissioner Lin, so we can persuade him to reconsider. There's a lot of money bound up in the trade, on their side as well as ours, and I've never known a Chinese administrator who can't be bribed. Stay here tonight and we'll find out where we stand in the morning. I have a fine Chinese cook and some finer malt whiskey, so I suggest we wait it out and see what tomorrow brings.'

Yet this time, James Matheson's optimism about the persuasive power of money was seriously misplaced. By early evening, Imperial troops had surrounded the factories, and all Chinese agents, translators, servants, cooks and water carriers had been ordered to leave the foreign factories on pain of decapitation.

'Damn it, not the cook!' Matheson exclaimed. 'What is to become of us? I have many talents, but the culinary arts are not among them. Damn the man! Double damn!'

Matheson rarely swore, but the occasion seemed to demand it.

'In that case, I think I'd best be off, much as I enjoy your company,' said Ronnie. 'But what about our contract?'

'Well, we'll work out what to do about that depending on how things develop here. I suggest you stay on a bit longer – we may yet get a satisfactory solution to this business.'

'I'm still o' a mind to leave,' said Ronnie, 'I have a bad feeling about it.'

The decision had already been taken out of their hands. A few moments later, they received a visit from Robert Forbes, the head of the American firm Russell and Co. After introductions had been made, Forbes broke the news.

'I just heard they've sent Imperial war junks to block the Pearl River, so they've got us boxed in. I suppose Lin means to force us into compliance. But compliance be hanged, I'm going to arrange a meeting with him and see if we can't get this sorted out. Will you join me James?'

'I'd be more than willing,' Matheson replied, 'although I don't know what good it would do us. I think we should give Elliot a chance to play his hand first – he has the authority of the British government on his side.'

'Fat lot of good that will do him – Lin and the Emperor don't give a toss about the British government. We're all a bunch of barbarians to them.'

'Looks like you'll be staying with us a bit longer than expected, Ronnie,' Matheson said. 'I hope you can cook, since we're going to be down to basics soon. Good thing we have plenty of wine and whisky. Don't worry about getting word to your wife and family in Singapore, we'll find a way to let them know you're safe.'

'That can be easily done,' Forbes interjected. 'Dunn's people can get word back for you, they've already signed the bond. They're Quakers and refuse to trade in opium, so are free to come and go as they please. I dare say some of their ships will put into Singapore.'

'A' very well, but are we safe?' said Ronnie, accepting a glass of malt whisky from Matheson. 'I dinna trust these crooks who seem bent on stealing our living.'

13

When he arrived in Canton, Commissioner Lin had been delighted to discover that the barbarian William Jardine, the Tai-Pan, had left for retirement in Britain. He reported to the Emperor that the Iron-Headed Old Rat, the sly and cunning ringleader of the opium smugglers, had left for The Land of Mist, xxxvi for fear of the wrath of the Middle Kingdom. Secretly he was glad that he did not have to deal with Jardine, who had a fearsome reputation. When Lancelot Dent sent word that he wanted to arrange a meeting, Lin had him promptly arrested. That will show them I mean business, he thought to himself. He pressed Captain Elliot for the surrender of the stocks of opium, and while he waited for a reply, he wrote a letter to Queen Victoria, imploring her to end the opium trade. It began:

> Let us ask, where is your conscience? I have heard that the smoking of opium is very strictly forbidden by your country; that is because the harm caused by opium is clearly understood. Since it is not permitted to do harm to your own country, then even less should you let it be passed on to the harm of other countries.
>
> In several places in India under your control opium has been planted from hill to hill. For months and years work has continued in order to accumulate the poison. The obnoxious odour ascends, irritating Heaven and frightening the spirits. But you, Oh Sovereign, can eradicate the opium

xxxvi Scotland.

plants in these places, hoe over the fields entirely, and sow in its stead the five grains ... This will be a great, benevolent policy that will increase the common weal and rid us of evil. For this, Heaven must support you and the spirits must bring you good fortune, prolonging your old age and extending your descendants.

. He had the long letter translated and posted on the notice boards of the British factories.

* * *

Sarah Simpson had also put the past behind her, but it was much harder for her. Although it was now four years since her sister and her family had been murdered at sea, it often seemed as if it were but yesterday. She still imagined their poor bones lying scattered on the ocean floor somewhere between Malacca and Singapore, without anyone to tend or care for them. She had pursued the pirates with grim determination, but their destruction had brought her no comfort or closure – it was just more death heaped upon death. But like Ronnie, she determined to get on with her life, and get on with her life she did. She was a strong woman who made the most of what she had.

She sometimes joined Ronnie on his occasional voyages to China, India and Penang, but she was not a great lover of the sea. While she did not suffer much from seasickness, she preferred a stationary bed, and found that looking out over the endless ocean got a bit monotonous after a while. Yet like Ronnie she was restless. Mrs Stables looked after the children, and managing the household was light work except when they had a large party or celebration. She had learned Malay, although not nearly so quickly and easily as Ronnie, and was learning some Chinese dialects, although she found this to be incredibly difficult, so difficult that she was considering giving it up. She had a vague notion that she might become a teacher, and that is in fact how things turned out, although not quite in the way she expected.

She had taken her son Duncan out into the jungle to teach him to shoot, first with her Baker rifle and then with the newer Brunswick rifle. They had set up a target in the clearing near Bukit Selegie, now named Mount Sophia after Raffles' wife and daughter, where she and Ronnie had their first pistol shooting competition, and where they had duelled with Harry Purser the gunrunner. Duncan was now thirteen years old, and although a natural, she was training him to be a first-class marksman, as she was a first-class markswoman, as he kindly put it. Some weeks after they began, Dr Oxley came across them while returning from a visit to a patient on one of the plantation estates. Dr Oxley fancied himself a great hunter and an excellent shot, but he was no match for Sarah and only just managed to hold his own with Duncan. Oxley's pride was deflated, but he swallowed it down and asked Sarah if she could help him improve his marksmanship, offering a generous amount of money in compensation. Sarah would not take his money, but she agreed to train him if he made a generous donation to the Singapore Free School, which he promptly did. Oxley was delighted by the improvement that Sarah made to his marksmanship, and also delighted in telling his friends. Soon Sarah had more eager students, merchants, sailors, soldiers, senior policemen, and the greatest honour of all, professional tiger hunters, who brought a wide variety of weapons to the range – the newer rifles, but also older muskets and flintlock rifles, and a range of army and navy pistols, including, she noted wryly, duelling pistols. Soon she was running two training ranges, one for muskets and rifles, and another for hand guns, including her own pride and joy, an 1836 Lafaucheux revolver.

14

In April, Mr Le Dieu, a French resident who had a large coffee plantation west of Serangoon Road, about five miles out of town, founded the Joint Stock Coffee Company with twelve other planters, with Bishop Courvezy of Penang as secretary. In May, another Frenchman, Mr Gaston Dutronquoy from the Channel Islands, arrived in Singapore. He opened the London Hotel in the High Street and placed an advertisement in the *Singapore Free Press* stating that he was available to paint miniatures and portraits. In May, Mr Melany launched the *Sri Singapura,* the first vessel built in Singapore in his yard – a schooner of 100 tons, contracted by Shaw and Stephens.

* * *

At one of their last meetings, Sarah had mentioned to Dr Oxley that a tiger had been terrorizing the local kampongs, and said she had a mind to hunt it down and shoot it herself. A few days later, Dr Oxley came to call. He told her that he had tracked down the tiger, and that he and the rest of his party wanted her to join them. Now this is excitement! thought Sarah. She was about to call for her horse to be saddled, but Oxley told her he already had a spare horse for her, so they could get back to the hunt as soon as possible. She set off with Dr Oxley, carrying her favourite Baker rifle. Older, but more reliable than the Brunswick, she thought. She did not want to take any extra risks with a tiger.

They had gone only a few miles along the road to Serangoon when they came upon a crowd of people assembled in a clearing at the side of the road. There was Major Low, Dr Montgomerie, Mr Spottiswoode and Mr Boustead, both merchants, with clerks in attendance, and assorted soldiers and policemen and a party of Malays. They had come in a variety of forms of transport: horses, ponies, palanquins [xxxvii] and gharries,[xxxviii] and in the case of the Malays, on foot. There was a festive atmosphere, and Oxley and Sarah were hailed heartily by Mr Spottiswoode, who was also one of Sarah's students.

'Ah Mrs Simpson, so glad you could make it to our first tiger hunt, courtesy of Major Low. My only regret is that we did not bring a picnic hamper, I'm afraid we're going to miss tiffin.'

'Thank you for thinking of me, Mr Spottiswoode,' Sarah replied, as she dismounted and removed her rifle from its holster, 'I'm sure we can survive a day without tiffin.'

'When do we start?' she inquired.

'Oh, no need to start, Mrs Simpson,' Spottiswoode replied with a laugh, 'we have the blighter here. The Malays dug a pit and caught him early this morning, then covered it with logs to keep him in. We wanted to give you the honour of first shot.'

He pointed to a methodically placed row of logs around which the hunters stood, their guns at the ready.

Sarah walked forward and approached the pit. It was about twenty-four-foot deep. The tiger stood in about a foot of water, glaring up at his tormentors with angry and bloodshot yellow eyes. As she got closer, the tiger let out a fearsome roar and leapt up the wall of the pit, but was prevented from escaping by the logs across its top.

---

xxxvii A covered litter for one passenger, consisting of a large box carried on two horizontal poles by four or six bearers.
xxxviii A wheeled cart or carriage (usually horse drawn).

After Mr Spottiswoode had assured the Malay hunters that they would receive their reward even though they had not killed the tiger, he gave orders for the logs to be removed, so the hunters could have a clear line of fire.

'Do you think that's wise, Spottiswoode,' said Dr Oxley, cocking his rifle. 'Just take a couple out and we'll be able to get a clear shot.'

'Not much sport in that, doctor,' Mr Spottiswoode replied. 'We ought to give the beggar a sporting chance!'

'As you wish, but you'll get my bill if he eats one of the merchants or natives,' Oxley replied.

They all aimed their weapons down into the pit, as the Malays cleared the logs and the tiger crouched in sullen silence, waiting for its chance.

'On your command, Mrs Simpson, we'll wait on you but please be quick!' cried Mr Spottiswoode.

'No, on yours!' Sarah cried back, raising her rifle to her shoulder. 'I cannot shoot!'

She could not do it. She had no compunction about shooting game – snipe, wild boar and the like – but she could not kill this defenceless animal, no matter how great a danger it posed to livestock and human life. It was a magnificent creature and deserved a better death. An honourable death.

She stepped back from the edge of the pit as the Malays withdrew the last logs and the hunters fired their first volley. It was not a great success, and few of the party hit their target. Mr Spottiswoode forgot to cap his gun, and one of the policemen fired off his ramrod at the animal. The tiger was wounded, but roared back at them, as in contempt. They reloaded and fired a second volley. The tiger ceased to roar. As the smoke cleared, Sarah stepped forward again and looked down into the pit. She saw that the tiger was badly wounded, perhaps dead. It lay motionless in the water at the foot of the pit, its striped coat soaked in blood from head to tail. Sarah turned away in disgust and started to walk slowly back to the horses.

'Do you think it's dead,' said Dr Oxley, peering down into the pit.

'Well, let's see,' said Mr Spottiswoode, who took up a long piece of bamboo and proceeded to cautiously prod the tiger with it.

At first the tiger did not respond, but then, letting out a blood curdling roar, it leapt up and its front claws reached almost to the top of the pit, causing great consternation among the hunters, who fled in all directions into the jungle. Except for Dr Oxley and Mr Spottiswoode, who stood their ground and levelled their weapons once again.

But the tiger was too quick for them. Before they could shoot, it leapt again in rage and desperation, and its front claws gained purchase on the edge of the pit. In a flash, the bloodstained beast scrambled over the edge and onto the solid ground. Dr Oxley and Mr Spottiswoode backed away in haste. Sarah turned on her heel and looked straight into the angry eyes and bared fangs of the tiger. She did not know why the great beast hesitated while she raised her rifle. Yet hesitate it did, then in a sudden frenzy leapt towards her. She shot it right between the eyes. It fell dead at her feet and Dr Oxley and Mr Spottiswoode roared their approval. They hoisted her above their shoulders and paraded her around the pit, as the others returned timidly from the jungle, to the great amusement of the Malays.

Sarah was shaking with delayed fear and exhilaration. The great beast had had its chance, but she had shot it fair and square. She would have its head mounted in the hall. The story of her cool head and crack shot soon spread, and her training classes attracted many more members. But she swore she would never go tiger hunting that way again, and having looked into the tiger's eyes, nor any other way again.

15

Six weeks after Lin's ultimatum they all met with Captain Elliot in Jardine and Matheson's merchant house – European, American, Parsee and Jewish traders, with the exception of the Quakers.

'I must insist on your compliance,' he informed them. 'We cannot go on like this, and we cannot move forward with any negotiation until you surrender your stocks.'

'But can't the ships of the Royal Navy force their way up the river and compel him to back down,' demanded the American Robert Forbes.

'I'm afraid I have no authority to do so, since after all the trade you are engaged in is illegal. And I certainly have no authority to start a war. However, I can assure you that the British government will eventually compensate you for your loss, and secure repayment from the Chinese. But we will have to wait a while for that.'

'He's right,' admitted James Matheson reluctantly. 'We'll soon be out of food, not to mention wine and spirits.'

'I agree,' said Ronnie grudgingly. 'I'm willing to take the loss for the moment, so long as I dinna have tae look at another tattie.'[xxxix]

They had been living off eggs, potatoes, rice and toast for the past six weeks, and it was playing havoc with their digestion, not to mention their evacuation.

Robert Forbes was not yet satisfied and vented his frustration on Captain Elliot.

---

xxxix Scots for 'potato'.

'What guarantees do we have that we will be compensated? Will Great Britain go to war to enforce continued trade?' he demanded to know.

Captain Elliot was preparing a cautious and careful reply, but James Matheson beat him to it.

'I can assure you they will, Forbes. Have no doubt about it.'

'How do you know that?' Forbes responded.

'Oh, I know, Forbes, believe me, I know,' he replied with a thin smile. 'Have faith in the Iron-Headed Rat!'

A few days later the merchants handed over their stocks of opium, some twenty thousand chests in all, about fourteen tons in weight, comprised of three-pound balls of opium extract wrapped in poppy leaves, valued at just over six million Spanish silver dollars. Yet they steadfastly refused to sign any bond committing them to a cessation of trade in opium. When Commissioner Lin released Lancelot Dent and withdrew the Imperial war junks from the mouth of the river, Elliot ordered the British merchants to leave Canton, which they did at the end of May. The other merchants soon followed, while they had the chance. Ronnie set off for home, but not before he had stopped off in Macau to stock up on chickens, fruit and vegetables, and a supply of castor oil.

He was no longer happy as a sand boy.

* * *

Towards the end of May, the British schooner *Royalist*, 142 tons, anchored in the roads, unheralded and unnoticed among the multitude of merchantmen and native craft. The captain of the ship was James Brooke, an Englishman embarked upon a great adventure. James Brooke drew inspiration from the life of Sir Stamford Raffles, and longed to follow in his footsteps.[8]

Some years earlier, James had read George Windsor Earle's

Eastern Seas, published in 1837, and was particularly taken with Earle's description of Borneo. Here was a true prospect for adventure and advancement, a virgin country that had not yet tasted the fruits of Western trade and civilization. It was much like, he thought to himself, the island of Singapore before the coming of Sir Stamford Raffles.

Before he left England, James had published a prospectus describing the goals of his voyage in the *Athenaeum*, a London literary periodical. He declared that his primary intention was, like Sir Stamford Raffles, to resist Dutch influence in the region, and to establish free factories in Borneo through the 'tender philanthropy' of British rule. He had no government sanction for his self-ordained mission, and his prospectus was generally ignored, except by the Dutch, who rightly saw him as another Raffles intent on interference.

James visited Governor Bonham, whom he found to be an amiable and hospitable fellow. Over tiffin, they bemoaned the situation in Canton, two million pounds sterling given up without a struggle, and all the clipper ships standing empty. Bonham took James on a trip around the island, but was lukewarm about his ambitions in Borneo, pointing out that the Armenian merchants in Singapore had already established a trade in antinomy with the region. However, Governor Bonham gave him a letter of thanks to present to Rajah Muda Hassim, who was serving as regent in Sarawak for his nephew, the Sultan Omar Ali Saifudden of Brunei. About a year earlier, the British merchantman *Napoleon* had been shipwrecked off the coast of Brunei. When Rajah Muda Hassim heard of this, he rescued the crew and salvaged as much of the cargo as was possible; he provided food and shelter for the sailors, and sent them back to Singapore at his own expense. This was in marked contrast to the usual practice of the local rajahs, which was to murder, ransom or enslave the crews, and sell the cargo to the highest bidder. Governor Bonham also gave James gifts for

Rajah Muda Hassim from himself and the grateful merchants of Singapore. After nine weeks in Singapore, James signed on some new crew members, including a Malay interpreter, and set sail for Sarawak on July 27.

* * *

Ronnie returned to Singapore at the end of May. All the way back home in the carriage Sarah had brought for him, he regaled her with his account of how he had been robbed and ill-treated by Commissioner Lin, and forced to live off eggs, tatties and rice for nearly two months.

'You do look a bit leaner,' she said, looking him over. 'But don't worry my love, we'll soon feed you up. Although it does suit you, you know.'

Ronnie grunted a response as he got down from the carriage. He was still in an ill temper. He had been in an ill temper since he left Canton. Then he checked himself.

'I'm sorry, Sarah,' he said as they left the carriage and climbed the steps to the entrance to their home. 'I'm sae mad at what happened that I've nae been thinking about anyone else. How are you? How are the children? Has anything happened?'

'Oh, we're all well,' Sarah said breezily as they entered the main hall, 'and it's been very quiet since you've been gone. Just the usual round of dinners, concerts and charity work.'

Ronnie was about to reply when he saw the tiger head mounted on the wall before him.

'Oh aye then, now would you like to tell me about that!'

And so she did.

16

Commissioner Lin had special pits dug and filled with seawater, with canals cut to the mouth of the Pearl River. The seawater was mixed with lime, and the opium tipped into the pits, where it dissolved. The first labourer who tried to steal some of the opium was beheaded on the spot, as a warning to the others. On June 1, when the work was almost complete, Commissioner Lin made a ritual apology to the Spirit of the Ocean and warned the fishes to swim far out to avoid the poison that was about to flow into their waters. Two days later he ordered the canal gates opened and flushed the opium solution out to sea. When Commissioner Lin informed Emperor Tao Kwang of his success, he was rewarded with a sumptuous venison dinner, and a message written by the Emperor in vermilion ink [xl] on a silk scroll wishing him good luck and a long life.

Meanwhile, Elliot had banned all trade with Canton and had withdrawn his naval squadron and the merchant ships to the anchorage at Hong Kong island, from which they received supplies of food and water from Kowloon. In September, Commissioner Lin cut off these supplies by blockading Kowloon. Elliot sent in his frigates, which sank two of the Chinese junks and broke the blockade. The Chinese protested, but did not respond in kind. A month later, the British merchantman *Thomas Coutts* sailed up the Pearl River to Canton, despite Elliot's prohibition. Captain Smith and the ship's owners were Quakers, who would not carry opium, and thought Elliot had exceeded his authority in banning all trade.

---

xl Made from a brilliant red or scarlet pigment.

To prevent a repetition, Elliot ordered a blockade of the Pearl River, and when a second British ship, the *Royal Saxon*, tried to enter in November, the Royal Navy frigates HMS *Volage* and HMS *Hyacinth* fired warning shots across her bows. Commissioner Lin ordered the Imperial navy to protect the *Royal Saxon*, and so began what came to be known as the First China or First Opium War. The British men-of-war outclassed the Chinese war junks, and five of the Chinese ships were sunk, although Commissioner Lin claimed a great victory in his report of the engagement to the Emperor.

Lin then sent out fifteen war junks and fourteen fire ships, which anchored opposite the Brogue forts at the mouth of the River Pearl. Elliot demanded that they be withdrawn, and when his demand was refused, he sent in his frigates again and destroyed more of the Chinese junks. Commissioner Lin reported the engagement to the Emperor as another great victory for the Imperial forces.

* * *

Father Jean-Marie Beurel came to Singapore on October 27.[9] He quickly took charge of the fledgling Roman Catholic community but found that the congregation had already outgrown the small chapel on Bras Basah Road [xli] that had been founded by Father Boucho in 1833. Father Beurel managed to obtain additional land from Governor Bonham opposite the chapel and set about raising funds for the establishment of a larger church, travelling as far as Manila in the Philippines to seek support.

* * *

---

xli On the site of the Bras Basah stream, meaning wet rice stream, because native traders used to unload their cargoes of wet rice on its banks to dry.

William Jardine was enjoying his holiday in Genoa when he heard the news that Commissioner Lin had blockaded the merchants in their factories and destroyed their opium stocks. He was not outraged, but rather grinned with secret glee, for he knew that the Chinese had delivered him just the sort of incident that he could use to persuade Lord Palmerston, the new foreign secretary, to go to war. He cancelled the rest of his holiday and boarded the first ship for London.

17

The *Royalist* arrived off the coast of Borneo five days after leaving Singapore. James Brooke looked out over the unfamiliar coastline, dark blue sea fringing sandy beaches and deep green jungle, and knew that his great work was about to commence. He had toiled and sacrificed, but now the moment he had waited for so long was close at hand, he wondered to himself if he was equal to the task. He was surprised to find that he was not in the least excited or anxious but suffused with a calm determination to make the best of things, however he found them. He would gird his loins, he told himself, and perform a great service that would be useful to mankind and true to his own nature.

On August 15, the *Royalist* anchored off Kuching [xlii] at the mouth of the River Sarawak. After a series of gun salutes, James and his party went ashore to meet with Rajah Muda Hassim in his audience chamber, an open structure made from plank and attap [xliii] and hung with bright cloth. They exchanged formal greetings, and James presented Rajah Muda Hassim with the letter of thanks and gifts from the governor and merchants of Singapore: silk for the Bruneians and velvet for the Malays, and sweets and Chinese toys for the children. James found Hassim intelligent and friendly, and was charmed by Pangeran [xliv] Indera Mahkota, the Governor

---

xlii Cat-town.
xliii Thatch made from the leaves of the attap palm.
xliv Prince or other male noble of high rank.

of Sarawak, who composed clever pantuns [xlv] for each and every occasion, including James' arrival in Sarawak.

James Brooke bore a letter from the governor of Singapore, commanded a heavily armed vessel, flew the ensign of the British Royal Navy and was dressed in a blue naval uniform and jacket (as was his right, the *Royalist* being an ex-Royal Navy vessel). This led Rajah Muda Hassim to believe, not unreasonably, that James Brooke was a representative of the British government. James himself did nothing to disabuse Hassim of this belief, and when Rajah Muda Hassim came on board the *Royalist* in the evening, James answered his questions with the authority of a government official. He advised Hassim against trading with the Dutch, who invariably exploited any region they managed to occupy, and promised him British protection in the event of a Dutch invasion. For Rajah Muda Hassim, these were not academic questions. Hassim was in Sarawak to suppress a rebellion of local Malays who were allied to the Sultan of Sambas, a neighbouring territory controlled by the Dutch. Hassim thought that an alliance with the English might serve as a useful bulwark, as did Prince Mahkota.

* * *

When he returned to Singapore, James Brooke learned that Governor Bonham was much less enthusiastic about his plans for Borneo and refused to endorse his negotiations with Rajah Muda Hassim concerning British protection against the Dutch. Taking great umbrage at what he perceived to be a small-minded insult typical of a Company official, James turned around and set sail again for Sarawak in August 1840.

---

xlv A Malay form of rhyming four-lined allusive poetry.

18

1840

Back in London, William Jardine was doing his best to start a war with China. He gathered signatures from traders, manufacturers and dignitaries for a parliamentary petition. He wrote letters to the press likening the blockade of the merchants in Canton to the horrors of the infamous Black Hole of Calcutta.[xlvi] Armed with a letter of introduction from Captain Elliot, who acknowledged him as leader of the merchant community in Canton, Jardine met with Lord Palmerston, the foreign secretary, and other members of the cabinet and House of Commons. Jardine offered Palmerston his 'suggestions' on how the war should be prosecuted: he presented him with detailed memoranda on how many vessels and soldiers would be needed, detailed maps of the region, and strategic goals from both a military and mercantile point of view. He also outlined the terms of the future treaty to be concluded with China when the war was won. There would have to be compensation for the opium lost, plus interest; the reopening of Canton for trade and the opening of additional trading ports along the China coast, such as Fuzhou, Ningpo and Shanghai; and an indemnity paid for the cost of the war. When Lord Palmerston asked him at their final meeting how such a treaty should be presented to the Chinese, Jardine answered him briskly:

---

xlvi Guardroom of Fort William in Calcutta in which over a hundred men, women and children perished while imprisoned by the Nawab of Bengal in 1746.

'It will gang roughly like this, yer Lordship. You tak my opium, and I tak yer islands in return. We are therefore quits! Let us live in communion and guid fellowship. You canna protect yer seaboard against pirates and buccaneers, but I can. So, let us understand each other and promote our mutual interests.'

'Capital!' said Palmerston. 'I think we understand each other, Mr Jardine, and what is in our nation's interest.'

On the basis of Jardine's 'suggestions', Palmerston decided to go to war with China. Given the persuasive rhetoric of Jardine's petition, Palmerston also had the support of the House of Commons, who voted to approve the dispatch of an expeditionary force to China. Nevertheless, the vote was close, with the young William Gladstone denouncing the 'infamous and atrocious' opium trade, and declaring:

'A war more unjust in its origins, a war more calculated in its progress to cover this country with permanent disgrace, I do not know and I have not read of. I am in dread of the judgments of God upon England for our national inequity towards China.'

However, Lord Palmerston was not in dread, and believed that God and international justice were on the side of the British Empire. He gave orders for the expeditionary force to assemble in Singapore by June 1840, and then proceed to Canton.

* * *

Aristarchus Sarkies was the first Armenian merchant to come to Singapore in 1820 and had gone into business on his own; his nephew Catchick Moses had come to Singapore in 1828 at the age of sixteen and had served in the offices of Boustead, Schwabe and Co as an apprentice before starting his own business. In March, Aristarchus and Catchick founded the firm of Sarkies and Moses. Both men were devoted servants of the Church of Saint Gregory the Redeemer, and Catchick Moses paid for the back porch of the church and the erection of the wall around the church compound. Catchick Moses came to be deeply respected by people of all races and creeds, and many would come to him in the early morning to ask for his advice or help them settle disputes. Catchick was a lefty, who played an excellent game of billiards with his left arm and had the entertaining habit of shaving himself in the morning with his left hand without the use of a mirror, while walking up and down the verandah of his godown.

In April, a great celebration marked the arrival of the large statue of Ma Cho Po that had been especially imported from China for the Thian Hock Keng Temple. A procession extending for nearly a third of a mile wound from Boat Quay to Telok Ayer Street, to the accompaniment of loud clashing gongs and brightly coloured flags that swung high in the air. A Buddhist priest led the procession, and yellow-coated devotees supported the statue of Ma Cho Po on a palanquin [xlvii] draped in yellow silk and crepe. On ornamental platforms supported precariously by iron rods carried by devotees, young girls dressed in shimmering silken garments smiled down upon the crowd, protected from the bright sunshine by the umbrellas they waived gaily around them.

---

xlvii Covered litter, supported by a pole.

19

Ronnie and Sarah Simpson rode in their carriage from Kampong Glam [xlviii] to the Esplanade, where they took their seats for the weekly performance of the military band of the 29th Madras Native Infantry. Then they walked arm and arm along the waterfront promenade under the spreading angsana trees, enjoying the light breezes from the ocean as the sun sunk over the island and spread its golden shadows over the gently rolling surf. They lingered at Scandal Point, where Lieutenant Ralfe had built his gun emplacement many years before, and whose stone dyke was now used as a resting place where the townsfolk exchanged the gossip of the day.

The gossip of the day was about the case of the Armenian merchant who had been imprisoned for debt; although not about his imprisonment for debt, but the fact that his wife had been allowed to accompany him to jail, a matter on which the townsfolk had widely differing opinions. There was also talk about the wife of a European merchant who had got herself into debt playing cherki with her Nonya friends, and how her husband had threatened to horsewhip her if she did not mend her ways. Then just before they were about to leave for home, there was some real news – the first ships of the China fleet had been spotted in the roads. They walked out on the nearby jetty and saw HMS *Conway*, HMS *Larne*, HMS *Cruiser* and HMS *Algerine* anchored side by side. The gun batteries

---

xlviii Village area occupied by Sultan Hussein and his followers, named after the Glam tree, whose resin was used for caulking ships, and whose leaves were used for medicinal oil.

on Government Hill and Fort Fullerton [xlix] fired salutes, and a host of native boats went out to greet them and offer their services.

Over the next few days more and more ships arrived, men-of-war, steamers, and troop and store transports. The troops and marines were disembarked while the expedition awaited the arrival of Rear Admiral Elliot's flagship HMS *Melville* and the rest of the fleet and transports. Rear Admiral the Honourable George Elliot was the cousin of Captain Charles Elliot, the British Superintendent of Trade in Canton, who had ordered the merchants to hand over their stocks of opium to Commissioner Lin. The tents of the infantry and marines were stretched out in neat white lines on the green grass of the Esplanade. The officers promenaded in their dress uniforms in Commercial Square during the day and took service in St Andrew's Church on the Sabbath, while the crews on shore leave indulged themselves in the hostelries and brothels in the backstreets of the town at night.

Governor Bonham, ever genial and hospitable, kept an open house on Government Hill for the officers and captains, where they dined with prominent members of the merchant and business community. Captain Scott and his good friend John Simpson were regular guests of the governor, for they both had a well-deserved reputation for lively conversation and storytelling. Tan Tock Seng and Whampoa were also frequent guests, since they were now established leaders of the Chinese community, and both men spoke excellent English. One evening John Simpson asked the commanding officer of the military force, Sir Gordon Bremer, what their plans were when they reached Canton.

'I'm afraid I can't disclose these, sir,' Bremer replied, 'which is not to say that I distrust our present company, including our

---

xlix Fort built on the Western mouth of the Singapore river in the 1820s, to protect the ships in the harbour. Now the site of the Fullerton Hotel.

Celestial guests. We will of course demand compensation for the opium they have destroyed and some form of reparation, which we will enforce if necessary. We certainly have a force sufficient to our purpose. But I can tell you one thing for nothing. That man William Jardine is the power behind all this. He put it all down in a letter to Palmerston, the number of ships and troops required, where they should be deployed, the amount of compensation and even the terms of the final treaty, down to the last brass tack. Quite a character is Mr Jardine.'

'He is indeed,' said Reverend Ogilvie, who had joined them. 'The Chinese call him the Old Iron-Headed Rat.' Reverend Ogilvie was with the London Missionary Society, en route to Siam, but hoped eventually to be able to spread the word of the Lord to China. 'But do you really think we have the right to force the Chinese to accept a drug that is banned in our own country as well as theirs? Do you know how Queen Victoria responded to Commissioner Lin's appeal that she put an end to the dreadful trade, which I recently heard has already claimed nearly two million poor souls as addicts in the coastal regions?'

'I know nothing about any letter to the Queen, Reverend Ogilvie,' Sir Gordon replied. 'And I'm not as well qualified as you to comment on the morality of the trade, but matters are rather more complicated than you suggest. There is of course the general question of our quite reasonable demand for expanded trade access to China, given the amount of trade in tea and silk we bring to them. Then there is the particular matter of the seizure and destruction of the private property of British merchants, which is an insult to us all. We cannot stand idly by and let that happen, so these people will have to be taught some sort of lesson. I also don't think you can take the high moral ground, Reverend, given that many of your Godly colleagues have rather lucrative investments in the opium trade themselves. Moreover, in opening up the country to trade we also open it up to the expansion of Christian civilization. I'm told that many of your colleagues travel up country with the opium traders distributing bibles and tracts to the Chinese.'

'I'm ashamed to admit you're right about that,' Ogilvie conceded, 'although I refuse to have anything to do with the trade myself. And I acknowledge that there are Christian benefits to the further expansion of trade with China. Yet don't you think ...'

But Sir Gordon interrupted him. 'No, sir, I don't think, and I don't think you should either, Reverend. Just you see to their souls and leave us to serve Her Majesty's government.'

After dinner was over, Sir Gordon stopped Tan Tock Seng and Whampoa on the verandah as they were preparing to leave.

'What do you gentlemen think about this expedition?' he asked them. 'You hardly said a word about it over dinner.'

For a moment neither man spoke, but then Whampoa said in his careful English.

'We are merchants, Sir Gordon,' he replied, 'so of course we support any action that will improve trade between our two countries. We only hope the situation can be resolved amicably, without unnecessary bloodshed on either side.'

'We also hope there will be no repetition of yesterday's incident,' said Tan Tock Seng, referring to the seizure of four junks in the Singapore roads by the over-zealous frigate HMS *Blonde*. 'It created a very bad impression in our own community, and we would appreciate some assurance that such a thing will not happen again.'

'You have my assurance, Tock Seng,' said Governor Bonham, who had overheard the conversation. 'Sir Gordon and I have discussed the matter and taken steps to ensure that it will not happen again. You have my word on it.'

'We accept your word, Tuan Bonham,' replied Tan Tock Seng, 'and bid you good night.' Then he and Whampoa descended the steps from the verandah of Government House and climbed into their waiting carriages.

'Do you think they mean it?' Sir Gordon said to Bonham. 'Do you think you can trust them not to create trouble if hostilities do commence?'

'Oh, I think we can,' Bonham replied. 'Don't you agree, John?' he asked, turning to John Simpson, who had come out with Captain Scott to join them on the verandah.

'Aye, I do,' John Simpson replied, 'for it's nae the Chinaman's love for China you hae to worry aboot, it's his love for this place. If we lose the China trade, he'll be up and awa afore ye can say Jack Robinson, and we'll be stuck here wi the last o' the sea gypsies.'

'They're both good men,' Captain Scott agreed, 'but like their fellow countrymen, they're completely inscrutable. I can talk to them both all night, but still have no inkling about what they really think. I certainly wouldn't want to play them at cards, that's for sure!'

20

The expeditionary force left Singapore in mid-June and assembled off Macau at the end of the month. The complete force comprised of sixteen warships, four armed steamers, and twenty-eight transports carrying four thousand soldiers and marines. A small flotilla was detached to blockade Canton, while the main body of the expeditionary force proceeded north along the coast, much to the consternation of the Canton merchants, who had expected that their first business would be to reopen the Canton factories. Rear Admiral Elliot, following the directive of Jardine and Palmerston, believed that the best way to promote British interests in China was to take their complaint directly to the Emperor Tao Kwang, by threatening him in Peking,[1] the Imperial capital. Elliot bombarded Zhoushan Island at the mouth of the Yangtze River, just south of Shanghai, and occupied the principal city, Dinghai. Then he took the ships further up the coast and anchored them at the mouth of the Peiho River, threatening the river approaches to Peking, and creating pandemonium in the Imperial court. The Emperor was furious that Commissioner Lin had failed to destroy the 'great rats' as he had promised to do. Lin was dismissed from his office as Commissioner of Trade, and sent into exile to Xinjiang Province, in the frozen north. The Emperor replaced him with Qishan, an aristocratic scholar and skilful diplomat, who managed to persuade Rear Admiral Elliot to withdraw his force and return to Canton to begin negotiations towards a peace convention. In the end it was

---

1 Beijing.

Captain Elliot who conducted the negotiations with Qishan since Admiral Elliot was forced to return to England in November due to ill health.

* * *

On August 11, Dr Robert Little, an Edinburgh surgeon, arrived in Singapore aboard the *Gulnare*. He went into partnership with his uncle, Dr M. J. Martin, an English surgeon who had founded the Singapore Dispensary in Commercial Square in the early 1830s. [10]

Dr Little quickly established his reputation in Singapore. He kept up with the latest medical discoveries and techniques by subscribing to the best medical journals, to which he also sometimes contributed – although his lengthy paper on the dangers of opium addiction fell on deaf ears in Singapore. Dr Little had two younger brothers, John Martin and Matthew Little, who later followed him to Singapore, although their own interests were strictly commercial.

In October, Edward Boustead and Joseph Balestier, the American consul, stood at South Point and watched the *Nemesis* anchor in the roads. She was the first steamer to have made the journey from London around the Cape of Good Hope. They discussed the letter they and other merchants had received from Mr Waghorn, proposing the raising of capital for a steamer mail service from London to Canton, using an overland route through Egypt, and passing by Ceylon [li] and the Straits of Malacca on the way to Canton. The East India Company and Her Majesty's Postal Service had rejected the idea of using steamers as mail packets, and the Admiralty was considering scrapping or selling their own steamers, which were considered to be unreliable in bad weather. Despite this, Boustead and Balestier recognized that the future of trade lay in steamships and they had agreed to serve on a committee to

---

li Sri Lanka.

explore the possibility of a steamer mail service. Eighteen steamers had passed through Singapore carrying troops and supplies for the China war, and there were about fifty steamers operating in the Indian Ocean and the South China Sea. They also recognized that in future years there would be heavy demand for docking and coaling facilities for these vessels, which was probably why the clever Chinese had bought up most of the land west of the river and out past Telok Ayer to New Harbour.

The town continued to expand, and the population continued to increase. By 1840 it numbered just under forty thousand, including military personnel and convicts, and the floating population, which comprised mainly Boyanese and Javanese pilgrims paying off their pledges to plantation owners, who covered the cost of their passage to and from the holy city of Mecca on their Haj pilgrimage. The rising price of gambier in the 1830s, when it was in heavy demand by British dyeing and tanning industries, led to a dramatic increase in the number of plantations. The consequent drop in the price of gambier in the 1840s led to an increase in coolie unemployment, which led to increases in vagrancy, poverty and crime.

21

1841

At a peace convention in January, Qishan met with Captain Elliot and agreed to the major British demands under the Convention of Chuenpi. The Chinese would pay an indemnity of six million dollars in compensation for the destroyed opium, reopen Canton to trade, and cede Hong Kong island to the British. Both men left satisfied with the arrangement and gratified that they had managed to avoid further bloodshed. The merchants returned to Canton and reoccupied their factories.

But the Emperor Tao Kwang and Lord Palmerston were far from satisfied, and both were furious at the actions of their representatives. The Emperor had Qishan arrested and taken in chains to Peking, where he was tried for his treacherous surrender of Hong Kong island to the barbarians. Qishan, formerly one of the richest men in China, had his lands and property confiscated. The Emperor repudiated the Convention of Chuenpi and sent an Army of Extermination to Canton, commanded by a triumvirate of generals. Lord Palmerston cursed Elliot for not securing an indemnity for the cost of the war and for failing to get the Chinese to open up additional ports to British trade. Palmerston dispatched Sir Henry Pottinger with a larger expeditionary force to replace Captain Elliot, and to prosecute the war in the vigorous manner that he and Jardine had originally intended.

* * *

Long before Sir Henry Pottinger reached Hong Kong, Captain Elliot realized that the Chinese were stalling, and saw that they were preparing to resume hostilities. In February he seized the initiative by attacking the Bogue forts at the mouth of the Pearl River. The forts contained many cannon that were aimed towards the British ships, but because they were built into the masonry rather than mounted on gun carriages, they were hopelessly inaccurate. They were quickly blown from their encasements by the heavy guns of the ironclad steamer the *Nemesis*, which had recently arrived in Hong Kong under the command of Captain William Hall. The steamship's shallow draught also enabled her to sail right up to the forts and shower the fleeing Chinese with grapeshot as they tumbled from the gaping holes in the masonry that her guns had blasted. Captain Elliot then moved his fleet up to Whampoa, where he captured and burned the nine-hundred-ton *Chesapeake*, which the Chinese had bought from the Americans to turn into a warship. When the flames reached the *Chesapeake*'s magazine, she exploded in a brilliant fireball that cast burning rigging high into the air, setting fire to the junks upriver and the houses on the river bank.

Elliot then moved his fleet up to Canton and ordered a second evacuation of the merchant factories. He did so in the nick of time, for a few days later a Canton mob looted the factories, smashing the windows, mirrors, china, furniture and wine and brandy stocks, then burning the remaining shells of the buildings. The Qing admiral sent out a hundred war junks and fire ships against Elliot's fleet in an attempt to drive the barbarians from the river. Then the imbalance of naval power was made humiliatingly clear to the Chinese, as the *Nemesis* and the other ironclad steamers blasted the fireboats from the water and sunk over seventy of the Chinese war junks.

Yet Elliot did not stop there. He realized that the shallow draft of the *Nemesis* and his other ironclads enabled them to steam upriver beyond Canton, where he landed General Hugh Gough with over two thousand British soldiers and Indian sepoys,[lii] who seized the strategic forts on the hills overlooking Canton. Elliot had the city at his mercy, but once again he entered into negotiations, this time with the triumvirate of generals that commanded the city and the Army of Extermination. As the negotiations dragged on, lawlessness reigned in the countryside while mobs rioted in the city. The British soldiers patrolling the hills above Canton marched through ripening paddy fields, stole livestock and vegetables, raped the local women and gleefully desecrated Chinese graves and temples. In response, the villagers formed themselves into local militias, whose numbers soon swelled into the thousands. Joined by the bandits and pirates who had been driven inland by the British advance, they attacked the barbarian invaders on the hills during a blinding rainstorm. The British held their positions with few casualties, but the militias regrouped and garnered new recruits, until by the end of May they were nearly twenty thousand strong, and ready to wreak their vengeance on their enemies.

Then, just as battle was about to be joined again, Captain Elliot came to an agreement with the prefect of Canton. The Chinese would pay an indemnity of six million taels [liii] of silver for the cost of the war, withdraw their Army of Extermination to sixty miles north of the city, and disband the militias. In return, the British agreed to abandon the hill forts and withdraw their soldiers and ships. Elliot then sailed back down the Pearl River to await the arrival of Sir Henry Pottinger. General Hugh Gough vigorously protested Elliot's action, since in his opinion the army could easily have dispersed the militias and captured Canton, demonstrating once and for all to the Chinese the consequences of insulting Her Majesty's government.

Gough was not the only one who felt cheated by the agreement.

---

lii Infantrymen.

liii Chinese unit of silver currency.

The villagers who made up the militias, and the citizens of Canton, all felt that their Qing masters had betrayed them, and cravenly surrendered to the barbarians to save their own skins. When the scholars entered the examination halls that spring, they flung their ink stones, pens and ink at the officials, while mobs in the streets hunted down the traitors who had helped the barbarians, driving wooden sticks through their ears and into their bleeding brains. Thus were the seeds of rebellion against the Manchu sown in Canton and in the countryside beyond.

22

George Coleman, the Irish architect, had come to Singapore in 1822. He was largely responsible for the town plan of Singapore, as well as many of its fine buildings and churches, including the Armenian Church and St Andrew's Church. Lately he had suffered from a variety of tropical fevers, and accepted Dr Oxley's suggestion that he return home to avail himself of the health benefits of a more temperate climate. Coleman put up his furniture, horses and carriages for sale, and leased his house to Monsieur Dutronquoy, who moved his London Hotel to the new premises. Before he left in July, Coleman supervised the construction of a nine-arched brick bridge between Hill Street and the northern end of Boat Quay. The bridge was originally known as New Bridge, but later came to be known as Coleman Bridge. Coleman also designed an elegant house on Victoria Street for H. C. Caldwell, the senior clerk to the magistrates of Singapore, and built a new Istana for Tengku Ali at Kampong Glam, which Ali hoped would elevate his social status and help promote his claim to the Johor-Riau-Lingga Sultanate.

Sometime after he arrived back in England, the 47-year old Coleman married 21-year old Maria Francis Vernon, the daughter of George Vernon of Clontarf Castle, Dublin.

* * *

In August Daing Ibrahim was rewarded for his cooperation with the government in helping to suppress piracy. In a ceremony presided over by Governor Bonham and attended by most of the leading merchants and local dignitaries, Bendahara Tun Ali of Pahang formally installed Daing Ibrahim as Temenggong of Singapore, with jurisdiction over Johor. Ibrahim had consolidated his position as leader of the Malays of Singapore and Johor, and protector of the sea-peoples. His properties at Telok Blangah had increased in value, in part due to their proximity to Commercial Square. He was on good terms with the mercantile community, particularly with leading merchants such as James Guthrie and William Wemys Ker, who had bought land from him and were now his neighbours at Telok Blangah – Guthrie at St James and Ker at Bukit Chermin.[liv] Joaquim d'Almeida also lived nearby, in a house further west at Raeburn.

When the ceremony was over and refreshments were being served, Ronnie Simpson and James Guthrie thanked Daing Ibrahim for his help in the destruction of the Illanun pirates who were responsible for the murder of Sarah Simpson's sister and her family.

'You make too much of this, my good friends,' he replied. 'All I did was make some inquiries and put out some information.'

'For that we remain very grateful,' Ronnie replied, 'and we congratulate you on your appointment as Temenggong. We're sure you'll carry on your late father's work to preserve the interests of the Malay peoples with great distinction.'

As they left the new Temenggong, Ronnie asked James Guthrie about Tengku Ali, the son of the former Sultan Tengku Long, and if he was now on better terms with Daing Ibrahim.

'Oh no,' Guthrie replied, 'he opposes our new Temenggong, and conspires against him at every opportunity. He still presses his own claim to the sultanate, but the government ignores him. Daing Ibrahim has done a lot for his people, but Ali has done nothing for his. He complains about the inadequacy of his pension, but never invests any of it in commerce or agriculture, unlike our new Temenggong. He just gets deeper and deeper in debt, like his

liv Mirror hill.

father before him – in fact, most of his money is pledged to an Indian Chettiar [lv] to cover the interest on his debt. Daing Ibrahim's estates at Telok Blangah are well managed, but the sultan's Istana at Kampong Glam is a public disgrace, overrun with distant relations and hangers-on who won't lift a finger to help Ali or themselves.'

* * *

In August Sir Henry Pottinger arrived in Hong Kong and took command of the new expeditionary force that had assembled there, which included twenty-four ships of the line, fourteen ironclad steamers, and support and troop ships carrying ten thousand soldiers and marines. With Rear Admiral Parker in charge of the naval force and General Gough in charge of the troops, Pottinger swept north and captured the port city of Amoy on August 26, after destroying fifty junks and three reputedly impregnable forts. He recaptured Zhoushan Island on October 10 and the port city of Ningpo on October 13, where he garrisoned the troops for the winter.

* * *

In December, Alexander Laurie Johnston retired from A. L. Johnston and Co, the firm he had established in 1820, and returned to Scotland.[11] Mr Christopher Rideout Read, his partner since 1822, retired in January of the following year, relinquishing his partnership to his son William Henry Read, who had arrived in Singapore three months earlier on the *General Kyd*. William Henry, or 'W.H.' as he was later known, was born on what the Chinese would have called a propitious day: February 7, 1819, the day after Raffles signed the treaty with the Temenggong and Sultan Hussein establishing the right to establish a trading post on the island.

---

lv South Indian trader and moneylender.

23

1842

As the Chinese New Year dawned, the Emperor Tao Kwang looked forward to the fight with the British barbarians, as most of his advisors had assured him that the British were incapable of fighting on land. Tao Kwang had appointed his cousin I-ching as commander in chief of the Imperial army, and within a few months he had assembled a force of over sixty thousand men, both regular troops and local militia, and prepared to march on Ningpo.

On New Year's Day, General I-ching visited the Temple of the God of War to pray for victory. He drew a slip of paper from the box held out by the priest, and read the inscription:

If you are not hailed by humans with the heads of tigers
I would not be prepared to vouch for your security.

Three days later a contingent of militiamen arrived from the Golden River region of Szechwan, all wearing tiger-skin caps, and then General I-ching knew he was assured of victory.

Inspired by the tiger omen, he determined to attack the barbarians at the tiger hour of the tiger day of the tiger month of the tiger year, between 3am and 5am on March 10. Unfortunately for General I-ching, the tiger month of 1842 was also the height of the rainy season. His advance columns had to drive through rain and mud to reach Ningpo, and lost most of their supplies and provisions when their wagons tumbled over into ditches and riverbeds. They were hungry, exhausted, and soaked to the skin when they advanced with their rusting matchlocks and muskets, to be slaughtered by the British mines, howitzers and grapeshot, and deadly volleys from the new Enfield rifles with which the British regiments had been recently equipped.

Having crushed the Imperial Qing forces before Ningpo, Pottinger advanced up the Yangtze River, captured the city of Chapu, and entered Shanghai, which he found abandoned. He was temporarily stalled at Chinkiang, where the Manchu Bannermen lived up to the reputation they had gained when their ancestors had ridden down from Northeastern Manchuria to seize the Middle Kingdom from the Ming dynasty in the seventeenth century. They fought a desperate action against the British infantry, until they finally saw that their position was hopeless. Then the Manchu killed their women and children, and hung themselves or fell on their swords. With Chinkiang captured, Pottinger now commanded access to the Grand Canal, through which all provisions for Peking were transported. As Pottinger advanced towards Nanking,[lvi] the former capital and China's second largest city, the Emperor sent Ch'i-ying, another of his aristocratic relations, to negotiate a peace settlement. General I-ching was arrested and taken back to Peking, where he was imprisoned and tried on the charge of wasting the resources that the Emperor had entrusted to him.

---

lvi Nanjing.

24

The Thian Hock Keng Temple was completed in August, in traditional southern Chinese architectural style. The timber, granite and statues for the temple were imported from China. The cast iron railings that surrounded the temple had been brought out from Glasgow, and the blue ornamental tiles that decorated many of its buildings had been shipped from England and Holland. The temple itself was constructed from pre-jointed wooden frames, without the use of a single iron nail.

The temple had a rich red and gold facade, with fine carvings, sculptures and tiled roofs surmounted with dragons. At the main entrance stood two giant stone lions: the right male dragon held a ball symbolizing wealth; the left female lion held a cub symbolizing fertility. The high threshold at the main entrance forced worshippers to look downwards as they entered, thus adopting the appropriate pose for entering the temple, and also served to protect the temple from wandering ghosts, by tripping their shuffling feet if they tried to enter. The front entrance led into two wide courtyards, with the main temple in the centre. The statue of Ma Cho Po was surrounded by burning incense and candles, and her lips were smeared black with opium to heighten her senses. The deities of health and wealth stood at each side of the goddess, and two tall stone sentinels stood guard over her shrine: one of these could see for one thousand miles; the other could hear for the same distance. On either side of the main temple were two octagonal pagodas, the one on the left housing a shrine to Confucius, the one on the right containing the ancestral tablets of the founders. Although the main temple was Taoist, a smaller Buddhist temple in the rear housed a statue to Guan Yin, the Goddess of Mercy, her many arms reaching out to all those who suffer on earth.

After the official dedications were completed, Moon Ling made her own offering to Ma Cho Po, thanking the goddess once again for saving her life so many years ago, and praying that she would guide her husband, long years since lost at sea, through the dark night to everlasting peace.

* * *

The Treaty of Nanking was signed by the Emperor's representative Ch'i-ying aboard Pottinger's flagship on August 29 and marked the end of the First China or First Opium War. The Chinese agreed to pay an indemnity of twenty-one million dollars, in compensation for the losses to the Canton merchants and the cost of the prosecution of the war. Canton was to be reopened to British trade, and four new ports were to be established at Amoy, Fuzhou, Ningpo and Shanghai. British consuls were to be established at these 'treaty ports', and British gunboats stationed in them. Britain was to have sole legal jurisdiction over her own nationals, and Christian missionaries were to be allowed to continue their operations unmolested. The island of Hong Kong was officially ceded to Her Britannic Majesty, and her heirs and successors. The treaty made no mention of the legality or illegality of the opium trade.

The United States and France entered into similar arrangements shortly afterwards, and with the opening of the new treaty ports, the trade in tea and silk and opium boomed. As the tea clippers raced to London and New York, raw Indian opium was consigned and processed in Singapore, and smuggled by square riggers, steamers and schooners up and down the coast of China, from Macau to

Shanghai. Shanghai's trade exploded and transformed the port city into the new metropolis of China.

The treaty was a shameful humiliation for the Emperor and his aristocratic mandarin ministers. Yet they had no choice but to surrender to the demonstrated superiority of British warships, ironclad steamers, modern artillery and Enfield rifles. The Emperor and his ministers decided to play a waiting game, initiating a policy of self-strengthening in the hope that through modernization of their armed forces they would eventually attain military and naval superiority over the barbarians. For the ordinary people – for the villagers who had flocked to the black banners in the countryside beyond Canton, and to his Hakka brethren to whom Hong Xiuquan returned after he failed his examinations in Canton again in the spring of 1843 – it was yet another betrayal by their Manchu masters to save their own skin.

25

1843

Tan Tock Seng was returning from tiffin with John Horrocks Whitehead at the new London Hotel, where they had been discussing the purchase of a fifty-acre parcel of land at Tanjong Pagar. Tan Tock Seng had become friends with Whitehead when he had worked for Graham Mackenzie and Co. The two men had gone into business together to sell wholesale local produce, and now exported pepper and gambier and imported building materials. Whitehead was later made a partner in Graham Mackenzie and Co, when it became Shaw, Whitehead and Co, but he continued to work with Tan Tock Seng, and both men made fortunes through their speculation in the property market.

Tan Tock Seng was walking along Boat Quay to visit his shophouse when he suddenly stopped in his tracks. On the ground a few feet in front of him a Chinese man lay on his back, so thin and undernourished that his skin hung from his bones like ill-fitting clothes. He was clad only in a pair of filthy ragged trousers and a torn singlet, which revealed his skinny rib cage. The bristled hair on his head was white as snow, and his face was deeply lined, but it was difficult to tell the man's age. He could have been an older man who had weathered life longer than most, or he could have been a younger man destroyed by backbreaking work and opium. His black eyes stared up blankly at the puffy white clouds in the deep blue sky – the man was stone dead. Tan Tock Seng stood for a few moments in silence, a short bespectacled merchant, with his black queue hanging down his back over his plain grey tunic.

He watched in mounting horror as merchants, lightermen and coolies walked around the body, giving it no more attention than a dead dog or a pile of rubbish. The driver of a bullock cart got down and pushed the body aside to clear a path for his cart, while another stole the dead man's ragged singlet. Tan Tock Seng sighed deeply and shook his head. He was a devout Taoist, and his heart was filled with *cí*, a deep compassion for the suffering of a fellow human being.

How can I, a successful merchant, ignore the fate of one so wretched as this poor dead man? he thought to himself.

Then he made his decision. He went into the nearest shop and asked the Chinese shopkeeper to send his boy for the undertaker. Then he asked the man to help him remove the body from the main thoroughfare. When the undertaker arrived, Tan Tock Seng paid him to arrange for the burial and funeral services for his dead countryman. After the undertaker had left with the body, Tan Tock Seng made his way to the Thian Hock Keng Temple to pray for the man's departed soul. Over the next decade Tan Tock Seng arranged for the burial and funeral services for over one thousand Chinese paupers and destitutes, including the provision of over one thousand black coffins.

* * *

William Jardine never returned to China and did not live long enough to enjoy his wealth and retirement. After he persuaded Palmerston to prosecute the China war, he bought an estate at Lanrick in Perthshire, Scotland, and was elected member of parliament for Ashburton in Devon in July 1841. He died on February 27, 1843, after a long and painful struggle with stomach cancer, and was buried in Lochmaben, the place of his birth. The fates were kinder to James Matheson. He retired to Scotland in 1842, where he bought the island of Lewis in the Western Hebrides for two hundred thousand pounds sterling. [12] The business of Jardine, Matheson and Co was carried on after his departure by William Jardine's nephews, David, Joseph, Robert and Andrew Jardine, and by his own nephew, Alexander Matheson.

PART TWO

THE WHITE RAJAH

1843 – 1846

1

1843

Captain Stephenson, the acting settlement engineer, was excavating the western mouth of the Singapore River, to clear the entrance for shipping and to make space for living quarters at Fort Fullerton, when he came upon a large sandstone rock that had been hidden by the surrounding brush. It was about ten-foot high, ten-foot long, and about five-foot wide. A single-minded government officer intent on the immediate task at hand, Captain Stephenson gave orders that charges be set. Shortly afterwards the stone was blown to pieces, the sound of the explosion echoing for miles around.

When Colonel Low heard the explosion in his office at the courthouse, he feared the worse. He immediately left the office and took a sampan across the river, where he found the remains of the stone whose ancient inscriptions had puzzled Raffles, Farquhar and Abdullah so many years before. The great rock, which according to Malay legend had been thrown across the river by Badang, the royal champion, now lay scattered in pieces across the ground before him. With the help of some Chinese labourers, but with no help from Captain Stephenson, Colonel Low had those fragments that still retained their ancient inscriptions chiselled down to manageable sizes. He arranged for three large pieces to be sent to the Royal Asiatic Society Museum in Calcutta, and sent another piece to Governor Bonham, who had it placed at the corner of Government House. This last piece was shortly after demolished by zealous convicts who had been employed to fill in some holes in the road. Fortunately, Colonel Low kept a portion for himself, which he presented to the Singapore Library when it was founded the following year in the Singapore Institution.[13]

* * *

Shortly after Dr Montgomerie had arrived in Singapore with Raffles in 1819, he had started a plantation on the track past Bukit Selegie. One morning in 1822, as he walked by the edge of his plantation, he came across a Malay woodcutter paring a log of wood with his parang. He was impressed by the firm grip the man had on the blade, despite the fact that the day was hot and both men were sweating profusely. When he questioned the woodcutter, the man told him that the handle was formed from the sap of the gutta percha tree. When the sap was collected, it hardened, but grew soft again when placed in hot water, and could be formed into any shape that would grow hard once again when it was removed from the water. The woodcutter had formed the handle of his parang by moulding it in the shape of his hand, which gave him its secure grip. The woodcutter had taken Dr Montgomerie into the jungle and showed him a gutta percha tree, which Montgomerie had sketched in his notebook.

At the time he thought the material would be especially useful for knife handles and surgical instruments, although he had thought no more about it for years. But this year, before his departure on furlough to Scotland, he remembered the Malay woodcutter and his parang and began to experiment with samples of gutta percha. He wrote an article on its properties and sent some samples to the Medical Board in Calcutta, and, through his brother-in-law, to the Society of Arts in London. The Society quickly recognized the potential of the material and awarded Montgomerie their gold medal the following year. That same year Jose d'Almeida, on a visit to London, described the properties of gutta percha to the members of the Royal Asiatic Society in London.

The introduction of gutta percha to Britain set off a craze for the substance, which was used in snuffboxes, walking sticks, dolls, chess pieces, bottle stoppers and temporary tooth fillings. The early attempts to use gutta percha for medical instruments were not so successful, because manufacturers usually treated it as an elastic form of rubber rather than a malleable plastic that could be moulded to a hard finish. While it became an important export,[14] there was not much use for the product in Singapore, although local Malays still used it to mould the handles of their parangs, and some syces [lvii] used it to make horsewhips.

* * *

Many benefited from the discovery of these varied uses of gutta percha, but none more than Daing Ibrahim, the newly recognized temenggong of Singapore. His friend, neighbour and business partner William Wemys Ker alerted him to the economic potential of gutta percha, or *getah taban* as the Malays called it, when large deposits were found in the forests of Johor. The first European shipment was sent out by Ker, Rawson and Co, who managed Ibrahim's commercial interests in Johor for the ensuing decades, to their mutual profit. Daing Ibrahim declared a monopoly on all gutta percha collected in Johor and sent gangs of orang laut [lviii] into the jungle under the supervision of his Telok Blangah followers. Soon farmers and labourers were gathering gutta percha from Penang to Pahang, throughout the Riau-Lingga Archipelago, and in the jungles of Borneo and Sumatra. A new Malay term was coined,

---

lvii Grooms.
lviii Literally 'sea-people'. The original aboriginal 'sea gypsies' of Singapore, who dwelt in boats along the coastline of Singapore.

menaba, meaning to collect gutta percha. Ibrahim then extended his monopoly to all the gutta percha that was gathered in the region and delivered to Singapore. His ships in the roads stopped all native craft carrying the product, and forced them to sell at prices considerably below the market value, creating huge profits for Ibrahim and Ker, Rawson and Co. Within a few years Daing Ibrahim had cornered about ninety percent of the gutta percha market in the region, a market that soon exceeded one million dollars per annum and was now rapidly approaching two million dollars per annum.

As he expanded his business and courted the government, Daing Ibrahim continued to cultivate friendships and partnerships with the European and Chinese merchants. In addition to his business dealings with Ker, Rawson and Co and Guthrie and Co, he helped to negotiate trading concessions and mining rights for Martin, Dyce and Co in Siak and Paterson and Simons in Pahang. He also established a partnership with the clothing merchant Tan Hiok Nee, who was second in command of the Ngee Heng secret society, a Teochew offshoot of the Ghee Hin. Through Tan, Daing Ibrahim developed relations with the predominantly Teochew gambier and pepper plantation owners on the island, who had been granted the right to farm the jungle by his late father, before Raffles and Farquhar had landed.

2

On February 23-25, the first organized horse races were held in Singapore, and the Sporting Club was formed. Mr W.H. Read of Johnston and Co won the first race, the Singapore Cup, for $150, and Clarence Goymour of the Royalist Hotel won the second race. In early March, the first full Regatta was held. The umpire was Captain Henry Keppel of HMS *Dido*, who awarded the first prize to the *Maggie Lauder*. The band of the *Dido* played for two to three hours each evening on the Esplanade, until she left in April.

* * *

Hoo Ah Kay, or Whampoa as the European community affectionately knew him, was now head of a thriving company, with offices on Boat Quay and a large godown on Telok Ayer Street. Whampoa was the main chandler for the ships of the British Navy as well as many private merchantmen; he owned nutmeg plantations at Tang Leng,[lix] and land and property in Chinatown and Serangoon Road. He had also formed a partnership with Mr Gilbert Angus, one of the Scottish merchants. Part of Whampoa's success was due to his proficiency in English, which made it easier for him to negotiate with ship's captains and European merchants, although he would occasionally confuse some English phrases, much to the amusement of his English friends.

One day when John Turnbull Thomson, the government

---

lix Meaning 'great east hill peaks', later known as Tanglin.

surveyor, was showing Whampoa some pen and ink sketches that the merchant Charles Dyce [15] had created of himself and his family, Whampoa told him how much he admired the 'scratches' of his family. When Thomson pointed out the difference between 'sketches' and 'scratches', they had a good laugh together. As Whampoa was leaving, the correction slipped his mind, and he asked Thomson if his artist friend could do some scratches of himself and his family to send to their relations in Canton. Thomson replied that he was sure this could be arranged, although he hoped the artist would not scratch too deep. Whampoa, remembering his error, laughed so hard that the tears ran down his face.

While he got on well with the European merchants, and frequently mixed with them socially, Whampoa did not adopt Western habits of clothing. He was a devout Taoist, and dressed in a traditional black tunic, trousers, and felt-bottomed slippers, with his long queue hanging down his back to his waist. He was a small man with a slim body, and a large head that was bald apart from his queue; he had dark eyebrows and moustache and sparkling black eyes. Mindful of the limitations of his own English, which was self-taught, Whampoa sent his son to study at the University of Edinburgh. When the young man returned three years later, he spoke excellent English, but had cut off his queue and embraced the Protestant faith. Whampoa immediately packed him off to Canton and ordered him not to return until he had learned to respect his ancestors and his Chinese heritage.

In 1840 Whampoa had built himself a bungalow about two and a half miles outside town at Serangoon, next to his orange plantation and fruit orchard. His two-storied house was unpretentious from the outside, but filled with magnificent lacquered furniture and silk hangings inside. Adjacent to his bungalow, Whampoa had laid out an extensive Chinese garden. He had brought in skilled horticulturists from Canton to lay out the pathways, which wound through mini-rockeries, through magical forests of dwarf bamboo trained into the shapes of animals, and by deep ponds whose waters were covered with water lilies of every colour of the rainbow, or brimming with gold and black carp. The air was filled with the perfume of chrysanthemums, dahlias, and a host of other flowers, which were arranged in groves around exotic flowering trees and plants. Waterfalls splashed down over rockeries and into miniature lakes, their dark waters reflecting the moon and stars in the night sky. Throughout the gardens and along the paths there were a multitude of brightly flowering plants and shrubs: brilliant ixora, delicately scented magnolias, and bright hibiscus. In the early evening, it was a magical jungle of dark tropical foliage and a kaleidoscope of colours. The gardens contained an aviary, with many species of singing birds – merbuks, white rumped shamas and mata putehs – whose sweet notes seemed to drift like musical threads between the bamboo and rockeries. Whampoa also maintained a sizeable collection of animals in his menagerie. Many were tame and wandered around at their leisure through the gardens, so it was not unusual to see a mouse deer nibbling on the bamboo or an orang utan [lx] lounging on one of the stone benches.

An ornamental open circular gate led into the garden, which Whampoa opened to the public during Chinese New Year, when people from all walks of life – rich and poor, Chinese, Malay, Indian and European – would wander among his rockeries and bamboo forests, and visit the food stalls, booths and merry-go-rounds that were set up for the occasion.

Whampoa regularly hosted dinners for ships' captains and merchants at his estate. He was extremely sociable and hospitable, but he always sat a little apart from the company, in a chair set

lx The word 'orangutan' comes from the Malay words 'orang' (man) and '(h)utan' (forest), literally 'man of the forest'.

back from the table, where he sipped his Madeira sherry from a tall-stemmed glass. One such dinner was held in May to celebrate the return of James Brooke after his remarkable adventures in Borneo. The guests included Governor Bonham, who was about to depart for his retirement in England, Captain Jameson of the *Liverpool Spirit*, Captain Green of HMS *Leander*, Captain Ney of the French Schooner *Liberté*, Captain Scott the harbour master, Captain Henry Keppel of HMS *Dido*, and John and Ronnie Simpson and his son Duncan.

Duncan, now age seventeen, had grown almost as tall as his father, and had inherited his slim, strong and wiry body. He also had his father's sharp angular face, with hawk-like features, enhanced by his wavy brown hair and sharply pointed sideburns. But he had his mother's bright blue eyes and her habit of sticking her tongue out when in deep concentration. Duncan had been educated at various schools in Singapore, where he had shown a remarkable facility in languages. He mastered the local Malay with ease, but also the various dialects of the Chinese and Indians. He also had a good head for figures, which made him a great asset to his father and grandfather at Simpson and Co, where he had served as an apprentice for the past few years. John and Ronnie Simpson hoped that one day he would be able to take over the company, and so far, he had shown every indication that he was willing to do so. At the moment Duncan's bright blue eyes were fixed on James Brooke, whom he thought a heroic figure.

James Brooke was six feet tall, slim and muscular, with dark wavy hair and sideburns that framed his bronzed face. His eyes and nose were well proportioned, as if they had been painted on a canvas. He had a small but sensual mouth, firmly set in an almost permanent half smile. Handsome and well spoken, he exuded the confidence of his adventurous spirit. He was dressed in a dark blue naval jacket with brass buttons, with a white shirt and black silk bandana, his tight flannel trousers held with a black belt and brass buckle – to all appearances a dashing naval officer in Her Majesty's Service, which he was not. Yet he was a presence, a force of human nature whose dark brown eyes burned with the intensity of his vision and purpose.

Brooke was describing to his audience how he came to be the Tuan Besar [lxi] of Sarawak.

---

lxi 'Great Lord.'

3

'When I returned to Kuching in '41,' Brooke recalled, 'Rajah Muda Hassim welcomed me with open arms. The war with the rebellious Malays still dragged on, although some of them had come over to Hassim's side, along with some local Chinese. I quickly discovered that his original story about threats from the Sultan of Sambas and the Dutch was complete fiction – the so-called war was really a dispute about the trade in antinomy. The Malays and Dayaks [lxii] use it as a dye and cosmetic, while the Europeans and Americans use it to make tin cans and bullets. The name of the state and the river on which Kuching is situated, 'Sarawak', comes from the Malay name for the silvery-white metalloid. Antinomy is known in the commercial world as 'Singapore stone', because your merchants control most of its distribution. Prince Mahkota had been trying to seize control of this lucrative market, which had led to a showdown with the local Malays who traditionally mined and traded it.

'Now I say "war" and "showdown", but it was really nothing of the kind. For years, both sides had built forts, which they constantly disassembled and reassembled in various places, while shouting insults at each other, screaming their war cries and clashing their gongs. It practically never came to anything. There were few casualties, most of whom were executed prisoners. I thought I could bring the affair to a speedy conclusion, and brought up four guns from the *Royalist*, which we used to blast a hole in the nearest fort. Mahkota and the Chinese were willing to follow

---

lxii Native peoples of Borneo.

through right away, but the Brunei and Malay chiefs were in no hurry. They debated endlessly over their battle plan and gave long speeches about their past exploits. They even performed war dances and whipped themselves into a fighting frenzy. But they would not attack! I packed up our guns in disgust and got ready to quit the place.

'Then a remarkable thing happened. As we were preparing to leave, Rajah Muda Hassim came on board and offered me the state of Sarawak if I would stay and help Prince Mahkota bring the war to a swift conclusion. I was frankly flabbergasted and a tad suspicious of Hassim's motives. I knew he was only in Sarawak because of the war, and was desperate to get back to Brunei, because he feared – and I believe on good grounds – that his enemies were plotting against him. I questioned his authority to grant me this great gift – surely he would need the approval of the Sultan of Brunei?

'Hassim assured me he had the authority, and that I would be in charge of the government and the revenues. When I pressed him, he granted that the sultan would of course make a small charge on the revenues, as demonstration of his authority, and said he would leave behind one of his brothers to help ensure the loyalty of the Malays and Dayaks. I remained cautious and suspected a trick. It just seemed too easy, my friends.

'Then I met the brother whom Hassim was proposing to leave behind, Pangeran Badrudeen. Oh, what a man was Prince Badrudeen! Tall and muscular, with dark flashing eyes and a sharp intelligence. He was, like myself, a born adventurer and romantic, and we got on like a house on fire. He came to share my fondness for wine, and even adopted European attire. We had some jolly times together and I decided to take up Hassim's offer and stay.

'We brought up our guns again. Feeling certain that Badrudeen's presence would spur them to action, I ordered a general charge against the rebel forts. But they would not budge for fear of endangering Badrudeen's royal blood, and we were back to square one again! Or so I thought. A few days later a Dayak tribesman came out of the jungle with a plea for help from the Temenggong of Lundu, who was trapped by the enemy in his half-finished stockade. We immediately set off in pursuit, without consulting anyone, and came upon the rebels as they advanced upon the stockade. We charged, and the rebels, taken completely by surprise, threw down their weapons and fled into the jungle. Without a casualty on either side, would you believe it!

'I could have left it at that, but decided not to, because I knew they would return again sooner or later. So, with the help of some holy sherips ^{lxiii} from both sides, I arranged a parley with the enemy. After a day of negotiations, we agreed terms of their surrender. I guaranteed the safety and security of their property on condition that they gave up their weapons and their forts. They were as good as their word, but Prince Mahkota, who had gotten word of our victory, almost ruined it all by demanding the right to plunder the defeated rebels' property. I would have none of that and fired over the heads of his men to stop them. Hassim backed me up, although I fear I made a lifelong enemy of Prince Mahkota.

'I was all set to take up my promised position as master of Sarawak, but to my disgust, now that I had won the war, Hassim was no longer willing to hand over control. He assured me it was only a temporary delay, and that I was free to stay and trade until he received the approval of the Sultan of Brunei, which, as you may recall, he had assured me earlier he did not need. As you can imagine I felt cheated and was very unhappy about the situation. Hassim advised me to return to Singapore to secure some trade goods while we waited for word from the sultan, and promised to build me a fine house for my return. I was disinclined to take

---

lxiii Noble men believed to be descended from the prophet Mohammed by way of his daughter Fatimah.

his advice, having already had enough of the false promises of Borneans. But Badrudeen assured me he was going to remain as promised, and Hassim further enticed me by offering to organize a shipment of antinomy. Since I had effectively seized control of that market by defeating the rebels, I saw the real commercial sense in giving it another go. So, I returned to Singapore to pick up some cargo. I purchased a new vessel, the *Swift,* and returned to Kuching as soon as we were loaded. I was eager to begin trading and hold Hassim to his bargain, and to be honest to see Prince Badrudeen again. But I should have known better. When I arrived, I discovered that no house had been built, no antinomy had been collected, and Hassim – who was happy enough to take my trading goods – was still waiting approval from the sultan.

'Then fate – or God – took a hand. Someone tried to poison me. My poor Chinese cook actually died, and I managed to pin the blame – fairly I am sure – on Prince Mahkota, who I know was opposing my appointment. Then all a sudden the *Diana,* the Company steamer, entered the river bristling with guns, and belching smoke like a fiery dragon! The very same *Diana* that I believe supported you in your battle with the Illanun pirates, Mr Simpson.'

'It was indeed,' Ronnie Simpson replied, raising his glass, and they all followed him in a toast to the *Diana.*

'Now the thing was, she had only put in for fruit and water, and had nothing to do with me. But they naturally assumed otherwise and were greatly impressed by the power she represented. So, I loaded the *Swift*'s guns with grape and canister in case of trouble and marched off to Hassim's compound with a bunch of armed men – my own crew and some Malay and Dayak warriors who seemed eager for a fight. I assured Hassim of my good will towards him, but denounced Mahkota as an evil man and demanded that Hassim keep his end of the bargain as I had kept mine.

'He looked towards me and my boys, and to the *Diana* on the river, and agreed! A few days later, in a pavilion hung with flags and bunting – a bit like Raffles on the day of the Singapore treaty – we signed and sealed an agreement designating my good self as the Rajah of Sarawak, with all the power and authority accorded to the title. And that is how I became the Rajah of Sarawak, or Tuan Besar, as they call me.'

'Hear, hear,' said Governor Bonham, who rose and led another toast to the new Rajah of Sarawak, or as some had come to call him, the White Rajah of Sarawak.

'Almost happened to me too, you know,' said Captain Keppel, who was sitting grinning at the end of the table.

Henry Keppel was an officer in Her Majesty's Navy.[16] If not as dashing as Brooke, he was certainly as brave, and definitely savvier. In 1832, he was sent to support British forces in the war against the Penghulu of Naning, north of Malacca, in HMS *Magicienne*, twenty guns. He was in command of a small force blockading the mouth of the Muar River, to prevent arms and supplies reaching the rebels.

'Pretty dull sort of duty,' Captain Keppel explained to the company. 'Almost impossible to patrol the length of the coastline, and I'm sure supplies got in most other ways than through the mouth of the river. But I got to know the Rajah of Muar pretty well; he had a large house facing the river a bit up country. One day I acknowledged his royalty with a twenty-gun salute, and he invited me to dinner. A sailing man himself, we got on very well, like two old chums out on a night on the town in Portsmouth. He loved to play chess, and we had a great many games together – rather evenly matched, I thought. Well, about three months later the war was over, after the Company and the Penghulu came to a financial settlement, but I was loath to part from my good friend. I went to visit him one last time, to bid him farewell, when to my great surprise he offered me his daughter's hand in marriage, on condition that I would solemnly promise to become his heir and succeed him on the throne of Muar. I have to say I was jolly tempted, even though she was a tall Malay beauty and me a rather tubby five-footer, but duty was duty, and I was ordered back to the Cape. So, you see, I could have been the first White Rajah, although I dare say James is doing a far better job of it than I could ever have done.'

Keppel sat back in his chair. He was, as he had said, rather stocky and no more than five feet tall. In his mid-thirties, his hair was already balding, and he looked more like an avuncular banker or broker than a naval captain. But his hazel eyes flashed with intelligence, and he was known to be a lion in battle.

4

Whampoa, who had been listening to the conversation with an expression of polite interest, posed a question to Rajah Brooke:

'Now that you are the ruler of Sarawak, Mr Brooke, how will you govern the fierce Dayaks and the rest of the Malays, and how will you treat my countrymen, who have business and mining interests in Borneo?'

'Oh, with a firm hand and understanding, in the way Sir Stamford treated the locals here. I mean to rescue them from barbarism and lead them on the road to civilization. I will impose firm rules based upon English law but adapted to local circumstances, which I'm having written up while I'm here in Singapore. We have a court that meets almost daily, and we get by pretty well, all things considered. We even tried a huge crocodile the other week, for having eaten a number of men and children. Some of the Malay nobles wanted to spare his life, on the grounds that he was a rajah among crocodiles, but I had him killed and hung up over the river as a warning to all the other crocodiles.'

What Brooke did not say was that the system worked well because his word was law, backed by the guns of the *Royalist* and those Dayaks and Malays who had sworn allegiance to him after he had won the war, and who remained fiercely loyal to their Tuan Besar.

'Of course,' Brooke continued, 'you need to distinguish between the hill Dayaks, or Bidayuh, who are industrious farmers, and a peaceful and honest people, and the sea Dayaks, or Iban, who are a race of ruthless pirates and headhunters, who prey upon the hill tribes, with the connivance of the Malay and Brunei princes. They sail up the rivers in their great war fleets, stealing the produce of the hill tribes, slaughtering their men and taking their heads, and driving many of their women and children into slavery. You may think I exaggerate, but I assure you, sirs, I do not!

'The hill Dayaks can be easily brought to a state of improvement, so long as they are protected from their pirate brethren, and I believe the same is true of the sea Dayaks and the rebellious Malays, so long as they can be persuaded to abandon their piratical ways and appreciate the benefits of free commerce in the archipelago. For they are in their own way a noble race, and their spirit of adventure reminds me of my own youthful days. They are really like a good breed of dogs, which need the firm hand of a kindly master. I warned one of the Skrang chiefs recently that he could not enter our country or pass up our rivers, and that could not take a single head or he would answer dearly for it. He was a tall, strong, and ferocious-looking man, tattooed all over his body, with an intelligent face and a reputation as a fierce fighter. He accepted my warning without demur, yet he kept nagging me over and over again, with a sheepish grin on his face, asking if I would not let him take just one or two heads – he was like a schoolboy asking for apples!

'I believe that we can advance these races further in the scale of civilization without sacrificing their freedom, so long as we can get them to embrace commerce, which will benefit both the native peoples and ourselves. The main obstacle to that is piracy, which is the curse of the region. And the main culprits are the Saribus and Skrang, a bunch of ruthless Dayaks who are the scourge of the coast and rivers. Once we've driven them out, we'll have a good shot at it.'

'Hear, hear,' echoed the company, who had had their own share of problems with pirates, and told him so.

'But I thought you'd dealt with the pirates around here,' Brooke responded. 'What about Stanley and Congalton? And Captain Chads? I thought they'd cleared out the place?'

'Well, they did a lot of damage to the Illanun, and my son and daughter-in-law helped them a good bit,' replied John Simpson, with not a little pride. 'You don't see much of them these days, but the local Malay pirates are near as bad, although they tend to restrict their attacks to the Chinese and native craft. But we're gradually clearing them out as well. The steamers are a great help – the native boats are afraid o' them, with their chimneys belchin' smoke and nae need for wind. Scares the divil out o' them!'

'Well, I promise to do my share, as I'm sure you'll do yours, and one day we'll have the seas around us safe for trade and travel. Death to the pirates!' James Brooke cried, raising his glass. They all joined him in his toast, including Whampoa's tame orang utan, who had wandered in and picked up one of the open champagne bottles.

After the toast was over, Duncan spoke up to ask Brooke a question.

'A fascinating story, Rajah Brooke, and you do your country great credit. I'm fascinated by the headhunters, though – could you tell me how they preserve the heads and why they take them?'

'Well, young Duncan,' Brooke said, 'the first order of business is of course to sever the victim's head from his torso. Easily done with a sharp parang. The second order is a nasty piece of work in which they scoop out the brains from the bottom of the skull with a piece of bent bamboo. Then the head is slowly dried, flesh and hair and all, over a low fire. This gruesome trophy is sometimes hung from the roof of the longhouse or borne on a rope over the shoulder during a war dance. Sometimes it is laid in the grave of the man who took the head, when he dies. But most often, it is presented to one's intended bride. Which more or less answers your second question – the true source of the custom are the Dayak women. They don't consider a man a man until he has accumulated heads, and they would not even think of marrying one without them. They are the root of this evil!' he laughed.

He held Duncan's gaze in his soft brown eyes and said: 'Now, young man, if you are so interested in these pirates and their ways, why don't you come back with Keppel and I to Sarawak? Then we could introduce you to some of these fine fellows in all their glory. I'm sure your father could spare you – you might even be able to drum up some business for the firm, what?'

Duncan asked his father if he could spare him for a few months. He said he was sure he could learn a lot from Captain Keppel and Rajah Brooke, and really might be able to drum up some business for Simpson and Co into the bargain. Ronnie was happy enough to agree and did so on the spot. He knew the trip would involve some danger, since Keppel's mission in the archipelago was to keep the shipping routes free of Malay pirates. But he thought Duncan was old enough for action, if it came to that, and he could probably have no better teachers in ship craft and war than Keppel and Brooke. Sarah would protest, but not very much, since she could hardly deny her son what he had never denied her. It was agreed that Duncan would accompany Keppel and Brooke to Sarawak, and that James would introduce him to the Dayaks and their customs, including, 'God forbid if it comes to it,' Brooke said, smiling his charming smile once more, 'head-hunting and pirating.'

'However, I must apologize,' he said, turning now to directly address Whampoa, 'for I have failed to answer my gracious host's question. We will of course look after the interests of the Chinese settlers, whose industry and commerce will provide the foundation of our settlement in Sarawak as it has here in Singapore. Your countrymen already mine much of the gold and antinomy and are making a very nice book betting on the outcome of our trials and legislative councils!' Whampoa nodded his acknowledgement and downed the last of his sherry, wishing the company good evening. He might falter in his English sometimes, but he knew the English word for it. *Hubris*.

As they went out to their carriages, Brooke asked the company about his former second mate, Clarence Goymour, who had quit his service while they were in Singapore five years before.

'I believe he opened a hotel, and called it the Royalist Hotel, after my own schooner. I expect you chaps know it quite well?'

'Hardly a hotel,' responded Captain Scott. 'Just a bar and billiard room really, with only a few tiny rooms for rent. But it's a cosy enough snug, and he does a fair tiffin if ye dinna mind being cramped up. The best hotel in town is the new London Hotel, even if it is run by a Frenchie who paints miniatures and the like. Used to be Coleman's house, 'afore he retired to England.'

5

Achmad Hassin was a bomoh, a Malay healer and magician. Achmad's father had also been a bomoh, but Achmad had not learned his craft from his father, who had died with the rest of his family when their home had been struck by lightning – some said for the evil that his father had wrought. After Achmad had performed the funeral rites for his family, he had prayed and fasted for endless days and nights. Then he recited the one chant that he had learned from his father – the chant that would summon the angels.

After many days and nights, when he was close to fainting with hunger and exhaustion, the vision had finally come to him. He had seen and spoken with the archangel Jibrail, the divine messenger of God. He had seen and spoken with the archangel Mikail, the guardian of land, sea and air. He had seen and spoken with the archangel Israfil, who keeps the records of the dead, and the horn that will sound on Judgment day when the world ends. He had seen and spoken with the archangels Ridhwan and Malik, who revealed the kingdoms of heaven and hell. And he had seen and spoken with Iblis, the fallen angel,[lxiv] who vouchsafed the knowledge that was given to him by the other angels. When he recovered from his vision he had the knowledge and the power of the bomoh.

The bomoh lived in an uneasy relationship with the official Muslim religion of the Malays, which had been adopted nearly five hundred years before, in the time of Iskander Shah, the last Rajah of Singapura and founder of Malacca. Most of the practices

---

lxiv Satan in Christian theology.

of the bomoh, which were rooted in the worship of ancient Hindu gods and rituals, were forbidden, since they were in violation of both the Tawheed doctrine [lxv] and the Sharia law of Islam. Yet the bomoh was tolerated within most Malay communities because he healed the sick, and blessed and protected the rice fields and fishing grounds, through his magical spells and incantations.

Yet today Achmad Hassin was not concerned with the sick, the rice fields, or the fishing grounds. All of his mind and magic was focused on a beautiful young woman named Nahu. She was the wife of Sadat bin Badang, who had won her heart one silver star studded night when he had participated in the Koran reading competition during the holy month of Ramadan. As he recited the sacred words it had seemed to Nahu that she heard the music of the heavens. Like the son of Moon Ling, Sadat bin Badang was a distant descendant of Badang, the famous warrior who had defended the ancient city of Singapura against the first Majapahit [lxvi] invasion. Sadat had not inherited the legendary strength of his warrior ancestor, but he was a good and devout man who made his living through fishing and rice cultivation, and he loved his wife with a quiet passion that matched her own. They lived in a cottage close by a kampong on the edges of the jungle beyond Kampong Glam. They were recently married and hoping for their first child.

Achmad Hassin lusted after Nahu, as a tiger lusts after its prey. He cursed the day that Sadat bin Badang had won her love and made her his wife. But today he had begun to work his magic spells on her. He had followed her along the shoreline and collected her footprint from the sand. He had mixed this with earth from the graves of a man and a woman, and cooked them together in a pot, with a mixture of black pepper and shavings of mambu, the hairs of the bamboo. Now he held her image in his mind and recited the

---

lxv The doctrine that God is one and unique.
lxvi Javanese.

charm to gain control of her love force:

> In the name of God, the Merciful, the Compassionate!
> Friend of mine, Iblis and all ye spirits and devils
> That love to trouble man!
> I ask you to go and enter the body of this girl
> Burning her heart as this sand burns
> Fired with love for me.
> Bring her to yield herself to me!
> By virtue of this rice and steam
> Place her here by my hearth
> Or else take ye heed!

6

A few weeks later Duncan set off for Sarawak with Captain Keppel and Rajah Brooke aboard HMS *Dido*. He looked back one last time at his home on the east beach, shimmering in the early morning sunlight, and then turned back and looked out towards the South China Sea, as the *Dido* headed northeast out of the roads and the Singapore Straits. He looked forward to the voyage and the adventures they were sure to have, at least if Mr Brooke had anything to do with it. And little did he know where that voyage would eventually take him.

* * *

Before they left for Sarawak in April, the crew of HMS *Dido* played a cricket match on the Esplanade against a Singaporean team, which was very well attended. That same month the Reverend Benjamin Peach Keasberry opened the Malay Mission Chapel on Prinsep Street, near Kampong Bencoolen, which had been built with funds he had raised from the Singapore merchants. In later years the chapel would be known as Tuan Keasberry punya Graja, or Keasberry's Church.[17]

When Keasberry and his wife first arrived in Singapore as American missionaries they became friends with John and Alexander Stronach of the London Missionary Society. The brothers advised them to learn Malay from Munshi Abdullah, who happily agreed to be their tutor. In 1839, the American Board of Commissions moved all their missionaries to China, but Keasberry and his wife declined to go, because they had fallen in love with the Malay people. Encouraged by the Stronach brothers, they joined the London Missionary Society, and lived in a rented house at the corner of Bras Basah Road and North Bridge Road. Keasberry started a small school for Malays at Kampong Glam, where he taught the boys printing, English, and arithmetic, and on Sundays he preached in Malay to his small congregation of Christian converts – both Malay and Peranakan Chinese – from an attap hut on North Bridge Road. He also taught the Malay classes at the Singapore Institution.

Keasberry took over the Mission Press in Commercial Square, which was transferred to the London Missionary Society when the American Board moved its operations to China. It published Christian literature in Malay, Bugis and Chinese, government documents and circulars, and had printed the *Singapore Chronicle* from 1824 to 1826.

Keasberry was happy with his life and work, save for his single sadness – his wife died from a fever the year after they had decided to remain in Singapore among their beloved Malays.

* * *

The Reverend Samuel Dyer of Penang preached the first sermon at the new Malay Chapel in Prinsep Street, to a congregation of Malays, Peranakan Chinese, and some of the merchants who had contributed funds for the chapel. The following week the sermon was delivered by Dr James Legge of the London Missionary Society, who was breaking his journey in Singapore en route to Hong Kong, where he had recently been appointed principal of the Protestant Theological Seminary.[18]

James Legge was a talented linguist and sinologist, who had been entrusted by the London Missionary Society with the task of translating the names of the Christian deity into Chinese. Throughout his distinguished career as a theologian and Chinese scholar – he was the first to translate Chinese classics such as the *Analects of Confucius* into English – Legge championed the use of the Chinese term 'Shangdi', meaning 'High Lord of All', as the meaning of 'God'. Since this term occurred in the early Chinese classics, Dr Legge believed that the Chinese classical thinkers had borne witness to the Christian message.

7

The three men sat cross-legged in the middle of the floor of the bamboo and attap house, while the women laid out their evening meal. They placed wooden bowls of rice before the men, and china bowls of curry and condiments on a brass tray. While the men ate, the women sat kneeling by them and ministered to their needs. Nobody spoke. The silence was only broken by the whirring of the cicadas, the croaking of the frogs, the occasional bird cry, and the gentle lowing of the cattle in their pens. After the men finished their meal, the women retired to make their own from the remains that the men had not consumed, and the choice portions that they had left in the cooking-pot. The men prepared their betel nut and rolled their cigarettes of sweet Javanese tobacco, and began to discuss the important topics of the day – the weather, the fishing, the yield of their rice paddies, and how life had changed for them since the coming of the British and the development of the settlement.

Eventually Abdullah broached the subject they had all been putting off.

'He of the hairy-face is abroad in our countryside,' he said, 'and has taken the bullock of my cousin Anwar. We should take care to protect ourselves against him.'

The others seemed reluctant to discuss such preparations, as if by doing so they might attract the tiger into their midst, which was also why they spoke in low voices.

'I have heard it said that hairy-face does not care to eat the meat of goats or cattle or ... men,' said Mohammed, 'but prefers to drink their blood and leave their bodies to the dogs and birds.'

As if to distract themselves from the present danger, they began to talk about the origins of hairy-face.

'It is said that he is descended from the magicians of Kerinci,[lxvii] who gazed at the full moon on the surface of the mountain lake, and by their blasphemous spells transformed themselves into tigers,' said Wan Bong.

'I have heard that story too,' said Abdullah, 'but I have also heard it said he was driven out by the negrito Semang of Terengganu and forced to live in the jungle alone.'

'I have heard that he sometimes lives with his fellow tigers in the jungle at night,' Abdullah continued, 'living as men do during the day. I once met a man who knew a man who had been lost in the jungle for two years. This man came across a secret kampong harimau,[lxviii] where tigers walked about by day in the form of men, and were served by ghosts and spirits, until night fell and they went out to kill.'

Then they heard the sound, the long low moan of the tiger, announcing his hunger to the fearful world of men and other animals, caring not about their reaction to his warning of the doom that awaited them.

* * *

They heard the terrified bleating of the cattle trying to break out of their pens, and the hideous shrieking of the goats straining on their tethers, with the smell of the giant cat in their nostrils. But the men said nothing, and the women came and huddled beside them in the middle of the floor. Wan Bong fetched his spear, but none of them dared step outside the house.

---

lxvii Forest in Sumatra.
lxviii Tiger village.

They did not have to wait long. They heard the sound of thrashing from the cattle pen, and the thumping of hooves as the lucky ones escaped. But they did not venture out to retrieve them until the sun had risen the next day, when they found the ravished carcass of a heifer in a pool of congealed blood.

The slaughter on their own doorstep forced them to talk about the precautions they ought to take. They agreed to dig a pit at the edge of the jungle from where the tiger had approached the cattle pen. When it was completed, they covered it with palm leaves. They agreed to take turns on guard at night, and to sound the alarm by beating a gong if the tiger fell into the pit. Then Abdullah would shoot it with his musket and they would finish it off with their spears. Wan Bong suggested that they ought to hire a professional hunter, but the others disagreed. It was too expensive, they said, and they would lose the reward if they did so. Their bravery had returned in the light of day, along with their confidence in Abdullah's marksmanship.

8

HMS *Dido* was a three-masted corvette, seven hundred and thirty tons, with eighteen guns. She had a crew of 145, including a company of marines, commanded by Lieutenant Henry. As they made their way across the South China Sea, everyone on board was on the lookout for pirates. This was not merely a matter of self-defence. Keppel's orders from the Admiralty were to attack and destroy Illanun and Balanini raiders from the Sulu Sea, who preyed on shipping bound for the Straits Settlements, and Governor Bonham and James Brooke had persuaded him that he could achieve this goal by attacking the pirates on the Borneo coast, in order to deny the Illanun and Balanini access to secure bases. From the Admiralty's point of view, a pirate was a pirate, whatever the subtleties of his race or origin. Under an act of parliament passed in 1825 to encourage the Navy to act against African slavers, the government had agreed to pay officers and men twenty pounds sterling for each pirate killed or captured. Consequently, nothing would have pleased the officers and crew more than to run across a small fleet of Malay or Dayak pirates on their way to Sarawak. For his part, James Brooke was delighted to have the British Navy as an instrument he could employ against his enemies.

The weather was fair, the sea was flat, and the wind was with them. They arrived off the coast of Borneo on May 5, and anchored close to the mouth of the Sambas River. Brooke took the *Dido*'s pinnace upriver with a party of blue jackets,[lxix] but found only

---

lxix British sailors in uniform.

traces of campfires left by pirates. A few days later they were more fortunate. As they rounded Tanjong Datu on the morning of May 9, they saw three prahus [lxx] in the bay – one close to the shore and two in the centre. First Lieutenant Jameson looked through his telescope and reported that from the descriptions he had read they looked like Illanun slavers. Captain Keppel and James Brooke concurred when they took the telescope, but nobody was going to argue the point.

With his foremost guns on either side loaded with shot, Keppel took the *Dido* into the bay until she came within musket range of the closest prahus, and then dropped anchor. But before he could bring his guns to bear, the pirates set to their oars and pulled away as fast as they could. The musketry from the forecastle of the *Dido* brought down some of the oarsmen, but the sleek prahus soon drew away from their fire and passed the mouth of the bay. By the time they had raised anchor and sailed out into the open sea, the pirate ships had disappeared from view.

* * *

On May 16 they arrived in Kuching, where the *Dido* anchored in five fathoms in the centre of the Sarawak River, the largest ship to have ever entered the waterway. Keppel ordered a twenty-one-gun salute in honour of Rajah Muda Hassim, which did much to impress upon the residents of Kuching the power of the Tuan Besar, which they had never really doubted. They came out to greet him in boatloads decked out in silk flags, until the waters around the *Dido* were completely covered with native craft.

Captain Keppel and Rajah Brooke went ashore to pay their respects to Rajah Muda Hassim, and three days later Hassim and his many relations came on board to inspect the *Dido*. The

lxx Malay boat that can be sailed with either end at the front.

following day Keppel received a request from Rajah Muda Hassim for an additional audience with the Great Captain. When Keppel arrived at the appointed time, Prince Badrudeen presented him with a yellow silk bag on a large brass tray, which contained a letter from Rajah Muda Hassim, along with the gift of a magnificent ivory-handled and gold-worked kris.[lxxi] Mr Williamson, a linguist in the employ of Mr Brooke, translated the letter for him, which included Rajah Muda Hassim's formal request to Her Britannic Majesty to adopt measures against the murderous Saribus and Skrang, who had been terrorizing his peoples.

Keppel replied, again through Mr Williamson, that he would be happy to join Rajah Muda Hassim in taking speedy measures to suppress these and other pirates, but apologized that he had no comparable gift to offer in return. Prince Badrudeen told him there was no need to be concerned, since Rajah Brooke had already presented Rajah Muda Hassim with an ornamental clock. Keppel smiled to himself. Of course, James Brooke had arranged all this.

For the next few weeks Keppel made repairs to the *Dido* and her boats, while James set about assembling a fleet for an attack upon the Saribus pirates.

---

lxxi Dagger with distinctive wavy blade favoured by Malays.

9

In the early summer, Hong Xiuquan had travelled to Canton for a fourth time, and for a fourth time he failed the state examinations. He returned home once again, to his family and his teaching, and life continued much as before. Then one day he was visited by his friend Li Jingfang, whose family he had been tutoring. Hong invited Li Jingfang into his study and asked his wife to bring them some tea. Hong's study was a mess, with books piled high on the floor surrounding his desk; when Li tried to find a place to sit down, he knocked over one of the piles. After he had restacked the books, Li started to read one of them, and asked Hong Xiuquan if he could borrow it. Hong readily agreed, and Li took it home that evening. The book was Liang Afa's *Good words for exhorting the age*, which Hong had brought back from Canton in the spring of 1836. A few days later Li Jingfang returned in a state of high excitement. He told Hong that he was amazed by the book and asked him to decipher its meaning for him. Hong agreed to do so, and as he pored over the forgotten pages, the scales seemed to fall from his eyes, and the truth shone out from the pages like a white-hot flame.

He recounted their meaning to Li Jingfang:

'Oh Jingfang, now I understand! I had a strange dream years ago that was a mystery to me. But now I have read this book, all is clear to me as a mountain stream, and I can reveal to you the truths that I only dimly perceived before. Let me tell you about the great Ye-huo-hua, the highest God in Heaven, who created the earth and all living things, including men and women. Ye-huo-hua created a paradise on earth, but the serpent-demon brought evil into the world and changed the originally good natures of men and women to evil, except for the few righteous souls who were pure in spirit. So Ye-huo-hua sent his own son down from Heaven to earth, implanting the child's holy spirit in the womb of a virgin, who gave birth to the Saviour of the World in a wooden hut. When the child Jesus was born, an Angel cried out "Glory to God in the highest, and on earth Taiping, great peace and goodwill to all men." When Jesus reached the age of thirty, he abandoned his former life to preach the word of God. He gathered a band of disciples to help him persuade the people to abandon their wicked ways, and to cast aside false idols, including images of ancestors and Buddhist gods and goddesses.

'But the enemies of Jesus conspired against him, and he was unjustly condemned and executed upon a wooden cross. Yet marvellous to relate, he rose from the dead and attained completeness with his father in Heaven. Before he ascended to Heaven, Jesus reminded his disciples of God's commandments. Do not kill. Do not commit adultery. Do not steal. Do not bear false witness. Honour your parents. Love your neighbour as yourself. Do not smoke opium.'

Then Hong understood the significance of his near forgotten dream, which now returned to him in all its vividness. The great Ye-huo-hua was his Heavenly father, for whom he had fought the serpent-demon and driven him and his followers down the levels of Heaven to earth. He, Hong Xiuquan, was the son of God, and Jesus was his older brother. He remembered how his Heavenly father told him that his mission was to destroy the followers of the serpent-demon on earth, along with their idols and false gods, and to establish Taiping, the Heavenly Kingdom of Peace on earth, through the word and the sword of God.

Hong recognized that he was now the same age as Jesus

when he began preaching, and set out upon his own mission right away. His first convert and disciple was Li Jingfang. Hong and Li Jingfang baptised each other after the fashion Liang Afa described in his book, by sprinkling water on their heads and praying to the Heavenly father. Hong's next convert was Hong Rengan, the cousin who had watched by his bedside during his confinement. Hong Rengan enthusiastically embraced Hong's teaching, believing it to be divine illumination of the poetry he had heard from Hong on his sickbed six years before. Hong's third convert was Feng Yunshan, a relative of Hong's stepmother, who lived in a village close by. Like Hong, both young men had failed their state examinations, and worked as village teachers.

10

Achmad was satisfied with his work. He knew that Nahu did not love him yet, but saw that his magic was beginning to take effect from the worried and puzzled look on her face. First, he had to draw her love away from Sadat, and then draw it to him. Now it was time for the second part of his plan, the gradual elimination of his enemy Sadat. He would not do it quickly, for that would arouse suspicion. He would trouble Sadat with pains and fevers, and minister to him before he finally killed him. And the kindness he would show to Sadat would help to draw her love to him.

He drew out the image of Sadat that he had made in wax from an empty honeycomb, and slowly slid the thin bamboo shards into its head. With the image of Sadat held before him, he uttered the chant:

It is not the wax that I slay
But the head of Sadat
I do not banquet you on anything else
But the head of Sadat.

* * *

Sadat screamed with the pain. He tried to bear it like a man, but the pain burned like a fire in his brain, threatening to split his skull like a betel nut in a steel press. Nahu went to him, but he pushed her away as he tried to bury his head in his hands. She brought him cloths soaked in cool water from the stream, and made him tea mixed with herbs, but nothing seemed to relieve the pain. His father came and saw his distress, and said they must summon bomoh Achmad Hassin, for he was the only one who knew how to deal with such afflictions. So Nahu sent her cousin to beg the bomoh to come to them as soon as he could spare the time, and to promise him that they would reward him handsomely if he could save her husband.

The bomoh came later that day and applied a poultice to Sadat's forehead, which seemed to temporarily ease the pain. Unlike most bomohs, who were white-haired and aged, Achmad was a young man with jet-black hair and eyes. He was not much older than her husband, and Nahu felt strangely drawn to him, as he prayed with great humanity and dignity for Sadat's recovery. His deep black eyes seemed to hold out the promise of Sadat's recovery, and indeed her husband did seem to recover as dusk was settling, when he managed to take the cup of warm milk that the bomoh had prescribed. She felt relieved, and her heart, so recently troubled, seemed to find peace again, as the bomoh's incantations echoed softly in her mind. Yet in the night Sadat's affliction returned, and his screams dragged her from her sleep.

* * *

Achmad was satisfied with his handiwork. Sadat's pain brought him the greatest pleasure, and he had caught Nahu's affectionate look as he had pretended to care for her husband. He drew out the wax image and drove the bamboo shard into its midriff, chanting:

> It is not the wax that I slay
> But the liver, heart, and spleen of Sadat
> I do not banquet you on anything else
> But the liver, heart, and spleen of Sadat.

Far off in the night Sadat groaned like a wounded beast as the pain sliced through his stomach, and Nahu feared for his life.

11

Kuching, May 28, 1843

Dear Mother and Father

Thank you once again for letting me accompany Captain Keppel and Rajah Brooke on their return to Kuching. I have already had some adventures, but assure you I am safe and well, and eagerly looking forward to joining them in their attack on the Saribus pirates, who have assembled a great war fleet in the higher reaches of the Sarawak River. At the moment, Rajah Brooke is organizing the native chiefs and their followers, while Captain Keppel is making repairs to his ship and long boats. Mr Whitehead allowed his yacht *Emily* to follow us with the mail from Singapore, so I thought I would take this opportunity of penning a quick letter before she returns to Singapore tomorrow.

We had fair weather and winds on the way out. Lieutenant Henry taught me how to use a cutlass. Not much to it, he says, just raise for the back-hand cut, stamp and slash, then thrust, stamp and slash, then thrust, stamp-slash-thrust! The trick is to do it in unison and in line with your mates, and the enemy will never stand a chance against determined jack tars.[lxxii] He also offered to teach me how to shoot my pistol, but I told him that I had been trained by the best – by which I mean my dear mother, of course!

A few days after we reached the Borneo coast we had a run in with three pirate prahus. Keppel tried to surprise them when

___
lxxii Colloquial term for English seamen.

we discovered them in a bay beyond Tanjong Datu. We got off a few shots and dropped a few oarsmen, but they pulled away very quickly and disappeared from sight before we managed to make our way out of the bay again. They did not escape us completely, however, as I will shortly relate, but I have to admit that I was greatly impressed by the speed of their craft, which are very sleek in their build. They raced across the bay like heron skimming across the surface of the sea.

The rest of our voyage was uneventful, except for a seaman who had to get a tooth removed and made such a fuss about it that we had to fill him with grog and hold him down; but he went around afterwards shaking our hands and thanking us for what we had done. Sailors are a strange breed, but they are generally good and honest men.

We arrived in Kuching on May 16, the *Dido* anchoring like a great giant in the river, dwarfing the surrounding houses and boats, her masts standing higher than the highest trees of the forest. We fired off a twenty-one-gun salute that boomed across the river and echoed from the mountains beyond. It must have impressed the natives, although it soon became clear they needed little impressing. They came out in boatloads, yellow flags streaming behind, with bands playing and gongs crashing. They climbed up the sides of the *Dido* and onto her deck, waving and bowing to James and calling out, Tuan Besar! Tuan Besar! They love him like a father and would go to the ends of the earth for him if he asked them to.

The next day, we went ashore to visit Rajah Muda Hassim. One hundred and fifty officers and seamen in their dress whites presented themselves, while the ship's band played 'Hearts of Oak'. Rajah Brooke was dressed in his Royal Yacht Squadron jacket with bright brass buttons, a crisp white shirt, black trousers and a black necktie – looking the very picture of a natural leader of men, his bright eyes flashing and his back straight as a ramrod. Keppel and his officers were in full naval dress uniform, with cocked hats and feathers, gold braiding and swords flashing silver in the morning sunshine. I had the great honour of being asked to join them, although all I could muster was a clean white shirt and clerical black. But if it was good enough for Raffles, I thought it ought to be good enough for me.

When we alighted from our boats before Rajah Muda Hassim's audience chamber, we had to climb up a long ladder – Captain Keppel had a little trouble with this! – into the chamber, which was really nothing more than a long wooden shed built upon piles, thatched with attap and hung with red and yellow silk curtains. Rajah Muda Hassim sat in the centre with his princes and advisors on one side, and our party on the other. Behind their nobles and ministers was a band of brightly plumed warriors armed with swords, spears, krisses and blowpipes, some sporting dried human heads hanging on ropes from their shoulders or tied around their waists; behind our dignitaries was a party of marines, in their blue jackets and white facings, muskets and cutlasses at the ready. But there was no friction between the two parties, and the meeting went off without incident, but also without any business being transacted as far as I could see. Polite greetings were exchanged, and we sat in a semi-circle drinking tea and smoking cigars, while Hassim and his party chewed sireh leaf and betel nut and spat their juices on the floor. The Rajah was courteous and polite but struck me as a very insignificant little man. He seemed much more interested in playing with his toes as he sat cross-legged on his chair than he was in discussing our expedition against the pirates of the Saribus and Skrang Rivers, and he never mentioned them during the half hour or so we were there. Indeed, he said hardly anything at all, then rose and wished us good day, expressing the hope that our friendship would last as long as the moon. But that is just the easy way of the Malay, for he knew exactly what he was about, as events later demonstrated.

On the second day Rajah Muda Hassim came on board the *Dido* with his princes, ministers and warriors, and the whole episode was repeated in Keppel's cabin. I could not attend because the cabin was too small to accommodate all our people and theirs, so I took up my duty on deck, which had been scrubbed and painted white for the occasion. I was later told that the meeting proceeded in much the same fashion as the previous day, except that Rajah Muda Hassim had taken a liking to Captain Keppel's cherry-brandy, although apparently it did not interfere with his near constant chewing on sireh leaves and betel nuts. I know this latter to my cost. When he left the cabin, Raja Muda Hassim made straight towards me and shook my hand with great vigour, then spat a great jet of dark red betel juice across the pure white deck and my trouser leg – thank goodness for my clerical black that day! He kept pumping my hand and gave me a great black-toothed grin – not the sort of thing one expects from royalty. But I just grinned back and he went off cheerfully enough, not wishing to be held responsible for a diplomatic incident.

But Hassim is no bumbling fool. The next day, he asked Captain Keppel to meet with him again and presented him with a formal request for help against the Saribus and Skrang pirates, along with a magnificent ornamental kris – 'his poor reward' he called it. Captain Keppel and I are sure that Rajah Brooke put him up to it, but whatever the cause, he seems steadfast in his commitment, and has been working with Rajah Brooke to gather the war chiefs and loyal Malays and Dayaks for the expedition.

The past few nights we had some wonderful times in Mr Brooke's house, or Residency, as he is pleased to call it. It is just a one-story wooden plank house built on stilts like all the other houses, a short distance behind Rajah Muda Hassim's own 'palace,' but well-furnished with tables and chairs, and bedsteads, pictures and books in the bedrooms. The main room in the centre of the house serves as mess room and audience chamber, decorated all around with British and native weapons and guns, where we all sat down to dinner each night while James presided at the end of the table, his bright eyes sparkling and his head flung back in laughter and merriment. While we sampled the delights brought forth by his wonderful Chinese cook, a host of meat and fish dishes, with fresh vegetables and fruits and a brilliant sweet bean desert, we drank the Rajah's champagne, wine, beer and brandy, and smoked his excellent cigars. All the men seemed to have travelled the world and have had great adventures (except for yours truly, although I do have a minor one to report) and regale each other with stories and anecdotes well into the night. One local tale I will relate since it is very short.

One of our company, Dr Treacher, who is a medical officer, thought that he had won the heart of one of the most beautiful girls in the harem of Prince Mahkota. This was because she had sent him a secret message via her servant, begging him to meet her in a secluded spot in the jungle at sunset. Dr Treacher got himself all decked up as if he was going to the Governor's Ball and set off to meet her at the appointed time. His heart leapt when he saw her waiting for him in the clearing, the last golden rays of the sun dancing on her jet–black hair and slim brown legs and ... well, you know what I mean! But when she looked at him imploringly with her big brown eyes, she did not ask him to take her away with him, but begged the good doctor to give her some arsenic so that she could poison Prince Mahkota, who had beaten her and her sister. When Dr Treacher refused and told her that he had sworn the Hippocratic Oath, she gave him such a look of contempt that he knew his own hopes of romance were well and truly dashed!

While they were telling these stories, groups of Malays and Dayaks slipped into the house to pay their respects to Rajah Brooke, creeping up to James and touching his hand, and then sitting silently on their haunches for an hour or so before slipping out again. All of them were armed with evil-looking krisses, which alarmed me at first, until I was informed that the natives would consider it a great insult if they came before their Rajah without their krisses.

While the preparations were going on for the expedition against the Saribus, Captain Keppel suggested that Lieutenant Hunt take a party in search of the pirates we had missed off Tanjong Datu, and I asked to go along. Lieutenant Hunt and I get along very well. We both admire Rajah Brooke and all he is doing for the native peoples of Sarawak, and of course dear Captain Keppel, who acts as if this pirate chase was all a jolly game rather than the serious business it is. Rajah Brooke offered us the use of the *Jolly Bachelor*, a large schooner he recently had built at Sarawak, with a brass six-pounder long gun mounted on the forecastle. With a crew of about fifteen seamen, half a dozen marines, and two weeks' provisions, we set off in pursuit of the pirates we had previously disturbed.

We were scarcely a few hours out at sea when we saw prahus far off in the distance and set off in pursuit. We lost sight of them for a while, and then saw them a second and a third time, but could not catch them. By this time, it was getting dark and we were all tired and hungry, so we pulled in close to the shore and lit a fire to cook our evening meal, with sentries posted on all sides in case of attack, each man taking turns to eat and then take his place as sentry. We brought the schooner back to her anchor close to some rocks and settled down for the night as best we could. We lay down on the deck of the *Jolly Bachelor* with our side arms close at hand and our muskets stacked and loaded around the mast; we placed sentries at both ends of the craft and a lookout on the mast. We were all soon fast asleep, including all the sentries I regret to say, and we were almost murdered in our sleep. For as we slept two pirate prahus crept up close to the starboard side of the *Jolly Bachelor*, and her crews were preparing to board us. But lucky we were to have

Lieutenant Hunt in command, for he woke to see the moon on the rise and flooding the deck with silver beams, which silhouetted the first pirate to climb on board with his wavy kris drawn. Lieutenant Hunt immediately leapt up and knocked the fellow overboard and raised the alarm.

We worked like madmen to cut the cable and get the oars going, while their small cannon sent balls into our rigging and musket-fire crackled all around. But we gave as good as we got, and once we were clear we could bring our six-pounder to bear, while the marines – and your sharpshooter son! – kept up such a deadly fire that the pirates were unable to reload. The fronts of their craft are faced with strong bulwarks for protection, but we quickly blasted those away with round shot, to deadly and bloody effect, while we poured musket fire into the mass of men milling aboard their decks. I fear we may have killed as many slaves and captives as we did pirates, since we had no way of telling who was who in the smoky moonlight, although we did later pick up some slaves who had managed to swim ashore. Yet truth be told, we also had no way of telling whether they really were slaves or pirates lying to us to save their own skins. One of the pirate prahus made its escape into the darkness of the night, but we later heard that their slave crew had overcome the pirates and killed them. Unfortunately, they surrendered themselves to the nearest native prince, who promptly seized them and sold them into slavery once again!

The other pirate prahu we boarded and captured. None of the pirates expected or asked for quarter, and those still living threw themselves at our men – who made short work of them – or dived overboard. The scene on deck was total carnage – about twenty or thirty bodies lay bloody and mangled across the boards. But then we came upon a singular sight. The young leader of the pirates, as noble a native face and of such brave bearing as I have ever seen – even I say, as noble and brave as James Brooke himself –

lay mortally wounded in the bow of the prahu. He was badly shot through in front and into his lungs, but he tried to raise himself up to face us, the blood flowing freely down his chest. He looked us straight in the eye, man to man, and made a great effort to speak, but it was in vain. Every time he tried, only blood issued from his lips, but his great effort reached the hearts of even the most hardened tars, who were moved to such pity that they raised him up to relieve his pain and distress. This seemed to make him easy in his soul, as he realized his life spirit was rapidly flowing from his wounds. He calmly folded his arms across his chest in a gesture of heroic defiance and resignation, while he fixed his eyes on the body of sailors surrounding him for one last time. Then he calmly turned his head and eyes to look out over the ocean that he had ranged as a pirate, and without a word or a sigh he died, his eyes staring blankly across the path of the moon shadow on the black water.

You may think me fanciful, but we all felt it was a tragic and moving death, despite our determination to rid these waters of pirates. It was the nobility of the Norseman of old, and even Mr Dobbs, the hard-bitten first mate, admitted before us all that the scene had moved him to such strong emotion as when he looked upon the painting of Lord Nelson dying below decks after the battle of Trafalgar. I know that we must harden our hearts to these fellows and know that they have brought great suffering to our family, but I also know that had you been there you would have felt his humanity as we all did. His name was Moon.

So, I have had my first adventure, and dare to opine that I have acquitted myself well, with no harm to my person other than a splinter from one of their balls that went into our mizzenmast. I am afraid I have not yet been able to explore the business opportunities of Sarawak, which do not on first impression appear very promising, but in the next few days I will seek out the Chinese merchants here and see what intelligence I can glean from them – not an easy task in any place or time!

I will write again soon when I have some more news and reflections, but please be assured I am safe and well, and thinking of you both and dear Annie and Grandpapa John.

Your loving son
Duncan

12

Achmad knew that he should leave the magic to work on its own but could not help himself. He wanted to witness its working at first hand. He made his way in the moonlight along the jungle path that led to the kampong. The moon was almost full, and on the morrow, when it was full at the midnight hour, he would complete the spell that would draw Nahu's soul to his. He saw the path open out into the kampong a little ahead, and thought he heard the sound of Sadat's screams, muffled by the bamboo walls of his stilted house. Eager in his anticipation, Achmad crept forward to get closer to the sound. Then he slowed his pace, for he sensed another following him from behind. He slipped his kris from the folds of his robe and turned to face the man. Yet it was no man he faced, but the yellow eyes and fangs of a tiger, which padded slowly towards him, paying no heed to his weapon. Achmad began a spell of protection, but it froze in his throat as the tiger let out its low hungry moan and opened its dreadful jaws. Achmad staggered backwards and tumbled into the pit the villagers had dug a week before.

Achmad struggled to his feet as the tethered goat brayed in fear and saw the tiger at the edge of the pit, poised to leap down upon him. But then a gong clashed, followed by a great clamour of voices, and the tiger took flight into the jungle, as the villagers woke and made their way cautiously to the pit, armed with what weapons they had. Abdullah carried his loaded musket, trying to hide the trembling in his hands and legs. Then, as he grew closer, his fear turned to puzzlement. He heard no roar or growling coming from the pit, and the other villagers were standing around talking in hushed tones. A few held lighted torches, which illuminated the mystery. For at the bottom of the pit was Achmad the bomoh, looking furious and fearful.

'How came you here, magician?' cried the headman of the village. 'Who invited you to come to us in the dead of night, like a thief in the darkness?'

Achmad swallowed his fear and anger, and replied in a controlled voice, 'I heard Sadat bin Badang calling out in his great pain and thought that I must come to his aid. You should ask his wife, who knows how hard I have striven to relieve his affliction.'

The headman called for Nahu to be brought before him, and she looked down at Achmad in the pit.

'The bomoh came to my house today,' she said, 'and did his best to try to heal my husband. For a few hours his pain seemed to pass, but it has returned again, and now I fear for his life. Please rescue this good man and do him no harm. We all have need of his services, but I most of all.'

Some of the villagers muttered their approval, and the headman was about to order his release when Abdullah cried out.

'A were-tiger! The bomoh is a were-tiger! Look at the hairy one's footprints leading to the edge of the pit! The bomoh is a were-tiger who drinks the blood of men and animals by night! We should kill him quickly before he escapes!'

They all rushed over to where Abdullah stood holding his torch over the tracks. They all saw it with their naked eyes. The tiger's tracks led to the edge of the pit, but the only creature in the pit besides the goat was Achmad.

The headman returned to the edge of the pit and looked down at the bomoh. 'You have deceived us, Achmad Hassin,' he declared. 'You who have blessed our paddy fields and prayed for our sick while wandering the night as hairy-face, and for that you must die.'

He then ordered the villagers to kill Achmad where he stood.

Abdullah cocked and aimed his musket, while the others drew back their spears, ready to strike him down dead.

'Wait, wait, you are making a great mistake!' Nahu exclaimed. Scarcely knowing what she was doing, she leapt down into the pit and stood before the bomoh. 'There must be some mistake, some explanation!'

'There is a simple explanation,' said Achmad, as he put his arm around Nahu's shoulders, as if to protect her, and smiling a secret smile to himself at the power of his magic. 'I came along the path for the reason I have told you, in the hope of relieving the pain of this poor woman's husband.' The warmth of Nahu's body aroused him and gave him confidence that he could escape this trap. 'As I came into the clearing I heard some movement behind me, and turning around, was frightened by the sight of hairy-face. I fell backward into the pit, where you see me now. The tiger was about to spring, but it fled back into the jungle when it heard the clashing of the gong. You will see my own footprints beside the tigers.' I am no were-tiger, only a humble magician. But if you do not release me,' he said, raising his voice in a threatening tone, 'I will put a curse on you that will pursue you into your very graves and the darkness beyond.'

'Heed me and release me!' he commanded, and the villagers looked at each other in fear and awe.

'He lies!' cried a new voice in the throng. When they turned their heads, they were amazed to see Sadat, raised from his sickbed, approaching the edge of the pit.

'I was in such pain that I thought I was going to die,' he told them, 'and then I heard the gong clashing and the pain began to subside. As my head cleared, I saw the evil face of Achmad the bomoh before my eyes, and knew that it was he who had set the affliction upon me, and he who has turned my wife's love from me.'

'No, no, it is not true!' Nahu cried in desperation, again trying to shield the man she loved. For in that swift moment she realized that it was true – she had lost the love of her husband and fallen in love with the magician who had tried to save her husband's life.

'You lie, husband!' she cried out. 'You make up lies against this good man, to whom you should bow down in gratitude for trying to save you from your grave sickness. But all you can do is spew poison from your black soul. I love this man, and if you kill this man you kill me also.'

'Then so be it,' said the headman, 'for I have heard enough. Kill the magician and try to save the woman. But if she gets in the way, she must die with her lover.'

'But what if the magician speaks true,' said Abdullah, pointing his musket at the bomoh's head, the trembling returning to his hands.

'But what if he lies?' the headman quickly replied. 'Then we release the were-tiger in our midst, free to rip out our throats and drink of the blood of our wives and children. I know these things to be true, and I trust not the word of a man who creeps in the darkness and charms a man's wife away from her lawful husband. Why take a chance with one who would strike at our first weakness and threatens to curse us, even beyond the grave. I do not trust such a man. Kill him, and do it quickly!'

'Hold your arms!' a great booming voice cried out behind them, stilling the muscles of their straining arms. Then the imam from the sultan's mosque, who had been staying the night with his brother in law, came forward, and they lowered their weapons and their heads before his authority.

'Enough of this blasphemy!' he thundered. 'You speak of things forbidden and denied in the Holy Book. Remember that you are followers of God and cast aside this sacrilegious talk. There are no were-tigers, save for those that live in the frightened minds of men.'

The villagers were subdued, including the headman, yet it was truly said by the imam that the were-tiger lived in their frightened minds.

'There are no were-tigers, but there are evil men who conjure up Iblis and his devils to serve their own dark purposes,' the imam continued. 'I know not if this man has practiced black magic on this woman and her husband, but God who knows all things will look into his heart and judge him. Return this woman to her husband and let him decide if he wishes her to remain his wife.'

'Release the bomoh, and let him go in peace,' he commanded, 'but first I have some words for him.' He looked down into the pit and addressed the bomoh directly.

'You may be a man of good intentions, Achmad Hassin,' he said, 'yet you came into this kampong like a man intent on evil at the dead of night. If not for your action, these good people might have captured and killed the tiger, which now remains free to prowl the jungle and terrorize their livestock and their dreams. For that you will recompense them for the loss of the heifer that was killed and for any other losses they sustain until the tiger is caught and destroyed.'

Achmad was furious, but made no response, for he knew that the imam held the thread of his life in his hands and could tear it asunder with a single word.

'And I say to you in the name of God the Great and Holy, that any man who conjures up the evil ones and invokes the name of the Prophet to command them to do evil, does blaspheme in word and deed and will have his evil thoughts and deeds returned to him by the dark angels. Say your prayers and humble yourself before God, or your soul will be forever lost upon the fiery sea.'

Achmad prostrated himself before the imam and begged his forgiveness, avowing that his life was less than a single grain of sand on the shoreline. The imam bade him rise and ordered a ladder to be brought and lowered into the pit, so that the bomoh and Nahu could climb out. He commanded Achmad to leave the kampong, and Nahu to return to her husband. She obeyed his command and followed Sadat in shame and confusion back to their home. She was glad that he had recovered, but she could not pretend that she loved him any longer – she loved only Achmad, her lord and master. They sat in the darkness on the floor, facing each other, but not a word was spoken between them.

13

Samuel George Bonham had begun his career in Singapore as a clerk to Colonel Farquhar in 1820, then as land commissioner and license revenue collector for Raffles in 1823. He had served as assistant and then resident councillor, as acting governor of the Straits Settlements between 1833 and 1835, and as governor from 1836 to May 1843, when he finally retired and returned to England aboard the Company steamer *Diana*. It was generally agreed that he had served the settlement well and that his steady hand had steered the port city through her difficult years of financial hardship to her recent prosperity. George Bonham was also fondly remembered for his conviviality and hospitality. His dinners were legendary, especially during the period when the ships of the China fleet were in the harbour. Thomas Church, who had been resident councillor for the past six years, and who had had previous Company service in Penang and Malacca, ought by right to have succeeded Bonham as governor. Yet although he was widely respected as an energetic and diligent administrator, he had one insurmountable impediment – he had a hard-earned reputation for hosting the worst dinners in Singapore. While George Bonham was governor, he always kept a large bottle of fluid of magnesia in his office, in case he was invited to dine with Tom Church in the evening.

Mr Edmund Augustus Blundell, a senior civil servant who had served as resident councillor of Malacca and Penang, was appointed to replace George Bonham. Blundell had excellent knowledge of the local languages and customs and was considered by the merchants and residents to be the ideal man for the position. He arrived on July 23, but the following day he received news that the Governor-General Lord Ellenborough had cancelled his appointment and had already appointed Colonel William John Butterworth of the Second Madras European Regiment as governor in his place on June 14. Colonel Butterworth was a career soldier in the Indian army, who had no knowledge or experience of the Eastern Archipelago. The *Singapore Free Press* bitterly opposed his appointment and complained about the injustice inflicted on the Straits Settlements by the extraordinary behaviour of Lord Ellenborough. Mr Blundell left two days later, not wishing to be present in Singapore when Governor Butterworth arrived the following month.

Governor Butterworth was a tall and good-looking man, slim and straight-backed, the very image of an officer and a gentleman. He had a long noble face with dark sideburns and was always immaculately dressed in his scarlet uniform and golden epaulettes. He had a strong commanding voice and impeccable manners. He was also extremely pompous and a stickler for propriety. He gave it out that the scar on his temple was a sabre wound, although the sceptical gave it back that his nursemaid had dropped him as a child, since they could not imagine such a prig would ever have soiled his immaculate uniform in warfare. To dispel doubts, Colonel Butterworth displayed his carefully preserved uniform in a glass case in his office and drew attention to the bullet hole in the breast as testament to his bravery. However, this only stimulated malicious rumours that the real hole could be found in the tail of his coat.

Governor Butterworth's administration quickly became embroiled in the intricacies of the land disputes with the Chinese, in the wake of the Straits Land Act of 1839, which had required proof of tenancy and the calculation of annual assessments on land leases. Butterworth left the complicated details of these disputes to Thomas Church, the resident councillor, and John Turnbull Thomson, the government surveyor, and then established their recommendations as law with a stroke of his pen. Governor Butterworth's favourite activity was presiding over official ceremonies in his military regalia, which gained him the nickname 'Great Butterpot'. However, his reputation improved when he was seen to work tirelessly to promote Singapore's trading interests, and to vigorously resist the introduction of port fees and taxes.

* * *

On June 18, the foundation stone for the Cathedral of the Good Shepherd was laid. Father Beurel had managed to secure donations from the Philippines and China as well as his native France, and from the largely Scottish Protestant community in Singapore as well as from local Catholics. Denis Lesley MacSwiney, a former clerk to George Coleman, won the competition for the design of the church, beating out the more expensive design submitted by John Turnbull Thomson. MacSwiney's design was based upon the Roman Doric form of St Paul's Church in Covent Garden and the temple-like interior and belfry of St Martin's in the Field, both famous London – and Protestant – edifices.

The elaborate ceremony began at six thirty in the morning, being the coolest part of the day. Bishop Courvezy of Penang presided over the dedication ceremony, which included a pontifical High Mass. Work began on the Cathedral of the Good Shepherd shortly after the bishop left Singapore.

14

Sarawak, June 30, 1843

Dear Mother and Father

Thank you so much for your letter and your news about Singapore. We are almost ready to move against the Saribus pirates. The local chieftains have assembled their canoes, and we have been joined by about four hundred Dayak men whose homes and families have suffered at the hands of the pirates. They are a tough-looking bunch, with strange whirling tattoos on their arms and legs, armed to the teeth with krisses, spears, blowpipes and muskets. They are out for revenge and heads, according to Rajah Brooke and Captain Keppel, and I'm glad they're on our side and not theirs!

Rajah Brooke has organized this little armada with great efficiency, while still managing to run the affairs of state and finding time to spend with his friends and associates. He holds a court almost every second day, in which cases are heard in a bewildering variety of languages – although Mr Williamson does a heroic job in communicating the content of these native tongues. I was surprised by the presence of so many Chinese in the courts, but George Steward, an old school friend of James who now seems to act as his informal adjutant in Kuching, told me they only come to make bets on the outcome of the cases; he said he wouldn't be surprised if they fabricated some cases for just this purpose. However, some of their cases are substantial. There is currently a dispute between rival kongsi [lxxiii] about the rights to gold and antinomy mining, which brings me to the main point of this letter. Despite Keppel's enthusiasm, and however much I admire Rajah Brooke's administration, neither of them seems to have any commercial sense when it comes to the prospects for trade in Sarawak. The Chinese have firm control over the only two commodities with serious export potential, namely antinomy and gold, and seem to be the only people with the expertise and energy needed to run the mines. The Dayaks and Malays are so poor that the prospects of any significant import trade are also pretty grim. There is coal on the island of Labuan, which the Rajah hopes to claim for Sarawak, but the rumour here is that the coal is very poor, and the island known to be dangerously pestilential. The Rajah has asked me to inquire if Simpson and Co would be willing to invest capital in such a venture, but I would strongly advise against it.

Still he is a great man, one of the best our country has produced. He is as noble as Raffles and as brave as Nelson, and he cares for his people and his young friends like a loving father. He manages to find time to spend with them, and always has a kind word and a warm smile. When the court is done, the great man can be found leap-frogging with the mids [lxxiv] from the *Dido*, and skinny dipping in the pool behind his house, much to the delight of the ladies of Rajah Muda Hassim's harem, who peer out from his 'palace' windows – you can hear laughter tinkling from their hiding places.

I went with Brooke and Keppel to visit some of the local chiefs who had agreed to provide men for the expedition. We had some good hunting of boar and deer along the way, with Keppel showing off his new Westley Richards rifle. We visited the chiefs in their longhouses, decked all around with hundreds of dried heads, and were made most welcome; the men and women danced before us,

lxxiii Chinese secret societies.
lxxiv Midshipmen – officer cadets in the Royal Navy.

and wished us good fortune in our fight against the Saribus. At the end of one of the longhouses they showed us a pile of magic stones. They told us that if the stones turn black, they will be defeated in battle, but that if they turn red they will be victorious (I suppose these colours represent death and the blood of their enemies). They also said that any man who touched these stones would die, and that if the stones were removed, doom will befall their tribe.

I must leave off now to catch the *Royalist*, which is taking the mail to Singapore. Please send my love to dear Annie and Grandpa John. I will write again after we have moved against the Saribus, but don't worry – I will take care of myself and return home safe to you.

Your loving son
Duncan

15

Achmad returned to his hut in the forest, relieved, humiliated, but unrepentant. He did not pray for forgiveness, but rather stoked the evil that burned like a hot coal in his heart. He would have his revenge and he would have it this night. He did not fear the villagers or the imam, and he would show them whose magic was stronger. Sadat would die before the night was through, and they would know his wrath and his power.

He took out the wax image of Sadat one last time. He took a bamboo shard, and with a cruel smile, drove it down through the head and body of the wax image, chanting:

> It is not the wax that I slay
> But the body of Sadat
> I do not banquet you on anything else
> But the body of Sadat.

Then he wrapped the wax image of Sadat in a fragment of shroud that he had taken from the grave of a man long dead. He covered the shrouded image in his own excrement and blood, then buried it in the earth some distance from the door of his hut. Then he called out to the spirits to aid him:

> Lo, I am burying the corpse of Sadat
> I am bidden to do so by the prophet Muhammad
> Because the corpse was a rebel to God

Do you assist in killing him?
If you do not kill him
You shall be a rebel against God
A rebel against Muhammad
It is not I who am burying him
It is Jibrail who is burying him.

Do you grant my prayer and petition, this very day that has appeared?

Grant it by the grace of my petition within the fold of the creed.

Then he began to say the prayers for the dead over the buried image of his enemy, his lips drawn taught over his teeth in a thin smile of anticipation.

* * *

Sadat tumbled forward and gasped in pain. He did not cry out – it seemed as if his scream was stifled in his throat, but Nahu could see the searing pain in his eyes and his gnashing teeth, and in his trembling limbs. As she knelt beside him and saw his suffering, she knew that he had not long to live. She also knew that she had been bewitched, although she could not turn her love away from the bomoh. But she knew what she had to do. She had to stop the bomoh working his evil. She got up and grabbed her husband's spear – she would kill the bomoh before he killed her husband, even if it meant killing the man she loved.

She pulled the door open and stepped out onto the verandah, but then stood frozen in terror. For before her a tiger lay sprawled upon the wooden plank steps, his two front paws crossed leisurely before him, with his dreadful hairy face leaning upon them, and his deadly yellow eyes staring up at her.

She stared back and tried not to move or tremble. The tiger

stared at her and she stared back at the tiger as the moon rose in the sky and the world turned and the night was silent all around them. No sound of cicadas or frogs, nor frightened goats or cattle, no murmur from the stream or birdsong. Just the still sound of silence as Nahu and the great hairy one stared into each other's eyes. Then suddenly, as she strained to keep her eyes fixed on the tiger, her vision blurred, and it seemed to her as if the lower regions of the hairy-one were not the legs of a tiger but those of a man, with bare white feet and toes curled around the wooden planks. But then as her vision refocused she once again saw the striped hind legs of the tiger.

16

Kuching, July 25, 1843.

Dear Mother and Father

You will be pleased to learn that I have returned safe from our expedition against the Saribus pirates, which resulted in total victory for Rajah Brooke and Captain Keppel. We set off on July 4 with a force of about one thousand men, Europeans, Malays and Dayaks, in an assortment of native canoes, the pinnace, two cutters [lxxv] and the gig [lxxvi] from the *Dido*, and the *Jolly Bachelor*. I travelled in the *Dido*'s gig with Rajah Brooke and Captain Keppel, the whole expedition being commanded by Lieutenant Wilmot Horton in the *Dido*'s pinnace, who had a hard time keeping us all together. Subi Besi, James' coxswain and bodyguard, also travelled with us. His name means 'iron anchor', and he is a singular fellow. He looks simple in the head, but he is very powerfully built and a fierce warrior in battle I am told. He serves only the Rajah, and will not speak or even pay attention to anyone else. He spends his days praying, eating, smiling and sleeping; before a fight he goes down on his knees to pray, rifle in hand.

We heard reports that the Saribus pirates had learned of our impending attack and were preparing for a vigorous defence of their forts and their fleet, but we also received assurances from the local sherips of their future good behaviour – including many of those

---

lxxv Ship's boats.
lxxvi Smaller craft normally employed as captain's taxi.

who had helped or harboured the pirates in the past.

We had a few light skirmishes with some of their craft on the way upriver, but otherwise our passage was not challenged until we approached the village of Paku, where the sound of gongs and cannon fire warned us that the Saribus were ready to fight. At this point on the river we came across a serious obstacle called the river bore – the tide comes in with tremendous force, and constricted by the narrow banks, roars upriver like a great wave carrying everything before it. We were forced to put in at the side of the river at a place called Boling, where we had to leave our commissariat and a sizeable party of men to guard it, since we were now deep in enemy territory. About half our force took on provisions for six days and prepared to advance on their capital Padi at dawn the following morning. Although we were a depleted force about to engage a pirate multitude that had never been defeated in a pitched battle before, there was no complaint from any man, except from those who were ordered to stay behind and guard the commissariat.

The night before the battle was one of uncommon beauty, the jungle deep green and fresh against a dark blue sky, reflected in the river that was still as the glass of a mirror, the smoke from the cooking fires drifting into the night air. We stood at the prow of the gig smoking our cigars and drinking our brandy, while the Musselmen [lxxvii] prostrated themselves on the decks of their craft in the direction of Mecca. We stood around talking and joking, with no spoken care for the fight on the morrow. Yet as the fires and lights went out, and the moonless darkness descended so deep we could not make out one boat from another, I am sure each man prayed in his heart that his god or gods would deliver him from death on the morrow. I know I did.

The next morning, we attacked at dawn, the moment the bore had past, riding with the tide waters behind us like Jason and the

lxxvii Archaic term for Muslims.

Argonauts of old, an easy feat but one that struck fear in the hearts of our enemies. We – that is Brooke and Keppel and I – were in the *Dido*'s gig ahead of the rest. The power of the tide gave us no option of retiring or retreating if we got into trouble, but none of us were in a mind to retire or retreat. As we rounded one bend in the river we exchanged fire with a party of natives who ran down to the river's edge shouting their fearsome war cries, and around another we passed a longhouse with warriors dancing on the roof, displaying the heads they had previously taken in battle. These were soon dispersed by round shot from the largest native craft following behind. Then just before we reached Padi, we came upon a great wooden barrier stretched across the river, made up of trees lashed together with rattan.

Luckily for us Keppel found a space and steered our gig through it, dropping off the native crew to work on the logs with axes, to clear a space in time for the pinnace and the larger craft to enter. But we soon found ourselves alone on the river facing a hot fire from the three pirate forts facing the bank, and a horde of warriors rushed down to the river's edge screaming their war cries and waving their weapons in the air, exalting at the prize they clearly hoped to take. We returned their fire with our muskets, rifles and shotguns as best we could, and I have to say I felt pretty small in the face of such overwhelming odds. We knew that if our men could not force a breach in the log-barrier in time to let our larger boats through, we would be cut off from our main body and would not long survive with our heads upon our shoulders! Luckily their shot went high, and only two of our men were wounded, and as we brought the long gig round – hard work in the tide! – the *Dido*'s pinnace came through the breached logs and opened up with her ten-pounders on the forts. Soon the cutters and native craft were alongside, and we felt a good deal safer, I can tell you!

Our parties prepared to land on the bank facing the forts,

and Mr D'Aeth was the first ashore, with his party of seamen and marines. They did not wait for the others to land and form themselves into units, but immediately drew their cutlasses and fixed bayonets and rushed straight up the hill to the first fort. I do not know whether it was from cowardice or surprise at this brazen form of attack, but all at once the pirates abandoned the fort and ran off into the jungle. The same pantomime was repeated at the other two forts, and all of us were hard pressed to get a shot at the rascals before they disappeared from sight.

We burned the forts, the outbuildings and the war-canoes in the river. All through the night our Malays and Dayaks pursued the fleeing enemy, who could not easily escape into the darkness of the jungle, since the fires from the burning forts soon revealed them. There was bloody hand to hand fighting late into the night. The Malays and Dayaks killed, burnt and, to use the Indian term, looted the surrounding countryside. I would like to think that they did it to teach the pirates a lesson they would never forget, which was certainly our intention – but I suspect they did it mostly for the loot and the heads. The most revolting thing about the Dayaks (this is not true of the Malays) is not their taking of heads from their slain enemies, but their desecration of the recent graves of their enemies. When Rajah Brooke complained to them about this, they simply grinned and said, according to Williamson's translation, 'Why should we eat the hard-caked rice at the edge of the pot when there is plenty of soft rice at the centre?' Make of that what you will – I try not to think on it.

The following day, we travelled upriver to join Lieutenant Gunnell, who had gone ahead with a scouting party, and found ourselves surrounded by pirates. Gunnell had fought them to a standstill that day, losing many men, and expected them to attack again the following morning. As night fell we posted marines on picket duty. I could tell that Keppel and Gunnell were concerned about our dangerous position – but Rajah Brooke, not at all. He was laughing and joking with the tars and said we would lick 'em in the morning, to show them who ruled the Saribus.

We spent a miserable night of it – it rained incessantly, and we struggled to keep our powder dry under our coats. When dawn broke we could see them all around us in the jungle, and upstream they were chopping down trees with some purpose in mind – perhaps to block our escape route. We were soaked to the skin like miserable water rats and braced ourselves for the worse. But, at first light an amazing thing happened! They sent one of their warriors to treat with us and said that they would accept any terms we dictated! We replied that we would treat only with their chiefs, and a meeting was arranged for midday. They came dressed in all their finery but looking very dejected and humbled. They said that they knew their lives were forfeit, and were prepared to die if we said so, but that they were also willing to live. They promised Rajah Brooke that they would never again resort to piracy and offered him hostages as their guarantee. Rajah Brooke made a great speech in his own turn, speaking to them like a stern but loving father. He told them that we had come not for pillage or plunder, but to punish them for their repeated piratical actions, and for killing and enslaving the crews of the vessels they had attacked. Then he told them how much better their lives would be if they were to devote themselves to honest trade instead of piracy, and invited them to a conference in Sarawak so he could demonstrate to them the superior benefits of commerce – although I thought this was a bit thick, coming from such a self-confessed failure in trade! Then he concluded by vowing that if they broke their promise and committed even a single act of piracy, he would return and wipe them from the face of the earth. They agreed to this on their part, although they said they could not vouch for the Saribus settlement at Rembas, where the pirates held heavily fortified – and, so they said – impregnable positions.

We had got off lightly, and the real fight came at the Rembas settlement, which we advanced upon the next day, with the support of Sherip Jaffar and his Lingga Dayaks, who had recently joined us. As we pressed on upriver the next morning, we came upon more barriers of logs – four in number – which it took some time for our crews to cut through. But they were unguarded, the enemy having retreated to their stockade, so we landed Sherip Jaffar and his Dayaks on the left bank of the river about a mile below the town, to work their way through the jungle and come up behind the enemy positions.

Our attack went off like clockwork. We slipped in past the last barrier close to the bank of the river unseen, until our larger boats with their guns came up. When they came through the last barrier we pushed out to come within point blank range of their stockade and opened up with our guns on the pirate forces arrayed along its walls. As we did so, we heard the blood-curdling war cries of Sherip Jaffar and his men falling upon them from behind, which took them completely by surprise. In their panic and confusion, they opened up the gates of the stockade and fled in all directions, without even firing a shot towards us; when we entered the stockade, we found their cannon primed and loaded, but they never got a ball off. The fighting was very bloody and hand-to-hand, and after it was over the battlefield was a gruesome sight to behold. Headless bodies littered the ground, some stuck through with multiple spears like grotesque porcupines. Mercifully most of the Dayaks had followed Brooke's orders to spare the women and children, although there were a few unfortunate casualties among them, especially children struck down by poisoned darts. These wounds are not usually fatal for adults, but almost invariably so for children.

But they have learned their costly lesson, and the survivors have sworn to obey Rajah Brooke's command that they cease their piratical activities on pain of extinction. They have come to respect

James as a great and powerful Rajah, and to revere jolly old Keppel as something akin to a river god! They believe he has supernatural powers, including the ability to command the river bore, and he has come to be known among them as Rajah Laut – the Sea King.

We returned to Sarawak to much rejoicing, heroic tales of war, and displaying of heads. I don't think I'll ever get used to the sight of men and women walking about in broad daylight with dried human heads – complete with flesh and hair – dangling from their bodies. We are now preparing to repeat our exercise against the Skrang pirates, although Rajah Brooke is not blowing his own victory horn. He hopes to avoid another fight and has sent out emissaries asking them to commit to the cessation of their piratical activities.

He is a great man, and I admire his bravery and passion for his people. I am honoured to call myself his close friend and love him like an elder brother. Perhaps you can come and visit him in Sarawak when things have settled down – you would be greatly impressed with what he has done for the native peoples. I will write again with news of our Skrang expedition, but do not worry – the White Rajah and the Sea King will keep me safe!

Love to Annie and Grandpa John.

Your loving son
Duncan.

PS A quick postscript, although I might arrive home before my letter! The Skrang expedition is abandoned for the moment because Captain Keppel has been recalled to Hong Kong. He has persuaded me to go with him. He says there are much better prospects for the company in Hong Kong than in Sarawak, and if Jardine and Matheson can have offices in Singapore, then Simpson and Co should have offices in Hong Kong. He made a lot of sense, so with your permission I have decided to go along with him. But you can tell me personally what you think about this when we get back to Singapore, where we will be putting in for water and stores in about a week's time.

17

Achmad Hassin was half way through the prayers for the dead when he heard the sound, the great rustling of wings as she settled on the rooftop of his hut, and he shivered at the sound. He turned and faced the pontianak [lxxviii] that perched on the mantel above his door, blocking the entrance. She had the body of a great bird, with long black-feathered wings hanging by her sides, ready to take flight in an instant. She had the wrinkled face of an old woman, a face that was grey as the face of a corpse, with bloodshot eyes and long sharp teeth that glistened in the moonlight. Her long black hair hung low over her shoulders, and he could smell her – a sweet sickly smell of perfume and death.

He knew who she was, for he had encountered her before. She was the undead soul of an evil woman who had died in childbirth two hundred years before, in a kampong in the jungle that was long since deserted. She normally appeared as a beautiful young woman, when she lured unwary men to their death when they lost their way – she would drink their blood and leave their bodies drained in the moonlight. But this night she appeared as her true self, for she knew that kind of easy trick would not work with a powerful bomoh like Achmad.

Bah, he thought to himself, recalling the pompous words of the imam. Only a bomoh could deal with pontianaks, and the dreaded penanggalan, the ghastly heads and entrails of female spirits that wandered the night and feasted on the living and the dead. The

lxxviii In Malay folklore, a female vampire.

holy imams forbade talk of such creatures as blasphemy, but only a bomoh knew the spells, the magic potions and the amulets that could protect a man against such horrors of miscreation.

Then he realized his mistake, and the horror of his own death gripped his heart for the second time that evening, for he realized he did not bear the amulets that protected him against the pontianak and the penanggalan. He had removed these talismans when he had performed his ablutions, in preparation for his prayers for the dead over the image of the corpse of Sadat. In his haste to complete his curse he had forgotten to replace them. Now he was like a naked man, unprotected from the carrion woman whose talons flexed in anticipation of her kill.

He had only one chance of escape. He had to lead her away from his hut, and then double back to gain the protection of the amulets, to give him time to cast a spell that would banish her into the darkness of the night. He rose cautiously and carefully, and then raced as fast as his legs could carry him towards the jungle. As he did so he heard the dreadful whoosh of her wings and turned in terror to see her flying alongside him, her bloodshot eyes fixed upon his eyes and her white fangs drawn in a ghastly grin. He forced himself forward, then stopped dead in his tracks and spun around, and raced back towards his hut. But she was too quick for him. He heard the great wings beating and saw that she was back perched above his door, her bloodshot eyes fixed upon him. Again, he ran towards the jungle, and again she flew alongside him. He made a feint, but she anticipated his feint; he ran in a shortening circle round his hut and she flew the circle with him, returning to her perch when the circle neared the door; he ran along the pathway back toward the kampong, only to find her perched upon a low tree branch before him.

He turned and ran back once again towards his hut, exhaustion and despair threatening to overcome him. He knew he must not stop, for when he did she would be upon him. Desperation drove him on, and for a hopeful moment he thought he might make it. But when he was only about fifty feet from the door of his hut he tripped upon a root and fell sprawling to the ground. He heard the great beating of her wings above him, and in his fear, he fainted outright.

18

Achmad woke to the sound of a bird shrieking in the jungle. He reacted with alarm, but in his first waking thought he realized he was alive. He had fainted in his fear that the pontianak would sink her talons into his back and drink his blood and his soul. Yet when he woke he felt no pain, only a soft hand gently pushing on his shoulder to rouse him. He breathed a sigh of relief and looked up to thank his saviour – and looked into the yellow eyes of the tiger. He smelt the putrid blood on the tiger's breath just before it sank its teeth into his head and dragged his body into the jungle.

* * *

A few moments later a wild boar came rooting through the clearing and disturbed the grave of the waxen image, dislodging the image from the shroud. The boar took the image into its mouth, but spat it out when he got the taste of the wax. The black sliver of bamboo fell away from the broken image and drifted over the lalang grass in the gentle night breeze.

* * *

Nahu stood in a daze, amazed and confused. He of the hairy face had stared at her for what seemed an eternity, and then, just as she was sure the great cat was going to strike, it had raised itself up on its haunches and turned away, padding softly into the night. She sat down on the steps and gave thanks to God for her deliverance, then rose to see if Sadat was still living or dead. When she entered the cottage, she was overjoyed to see him sitting in the corner of the front room, smiling up at her. Her love for him was now returned as strong as it had ever been, and Sadat could tell that this was so. Without a word or question or rebuke from each to the other, she followed him as he took her by the hand and led her into their bedroom. And they were strangers to each other no more because the evil had gone out of their lives. A year later Nahu gave birth to a healthy baby boy, whom they called Adi, the first.

19

In September, Governor Butterworth appointed Thomas Dunman as Deputy Magistrate and Superintendent of Police. Born in Belfast in 1815, Dunman came out to Singapore in 1840 to work as a clerk for Martin Dyce and Co in their offices on Boat Quay, where he remained for three years. His appointment to take charge of the police at the age of twenty-eight surprised many, since he had no civil or military service with the East India Company or the Straits government, and no police experience of any kind. Yet Dunman quickly earned a reputation for his excellent relations with the various ethnic communities. This was in large part due to his ability to master the rudiments of most of the local languages, as well as his good nature and genial personality. He was a short stocky man, with a round face surmounted by a shock of curly brown hair, and he walked around with his thumbs in his waistcoat like some Ulster farmer.

Yet his sharp eyes and attentive ears missed very little, and he proved to be an inspired appointment. He had spent most of his time in his office while clerking for Dyce and Co, but as superintendent of police he was usually out on the streets making sure his men were alert at their stations – he was sometimes to be seen driving his buggy late at night without any lights, to check that his men were at their posts – and picking up as much information as he could from his contacts in the Chinese, Malay, Indian, Bugis and Arab communities. Although he was a strict taskmaster, he took good care of his men, conducting evening classes at the stations to teach them the basics of reading and writing, a requirement for promotion to the higher ranks. The Malays who reached the rank of sergeant major under Dunman's tutelage won the approval of their communities, which in turn attracted superior recruits into the force. The police came to be respected and to respect themselves under Dunman's leadership. Perhaps most important of all, he managed to gain the confidence of the heads of the Chinese secret societies, by demonstrating on numerous occasions that he could be absolutely trusted to protect his sources, and he created an excellent working relationship with them.

Dunman built himself a house and three seaside bungalows at Tanjong Katong, where he managed a four-hundred-acre coconut plantation. There he slept soundly in his bed without any concern for his own safety, having few enemies and a loaded shotgun by his bed. In any case, he rarely spent more than a few hours in his bed each night, for he normally rose at four to travel into town and did not usually return until after midnight. The man and the job were made for each other.

* * *

When Bishop Wilson arrived in Singapore in October 1843, he conducted a service in St Andrew's Church. The following day he sent out a circular letter suggesting that the gentlemen of the town might consider a minor improvement to their beautiful church – a small tower and spire that would serve to distinguish it from other secular town buildings such as the courthouse and the London Hotel. Once again, the merchants reached into their pockets, and a tower and spire were added by the end of the year, designed by John Turnbull Thomson.

The merchants were not the only ones to contribute to the newly towered and spired church. Mrs Maria Balestier, the wife of the American consul, donated a large cast-iron bell, thirty-two inches in diameter and twenty-six inches in height, on condition that it be used to ring the curfew for five minutes each evening. Maria Balestier was the daughter of the American patriot Paul Revere, who made his famous midnight ride in 1775 to warn the Sons of Liberty that the British were advancing on Lexington and Concord. The bell was cast in Boston by the firm of Paul Revere and Sons, founded by the patriot at the turn of the century, and continued by Maria's brother Paul Revere Jr, who had expanded his father's silversmith business and now specialized in the casting of church bells. The inscription on the bell read:

> Revere Boston 1843. Presented to St Andrew's Church
> Singapore, by Mrs Maria Revere Balestier of Boston,
> United States of America.

Thomas Church, the resident councillor, donated a large and expensive clock, made by the famed London clockmaker Barraud and Lund.

* * *

After spending so much time in the East, George Coleman could not settle in England. He and his pregnant wife Maria arrived back in Singapore in November, with plans to establish permanent residence. Maria gave birth to a healthy boy on December 27, two days after the splendid Christmas day dinner Coleman hosted for his old friends and servants. Yet his joy was short-lived. Coleman developed a fever in March the following year and died within a few days. He was buried in the Christian cemetery at the foot of Government Hill, where his tombstone expressed the indebtedness of the townspeople for the many 'elegant buildings, both public and private, which adorn Singapore'.

Coleman's friend and newspaper partner, the lawyer William Napier, married Maria six months later, and adopted Coleman's son, whom he named George Vernon Coleman Napier.

* * *

In December, Gaston Dutronquoy, the proprietor of the London Hotel, who also had a side business painting portraits and miniatures, ventured into photography, and placed the following advertisement in the *Singapore Free Press*:

> Mr G. Dutronquoy respectfully informs ladies and gentlemen at Singapore, that he is complete master of the newly invented and imported Daguerreotype. Ladies and gentlemen who may honour Mr Dutronquoy with a sitting can have their likenesses taken in an astonishing short space of two minutes. The portraits are free of all blemish and are in every respect perfect likenesses. A lady and gentleman can be placed together in one picture and both are taken at the same time entirely shaded from the effects of the sun. The price of one picture is ten dollars, both taken together in one picture is fifteen dollars.

In March the following year, Mr Dutronquoy moved the premises of his London Hotel once again, to the building on the corner of High Street and the Esplanade, which was formerly owned by Edward Boustead. Later in the year he set up a small theatre in the hotel, which he called the Theatre Royal, in an attempt to revive theatricals in Singapore. The first theatre in Singapore had opened in Cross Street in the 1830s, but it had not been a great success. The actors had no talent, spent little time rehearsing their lines, and seemed to have great difficulty remaining sober.

The initial success of the Theatre Royal owed a lot to Thomas Dunman, who demonstrated his comedic talents as Mr Johnston in *The Spectre Bridegroom*, one of the first plays produced at the theatre. He was ably supported by the delightful Miss Potowker as Lavinia, whose sparkling performance made her the envy of every young woman in the audience. She had the smallest waist and daintiest feet in Singapore, and nobody guessed that 'she' was in actuality played by the merchant W.H. Read. Other community stalwarts such as William Napier and Captain Scott featured in later productions, and the theatre got a special boost when Mrs Deacle, an English actress who had been playing in Calcutta, came out to Singapore and gave a number of performances. These included a production of *The Merchant of Venice* in which she played Portia, with John Horrocks Whitehead of Shaw, Whitehead and Co playing Shylock.

Unfortunately, Thomas Dunman had to abandon his budding thespian career. Governor Butterworth, who was in the audience one evening, identified the intrepid Captain Cobb as his superintendent of police. The governor, who was a stickler about these things, did not think such activities compatible with Dunman's official position, and he was forced to abandon the stage.

20

For six long months Hong Xiuquan, Feng Yunshan and Hong Rengan pored over Liang Afa's text, which Hong interpreted for them. They converted and baptised more villagers and began to take action against the idols and demons. They removed the Confucian ancestral tablets from the schools in which they taught and promptly lost their jobs. Hong decided that the time had come for him to travel the world, like his elder brother before him, to teach the people the doctrine of repentance. He set off with a small party of followers in April, with little money, and indifferent to the fact that his wife has just borne him a second baby girl. Feng Yunshan accompanied him, but not Hong Rengan, whose parents forbade him to make the journey, after having beat him mercilessly for having defaced the revered Confucian tablets.

Hong Xiuquan and Feng Yunshan travelled first to Canton and the southern delta region, then north and northwest through Guangdong, preaching Hong's gospel of redemption. They continued west into Guangxi province until they reached Sigu, where they were welcomed by two of Hong's relatives. While in Sigu, Hong began the first of the many religious tracts that he would write during his lifetime, and refined the basic rituals of his faith. Hong preached his sermons on sin, redemption and remorse to congregations of Hakka men and women before a simple altar – a table upon which two lamps were placed, with three cups of tea as offering. The congregation sang hymns to God's grace, and then prayed for their redemption on their knees with their eyes closed, each taking turns to recite their prayers aloud before the congregation, ending with the exaltation:

'Blessed by the merits of the Saviour and Heavenly Elder Brother, Jesus, who has redeemed us from sin, we pray through him to our Heavenly Father, the Great God, who is in Heaven, that His will be done on earth as it is in Heaven. Look down and grant my request. Amen.'

Hong gained over a hundred converts through his preaching. They confessed their sins, abjured the worship of evil spirits, and swore to obey the Heavenly commandments. Hong baptised them by pouring water over their heads, as he had learned from Liang Afa's tract and as he had practiced in Guanlubu. When their baptism was complete, the converts bathed in the river, drank the tea offering, and washed the area around their hearts, to signify their inner cleansing.

* * *

Joseph Balestier met his son at his godown on Boat Quay, where they had tiffin together in his office. They dined on mutton curry from a street vendor and pineapples from the American consul's own estate. Joseph Balestier was proud of his son, who was named Joseph Warren, after the American patriot who had instructed Paul Revere to make his midnight ride. He was an upright and intelligent young man, always eager for new challenges, and with many interesting ideas on how to develop his father's sugarcane plantation and other business interests. He seemed to have inherited his technical know-how from the Revere side of the family, and Joseph looked forward to the day when he could hand over the business to his son and retire as the senior representative of the United States in Singapore.

After tiffin, father and son walked down Boat Quay to Commercial Square, where a horse auction was in progress. Joseph successfully bid on two feisty Sydney ponies, and gave one to his son, joking that he never knew when he might have to make his own midnight ride.

'To warn against whom?' his son quizzed him.

'Oh, the Chinaman, the Malay, the Bugis or the Hindoo!' replied his father. 'You never know when a war might break out among them or between them and us. Although hopefully we're back in the good graces of the British government for the time being!'

Cast iron railings had recently been erected in Commercial Square, to fence off the central area that had been planted with flowers. The local Chinese consequently came to call Commercial Square *tho kha hue hng*, the 'flower garden by the godowns'.

21

Duncan walked down to the harbour's edge at Hong Kong island and took a sampan out to the *Dido*. The sun was shining bright in the clear blue morning sky, and he had to shade his eyes to make out the ship. He had received a message that morning stating that Captain Keppel wanted to meet with him. Duncan had been staying with David Jardine, who had given him lots of excellent advice on the China trade and the commercial prospects of Hong Kong island. These had originally been pretty grim, Jardine admitted, when the British took occupancy in 1841 under Sir Henry Pottinger, the first governor. The settlement had been devastated by regular outbreaks of fever and bubonic plague, which decimated the original settlers and troops to such a degree that a posting to Hong Kong was considered a death certificate, and their early wooden buildings had been battered by typhoons. The new settlement attracted as many criminals as legitimate merchants, and the waterfront area of Victoria was soon home to opium dens, gambling clubs and brothels. Jardine estimated that about four hundred and fifty prostitutes plied their trade in about two dozen brothels, and that most of the vice trade was controlled by the secret societies that had come across from Canton.

But things had much improved in the past year or two, Jardine assured him. The British government had invested a significant amount of money in the settlement, which had enabled the Royal Engineers to install proper drains, roads and harbour facilities. This, along with the recently planted shrubs and bamboo groves, had greatly improved the quality of the air, which led to a significant reduction in disease. The newly instituted police force was beginning to bring order to the settlement, which was certain to thrive, Jardine assured him, because of its greatest asset – the deep, well-sheltered harbour which the Cantonese called *hèung-gáwng*, or fragrant harbour, because of the smell of sandalwood incense that drifted across the harbour from the factories on the west coast of the island. Indeed, in the past year, Hong Kong had developed into something of a boomtown, as a consequence of the opening up of the new treaty ports after the Treaty of Nanking; new and solid brick houses and godowns were going up all over Victoria and the waterfront. Jardine said the Treaty of Nanking was only the beginning, and that the British government and the other European powers, and also the Americans, were planning to open up the whole of China to outside trade – through diplomatic negotiation if possible, but through force if necessary. That was why Britain had invested so much money in the settlement, not only because it was well-situated for the China trade, but because it was ideally suited as a safe and sheltered base for the Royal Navy.

As he sat in the sampan heading out to the *Dido*, Duncan thought to himself that he must persuade his father to open an office of Simpson and Co in Hong Kong. Such an investment would not only be a prudent expansion of their present business but might eventually prove to be a necessary one to the survival of the company. Given its location and the British government's commitment to develop it as a naval base, Hong Kong might soon eclipse Singapore as the major British trading port in the East. He was not unduly concerned, however, for as he reasoned to himself, if Jardine and Matheson had seen fit to open an office of their own in Singapore, they must still think it had a viable future. Yet he wondered how much faster Singapore might have developed had the British government been as financially committed to its support from the beginning.

'Good to see you again, Duncan,' said Captain Keppel, when Duncan arrived on board and was shown to Keppel's cabin.

'You're looking well, I must say! It must be all that good food and drink you've been getting from my friend David Jardine. He keeps a very good table, he does, very good indeed. It's great to see you again, my boy, and I have some good news. We're done with our China service, so we are going back to Sarawak to help Mr Brooke sort out the Skrang Dayaks. Admiral Sir William Parker has given us formal approval, and we sail tomorrow morning.'

'Good news indeed,' Duncan replied. 'I'll pack my things tonight and write a quick letter to my family – I take it we can continue on to Singapore after we have dealt with the Skrang. Have you any news from Brooke?'

'Yes, yes,' Keppel assured him, 'certainly I'll take you back to your family after we've taught the Skrang a lesson! Mr Brooke's been off fighting pirates in Ache with Admiral Parker. He's charmed the pants off the Admiral, so we have carte blanche to attack pirates anywhere we find them, including Sarawak and the Skrang river. We don't even need Hassim's approval, although we will of course secure it. James also managed to persuade Mr Church, the acting governor of Singapore, to let us use the Company's *Phlegethon*. She's an armoured steamer with a very shallow draught – just the sort of craft for our line of work. I'm not sure Colonel Butterworth would have approved its use, or if he did, he would have made us jump over fences to get it.'

'Ah, come in Lieutenant Wade,' said Keppel, noticing the young man at the door, 'I'd like you to meet Duncan Simpson. Duncan, meet Francis Wade, who's just been appointed First Lieutenant of the *Dido*. They promoted Lieutenant Horton for his action against the Saribus pirates.'

Duncan and Francis shook hands. Francis Wade was about

Duncan's height, with curly blond hair and bright blue eyes, and a warm smile. He was also about the same age as Duncan, and the two young men bonded quickly, especially after they discovered they shared a love of chess, which Duncan had learned from his grandfather.

Over dinner that evening, Duncan asked Francis how he had come to join the navy.

'I was born in Tipperary, where my father was a Protestant minister,' Francis replied. 'I always loved the sea, and dreamed of joining the navy, but my family discouraged the notion. They had no money to send me to naval college, and no friends who could secure me a place as a midshipman. However, one day, when I was fourteen, my father sent me to London with some letters and books for my uncle. While I was staying with my uncle, I overheard him mentioning that the Earl of Huntly was about to leave for the West Indies on HMS *Valorous*. I waited all day outside the Earl's house, and when he came out to go to his club I introduced myself, and told him of my dream of joining the navy. A bit of a nerve, I know, but he seemed to approve of that, and offered me a place on the *Valorous*. He became my patron and eventually my friend, and he helped me secure my first position, as artillery officer with the British Legion in Spain.'

'Where he received the St Ferdinand and Isabella the Catholic crosses for valour under fire,' interrupted Keppel, pouring them both a glass of port. 'Then service in the Mediterranean and the Pacific, until he ended up as first lieutenant at my table. Your good health, gentlemen, and to a successful war against the Skrang!'

'To a successful war,' replied the two younger men, raising their glasses.

22

Hong Kong, June 22, 1844

Dear Mother and Father

I write to say that Captain Keppel has returned from his China service, and that we sail tomorrow to join Rajah Brooke on his expedition against the Skrang pirates – we hope to help him finish the job we started last year.

I am more convinced than ever that we ought to open an office in Hong Kong, as I intimated in my previous letters. I will explain the situation in detail when I return to Singapore, which should be with Captain Keppel in late September.

Be assured that I will keep myself safe, and look forward to seeing you all again soon. Love to Annie and Grandpapa John. Must dash.

> Your loving son
> Duncan.

* * *

They left Hong Kong on June 22, but did not reach Sarawak until July 29, because they had to beat down against the southwest monsoon. On the journey Duncan and Francis became good friends. They found they had similar interests besides chess, at which they were evenly matched, including a shared longing for female companionship. Francis complained about the romantic constraints of life in the navy, while Duncan complained of the paucity of suitable European girls in Singapore. When Francis suggested that he might think instead of a suitable Chinese girl, Duncan replied that there was a paucity of them as well. Duncan asked Francis if his father had forgiven him for running off to the navy, to which Francis replied that he had. Francis then asked Duncan jokingly if his father would forgive him if he married a Chinese girl, and Duncan replied, in earnest, that he was sure he would. They spent many a night watch together, in silent friendship during the howling monsoon winds and pitching seas.

When they arrived in Kuching, they were greeted with the usual gun salutes and clashing of gongs. That evening they dined at Rajah Brooke's new residence, which he had seized from Prince Mahkota in retaliation for his failed attempt at poisoning him. The Rajah's Chinese cook produced a multi-course feast fit for a king, washed down with copious amounts of champagne and claret.

'My old enemy, Mahkota – the Serpent! – has been working against me in my absence,' James informed them. 'He has helped Sherip Sahib and his brother Sherip Muller raise a pirate fleet of over two hundred prahus, and they have brought murder, rape, enslavement and destruction up and down the coastline. Our job is to hunt down this nest of vipers in their Skrang lairs. My spies tell me that they think we are weakened because Captain Keppel and I have been away this past year, but we are back now and they are in for a bloody nose! We'll show 'em, won't we Charlie?' he concluded, addressing his nephew Charles Johnson, who James had arranged to have transferred as midshipman from HMS *Wolverine* to HMS *Dido*.

Preparations for the expedition began the following day. While Keppel met with Rajah Muda Hassim in an extended council of war that resulted in the anticipated invitation to protect Sarawak against the Skrang pirates, Lieutenant Wade prepared the *Dido* for war and Rajah Brooke and George Steward organized the native contingents. Despite James' protests, Prince Badrudeen, Hassim's brother, determined that he would lead a war party himself, since he had an old score to settle with Mahkota. Like Keppel and Brooke, Duncan and Francis were greatly impressed by Badrudeen. A tall, bronzed and muscled Malay warrior, with a noble brow and hawk-like nose, he looked the epitome of Brunei royalty. He was also, they were pleased to recognize, intelligent and charming to boot, and an excellent chess player.

* * *

'What is it, my dear,' Ronnie asked Sarah, when he saw her frowning over the letter she was reading at the breakfast table. 'Is there anything wrong?'

'Oh nothing,' she said. 'It's a letter from Duncan. He says that Captain Keppel has returned and that they are going to join Rajah Brooke on another expedition, this time against the Skrang pirates. He still thinks we should open an office in Hong Kong, and says he'll be back in September to persuade us of it.'

'Well, that's good news,' Ronnie replied, 'and I'm sure he'll be safe enough with Keppel and Brooke, especially since I heard the other day that Church had authorized the use of the *Phlegethon* to support the expedition.'

'I hope you're right,' Sarah replied, 'you know how I worry about him.' She did not mention the black shadow that had seemed to descend upon her when she read that Duncan was going to join the expedition, the same black shadow that still descended upon her whenever she thought of the dreadful fate of her dear sister and her family.

'As I do, but I'm sure he'll be fine,' Ronnie assured her. He did not mention the chill that ran through him when she read him the news.

23

Tan Tock Seng continued to arrange for burial and funeral services for the Chinese paupers, and to attend to the general welfare of the coolies. Yet he recognized that this was not enough. There were few doctors in Singapore. The British senior surgeons such as Drs Montgomerie and Oxley looked after the officials of the East India Company, and a number of private doctors looked after the wealthy merchants. There was a small Company hospital, but otherwise there was only the poorly staffed Pauper Hospital on Hospital Road, which was formerly nothing more than attap sheds funded by revenue from the pork farm tax. Coleman had built a brick building to replace them in 1833, which had then served as a convict as well as a pauper hospital. However, it was overcrowded with lunatics and destitutes as well as sick convicts, coolies and European sailors, and was poorly staffed. When the Indian government abolished the pork farm tax in 1837, which had been used to fund the hospital, it degenerated into little more than a poor house. Many died of leprosy, smallpox and cholera in the dark corners of the building, packed in rows of fly-infested wooden bunks that stood upon the mud floor. The plank structure that made up the European Seaman's ward hovered precariously over the open and foul-smelling latrines at the end of the building. If the poor and lunatic were not sick when they entered the hospital, they invariably became so within a short period of time and died soon afterwards. The lepers were in charge of cleaning the hospital. Lacking a proper kitchen, they placed the cooking pots on the beds besides the patients and convicts when they were not being used to cook the mid-day meal of fish-curry and rice. The grand jury and the leading merchants followed the Company and private doctors in petitioning the Indian government to reintroduce the pork farm tax to support the funding of a superior facility, but as usual baulked when the Indian government suggested that such a facility be supported by a levy on the merchants themselves.

Yet Tan Tock Seng could not stand idly by and watch his countrymen die. He arranged for the distribution of food and clothing to the poor and unemployed, and set an example by pledging five thousand dollars to the founding of a new hospital dedicated to 'the sick and poor of all nations', to be built on land he donated at the foot of Pearl's Hill. At a public meeting in February, Tan Tock Seng, newly appointed as a justice of the peace by Governor Butterworth, announced that a further two thousand dollars had been pledged from the estate of Cham Chang Sang, who had died the previous week. The leading Chinese and European merchants agreed that funds for the maintenance of the hospital should come from the general revenue, based upon a two percent tax on houses and an annual grant from the Indian Government. Further donations were secured from leading Chinese merchants such as Seah Eu Chin, Tan Kim Seng, Tan Hong Chuan and Hoo Ah Kay. John Turnbull Thomson submitted a design for the hospital, which was unanimously approved, and the foundation stone of the 'Chinese Pauper Hospital', which later became known as Tan Tock Seng Hospital, was laid in July.

The government had earlier approved the construction of a European Seamen's Hospital, also at the foot of Pearl's Hill. For years the merchants had petitioned the government for the provision of such a facility, given the development of the port, but had been reluctant to contribute to the cost themselves. But after a number of serious cholera outbreaks among visiting sailors had impressed upon them the desperate need for such a facility, the Chamber of Commerce raised nearly three thousand dollars and the government agreed to pay the remaining cost of the building. The foundation stone was also laid in July.

24

The expedition departed August 5, and a huge crowd assembled to see them off, including families that had travelled great distances to witness the departure of Prince Badrudeen, in his royal barge decked out with silk canopies and colourful streamers. Guns saluted, gongs crashed, and the Arab imam Mudlana gave the Muslim blessing. They sailed up the coast without incident and anchored at the mouth of the Batang Lupar River, where they warned Sherip Jaffar not to give aid to Sherip Sahib and Sherip Muller. They learned that Sherip Sahib had removed his harem from his fortified position at Patusan, some fifty miles upriver. There he and Prince Mahkota were preparing a strong defence, having been informed by their spies of the expedition that was being prepared against them.

The following morning, they sailed up the river on the flood tide, the *Jolly Bachelor* leading the way, with the *Dido* and *Phlegethon* close behind. That night they anchored just below Patusan and prepared the ships for battle the next morning.

The boats from the *Dido* and the cutters from the *Phlegethon* lined up with the native craft in the misty dawn, with Lieutenant Wade leading in the *Dido*'s pinnace. The plan was for the boats to land the marines and sailors close into the shore, with Prince Badrudeen and the war-chief Patinggi Ali supporting with their force of Malays and Dayaks, while the *Phlegethon* and the *Jolly Bachelor* provided covering fire with their guns. When the mist cleared, they moved forward, the boats hugging close into the riverbank, until they pulled in front of the five forts that stood menacingly before them, which suddenly erupted with canon fire and musketry. Keppel and Commander Scott aboard the *Phlegethon* cursed when her guns failed to fire, because of problems with her detonating priming-tubes, leaving the landing party unprotected on the shore. James brought the *Jolly Bachelor* around so her bow gun could bear, as George Steward called out to Duncan to go back and fetch up more shot for Mr Ellis, who was manning the gun. But as Duncan turned to do so, he heard a loud and sickening thump and stumbled forward as a missile struck him in the small of his back. He reached behind and felt the blood that soaked his shirt – he wondered how badly he was wounded. But then Charlie Johnson, Brooke's nephew, knelt beside him and yelled:

'Don't worry, Duncan, you're not hit! You're only hit by poor Ellis's arm!'

Duncan turned around and saw Charlie clutching Ellis's severed arm. A cannon ball had made a direct hit and cut Ellis to pieces, and the forward deck was awash with blood and body parts.

'Don't just stand there, men,' screamed George Steward, 'help me clear the deck!'

Duncan stood transfixed for a moment as he watched Steward toss body parts and guts over the side of the schooner, but he managed to overcome his horror and grabbed the sand buckets, whose contents he emptied over the blood-stained decks so that the fighting men could keep their footing. James brought the *Jolly Bachelor* round again so he could bring her swivel guns to bear.

On shore, the landing parties seemed oblivious to the lack of protective fire. They had been waiting for the attack since before dawn, and their blood was up. Lieutenant Wade landed first and immediately set off for the largest fort, waving his drawn sword above his head to encourage his men. They needed no encouragement. They fixed their bayonets and drew their cutlasses and did their level best to drown out the ferocity of the native war cries with their own blood-curdling chants and cheers. If the pirates had held their ground and maintained their fire they might have inflicted heavy losses on their attackers, but they did not. When the marines and blue jackets approached, the pirates streamed out the rear of the forts, thousands of men running into the jungle. As Wade's men took possession of the forts, the Dayaks pursued the pirates into the jungle, and after some fierce hand-to-hand fighting, returned victorious with many of their heads. The expedition's casualties were remarkably light, given the assembled firepower of the enemy. Although a few men had serious wounds, Mr Ellis was the only fatality of the day.

For two days they laid waste to the forts. They spiked the sixty guns and destroyed tons of gunpowder and ammunition, and gathered up quantities of gold, silver and precious stones. They sent two divisions upriver in pursuit of Sherip Sahib and Mahkota, but when they came upon the home village of Sherip Sahib, they found it deserted. Sherip Sahib had fled to the mountains, leaving behind his extensive wardrobe and his harem, and more stores of treasure and gunpowder. Keppel ordered the women sent downriver to safety, the treasure brought on board the ships, and everything else destroyed.

'Pretty rum sort of fight,' Brooke complained that evening. 'We hardly killed any of the buggers, and Mahkota got off scot-free with Sherip Sahib.'

'Hardly scot-free,' replied Keppel. 'We've destroyed his forts, his cannon and his gunpowder, and seized his money and his harem. He'll be in no position to create any trouble for a while.'

'Don't you believe it,' James replied. 'They still have their boats, and they can steal everything else back quick as a flash. But we're not through with them. I'm told Mahkota has headed further upriver to join up with Sherip Muller and the Skrang Dayaks and Malays – we might still find that Sherip Sahib has joined forces with them. We'll pursue them in the morning.'

'As you wish, James,' said Keppel, 'you know these people and the country better than I do.'

25

The following morning, they set off for the country of the Skrang Dayaks, led by Patinggi Ali and his native division of scouts. Fifteen miles above the Patusan forts they came upon a branch of the river called Undop, where Patinggi Ali informed them that he had successfully routed a large force of Malays in the service of Sherip Muller.

They drove on upriver but came across a series of barriers made from trees that had been felled from both sides of the river, with their trunks interlaced with rattan. They cut through the first barrier and most of the second before pitching camp in a large farmhouse at the edge of the river, where they posted sentries and settled down for the night. The next morning, they cut through the second barrier, and quickly came upon Sherip Muller's home village, but finding it deserted, they set fire to the buildings and pressed on. They cut through three more river barriers and spent another dreary but uneventful night camped on the riverbank, as the rain fell in great sheets of water and turned the ground into a sea of mud.

After they set off the following morning, they came upon yet another barrier, this one uncompleted. Pressing through, Patinggi Ali's men spotted the war-prahu of Sherip Muller in the distance, and quickly set off in pursuit. They captured the war-prahu, but Sherip Muller made his escape in a fast sampan to his refuge further upriver.

That evening they discussed their strategy aboard the *Jolly Bachelor*. According to Patinggi Ali and Prince Badrudeen, Sherip

Muller's fortified stockade was on a hill a few miles ahead. It was perched on top of a bend in the river that looped for five miles around the hill. There were two landing places, they had been told, the second offering a more direct route to the stockade. It was decided that Keppel, Duncan and Lieutenant Wade would set off early the next morning and try to find the second entrance. Yet when they explored the river shortly after dawn, they could not find it, and eventually turned and made their way back up the river. After a few hours of fruitless search, they pulled into a small clearing to have breakfast, and wait for the other boats to come up.

They were in the process of making a small fire when Francis told them to hush – he thought he heard voices in the jungle behind them. They strained their ears and did hear sounds coming from the jungle, but whether these sounds came from pirates, birds or monkeys they could not tell. Francis posted sentries around the camp, then he, Duncan and Keppel took up their weapons and set off into the jungle with a small party of marines.

They did not have to go very far. As they cut their way through the undergrowth it became clear that the sounds were of men calling out to each other, and within a short time they came across a huge armada of pirate prahus hidden in a wide inlet, whose entrance they had missed because it had been concealed by hanging branches.

'So that's where they're hid,' whispered Keppel, holding up his hand to caution Francis against breaking cover. 'Let's send someone back to bring up the others.'

Duncan looked at Francis, whose eyes were fixed straight ahead. He did not seem to hear what Keppel had said. For instead of sending one of the marines back for help, he dashed straight out of the jungle and charged towards the pirate fleet, firing off his pistol as he went.

'Damn and blast!' said Keppel. 'Brave as Brooke, but just as daft.' They had no choice but to follow, firing their weapons and drawing their swords and cutlasses as they charged out of the jungle. They were hopelessly outnumbered, but the pirates did not know that – they abandoned their ships and fled up the hill toward Sherip Muller's stockade, believing that Francis and his men were the advance guard of a much larger force. As they reached the prahus at the foot of the hill, Keppel called out to Lieutenant Wade to wait up. He had heard firing coming from the river, which meant that the rest of their squadron had caught up with them and would soon be able to support them in an attack upon Sherip Muller's compound.

But Francis' blood was up and he charged off up the hill after the pirates, with Duncan in close pursuit. Duncan paused only to fire his rifle to bring down a pirate who had stopped to fire back at them, then raced alongside his friend as they scrambled up the jungle track. Suddenly the track opened into a clearing, where they found a young Malay girl, clutching her baby in terror. Francis stopped and spoke to her softly to reassure her, then led her off to the edge of the clearing to safety. But as Francis walked back towards him, Duncan saw a sudden frown on his face. He looked around and understood why. They had outrun the rest of their party, and were now surrounded by armed Dayaks, who blocked them front and back, and lined the edges of the clearing. The eyes of the two young men met in the frozen moment, as they shared the knowledge that certain death awaited them. Duncan felt his insides turn to liquid, and his legs begin to tremble beneath him, but he managed a grim smile as Francis raised his eyebrow and his pistol, as if affronted by the audacity of their enemy. Duncan tried to call out to his friend but found he could not – his voice was choked with the fear in his throat. Then he gasped in horror as he watched a musket ball blow off the back of his friend's head and saw Francis crumble to the ground.

Then the rage overcame him. He turned and shot one man dead with his rifle, then drew his cutlass and ran screaming at the pirates who blocked the path that led back down to the captured pirate fleet and his comrades. As he charged towards them he wondered if there really was a heaven, and if he would meet his friend Francis there. He drove into the Dayak warriors who he knew were racing to take his treasured head and brought the first man down with a deep cut to his neck. But as he struggled to withdraw his blade, he was bowled over by a vicious blow from a Dayak war club. He staggered backwards and lost his grip on the cutlass. He tripped over the body of the Dayak he had shot and fell spread-eagled to the ground. In an instant his attacker was upon him, pinning his outstretched arms with his knees. Duncan struggled to maintain consciousness and tried desperately to free his right arm so he could reach the dirk in his boot, but the man's weight was too great for him to shift his arm more than a fraction. The Dayak was heavily tattooed, great whirls of black and blue that spun before Duncan's eyes, spiralling and dancing into a darkening mist. Duncan's senses were failing fast, but he snapped back to alertness when he saw the deadly black kris in the pirate's hand, poised for the kill. He knew he was going to die along with his friend. He had a final foolish thought – he wondered what their heads would look like in a Dayak longhouse.

26

The pirate froze and clasped his hand to his right eye, from which a slim feathered dart protruded. Then there was a sudden whooshing sound, as his severed head tumbled from his shoulders and bounced off Duncan's chest. As he gazed in horror, Duncan saw another head appear above the dead pirate's bloody neck, as two gnarled hands grasped the dead man's shoulders. The face grinned, an ugly, black-toothed grin, like the grin of the hellish demons in the paintings of Hieronymus Bosch. But Duncan was overjoyed when he recognized it as the grinning face of Subu Besi, iron anchor, the ugly Dayak who was James' coxswain and executioner.

As Subu Besi threw the dead pirate's body aside and pulled Duncan to his feet, he saw James and Prince Badrudeen leading a Dayak and Malay war party that had fought their way across the clearing and were pursuing the pirates up the hill-side.

'Easy, easy now,' Duncan heard a voice behind him. It was Captain Keppel, who grasped him firmly by the arm and asked what had happened to Lieutenant Wade. Duncan was too choked with emotion to answer and simply pointed to the place where Francis' body lay. They walked over to him together, where he lay face down in the long grass. The back of his head was a mass of blood and brains, but when they turned him over they found that his face was unmarked and wore an expression of white serenity – like a sick young man deep in peaceful sleep. Duncan could not hide his tears, and Keppel put his arm around his shoulder to comfort him.

'He was a brave man,' Keppel said softly. 'Some might say he was rash and impetuous, but I say he had the Nelson spirit that has seen us safely through our wars, and he was a credit to his profession. He gave his life in the service of his country – one of those young men who die too young to taste their own glory. But we will remember him well, Duncan, and commend his valour to his family and friends.'

While Keppel got two of the marines to fashion a makeshift stretcher to carry Francis back to the boats, James returned with Prince Badrudeen, both men with their swords drawn and covered in blood.

'A pretty fight we had of it, Keppel!' James exclaimed. 'The rascals were ready for us, but we fought them point to point, and sent a good few to their makers. Most of 'em will be without their heads by now, if my experience of my Dayak brethren is anything to go by. We've destroyed the fort and village, and we'll burn their boats before we leave. But we missed that black-hearted villain Sherip Muller, who seems to have fled at the first sign of action. Why can't they stand and fight like real men? We can still catch up with him, I hope, and we did nab his war chief, who's been bragging to Prince Badrudeen about how he killed the sailor with the golden hair. Badrudeen is demanding his execution, and this time I'm going to oblige him.'

The chief was dragged forward and made to kneel before them with his hands tied fast behind him. He was a magnificent specimen of a man, broad and bare-chested, with a blood red skirt around his waist and blood red feathers in his headdress. He held his proud head high, his black eyes expressing defiance and contempt for his captors. Subu Besi came up behind the chief with a short spear in his hand. He placed the tip very carefully on the left side of the man's neck and then drove the blade quickly down into his heart. Duncan watched the life go out of the man's black eyes but took no pleasure in it. Francis was dead, a casualty of war, and nothing could bring him back. He even regretted that the chief had been killed as well – it made no difference to him, although he supposed it had been done as an example and a warning. They carried Francis back to the waiting boats and wrapped his body in a Union Jack. The Dayaks burned their dead, while the Malays made makeshift coffins for their own. After firing the pirate ships, they made their way back to where the *Phlegethon* was stationed at the Undop fork in the river. They tended to the wounded and prepared to commit Lieutenant Wade's body to the deep.

Captain Keppel asked Commander Scott for a Bible to conduct the service. Scott sent out for one, but none could be found aboard the *Phlegethon* or the *Jolly Bachelor*. When Duncan heard the reason for the delay in the service, he quickly went down to the cabin that he and Francis had shared aboard the *Phlegethon* and hunted through Francis' knapsack. When he returned to the starboard deck where Francis' body was prepared for burial, he handed Keppel Francis' own Bible.

'He told me he had taken it along in case of an accident,' Duncan said quietly.

Captain Keppel read the service while the marines, sailors and natives stood in silent respect.

'Lord God, by the power of your Word you stilled the chaos of the primeval seas, you made the raging waters of the flood subside, and calmed the storm on the sea of Galilee. As we commit the body of our brother Francis Wade to the deep, grant him peace and tranquillity until that day when he and all who believe in you will be raised to the glory of new life promised in the waters of baptism. We ask this through Christ our Lord. Amen.'

Then the body of Lieutenant Wade, sewn up in the Union Jack, was sent to the bottom of the river, weighed down by two cannonballs. Duncan hoped that the crocodiles would not take his body, but all the men on board knew they would.

27

They rested for two days, then proceeded upriver against the Skrang Dayaks, who they learned were preparing to meet them just south of their capital city of Karangan. They also learned that both Sherip Sahib and his brother Sherip Muller had made their way there, and that Prince Mahkota and his followers had joined them. Prince Badrudeen was desperate to lead the attack, because he was determined to capture Mahkota and put him to death, but Keppel and James decided instead to let Patinggi Ali scout upriver, since the old warrior was greatly upset at having arrived too late for their last fight. James told him to report back immediately he spotted the enemy and not to engage them until their whole force had been brought up. James sent George Steward forward in Patinggi Ali's boat to make sure he followed his command, but he ought to have known better. Patinggi Ali was eager for a fight – he would not be denied this battle with his ancient enemies.

The first day passed peaceably enough, and they often caught up with Patinggi Ali, who was intent upon burning every village and abandoned pirate prahu along the way. They passed through countryside of incredible beauty, as the river narrowed and they drifted through cathedral-like canopies of trees and rocky gorges. They stopped together that night and ate a meal of curry and rice, taking what shelter they could from the rain that fell in slashing torrents from the sky, leaving a steamy mist over the river and jungle when they set out the following day.

Once again Patinggi Ali drove ahead in his scouting canoes,

with the boats and cutters from the *Dido* and *Phlegethon* and *Jolly Bachelor* coming up behind. Duncan was with Brooke and his nephew Charlie Johnson on the *Jolly Bachelor* while Keppel was in the *Dido*'s pinnace. They stopped for breakfast while Patinggi Ali continued to scout ahead. Brooke was grumbling about how likely it was that the pirates would all run away again and they would miss a good fight, when they heard shots and shouting upriver. Tossing their food aside, they ran to their boats and rowed and paddled up the river as fast as they could. As they rounded the first bend in the river, they came across a scene of chaos and carnage. Patinggi Ali had come across a fleet of war prahus, blood red banners and pendants streaming from their mastheads, and had driven right into the middle of the war fleet. His boats were trapped between twelve huge pirate prahus, six on either side, and the pirates had sent out armed rafts from both sides of the river, trapping their escape from behind, while hundreds of Dayaks streamed down from the surrounding hills to join in the bloodbath. Patinggi Ali and his men were fighting like demons, but their canoes were sinking, and they were leaping aboard the pirate prahus and selling their lives dearly. As the boats from the *Dido* and *Phlegethon* pushed forward, they came in behind the rafts, but could go no further, since they could not use their oars in the tight melee of boats that were bound together in mortal combat.

Brooke ordered his bow-gun to fire into the pirates, but it jammed, and he stood fuming on the deck of the *Jolly Bachelor* as he watched his old school friend George Steward cut down by a stroke from a battle-axe. Steward tumbled into the bloody waters of the river, where heads and headless corpses were crushed between the prahus and upturned canoes in a gruesome logjam. It was pandemonium, and Patinggi Ali and his men were being slaughtered. Suddenly Keppel signalled them to come on board his gig, the only paddle driven vessel among them, and the only craft able to force its way into the melee. The swell of the river had driven one of the rafts into a submerged tree trunk, forcing it to come adrift, and Keppel steered his vessel into the gap, heading for the spot where Patinggi Ali and his remaining men were making their last stand aboard one of the pirate ships. They fought like madmen – James, Duncan, Keppel, Charlie Johnson, Prince Badrudeen, Subu Besi, the marines and blue jackets, and the Dayaks and Malays – and they cut a bloody swathe through the enemy, but they saw Patinggi Ali cut down before they could reach him. Prince Badrudeen had rashly forged ahead towards the old warrior, and now found himself surrounded by four pirates at the head of one of the prahus. Without a thought for his own safety, Duncan leapt aboard, and dispatched two of them from behind with his cutlass. Badrudeen flashed him a quick grin of gratitude, then turned to cut down a pirate who was about to spear Duncan in the neck. The two men fought their way across the blood-slicked decks to Keppel's gig, which was now surrounded on all sides by pirates. To James' great outrage, Keppel gave the order to reverse paddle. As the *Dido*'s gig reversed its course, they fought their way backwards out of the mess of boats and bodies, as ever-increasing numbers of Dayaks lined the shores and showered them with musket fire, spears, and poisoned darts. They also threw long spears of bamboo filled with stones, which could crush a man's skull if they caught him in the head.

Things were looking desperate until Mr Allen came up in the *Phlegethon*'s rocket-launch and began sending Congrave rockets into the pirate prahus, still jammed together in the river. As the rockets exploded among the close packed warriors and set fire to their ships, those that were not killed outright by the rockets were burned alive on their decks, or drowned or crushed when they tried to escape into the river. The rockets showered into the warriors on shore, who fled in panic back up the hillsides. Congrave rockets were notoriously unreliable when fired at long range, but at this close range they could not miss, as explosive, shrapnel and incendiary material blasted into the mass of screaming bodies. The result was a slaughterhouse on the river, and the surviving pirates quickly fled back upriver or into the hills. When the rocket barrage ceased and the smoke cleared, there were bodies everywhere; the air was thick with the smell of gunpowder, and heavy with the low moans of the wounded and dying. The Dayaks went about their bloody work of claiming the heads of their enemies, while the surgeons attended to the dead and wounded. All seventeen men of Patinggi Ali's scouting party were killed, including George Steward, with twenty-nine men dead and fifty-six wounded from among those who had gone with Keppel to their rescue. The enemy dead were countless, although the Dayaks provided a count of their heads, which Duncan thought must surely be exaggerated until he saw them piled up at the river's edge.

They cut through the pirate wreckage and fell upon the Skrang capital of Karangan. They looted and burned the city, although once again most of the inhabitants had already fled. But this time as they pursued the stragglers beyond the city, they managed to capture Prince Mahkota before he had time to join Sherip Sahib and Sherip Muller in their flight across the mountains into the Dutch governed provinces of Borneo. When Mahkota was brought before them that evening, Prince Badrudeen demanded his execution, but Rajah Brooke refused to execute a royal prince of Brunei, however treacherous, and the two men argued for almost an hour. Eventually Badrudeen accepted James' decision, and even applauded the Rajah's speech, delivered in Malay to the farmers and their families who had come out of the jungle. The White Rajah declared that he had no quarrel with anyone but the pirates and their leaders, and that they had nothing to fear from him. He talked to them of the benefits of peace and free trade, and they assured him of their future cooperation. Only Subu Besi, the public executioner, looked unhappy, as he twisted the length of rope that he had intended to use to strangle Prince Mahkota. Mahkota got off with a stern lecture from the Rajah and was allowed to return with them to Kuching.

'You made a mistake sparing Mahkota,' Keppel told James later that evening as they sat down to dinner aboard the *Jolly Bachelor*. 'He's a snake, all right, and he'll give you trouble for as long as he lives.'

'Perhaps you're right,' Brooke replied, 'but I think we've had enough killing for one day. And I have great faith in the redemption of man, or at least in common sense – surely Mahkota knows by now that we have the stronger hand.'

'You might as well have faith in a stone,' Keppel replied.

They spent the next few days tending to their dead and wounded. Mr Beth, the assistant surgeon from the *Dido*, treated many sumpitan dart wounds, but only one proved fatal. Then they made their way back down the river to meet up with the *Phlegethon*, which fortunately had not come under attack.

On their way back to Sarawak they stopped over in the Dayak village of Lundu, where their now famous great victory over the Skrang was celebrated. They sat down to a great feast in the communal longhouse, while ancient warriors with gnarled faces and bodies pranced before them with the heads of their enemies draped around their shoulders like ghastly necklaces; nubile servant girls, naked from the waist up, and wearing only the flimsiest of cotton skirts, sprinkled them with yellow rice and gold dust. As the girls took over the dancing from the old men, Duncan was bewitched by one of them, who danced only a few feet before him, her tiny feet gliding softly across the earthen floor. He looked up into her eyes, which were dark and wicked. Her hair, which was jet black and luminous in the torchlight, hung down her back to her hips. Her nose was small but her mouth was large and her lips were full.

Her smile was positively lascivious, he thought to himself, as she laughed at his fumbling attempts to hide his rising member beneath his pants. He blushed bright red, while his friends roared in laughter at his discomfiture.

Prince Badrudeen leaned over to him as the girls left and whispered, 'She is yours, Duncan, and she will come to you tonight.'

Duncan began to protest, but Badrudeen raised his hand to stop him, his hawk-like face refusing any argument.

'You must accept her. You will dishonour the memory of the men who died in battle if you refuse her.'

Duncan did not argue, but did not feel any less embarrassed.

And so that evening Duncan lost his virginity to the Dayak girl, in the darkness of the longhouse, amid the sleeping naked families, the warriors and his closest friends. He thought he would be embarrassed again, but he was not; it seemed the most natural thing in the world, and no one paid the slightest heed to his or her moans of pleasure throughout the long night. Duncan remembered the lines from Ovid's *Amores*, in which the lover wished that time would slow down and prolong his night of pleasure: *Lente currite*, noctis equi! [lxxix] In the morning he woke to find her gone, but he lay in deep contentment, thinking of the girl and of Francis – he wished that his dear friend had lived long enough to experience such a night of bliss.

---

lxxix Run slowly, ye horses of the night!

28

In November, after five months in Guangxi, Hong Xiuquan returned home to visit his family in Guanlubu, who were delighted to see him. He thought that Feng Yunshan had gone on before him, but discovered on his return that he had not, and Feng's parents berated Hong for abandoning their son.

Instead of returning home, Feng had set off north toward the mountains, eventually arriving at a remote village deep in the Thistle Mountain range, from which he preached Hong Xiuquan's message of redemption and described his master's dream to all who would listen. He managed to gather together a group of zealous converts, whom he baptised in the fashion that Hong had taught him. He called his group the 'God-worshipping society.'

Like Hong Xiuquan, Feng Yunshan was a Hakka, and found it easy to communicate with the other Hakkas who dwelt in the mountains. Although they were simple country folk who believed in ghosts and female fox spirits who could steal a man's soul, they were also open to the message of Jesus, who Feng assured them had come to deliver the poor, the afflicted and the oppressed. His message appealed not only to his Hakka brethren, but also to the poor farmers, miners, blacksmiths, herdsmen, charcoal burners, boatmen, peddlers and labourers who subsisted through the summer droughts and harsh winters. They were oppressed by mankind as well as by nature, terrorized and exploited by local bandits and bands of pirates who had been driven upriver from Canton by the British, who, from their base in Hong Kong, were intent on clearing the pirates from the South China Sea. They were deeply moved when Feng told them that Hong Xiuquan's older brother, Jesus the redeemer, had been a humble tradesman like themselves, a carpenter who had worked first by the labour of his hands before he worked on the souls of men. And they felt Jesus spoke directly to them when he proclaimed these words from the top of another mountain centuries before:

Blessed are the poor in spirit: for theirs is the kingdom of heaven.

Blessed are they that mourn: for they shall be comforted.

Blessed are the meek: for they shall inherit the earth.

Blessed are they who hunger and thirst after righteousness: for they shall be filled.

Blessed are the merciful: for they shall obtain mercy.

Blessed are the pure in heart: for they shall see God.

Blessed are the peacemakers: for they shall be called the children of God.

Blessed are they that are persecuted for righteousness' sake: for theirs is the kingdom of heaven.

And they knew he spoke of them when he called them the salt of the earth.

* * *

Keppel had received orders to return to England and was planning to put in to Singapore for stores, so Duncan was returning with him. Before doing so, he went to the Rajah's home to take his leave.

'A great pity to see you go, Duncan,' said James, putting his right arm around Duncan's shoulders as he led him out onto the verandah, where they could see the *Dido* preparing for departure. 'You and Harry Keppel both, my good friends and companions.'

'You know,' he continued, tightening his hold on Duncan's

shoulders, 'I have to admit that I was jealous of your friendship with Lieutenant Wade. But he was a good man, and I am very sorry that he had to die so young. He was a noble warrior, like our own Prince Badrudeen.'

They wished each other good fortune.

Duncan also took his leave of Prince Badrudeen, who told him he was returning with Rajah Muda Hassim to Brunei, to support his brother's position as heir to the aging Sultan Omar Ali Saifuddin. Prince Mahkota and his ally Pangeran Usop, an uncle of Sultan Ali, were working to undermine Hassim's claim of succession, and James thought it best for them to return and re-establish their authority and rights. Before he left, Prince Badrudeen presented Duncan with a beautifully jewelled kris, as a token of their friendship and his gratitude for saving his life. Duncan was caught by surprise and was greatly embarrassed because he had nothing of value to offer Badrudeen in return, especially since the prince had also saved his life. He drew his dirk from his boot, a black bone-handled blade with silver clasps upon the sheath. It was a poor thing in comparison to the jewelled kris, but it was a handy weapon in a close fight. It was to prove its worth sooner than both men imagined.

29

1845

When Captain Keppel and Duncan reached Singapore, they heard that Rajah Brooke had been appointed Confidential Agent to Her Majesty's Government in Borneo. They dined with Duncan's parents the first evening, and with Whampoa the second, before Captain Keppel set sail once again for England.

As the *Dido* slipped out of the Singapore roads, Sir Edward Belcher departed Kuching for Brunei, with Rajah Muda Hassim, Prince Badrudeen and their royal entourages, screened from the eyes of the mariners by carefully placed screens on board HMS *Semarang*. The *Phlegethon* followed in support. When they arrived at Brunei, Hassim was reconfirmed as heir and principal advisor to the sultan. The White Rajah's influence now seemed to extend to the kingdom of Brunei itself.

* * *

On Thursday, May 1, the Singapore Criminal Sessions of the Court were closed. They had lasted four weeks but were not considered a great success. Eighteen accused persons were discharged due to lack of evidence, because no witnesses would come forward to testify against them. Bribery and intimidation were suspected in most cases but could not be proven; in one case of murder, the widow of the deceased, who had twice given evidence to the police, failed to appear in court and seemed to have vanished from the town.

One Chinese boatman was found guilty of murder, and sentenced to be executed a week later, along with three Malays convicted of the murder of Captain Robinson of the *Black Cat*. The three Malays admitted their guilt and met their death with resignation, but the Chinese boatman protested his innocence. He made a long speech on the scaffold, in which he condemned the witnesses against him, accused them of perjury, and threatened to return to take his revenge as a ghost after his death. But he declared that he bore no ill will to the judge and jury, since they had merely acted on the basis of false evidence. To demonstrate his sincerity, and to absolve them of guilt, he declared that he would hang himself, and stepped forward and put his head through the noose. He remained cool, calm and collected to the end – he bowed to the duty policemen and shook hands with the hangman before he was launched to his death. Whether or not they believed his story, all those present thought he acquitted himself well on the scaffold.

* * *

On July 1, Catchick Moses founded the *Straits Times and Singapore Journal of Commerce*, with the first issue published on July 15. He had not intended to found a newspaper, but he had recently taken over the printing presses that had been ordered by his friend Martyrose Thaddeus Apcar, who was forced to declare bankruptcy. When Mr Robert Carr Woods arrived from Bombay shortly afterwards and approached Catchick for advice on securing employment in the settlement, Catchick made him editor of the newspaper, which was printed weekly at the press offices at 7 Commercial Square. Each paper contained eight pages, half of which was devoted to general news of interest to the local community, with the other half devoted to current prices and market information. The newspaper was not an initial commercial success, and Catchick sold the paper to

Woods the following year. In his opening article, Woods promised his reading public a 'pleasant ride of it'.

* * *

Dr Clark the coroner had his work cut out for him, and he thought as much to himself. Forensics was an infant science, positively premature, he grumbled, as he tried to determine as best he could whether the Chinaman who lay dead at his feet had suffered his fate through hanging or strangulation – the red marks on his neck were consistent with both. After rubbing his chin in frustration for some moments, he decided upon a disjunctive verdict: 'Death by hanging or strangulation by person or persons unknown.'

Apart from gross injuries to the body, and detectable poisons like arsenic, it was often very difficult to determine the cause of death. Matters were not helped by the fact that in many cases where murder was suspected, the corpses were only discovered days or weeks later, and given the tropical climate, they were often in an advanced state of decomposition, making an objective diagnosis almost impossible. Then there were the perfectly ridiculous conventions that he was supposed to follow in recording the deaths of Europeans and other races. If it appeared that a native had taken his own life, the verdict to be recorded was 'felo de se' [lxxx] ; in the case of a European who appeared to have taken his own life, the verdict to be recorded was 'temporary insanity'.

It was enough to drive a man to temporary insanity. Then there was the embarrassment and humiliation of last weeks' inquest, which was held on October 27. Two days previous a boy had reported that he had been taken out into the harbour on a trip with his two brothers and older sister. A party of Johor Malays in a pirate prahu

lxxx Archaic legal term for suicide meaning 'felon to himself'; a self-murderer.

had attacked them, and only he had escaped. The following day a female body washed ashore and the tearful boy had identified it as his lost sister, dressed in the same red sarong she had worn when they had been attacked. It seemed likely that the pirates had killed her and his brothers, and Dr Clark had recorded a verdict of 'wilful murder by person or persons unknown'. Then he had heard that a few days after the inquest – and after the girl's funeral, which had been well attended – the boy had found his brothers and sister alive and well when he returned to their home! What a state of affairs!

And now, only two days later, a Malacca Malay had gone to the police and reported that his sister had been missing for days, and suspected that her husband had murdered her. He told Dr Clark that she could be easily identified by her black teeth, the deep scars on her right arm, and the fact that her left hand was shorter than her right. The police sergeant on duty speculated that the women who had been misidentified and buried two days before might be the Malay's sister, and said that there was an easy way to find out. So, reluctantly, Dr Clark agreed to accompany the policeman and the Malay to the burial ground, where the body was disinterred. There seemed to be no question about it: the corpse's teeth were black, there were deep scars on the right arm, and the left hand was shorter than the right. Dr Clark concluded that her husband had wilfully murdered the woman, and the three men hurried to the husband's house to make the arrest. The police sergeant hammered on the door and demanded that it be opened in the name of the law, but as the door was duly opened, Dr Clark's heart sank. For there before him stood a Malay woman displaying her prominent black teeth in a foolish grin. He noticed the deep scars on her right arm and the shortness of her left hand. There was no doubt about it. This was the Malay's sister, and he felt as foolish as ever a man could feel. He never established the identity of the dead women or the cause of her death.

30

Although Raja Musa Hassim had been confirmed as the heir to the Sultan of Brunei, James knew his position was not secure. Hassim managed to persuade the sultan to issue an edict calling for the suppression of piracy in the kingdom. The powerful Sherip Usman, who was allied with Pangeran Usop and Prince Mahkota, and whose heavily fortified stronghold at Maradu Bay on the north east coast of Borneo posed a threat to both Brunei and Sarawak, replied by pillaging the marooned European schooner the *Sultana* and enslaving her crew.

James knew that the combined forces of Sherip Usman and Pangeran Usop – and Prince Mahkota – could easily depose Hassim and Badrudeen, or worse, have them executed as usurpers. He managed to persuade Thomas Cochrane, Commander of the Far Eastern Fleet, to take action against the pirates who threatened the peace and stability of Brunei. After some anxious months of waiting, James was relieved when Cochrane arrived with an impressive force, which included the armoured steamers *Pluto* and *Nemesis*, carrying large cohorts of blue jackets and marines.

When he was summoned to appear before the sultan, Pangeran Usop fled into the jungle. Yet he did not admit defeat, and returned with his brother and two hundred followers two days later, after Cochrane and James had left to deal with Sherip Usman at Maradu Bay. There was fierce fighting in Brunei, but Prince Badrudeen soundly beat his enemy, and once again Pangeran Usop fled into the jungle. There he was betrayed by the chief of the Kaminis, who knew there was a price on his head and danger to any who harboured him.

Pangeran Usop was taken back to Brunei and executed with his brother in the respectful manner owed them by virtue of their relationship to the sultan. They were provided with mosquito nets, which they wrapped around themselves before they knelt on the ground and said their prayers. When they signalled that they were ready for death, the executioner placed a cord around each man's neck and strangled them.

Cochran's blue jackets and marines killed Sherip Usman and laid waste to his stronghold at Maradu Bay, with great loss of life among his followers. After their great victory, James and Cochrane returned to Brunei in good spirits. James' spirits were raised higher when he learned how Pangeran Badrudeen had repulsed the attack by Pangeran Usop, and of Usop's subsequent execution. James wrote a letter to Duncan praising their friend for his bravery:

'I tell you Duncan, Pangeran Badrudeen fights like a European; the very spirit of the Englishman is in him; he has learned that at Sarawak.'

More like the very spirit of the Scotsman, Duncan thought to himself as he read the letter a few weeks later. Yet he was glad for Badrudeen and for James, who now seemed to have achieved his final ambition. After the death of Pangeran Usop, Sultan Omar Ali Saifuddin officially appointed Rajah Muda Hassim as his successor, and bestowed upon him the title of Sultan Muda.[lxxxi] Soon James and Hassim would rule together, and owe allegiance only to the Queen of England. As his Malay servant filled his cup that night aboard the *Jolly Bachelor*, James Brooke thought with a grin that his cup surely did runneth over.

But he reckoned without Prince Mahkota, the Serpent.

---

lxxxi Young Sultan.

31

When John Turnbull Thomson added the tower and spire to St Andrew's Church, he unfortunately neglected to add a lightning conductor. One night in August the spire was struck by lightning, which splintered one of the tablets next to the communion table. Fortunately, no one was injured, the church being empty at night, and no other damage was caused. However, it did lead to a resurgence of rumours among the Chinese, Indians and Malays, who believed that the God of the Christians was angered because insufficient heads had been offered in sacrifice, despite the governor's public assurance that Europeans did not require human sacrifices for the consecration of their churches.[lxxxii]

. Earlier in the year a regular steamer mail service had been set up between Bengal and Batavia, and on August 4 the *Lady Mary Wood* inaugurated the Peninsular and Oriental (P & O) Navigation Company's Far Eastern Service by completing the mail run from London to Singapore in forty-one days, using the overland Egyptian route between Alexandria and Aden. By way of contrast, it had taken Charles Singer nearly two hundred days to travel from Liverpool to Singapore around the Cape of Good Hope in the early 1830s. The institution of the new steamer service created something of a social revolution in Singapore. Merchants and their families

---

lxxxii When St Andrew's Church was being built, a rumour spread among the Chinese, Indians and Malays that the government required the taking of heads as a blood sacrifice for the consecration of the church.

eagerly awaited the monthly arrival of mail and newspapers from Europe, and raced to complete their own correspondence before the steamer left on its return voyage. On the day of departure finely dressed European and Parsee wives could be seen dismounting from their gharries and racing to get their last letter aboard before the steamer sailed. It also gave many wives a useful excuse for avoiding the interminable bridge and tea parties, by claiming that they were behind with their letters or were rushing to finish them before the packet sailed.

In August, John Martin Little, the brother of Dr Robert Little, formed a partnership with Cursetjee Fromurzee, to form Little, Cursetjee and Co. They served as commission agents and opened an auction house and retail store in Commercial Square, which also operated as a ticket outlet for local plays and musical performances. Cursetjee Fromurzee was the son of Fromurzee Sorabji, a Parsee merchant who had set up in business in Singapore in 1840, and was one of the original trustees of the Parsee burial ground at Telok Ayer. Cursetjee was married to an Englishwoman, and was a well-respected member of the merchant community.

* * *

Paul Revere Balestier never made his midnight ride. Only a year after his father had made his purchase at the auction in Commercial Square, a distraught servant rode the young man's pony at breakneck speed from the American consul's estate in Serangoon to his godown on Boat Quay. He tearfully informed Joseph Balestier that his son had collapsed and died while working on a piece of machinery. Paul Revere Balestier died at the age of twenty-four. The coroner, Dr Clark, performed an autopsy and certified his death as due to a brain tumour. Joseph and his wife Maria were devastated, and grieved deeply over the loss of their only child.

* * *

The Seaman's Hospital was completed in July, close by the almost completed Tan Tock Seng Hospital at the foot of Pearl's Hill, and began admitting patients in November. Although the government had covered the remainder of the cost of the building, the hospital was immediately beset by financial difficulties. Some merchants who had pledged continued support failed to honour their pledges, and many ship's captains returned to sea without paying for the medical care of their sailors. Thieves regularly broke into the hospital, stealing everything they could get their hands on, including the bed linen. A thriving black market kept sailors liberally supplied with grog, which often led to riotous behaviour, so that some local wits came to call the new hospital the 'Drunken Sailor's Hospital'.

32

A waning moon shone like a silver tear in the black velvet night. Many of the stars were hidden behind the gathering storm clouds, as if they feared the armed parties of men who slipped out of the sultan's palace and made their determined way through the streets in the midnight gloom.

Badrudeen woke with a start. He smelt the acrid smoke and heard the crackling fire, and raced to the balcony overlooking the street. The assassins were below, putting torches to the walls of his house, and now beating down his door with heavy wooden clubs. He called for his servant to sound the alarm, and raced with his few fighting men to meet them as they burst through the door. Badrudeen and his followers fought like demons, and for a while they managed to hold the attackers at bay in the narrow doorway with their swords and krisses. Then a pistol ball struck Badrudeen in his left wrist, and as he stumbled backwards in pain, a sword cut deep into his right shoulder. His kris tumbled from his grasp as he fell to his knees, and his followers, thinking that he was mortally wounded, fell back in disarray. A tall black-cloaked assassin stood before Badrudeen, and raised his sword over the wounded prince's exposed neck. But as the man readied himself for the killing stroke, Badrudeen reached into his tunic and drew out the dirk that Duncan had gifted him, and drove it up into the man's groin. As the assassin staggered back in agony, Badrudeen leapt up and urged his men on again in a final assault, hoping to cut a way free so that one of his servants could escape and warn the sultan that he was under attack.

But to no avail. The narrowness of the doorway now worked against them, and Badrudeen's brave servant was cut down before he could escape. In any case, it would have been to no purpose, for, unbeknown to Badrudeen, the assassins were acting on the orders of the sultan. The last of his men sold their lives dearly, enabling Badrudeen to escape to the back of the house with his sister, his concubine Nur Salum, and his slave-boy Jaffar.

In a small room that was built upon stilts over the river, Badrudeen instructed Jaffar to take down a barrel of gunpowder from the shelf and lay a trial of powder as a fuse. Then he took a ring from his finger and handed it to Jaffar. It was a signet ring with the Brooke crest that James had given him as a present some years before. Hearing footsteps approaching, Badrudeen told Nur Salum to close the outer door, and to secure it with the wooden beam that lay beside it.

'Here Jaffar, my loyal servant,' he exclaimed. 'Take this ring, and make your way to Sarawak. Give it to the great White Rajah Brooke, and beg him never to forget his friend, but tell him and the Queen of England of the dark fate that has befallen their servant. Go with God!'

As Badrudeen helped Jaffar rip up the wooden flooring so he could jump down into the river, Nur Salum discovered to her horror that someone had removed the wooden beam for securing the door. As she heard Jaffar drop down into the river behind her, she pushed her arm into the iron brackets and gasped in pain as her bones were crushed when the assassins crashed into the door. Badrudeen's eyes brimmed with tears at the bravery of his lover, as he hugged his sister close and put fire to the gunpowder. Then the cares of their world were blown away with the souls of their would-be assassins.

* * *

Rajah Muda Hassim managed to escape his attackers and fled across the river in a canoe with his wife, his brothers and his children. When the assassins followed him, he shouted out to them to take a message to the sultan, begging that their lives be spared. They replied that the sultan himself had signed their death warrant, and that they were coming to kill them. Hassim took his family aboard a ship that was moored close by the river, and cast down the gangplank in order to gain them more time. He led them weeping down to the captain's cabin, where he placed a small keg of gunpowder in the middle of the room, and then laid a short train of powder as a fuse. He was ignorant of the fact that Prince Badrudeen had chosen the same fate. He had paid no attention to the muffled explosion across the river, so intent was he on trying to save his family. He bade a tearful farewell to them before he lit the fuse, and the explosion blasted arms and legs and heads in a dark red mist around the cabin.

As the smoke cleared, Hassim sat in amazement amidst the bloody gristle and bone. He had survived the blast without a scratch upon his person. In different circumstances, he might have seen his miraculous survival as a divine sign, but Hassim only saw the horror before him. In a corner of the cabin, a single bloody eye, torn from the socket of one of his brothers, stared up at him in accusation. Hassim drew his pistol from his belt, primed the weapon and placed it against his head. Then he blew his brains out over the remains of his family in the bloody morgue that was the captain's cabin, as his assassins boarded the ship.

* * *

Jaffar managed to swim out into the river far enough to avoid the blast at the home of Prince Badrudeen, and to slip upriver in a canoe. He hid at the edge of the town for a few days, planning his escape, but he was captured and brought before the sultan. When the sultan saw the ring on the boy's finger, he ordered that it be removed and brought to him. When he saw that it bore the crest of Rajah Brooke, he flew into a great rage, and determined to have the boy put to death immediately for his treachery. Yet his guilt for the blood of his relatives that he had lately ordered shed lay heavily on him, and he relented and dismissed the boy from his presence. Jaffar managed to find protection in the home of Pangeran Muda Mohamed, who promised to help him get Badrudeen's message to Rajah Brooke.

PART THREE

GHOSTS

1846 – 1852

1

1846

If asked, Poh Neo would have said she was content in her marriage. Her husband was a caring if not very passionate lover. He had secured a position as a clerk with the firm of Boustead, Schwabe and Co, in their offices and godown on Boat Quay opposite Thomson's Bridge.[lxxxiii] He had told her that the way to get on in Singapore was to find a position with one of the European merchant houses, a goal he had successfully achieved. Unfortunately, he showed not the slightest desire or intention of advancing beyond it. He was happy in his job, his superiors respected him, and that was that, he said. Her father had hoped that Lee Seng Huat would work for him in his business, and perhaps become a partner, after he had learned his trade while working for Boustead, Schwabe and Co; he had thought his experience with the European firm would prove a valuable asset. But Lee Seng Huat showed not the slightest interest in doing so.

Yet he was a dutiful husband and father. Their first son had been born just ten months after their marriage, and two daughters had followed. Seng Huat did not drink heavily or smoke opium, and although he gambled, he did not incur heavy losses because he did not wager heavily. His position at Boustead, Schwabe and Co brought in a modest income, if not enough to support their

---

lxxxiii Thomson's Bridge was a wooden footbridge built in 1844 by John Turnbull Thomson, which replaced the older wooden Presentment Bridge (also known as Monkey Bridge), which had been built in 1822 by Lieutenant Philip Jackson.

family without her father's contribution, but there was the chance of promotion and the hope that one day he would consent to join her father's business.

She enjoyed the freedom that her marriage had brought. She ran her own household and was able to visit her friends. She was popular with the other Nonya wives, because of her lively spirit and the witty pantun poems she could compose for almost any occasion. She had continued with her study of English and mathematics, although she now employed these skills to help her father with his correspondence and accounts, rather than her own husband as her father had intended. How she wished he were more ambitious! But she was not going to think about that today. Her sister Poh Ling was getting married, and she was going to attend the chia lang keh banquet with the other female relatives and guests.

Everyone agreed that her sister had made a good match. She was going to marry Gan Eng Seng, a merchant from Canton, who owned a number of businesses and shophouses in Singapore and had come to expand his investments in the town. He already had two wives and a concubine in Canton, but had decided to take another wife from among the Peranakan Chinese while he lived in Singapore. There were no respectable Chinese women from the mainland living in Singapore at that time, and female immigration was prohibited by the Emperor. Tan Poh Ling was very plain, but she had a good nature, and she came from a well-established and respected family that Gan Eng Seng hoped would help further his business interests with the Chinese and European business communities. Moreover, her two other sisters had married and had both produced healthy sons.

* * *

The wedding was the usual prolonged Peranakan affair, but Poh Ling handled herself well, and performed to Gan Eng Seng's satisfaction in the bridal chamber. Since Gan Eng Seng was a pure-bred Chinese from mainland China, Poh Ling went to live in his house, rather than Gan Eng Seng coming to live in her father's house, as was the usual Peranakan custom. She did not mind, and in fact relished her independence, even though she loved her family dearly and visited them frequently. And she was overjoyed when a few months later she became pregnant, and all the elderly Bibik relatives declared that it would certainly be a boy, since her stomach was pointed rather than round.

2

When he heard the news, James Brooke ranted and raved. He stormed and he swore. He cursed the sultan the traitor, the sultan the villain, the sultan the murderer! He howled at the moon and the empty night like a wild animal, and his loyal servants feared for his sanity. He could not sleep, so full of grief and rage was he. He began a letter to Duncan but could not bring himself to describe in cold prose the bloody death of their dear friend Pangeran Badrudeen, the noblest, bravest, most upright prince that ever lived.

When the tempest finally passed, James wrote to Duncan, and also to Admiral Sir Thomas Cochrane, requesting his help to punish the sultan for his murderous and treacherous acts against the British government.

* * *

Early in the year the London Missionary Society moved its operations to China, along with the Mission Press. Before they left, they deeded Reverend Keasberry the plot of land on River Valley Road on which the Mission chapel stood and allocated him an allowance of fifty pounds a year. They also arranged for the type from the Penang Mission and the press from the Malacca Mission to be shipped to Singapore, so that Keasberry could set up a new press. Keasberry converted one section of the old chapel into a commercial printing and binding shop and used part of the profits to set up a school for Malay boys in another section. The boys were taught in English and Malay, but also learned the printing trade, with the older boys working as paid employees of the press. Munshi Abdullah and his son helped with the teaching and with translations of Malay and Arabic texts.

* * *

Tan Tock Seng Hospital was completed in March. It was built to John Turnbull Thomson's classical design – a magnificent stone structure fronted with tall palladium columns – and was signed over to the East India Company that same month. Unfortunately, the hospital did not admit patients until some years later, because the Indian government had not approved funds for its maintenance, much to Tan Tock Seng's disappointment and Governor Butterworth's embarrassment, since the governor had assured him that such support would be forthcoming. In the meantime, the paupers, vagrants and sick of all nations were housed in attap sheds beside the hospital at the foot of Pearl's Hill.

When Tan Tock Seng's friend and business partner John Horrocks Whitehead died later that year at the age of thirty-six, Tan Tock Seng erected a tombstone to his memory in the European cemetery at the foot of Government Hill, 'as a token of affection on the part of a Chinese friend, Tan Tock Seng'.

3

Singapore, April, 1846

Dear James

I have just received your letter with the tragic news of the murder of Pangeran Badrudeen and Rajah Muda Hassim and their relations. What a cruel act of treachery, and one that must surely be avenged. I stand willing to join you at any time if you believe you can reach the evil Mahkota. I am sure you are right that he was behind the massacre. The sultan is a weakling and would only have done this dreadful thing at Mahkota's bidding, and only his blood can wash away the crime.

I remain in Singapore at present, although I have persuaded my father and grandfather of the wisdom of setting up an office in Hong Kong. Captain Keppel helped a great deal when he joined us for dinner before leaving for England. But I will keep you posted of my whereabouts and remain ready to join you at short notice.

Remember the good that Pangeran Badrudeen and Rajah Muda Hassim have helped you achieve in Sarawak and remember them with gratitude and honour. I will miss Badrudeen especially – he was like a dear uncle to me and saved my life in the fight against the Skrang pirates.

I remain, always, your good friend
Duncan Simpson.

* * *

Sir Thomas Cochrane answered James' request and arrived off Sarawak on June 24 aboard his flagship HMS *Agincourt*. He was accompanied by HMS *Iris* and HMS *Hazard*, and the armoured steamers *Spiteful* and *Phlegethon*, which Colonel Butterworth had sent from Singapore, after James had given him the misleading impression that Sarawak was under attack.

James wanted Sir Thomas to steam into Brunei to destroy the sultan and his palace, then set up the son of Muda Hassim as the head of a new government under James' supervision. Sir Thomas was reluctant to do so. As he pointed out to James, Brunei was an independent and sovereign state, and the sultan had the legal right and authority to sign and execute death warrants against his own citizens, including his own family, however distasteful that might be. After much persuasion, Sir Thomas agreed to investigate the situation in Brunei, to determine the sultan's disposition towards British interests in the region, but absolutely refused to act against the sultan.

The sultan persuaded him otherwise. When Sir Thomas made his way cautiously and diplomatically up the Brunei River with the steamers *Spiteful* and *Phlegethon*, with the boats of the *Royalist* and *Hazard* in tow, the sultan obliged and delighted James by firing on the *Spiteful*, to which Sir Thomas had transferred his flag. Sir Thomas was outraged and ordered an immediate general engagement. The sultan's men managed some direct hits on the *Phlegethon* from their heavy guns on the hillside, but eventually fled from the barrage of shot and grape and rockets from the British ships. In his outrage at the attack, and flushed with victory, Sir Thomas was tempted to install James Brooke as Sultan. Yet he quickly thought better of it. He issued a proclamation assuring the population that their lives and property would be respected, and that no action would be taken against the sultan so long as he agreed to govern his people justly and to support the British government in the suppression of piracy. Within a few days the populace and merchants returned, and the effusively contrite Sultan Omar Ali Saifuddin pledged his undying allegiance to the great Queen of England.

James did not come away entirely empty handed. He secured for the British government possession of the island of Labuan as a coaling station. It would turn out to be an unmitigated disaster. The coal was very poor, and the place was pestilential. The new governor arrived in late December and died of malaria on the first week of the new year.

4

In July, Ronnie and Sarah and John Simpson received an invitation to attend the wedding of Captain Scott's niece Ellen Scott to the Reverend Keasberry. The wedding ceremony was held inside St Andrew's Church, which sparkled in the morning sunlight. The interior of the church was decked out with a riot of magnificent flowers from Captain Scott's garden, whose colours contrasted brightly with the white plastered walls. Captain Scott walked down the aisle with his white hair flowing behind him and his sharp blue eyes filled with happiness. He walked with his niece on his arm and pride and contentment in his heart – he knew that Keasberry was a good man, even if he was English. It was a day of joy for all.

The reception was held in the London Hotel, at the corner of High Street and the Esplanade. As the guests mingled, John Simpson overheard Dr Oxley expressing his disgust to James Guthrie over the governor's treatment of Captain Scott. He turned to Oxley and asked him what he meant by that, and what had happened to his good friend.

'He fired him yesterday, that's what he did,' replied Oxley, 'although he planned it sometime before. The confirmation from Calcutta and Captain Scott's replacement – a very peculiar young man – arrived yesterday. The governor represented it as a routine matter of replacing older men with younger men, but that's not the reason for it – at least not according to Mr Church, although he has sworn me to secrecy.'

'I'll tak' it to the grave, if you want me to, but you have tae tell me man,' insisted John Simpson.

'Well, John,' Oxley replied, 'as you know, the master attendant's office is next to the governor's office, and Willie was fond of a cigar while he worked through his paperwork, as I know do many of our present company.'

Simpson and Guthrie nodded their agreement, puffing on their own.

'This never bothered George Bonham all his years as governor, but Colonel Butterworth took it as a personal affront, and ordered Willie to cease his filthy habit. But our dear friend merely smiled and carried on puffing away as leisurely as if he was standing on the poop deck of a ship. That was bad enough, but what really clinched it was Willie turning up in his whites. They may have been sparkling, and he may have been wearing them since he took up his appointment years ago, but Colonel Butterworth decreed that all officers of the Company should wear the clerical black of Leadenhall Street – a daft idea in a tropical climate, even if Sir Stamford was that way inclined himself. When Willie ignored his decree, Butterworth considered it yet another affront to his authority and dignity, and immediately issued a critical report of his offenses to the Bengal government, with a request for his dismissal and replacement, which was confirmed yesterday.'

John Simpson went over to console his old friend but found him in high spirits advising the new groom on how to plant his garden.

'Och, dinna worry about me John,' said Captain Scott when John Simpson finally managed to get a word in edgeways. 'It's a great injustice to be sure, and I feel it keenly enough, but there's nothing tae be done aboot it.'

'Can't you appeal to the Bengal government?' John asked.

'A waste of time and you know it. About as useless as Raffles appealing his bill from the Company, or Farquhar appealing his dismissal by Raffles. Nae John, they've given me a wee pension and

I've some money put by, plus a good sum I made recently selling my nutmeg plantation. I tell you there's a kind of craze aboot nutmegs at the moment, a' body wants them, but especially the Europeans and Chinese. I'll be quite happy with ma wee hoose and garden, and my guid friends and relations. Come on John, let's drink to the happy couple. They don't drink themselves, being of the temperance persuasion, so we'll hae to make up for them! He charged John Simpson's glass with whisky, and they raised their glasses high, two white haired old men in their white suits.

'To the bride and groom!'

* * *

Captain Scott was right about one thing. There was a positive craze for nutmegs, and by the end of the decade virtually the whole area around Orchard Road was given over to nutmeg plantations, with a few pepper farms scattered among them. Thomas Oxley had a large plantation on his Killiney estate; Charles Carnie a plantation on Cairn Hill; and William Cuppage a plantation close by at Emerald Hill. Orchard Road itself presented one of the most beautiful vistas on the island, with tall flame trees forming a shaded canopy for almost its full length, like the inside of some great natural cathedral.

Jose d'Almeida had a plantation at Mount Victoria and Serangoon Road; Alexander Guthrie had a plantation near Telok Blangah. Tan Tock Seng had a plantation at Tanjong Pagar, and Whampoa had plantations at Tanglin village and Serangoon Road.

As the merchants developed their plantations, they began to build their houses outside of the town. Some moved west of Temenggong Daing Ibrahim's compound at Telok Blangah, such as William Ker at Bukit Chermin and James Guthrie at St James, while others preferred to live further north towards Tanglin village.

5

Father Anatole Maudit was proud of his achievement. His bamboo and attap mission church, which he had constructed with his own hands with the help of some of his parishioners, was finally complete. It stood in a small clearing in the jungle at Kranji, in the north of the island, close to the Johor Strait. Father Maudit was a missionary with the Society of Foreign Missions in Paris, who had come down from Tonquin in Cochin China in 1844 to assist Father Beurel. Father Beurel had sent him to Kranji to minister to the Chinese gambier and pepper farmers, or, as Father Beurel called them, the 'jungle Chinese'. At Father Beurel's request, Father Maudit had dedicated the church to Saint Joseph, and it became known as Saint Joseph's Church. The church was eleven miles north of the town, and could only be reached easily by boat, so Father Beurel rarely saw his missionary brother.

In the years that followed, Father Maudit made many converts, and his congregation grew from about one hundred to three hundred souls. His income was so meagre that he was scarcely better off than the Chinese plantation workers to whom he ministered, and whose love and respect he won by living in poverty and humility like the saviour whose gospel he offered. He preached in Chinese on Sundays, and kept an open house during the week, when the poor labourers would come to him with their problems and misfortunes. He would give them comfort and advice, and try to rekindle their hopes and dreams by assuring them of the love of God the father and his son. He visited them when they were sick and arranged for their burial when they died. It was small wonder that he made many converts, since everyone could see that he was a sincere and genuinely good man who cared only for the welfare of his Chinese brothers. When one of his parishioners came to him and said he had no rice to feed his family, Father Maudit would give him half of what he had himself, no matter how small that amount might be. When one of his parishioners came to him and said he had no money, Father Maudit would give him half of what he had in his purse, no matter how little that might be. Such generosity meant that Father Maudit would eventually end up with no rice or money for himself or his parishioners, but then one of the wealthier plantation owners would usually step in with a generous donation, and Father Maudit's cycle of goodness and giving would begin again.

* * *

If there was one thing Governor Butterworth liked doing, it was presiding over an official ceremony, and the more lavish and glittering the better, since it gave him a perfect opportunity to display his splendid uniform and cocked hat. Today's ceremony was just the ticket. Before an assembled crowd of merchants, government officials, soldiers, marines, and visitors on Government Hill, he presented Temenggong Daing Ibrahim with an engraved sword in recognition of his services in the suppression of piracy.

The day was perfect. A few powder puff clouds drifted across the clear blue sky, borne by the sea breezes that cooled the brows of the onlookers. The band of the 27th Bengal Native Infantry played as the Temenggong knelt to receive the sword of honour from Governor Butterworth, to rousing applause from the assembled guests.

Not everyone joined in the approving applause. W.H. Read raised an eyebrow and muttered to his colleague James Guthrie.

'Bah! Suppression of piracy indeed! Just you take a look out there over the harbour. I can count three … no four … of Ibrahim's boats, just waiting to seize any gutta percha that the natives are bringing in. The Temenggong's men will buy it for next to nothing, or nothing at all! Tell me how that is different from piracy, eh?'

'Well,' replied Guthrie, who admired Daing Ibrahim's business acumen, 'I believe when Malays enforce prices on other Malays it's called a monopoly. Calm yourself, W.H., and let's go and have a drink!'

He led W.H. off to the trellised tables that had been set up before Government House, which were laid out with cold cuts and curries and fruit, and where Malay waiters in formal attire were serving champagne, wine and beer.

After the ceremony, Colonel Butterworth made the Temenggong what he considered to be a very generous offer. He offered to pay for the Temenggong's sons to be educated in England and was surprised when Daing Ibrahim politely refused.

'But why?' Butterworth exclaimed. 'They'd get the best education in the world! Surely, you're not going to give me the line that your father gave Raffles, about your family not being interested in trade. Why, man, your gutta percha business is the envy of many a merchant!'

'I agree that they would get the best education in the English world, Governor Butterworth,' Daing Ibrahim replied politely, 'but I want them to remember their people and continue to follow the word of the Prophet. In Singapore I can give them the best of both worlds – I intend to send them to Reverend Keasberry's school at Mount Zion. There they can learn their English and how to do business with the English, but they can also study the Malay classics and receive religious instruction from Munshi Abdullah and his son, who are both employed as teachers at the school.'

'Whatever you think best,' Butterworth replied, 'but the offer remains open. Perhaps you will reconsider when they come of age to go to university.'

'I will wait and see,' said Daing Ibrahim. 'For myself I think the world of men is the greatest university there is. If Reverend Keasberry can equip my sons to rule our people with wisdom and justice, then I will be well-satisfied.'

6

Poh Ling was so happy. Everybody made such a fuss of her, including her husband Eng Seng, since none of his other wives had given him a son. Preparations were made for the anticipated celebration, but in the end Poh Ling gave birth to a daughter instead of a son. Far worse, the baby girl was born with a harelip, which was known to be an evil omen, and Gan Eng Seng insisted that the child be removed from the house. Although Poh Ling was by nature demure and submissive, she fought like a wild cat when they took away her baby, scratching and spitting at the servants who pinned her down while they prised the screaming infant from her grasp.

The next day Gan Eng Seng visited Poh Ling in the birth room, where she remained, huddled up in bed, clutching the piece of swaddling cloth that still retained the smell of her baby. He told her that he did not blame her for the birth of a girl any more than he blamed his other wives – a fine piece of condescension, Poh Ling thought to herself – but there was simply no question of keeping it in the house. If the child had been born healthy and whole, he assured her, he would not have had it removed; he had allowed his other wives to care for their own daughters. Gan Eng Seng assured Poh Ling that the baby would be well taken care of – he had instructed his servant to take the child to a woman who had a good reputation for looking after orphans until she found them a decent home. The child would not of course be placed in a noble house, but he had provided enough money to ensure that she would find a place in a home where she would be well-treated. Gan Eng Seng told Poh Ling that he would continue to treat her with respect, but that she must act as a dutiful wife and accept his decision.

When he had finished speaking, Poh Ling answered him in a low voice:

'I accept that you could do no other, husband. I will continue to be a loving and dutiful wife.'

Her face was sullen, and he was not sure that she meant it, but he understood her grief and did not press the matter.

7

1847

On February 12, a fire broke out in Kampong Glam. Before long, the flames spread to the neighbouring European houses along Beach Road. Gilbert McMicking's was the first to catch fire, and the flames threatened to spread to the adjacent home of Jose d'Almeida. Fortunately, Mr Dutronquoy of the London Hotel was visiting Dr d'Almeida with a party of French sailors, and they quickly roused the other householders along Beach Road. Dutronquoy located some ladders and set up a human chain transporting buckets of water to the roofs of the two houses, while he and some of the French sailors poured water over the hot roof tiles and down the sides of the buildings. Everyone joined in to maintain a constant stream of water buckets – Ronnie, Duncan and John Simpson, whose own house was threatened, but also Sarah, Annie and most of the servants, and the same was repeated at every beach mansion, as every man and woman, master and servant, strived to maintain their homes and livelihood. Eventually the fires were put out, with only minor damage to the two houses. Dutronquoy was paraded on high as the saviour of the day and toasted with the beer and champagne that had been brought up from Jose d'Almeida's cellar. Everyone's attention was upon him, as he gave an only half-joking little speech about the need for a proper fire company – except for Duncan, whose attention was fixed on the raven-haired Portuguese beauty who had come out of d'Almeida's house and stood in the bucket line with him.

She was about sixteen or seventeen years old, with deep olive skin. She had large black almond-shaped eyes, with long silken lashes and high arching brows. Her nose was long and straight and perfectly formed; her mouth was small with a full upper lip. Her smile was warm and expressive, and revealed a set of pearl white teeth. She was about five foot six, lithe and graceful, with full breasts and long slender legs – which he had noticed when her skirts had billowed in the sudden Sumatran squall that had fanned the flames.

Her name was Marie. That was all he knew about her, other than that she was Portuguese and spoke no English, so they had not much to say to each other when they had laid down their buckets after the fires had been put out. Yet they held each other's eyes for a long, lingering moment, before Dr d'Almeida had fetched her away, and she flashed him a warm smile before she left.

The inhabitants of Kampong Glam were less fortunate and would have been well-served by a proper fire service. Many of the poorer plank and attap houses were consumed in the flames, as were a number of brick bungalows owned by Arab and Chinese merchants.

* * *

Duncan visited Joaquim d'Almeida in the offices of Jose d'Almeida and Sons in Commercial Square the very next day.

'Good morning, Duncan,' Joaquim said, rising from his chair as Duncan was shown into his office, 'and what can we do for you this fine morning? We were very grateful for your assistance with the fire last night, by the way.'

Joaquim was fairly sure why Duncan was visiting him but did not say.

'I'm sure you know why I'm here,' Duncan replied. 'I'm

surprised you don't have half the eligible men in Singapore banging on your door this morning. Who is she, the girl who is staying with your father and calls herself Marie?'

'Ah, Duncan,' Joaquim replied, 'not everyone is as quick off the mark as you young Scots. But about our Marie, she is a sad case, but my father has taken her under his wing. She is the daughter of a Portuguese couple in Macau who perished when cholera ravaged the city ten years ago. She was brought up by her uncle and aunt, with whom she got on tolerably well, until they arranged for her to marry a young man. He was supposedly of royal blood, but a perfect boor of a man, with a pock-marked face to boot. Marie refused to marry a man she did not love, but her uncle insisted upon it, so she took her jewels and what little money she had and fled to Singapore on a merchant ship. She was presented to my father when he visited the Portuguese community in Macau a few years ago, in his capacity as consul general for Portugal in the Straits. She thought he seemed a kind man, and she just turned up one day and threw herself at his mercy. My father knows her uncle, who is a distant relation, but has refused his demands that he return her. He is an incurable romantic who does not think anyone should marry except for love, and has told her she can stay with us for as long as she wants.'

'Well, I certainly agree with that sentiment!' Duncan exclaimed. 'But am I correct that she does not speak English.'

'That is correct,' Joaquim replied, 'although we have started to teach her a few phrases. She speaks a little French, and is an accomplished musician, which is another reason why my father is so keen for her to stay – you know how much he enjoys his little concerts at home.'

'Well, I am volunteering myself as her tutor in English,' Duncan said, 'and I mean to offer my services as soon as possible.'

'But how can you?' Joaquim responded. 'You don't speak much

Portuguese, do you?'

'That's true, but that's exactly where you can help me Joaquim, by teaching me the language. I'm a quick learner, having already mastered Malay, Hindustani, and most of the Chinese dialects. I've just had little call to learn Portuguese, with your family taking most of the Macau custom. How about it? I'd be willing to pay you.'

'Oh, I could not take money from you for that,' Joaquim replied. He paused for a moment and then said:

'But there is something you could do for me.'

'And what is that? I'd be happy to do anything – you know you have me over a barrel.'

'I'd like you to teach me how to shoot!' Joaquim said.

'You have yourself a deal!' Duncan replied.

8

Captain Adil bin Mehmood was the son of Mehmood bin Nadir, an Indian Chulia [lxxxiv] who gave up his job as a lighterman on the Singapore river when Captain Flint, Raffles' brother-in-law and a dictatorial harbour master, monopolized the commerce on the river. Mehmood bin Nadir had taken a job as a peon [lxxxv] on the police force when Mr Bernard, Colonel Farquhar's brother-in-law and then chief of police, had offered it to him. Shortly afterwards, Mehmood had been murdered by Syed Yassin while escorting him to negotiate a debt with Syed Omar. When his father died, Adil, who had begun work with his uncle on the river, made a solemn promise to the Prophet that when he was old enough he would be a policeman like his father. When he joined the force, he quickly distinguished himself, and had risen to the rank of sergeant and then to captain.

Adil and two police peons were investigating an early morning burglary at the Boustead, Schwabe and Co godown on Boat Quay, which the night watchman had reported. They arrived just in time to see the Chinese burglars emerge into the shadows from a door at the back of the godown and pursued them through the back streets. They chased one man down a narrow alley between two shophouses and had almost gained on him, when he suddenly disappeared, as if into thin air. Captain Mehmood suspected a hidden doorway in one of the shophouses and ordered the peons to conduct a search of

---

lxxxiv South Indian Muslim from the Coromandel coast.
lxxxv Constable.

both, while he waited in the alley in case the thief tried to escape back the way he had come. As he waited in the shadows, Adil thought he heard a very low moan, like the anguished mewing of a cat. He pricked his ears and peered up and down the alley, but could see nothing. Then he heard the sound again, softer than before, coming from a pile of firewood and rags a few feet away from where he stood. He stepped forward and on closer inspection saw that it was not a pile of rags at all, but a young boy clothed in rags who lay face down in the alley with his body concealed by firewood.

Adil pulled the firewood away and gently turned the boy over. He was horrified by what he saw. He was an Arab boy about twelve years old, who had been badly beaten and burned – the blisters on his body could only have been caused by burning irons applied to the flesh. The boy had also been stabbed and slashed with a kris or some other blade, and his rags were bloody from his wounds. Adil put his hand over the boy's heart and his ear to the boy's lips, and was relieved to feel his faint heartbeat and his breath on his cheek. The boy had been left for dead, but there was life in him yet. He lifted up the boy's head and gave him a little water from his canteen, which caused the boy to moan softly again and open his eyes briefly, before lapsing back into unconsciousness.

The two peons returned and reported no sign of the burglar or any concealed doorway. Captain Mehmood told them to return to the station and bring back a stretcher, so the boy could be taken to the hospital. He told them to arrange for him to be taken to the European Hospital, not the Tan Tock Seng hospital for paupers, and that he would try to interview the boy there later in the day after he had made his report. When Adil visited the boy later that afternoon, he was still unconscious, although the hospital orderlies had washed and dressed his wounds and the doctor on duty had determined that none of them were mortal. As Superintendent Dunman had advised, Captain Mehmood left instructions that word should be sent to the central police station the moment that the boy regained consciousness. He also advised the duty officer that when the boy recovered he was to be released from the hospital into police custody, on receipt of an authorization letter from Superintendent Dunman.

* * *

A few days later Captain Mehmood received word that the boy had regained consciousness, and seemed to be on the road to recovery, although there was still danger of a relapse. Adil went to the hospital to interview the boy and was horrified when he saw once again the dreadful burns and cuts to his body. He talked to him in Malay, which the boy understood, and discovered that his name was Aswad. He had been frightened of Captain Mehmood at first, as he seemed to be frightened of any person that approached him. Through calm questioning and warm assurances of his safety, Adil eventually managed to get Aswad to describe his persecution and torture, and finally to identify the men who had done these dreadful things to him. Aswad had been bought as a slave, despite Raffles' legal prohibition some thirty years before, and had been treated worse than most slaves. Captain Mehmood cursed silently when he heard who his master was.

* * *

Few Malays in Singapore had exploited the new opportunities for trade and commerce that the expansion of the port had offered; most had maintained their traditional occupations such as farming, fishing and boat building. Some were employed as police peons, and a few with learning were employed as clerks for the government or merchants, but few had advanced to positions of much importance in the community. Haji Safar Ali was one of the exceptions. He had a talent for languages and had quickly mastered English at the Reverend Keasberry's school. He had also mastered Tamil, which earned him the salaried position of Chief Malay and Tamil Court Interpreter. He was well-respected by both the Malay and European communities and lived with his wife and three sons in a fine brick house on the northern reaches of the Singapore River. He travelled by sampan to the courthouse when his services were required, and supervised his small cocoa plantation when they were not.

This day he was in his office at the courthouse when Captain Mehmood and a police peon visited him.

'Good morning, sirs, and what can I do for you gentlemen?' he inquired, as he rose from his chair and placed his thumbs into his waistcoat, as he had seen the English lawyers do. 'Is this about the Hussein deposition? You know he does not admit any part in the embezzlement scheme.'

Captain Mehmood did not return the greeting, but instead announced: 'Haji Safar Ali, I arrest you for the attempted murder of the boy who answers to the name of Aswad, and for the purchase of a personal slave. You must come with me to the police station.'

Haji Safar Ali protested vigorously and demanded to see Superintendent Dunman, whom he claimed to be his friend. Captain Mehmood told him he could speak to Superintendent Dunman at the police station, where he learned from Superintendent Dunman that he was no longer a friend.

Haji Safar Ali was committed for trial at the assizes in October, as were his eldest son and two other Malay men whom Aswad had identified as his tormentors. Aswad was anxious and nervous when he was told that he would have to appear as a witness in the case, but Captain Mehmood assured him that the police would protect him, and that once the trial was over he would have nothing to fear from Haji Safar Ali. Superintendent Dunman employed a

Sikh ex-convict, who had recently won his ticket of leave,[lxxxvi] as a bodyguard to watch over the boy until the trial. Dunman knew the man could be trusted, since he had used him successfully in other cases that had required witness protection.

lxxxvi In Singapore, convicts who were well behaved could be released on a probationary 'ticket of leave', which they had to carry at all times.

9

Over the next few months Poh Ling behaved as if everything was normal. She had come to accept the loss of her baby, although now and then she was overcome with a terrible sense of unease – as if she had left some vital service undone, which she confessed to her sister Poh Neo when she visited. Poh Ling continued to behave dutifully in the marriage bed, although she no longer took any pleasure in the act. Yet each and every day she wondered what had happened to her baby, and it became an obsession with her. Although she did not doubt her husband's good intentions, she could not help worrying about the fate of her baby.

Eventually she could stand it no more. She pestered and threatened the servant who had removed her baby, until he told her the name of the woman to whom he had taken the child and where she lived. He said that her name was Madam Ang, and that she lived on the top floor of a house in Hokkien Street in Chinatown. Poh Ling went with Poh Neo to visit her. She was an aged woman with mousy brown hair, but with fine skin and a healthy complexion, who smiled sweetly at them and offered them tea. They had to admit to themselves that she was very motherly. She was nursing two babies and looking after four infants, the oldest of which was a boy of about three years who sat in the floor playing with some coloured stones. Madam Ang told them that her husband and children had died of cholera some years before, and that she eked out a living by buying and selling children, and finding unwanted babies homes. When Poh Ling and Poh Neo frowned at her description of childcare as a commercial transaction, Madam Ang reassured them by telling them how much she loved the children, and how much pleasure it gave her to save them from the dreadful fate that befell many other unwanted children. Some, both male and female, were sold into prostitution or slavery, and others were dumped into a ditch or the river. They believed her, and Poh Ling shuddered at the thought of what might have happened to her baby. She asked Madam Ang if she remembered the baby that had been brought to her some months before with a harelip, and what had happened to her. Madam Ang replied that she did, and that she found every baby a good home. Poh Ling then asked Madam Ang if she could tell her who had taken her baby. She did not want to cause any trouble, she said, she simply wanted to assure herself, for her own peace of mind, that the baby was being well-cared for. Madam Ang smiled kindly, and said that she understood, but that Poh Ling must understand she could do no such thing. The business had been transacted and that was the end of it. The baby belonged to her new family now.

When they left, Poh Ling was disappointed, but she felt easier in her mind. She felt that a great burden had been lifted from her. She still felt sadness for the loss of her baby, but Madam Ang's kind words had comforted her, and she was satisfied that her baby girl was with a caring family. She said this to her sister as they parted, and Poh Neo was greatly relieved to hear it. She had been worried about her sister, but now she was confident that she would get over her loss and begin her life anew. She looked forward to the good times they would have together, and the stories they would tell each other about their own children. Poh Ling was young and healthy, and was sure to become pregnant again soon. The joy of a new baby, boy or girl, would soon compensate for her loss.

10

Poh Ling returned home from her visit to Madam Ang with a lighter heart, and immediately began to take a more active interest in the household and her husband's happiness. She instructed the cook to prepare special dishes for him that evening, and when he returned she whispered an invitation to join her in her bedroom that night, conveyed with a measure of warmth and sincerity that moved and gratified him. Eng Seng was glad that things were back to normal and went to his wife that evening with a glad heart.

When he left her, she lay back in her bed, with the sense of relief and relaxation of one who has left behind the troubles of their mind. She began to drift off into a deep sleep, but as she was doing so, at the very edges of her consciousness, she heard a baby cry – faintly, in the distance, but sharp and clear as the song of a tiny bird. She snapped awake with a start and sat in the gloom of her bedroom trying to locate the sound. She left her bed and pulled on her gown, then walked barefoot out of her bedroom into the hall, straining her ears to the sound. She followed the crying, but curious as it seemed to her, the lamentation seemed to move around the house. She would stop outside a door, and distinctly hear the crying coming from inside, but when she entered the room there was only silence, and then she would hear the crying in another part of the house. She became frantic, for she knew in her heart that the baby that was crying was her own baby, and that something dreadful had befallen her. She grabbed hold of the night watchman and demanded that he lead her to the source of the crying, but he just looked at her in puzzlement and then alarm, declaring that he could hear nothing but the wind rustling through the willow trees and the occasional croaking of frogs.

'But you must hear it,' she cried out to him, 'it is so shrill and sad!'

Then she went and woke her husband, who was sympathetic, but also declared that he could not hear a baby crying. 'You're just having a bad dream,' he told her. 'You're probably still upset about the loss of your baby. Maybe you should take a little opium to help you sleep – I'll ask Mr Lee to send you up a pipe.'

She shook her head. She did not believe him. She could not believe him, for the tiny voice was so painfully shrill and insistent.

'But you must hear her, husband!' Poh Ling pleaded. 'How can you not! She calls out to us in her small sad voice, she calls out to her parents to help her! We cannot abandon her again, so please help me find her! Please Eng Seng, please help me find her!'

Then Eng Seng grew angry and told her very firmly that he did not hear anything, and that he did not want to hear anything more about the baby girl that had been removed from the house.

'She is not here,' he said, 'and she can never return. You must get a hold of yourself, Poh Ling, and forget all about that unfortunate incident. I forbid you to speak of it again.' And he dismissed her from his presence.

Poh Ling returned to her bedroom, but as she approached it, a shiver of excitement ran down her spine as she recognized the crying was coming from inside. She entered cautiously, looking carefully about her, but although the crying grew louder and more insistent, she could see no sign of her baby. Then she knew that her baby was dead, and that her ghost had come to warn and torment her. She climbed into bed and pulled the silken sheets over her head, but they did nothing to block the baby's cries – she lay in the darkness as the pitiful wailing cut through her like a knife. As the night wore on, the baby's cries became fainter and fainter, and eventually Poh Ling drifted off into a troubled sleep. She dreamt she was on a boat on a river, drifting over its still waters in the early morning mist. The world was silent all around – there was no bird-song, no chatter of riverboat traffic, not even the gentle lapping of the water against the edge of the boat. Then she saw something horrible floating in the water – the tiny skeleton of a baby girl, the flesh stripped from her bones, her tiny jaw twisted in hellish anguish, her eye sockets staring empty at her. It was her baby! She recognized the silver bell she had attached to her ankle to ward off evil spirits. Now she was dead and had come back as a spirit to haunt her! She woke screaming. The room was silent, but she could hear the crying in her head and in the very depths of her soul.

And thus it continued throughout the nights that followed. Every night the cries seemed to come from within the house, which she searched from top to bottom, only to find that they had returned to torment her in her own bedroom. She questioned all the servants, but none had ever heard the crying. She dared not ask her husband again, for she knew what his answer would be. She lost all interest in life, and spent her days and nights searching the rooms for her baby. She did not eat or drink. She had no time for her husband, and after she refused him three times, he told her he would replace her with a concubine if she did not quickly change her ways.

On the days when she came to visit her sister, Poh Neo was surprised and increasingly concerned at the change that had come over her. When once Poh Ling had been pleasantly plump and her skin had glowed with girlish youth, her flesh now seemed to hang on her bones and her skin was a pasty, deathly colour. When Poh Ling told Poh Neo her story her sister tried to comfort her, but Poh Ling would not be comforted. She begged Poh Neo to stay the night with her, which she reluctantly agreed to do. But Poh Neo did not hear even the faintest cry, although she followed Poh Ling all through the house and then back to her bedroom, where she held her sobbing sister in her arms. Poh Neo feared for her sister and felt a troubling presence in the house.

11

Six weeks of intensive tuition later, Duncan had mastered the rudiments of Portuguese to sufficient proficiency to present himself to Miss Marie Abreu Melo at the home of Dr Jose d'Almeida. They sat politely in the presence of Dr d'Almeida and his wife Rosalia, and took tea with them, while Duncan demonstrated his new proficiency in the language, which impressed them all. After some polite conversation about the weather, the fire, and how she was finding the people of Singapore, Duncan asked if she would do him the honour of meeting with him again, so that he could improve his Portuguese, and perhaps help her with her English. She consented with another flashing smile, while his brown eyes and her black eyes met as if across a starlit highway over the world. They were in love, and they both knew it.

* * *

On June 6, on the feast of Corpus Christi, Father Beurel blessed the newly completed church, which he dedicated to Christ the Good Shepherd. He did this in memory of Father Laurent Imbert, the first priest from the Society of Foreign Missions to visit Singapore.[19]

The Cathedral of the Good Shepherd was laid out in Renaissance cruciform style oriented to the east, bounded by Queen Street and Victoria Street, with Palladian porticos and rounded Tuscan Doric columns. Later in the year Charles Dyce, the watercolour artist and partner in Martin, Dyce and Co, designed the eight-sided steeple and spire modelled upon the steeple and spire of St Andrew's Church. Like St Andrew's Church, the Cathedral of the Holy Shepherd was constructed in granite and plastered with Madras Chunam, which sparkled in the bright morning sunlight.

During the consecration ceremony, Father Beurel sprinkled holy water over the building while the choir sang psalms. He then removed the holy sacrament from the old chapel and carried it to the new church, ahead of a procession of fifteen hundred exultant parishioners and celebrants, including Father Anatole Maudit and some of his flock, who had taken a boat down from Kranji so they could attend the ceremony. After the holy sacrament was laid upon the cathedral altar, Father Beurel conducted a Mass before a congregation who wept tears of joy and gratitude.

Father Beurel was gratified with his achievement, but he was not satisfied. There was still much work to be done, including the provision of church schools for boys and girls.

12

The next day Poh Neo took Poh Ling to visit a medium she knew who lived at the Thian Hock Keng Temple, who could communicate with the spirits of the dead. She was a young woman, who looked quite normal when they paid their money and explained their troubles to her. She asked them to sit beside her before a small altar, where she burnt incense and uttered some incantations. Then she flung her head backwards and her eyes rolled in their sockets until only the whites were revealed. From her open mouth came the sound of a baby crying, which they both heard quite clearly. Poh Neo was shocked, for now she believed her sister. Eventually the crying ceased, and the medium returned to her normal self. She told them that the baby was dead, and that it was suffering in Hell because her parents had abandoned her.

'But what can I do?' Poh Ling begged, desperate through her tears.

'You have two choices,' the medium said, taking her by the hands, and looking deep into her eyes.

'You must find her body and give her a proper burial. Or you must go to her and comfort her.'

'What do you mean by that?' Poh Neo asked sharply.

'You both know what I mean,' replied the medium, who then rose, bowed briefly to them and walked away.

* * *

Poh Neo took her sister home and promised that she would return shortly, after she had conducted some urgent business for her father. Then they would revisit the old lady in Chinatown and demand to know what had happened to Poh Ling's baby. If necessary, they would offer her money for the information. She put her sister in the care of a servant, with strict instructions to watch over her carefully. But Poh Ling would not wait. The moment the servant's back was turned, she slipped out of the house and ran down the street and did not stop until she came to Madam Ang's house in Hokkien Street. Breathless, she ran up the stairs and knocked sharply on the door.

A few minutes later the door opened, and the mousy-haired woman opened it, with a baby in her arms.

'Oh, it's you again,' she said, a little surprised. 'I'm sorry, but I already told you there is nothing more I can do for you.'

'I want my baby!' Poh Ling shouted. 'I want to know where she is! You must tell me!'

She pushed her way past the woman into the room, which was as she had left it. Some small children were playing on the floor, with a number of infants lying in cribs.

Madam Ang laid the baby she was carrying in one of the cribs, and then turned to face Poh Ling.

'You have no right to storm in here like this,' she said. 'Now leave, or I will have to call the police.'

'I hear my baby crying, night and day,' Poh Ling replied in a shrill voice, which grew louder by the moment. 'I went to visit a medium, and she said my baby is dead. Did you kill her? Or did you give her to people who killed her?'

The woman continued to smile sweetly, but a malicious look flashed across her dark eyes. Despite the heat of the day and the gurgling cries of the infants, Poh Ling felt as if she was standing in a cold tomb and looking into the eyes of death.

'How dare you question me like this?' Madam Ang retorted.

'Get out of my home this instant, or I will call the police!'

She grabbed Poh Ling by the arm in a vice-like grip and forced her out of the room and back down the stairs. Poh Ling was amazed by how strong the woman was, but she fought back, scratching at the woman with her nails, and screaming 'Murderer! Murderer!' at the top of her voice. But it was no use. The woman forced her all the way down the stairs and flung her out onto the five-foot way. [lxxxvii]

'Get out, and never, never come back! I don't want you disturbing my children ever again!'

The noise of the fight attracted a small crowd. Captain Adil bin Mehmood, who had been patrolling the area at the time with two police peons, stepped through the tightly packed bodies to discover the cause of the commotion. Poh Ling was hysterical by now and he could get little sense out of her, except that she believed that Madam Ang had killed her baby daughter. Madam Ang seemed very reasonable and explained the situation to him. Poh Ling's husband had taken the baby away from her because it had a harelip and had asked Madam Ang to find a good home for it. This was her livelihood, and she loved the poor children and did her best to find them good homes. She had a good reputation, as a number of her neighbours in the crowd attested. And it was on account of her good reputation that unfortunate parents took their children to her, rather than taking more drastic actions. The young woman was obviously upset over the loss of her daughter, and this had caused her to have bad dreams and fantasies – or perhaps she was possessed by some demon, she could not tell. But Madam Ang would not let her in her house again, for she had created a disturbance and frightened her poor children.

Captain Mehmood ordered one of the peons to watch over Poh

lxxxvii The Town Plan of 1823 specified that each house should have a covered passageway with a depth of five feet, which became known as 'five-foot ways'.

Ling and followed Madam Ang upstairs to inspect her premises. He found nothing untoward. The room was neat and clean; the children played happily on the floor and the babies peered up at him contentedly. Captain Mehmood was satisfied that this was a good woman making the best for herself in a difficult world, and there seemed to be no danger to the children. He thanked Madam Ang for allowing him to inspect her premises, and told her that he would take Poh Ling home, and caution her never to return again, on pain of arrest. Madam Ang thanked him and saw him to the door.

When Captain Mehmood returned to the street, Poh Ling had calmed down, and she allowed him to escort her home without any trouble. Indeed, she said nothing at all, but retraced her steps like a woman in a trance, as Captain Mehmood followed behind. When they reached her home, Gan Eng Seng came out to meet them. He was furious. He had heard from his servants about Poh Neo staying the night to help search for the ghost, and of their visit to the temple medium. When Captain Mehmood told him about the fight at the home of Madam Ang, he started to curse and scream at his wife.

'You worthless, stupid woman! You will not leave your room until you have come to your senses and forgotten this nonsense. I don't much care whether your brat lived or died, but I won't have my wife making a laughing stock of me. Get out of my sight!'

He ordered his servants to take her away and lock her in her room until he decided how best to deal with her. Poh Ling said nothing in reply and went off meekly with the servants. Captain Mehmood took his leave of Gan Eng Seng and returned to his duties. He felt sorry for the girl, but she was plainly disturbed, and there was nothing more he could do for her.

* * *

As they locked the bedroom door behind her, Poh Ling stood in the middle of the room, watching the motes of dust dancing in the afternoon sunshine that streamed through the open shutters. She looked out at the clear blue sky and marvelled at the shadows of the willow trees dancing on the wall. She heard a black and white dial bird singing outside her window, sweet as any nightingale. How beautiful is this world, she thought, a world my baby will never know. She heard her crying softly in the room, and now the gentle sobbing seemed to give her comfort. She went to her closet and removed a silk tie from one of her robes. She tied a tight knot on one end, then pulling up a chair, slipped it over the hook that supported one of the roof lanterns, and formed the other into a makeshift noose, which she slipped around her neck. She pushed the chair aside with her foot and the silk cord tightened round her throat. Then she and her baby were at peace forever.

13

Poh Neo ran into Poh Ling's house. She had come earlier, only to be told that Poh Ling had left. She had gone to Madam Ang's house, but had only arrived in time to hear about the commotion, and that the police had taken Poh Ling home. Now she must go to her sister, for she knew Poh Ling would be in a desperate state of mind. As Poh Neo ran into the house, Gan Eng Seng blocked her path.

'What do you mean by entering my house unannounced, Poh Neo? You are my sister-in-law, but that does not give you the right to disrespect me. By whose authority did you stay with my wife last night and put those notions of ghosts into her head? She is a weak and foolish woman and cannot bear the strain. Please leave my house this instant.'

'I am truly sorry, brother-in-law, but I was only trying to help you both by getting to the bottom of the matter,' Poh Neo replied in earnest. 'I was hoping to convince Poh Ling that the crying she heard was only in her imagination. But I must see her! Where is she? Is she alive?'

'She is locked in her room until she comes to her senses, if she ever comes to her senses,' he said coldly. 'But you must leave now, you have no further business here.'

'Please Eng Seng,' she pleaded, falling onto her knees before him, and laying her head at his feet. 'Please let me see her. I fear for her life!'

'I do not much care if she lives or dies,' he sneered in response. 'But I will indulge you for the moment it will take to satisfy you that she is safe in her bedroom, and then you must leave immediately. Get up and follow me!'

He turned and led Poh Neo into the house and upstairs to Poh Ling's bedroom, and ordered the servant to unlock the door.

She heard him roar in anguish and anger as he entered the bedroom, and Poh Neo screamed when she followed him in. Poh Ling hung creaking in the late afternoon sunlight from the lantern hook, her eyeballs protruding and her black tongue sticking out from her mouth. Poh Neo rushed forward and put her arms around Poh Ling's frail body, but Gan Eng Seng pushed her aside. He jerked the body quickly down, snapping the cord, and flung it like a rag doll upon the bed.

'Get out!' he yelled at Poh Neo. 'See what you have done with your ghost stories! She is dead, and for what! Go now and tell your husband and father what has happened here and arrange for them to have your sister's body removed by tomorrow. If it is not removed by then, I will throw it in the gutter alongside the other vermin. I will not waste a penny on that wretched girl's funeral, and I hope the King of Hell orders that she be fried in a cauldron of oil!'

He roared and screamed and spat upon the corpse of his dead wife.

'I curse you, wife, and I curse your family!' he cried out in his rage.

Knowing there was nothing she could do, Poh Neo backed out of the room, and returned home to tell her father and her husband.

* * *

The next day the undertaker came and arranged for Poh Ling to be borne to her father's home in a casket. While Buddhist priests said prayers over her body, Poh Neo, her older sister Poh Chee, and her mother and father entered the house of Gan Eng Seng carrying brooms. They proceeded to sweep the house, while Gan Eng Seng stood watching them in sullen silence. It was the custom and their right. They were sweeping the luck from his house and his life. He watched them leave with the casket with a solemn expression on his face, but as he re-entered the house he shrugged his shoulders. Well, at least I am rid of her, he thought to himself, and I will make my own luck. He resolved to find himself a new wife, which he did within six months of Poh Ling's funeral.

14

The American consul Joseph Balestier had benefited from the increase in American trade since British restrictions were lifted in 1840, and had managed to supplement his paltry consular income by serving as agent and chandler for most of the American shipping. Unfortunately, the British doctrine of free trade only extended so far, and his investment in his thousand-acre sugar plantation at Serangoon suffered badly when the British government introduced an import tax on Singapore-grown sugar, to protect their own sugar interests in the West Indies. Then, on August 22, tragedy struck again. His beloved wife Maria Revere died, only two years after the death of their son. In its obituary, the *Singapore Free Press* commended Maria for her untiring zeal in serving the 'poor, the sick, and the needy of the community'. Joseph, normally in robust health, grew sick in body as well as in mind, and planned to take a temporary leave from Singapore to recuperate from his loss.

* * *

James Brooke decided it was time he returned to England for a visit, having been away from home for nine years. He arrived in Southampton in October and was surprised to find himself a national hero. His friends had done an excellent job of representing his achievements during his absence. They had promoted the cause of British interests in Borneo, particularly among the northern free-trade merchants, who were always searching for new markets for their surpluses. They had also cultivated a romantic image of James as an idealistic adventurer following in the footsteps of Sir Stamford Raffles, a man committed to extending the benefits of civilization and trade to the native peoples of the East – an image that James himself had carefully crafted in his letters to his friends, extracts of which they had published. They worked with Captain Keppel to edit and publish selections from James' journals in Keppel's 1846 book *The Expedition to Borneo of HMS Dido for the Suppression of Piracy, with Extracts from the Journals of James Brooke, Esq. of Sarawak,* which was well-received. It had prompted the London *Times* to editorialize in favour of government support for the 'heroic and indefatigable Mr Brooke' and his noble efforts to bring peace and civilization to the Borneans.

James was wined and dined by lords and merchants, army and navy officers, ministers and bishops. He gained effortless membership of the best London clubs, and was even offered a dinner in his honour by the King Edward VI Grammar School, from which he had run away at the age of twelve. He held court from his suite of rooms at Mivart's Hotel [lxxxviii] in Brook Street, which functioned as a general mess room for James' male friends and companions, where his dinner parties and brandy-fuelled skylarks with his young friends continued well into the small hours.

Wherever he went, James talked about Sarawak, and about his own firm but humane role in its civilized development. And finally, the government seemed to be listening. His appointment as Confidential Agent to Her Majesty's Government in Borneo was upgraded to the title of Consul-General of Borneo. It was another hollow title, since the government did not recognize Sarawak as a sovereign state or a British protectorate, but it carried a salary of two thousand pounds a year.

And then, to crown it all, he was introduced to the Queen and

---

lxxxviii The forerunner of Claridge's hotel.

Prince Albert at Windsor Castle. He kissed the young Victoria's hand and knelt before her. She told him that she was very pleased to make his acquaintance, and he replied that he was honoured that she would consider him so. Yet in his heart he was also deeply disappointed, for the Queen did not knight him for his administration of Sarawak as the Prince Regent had knighted his hero Sir Stamford Raffles for his administration of Java. His friends said it was a national disgrace, but James swallowed his humble pie and returned to the social swirl. Humility had its limits, however, and James had his portrait painted by the Royal artist Sir Francis Grant, RA. He stood against a backdrop of Sarawak in his dark Royal Yacht Squadron jacket, tight britches and navy buckle, white shirt and black neck-scarf, looking every inch the Byronian hero.

15

In August, Hong Xiuquan headed west in search of Feng Yunshan. When he reached Guangxi he learned that Feng was to the north at Thistle Mountain.

Hong was bone-weary from travelling, but immediately set off for Thistle Mountain. He was thin as a rake, dressed in rags, with only a few coppers to his name, but he felt the strength and power of his Heavenly father fill his heart and soul as he journeyed north. He felt that his elder brother Jesus walked beside him as he journeyed through the rivers and valleys and forests and fields on his journey to Thistle Mountain where, bright-eyed with joy and triumph, he greeted an amazed Feng Yunshan and his Society of God-worshippers.

* * *

During the autumn Hong Xiuquan and Feng Yunshan devoted their time to the preparation of written descriptions of the Heavenly Way. The God-worshippers grew steadily in number, and God the father spoke to Hong again, not in his dreams as before, but through the mouth of Yang Xiuqing, a poor Hakka charcoal burner who would enter into a trance and declare the word of God. His elder brother Jesus also spoke to him, through the mouth of Xiao Chaogui, a Hakka peasant.

They brought news of events in Heaven since Hong had left eleven years before. The voices told him he had a son by First

Chief Moon, who lived with his grandmother, the wife of God. His wife First Chief Moon yearned for his return, for his son was still unnamed, but she understood the importance of the mission his Heavenly father had set for him.

As the God-worshipping congregations knelt and prayed in their bare mountain churches, and recited the poems handed down by God the father, many entered into states of trance and ecstasy, and some were transported to Heaven, where, like Hong Xiuquan before them, they saw the Heavenly father arrayed in his black dragon robes and golden beard, and below them in hell the red-eyed demon king of the devils.

16

As the date of the trial drew near, Captain Mehmood visited Aswad almost every day, to reassure him of his safety and to prepare him for what would happen at the trial.

'All you have to do is tell the truth, Aswad, and describe to the magistrates what these dreadful men did to you. And do not fear them, for they cannot reach you or harm you.'

Adil had grown fond of the boy and used to take him treats such as dates and figs from the market. If time permitted he would read to him, tales of bravery from the *Malay Annals*, which seemed to fortify his spirit for the forthcoming trial, which was now two days away.

The story Aswad liked best was the tale of Hang Tuah and Hang Jebat, which Adil read to him on the night before the trial.

Hang Tuah was a famous warrior in the court of Sultan Mansur Shah of Malacca. His sultan knew him for his bravery and his unswerving and unconditional loyalty. Hang Tuah saved his master's life on many occasions and the sultan came to regard Hang Tuah as his most trusted servant.

One day, when Hang Tuah was accompanying the sultan on a visit to the court of the Rajah of Majapahit, the champion of the Majapahit, Taming Sari, challenged him to a duel. After a furious battle that lasted all of a long hot afternoon, Hang Tuah triumphed over the Majapahit champion. When Taming Sari smashed Hang Tuah's kris into fragments, and was about to kill his opponent, his own blade flew from his hand and set itself in Hang Tuah's hand, forcing him to drive the blade into Taming Sari's throat. The kris, which now quivered in Hang Tuah's hand like a living thing, had quit the man who had for so long abused its power, in order to serve the noble warrior Hang Tuah. The Rajah, amazed by Hang Tuah's victory over his defeated champion, awarded him the kris that had miraculously delivered his victory, named Taming Sari, after its owner.

It was a magnificent and magical weapon, forged from twenty-one different types of metal. These were remnants of the bolts that were used to bind the holy Kaaba, the great cubic place of pilgrimage that stands at the centre of the Great Mosque in Mecca, built by Abraham and his son Ishmael from a block of black stone that had been delivered to them by a Heavenly angel. The handle and sheath of the kris were encased in gold leaf, and the blade shone with the silvery grey of moonstone.

Hang Tuah and his warrior companion Hang Jebat fought and won many battles for their sultan, Mansur Shah, and they kept the seas around Malacca safe from pirates and from hostile neighbouring states. Yet Hang Tuah's martial success and favour with the sultan caused some of the older nobles to become jealous of him, and one powerful lord, Pateh Karma Wijaya, informed Sultan Mansur Shah that Hang Tuah was having an affair with his favourite concubine. The accusation was false, but Pateh Karma Wijaya swore that it was true. The sultan, who was a jealous man, believed him.

Sultan Mansur Shah ordered that Hang Tuah be

brought before him, and publicly accused him of treachery. Hang Tuah knew he was innocent and did not think he needed to offer any defence.

The Sultan took Hang Tuah's failure to offer any defence as a sign of his guilt and was greatly angered.

'Have you nothing to say for yourself!' the sultan cried.

'Nothing,' Hang Tuah replied. 'I have always been loyal to you, Highness. I am yours to command as you will.'

Then Sultan Mansur Shah ordered that Hang Tuah be taken to the palace prison and executed before the sun had set. Chief minister Bendahara Sri Nara led him away, before a hushed and shocked court.

That afternoon, as his friends came to make their last farewells to him, Hang Tuah surrendered his Taming Sari kris to Hang Jebat, who with tears in his eyes embraced and kissed his old comrade in arms. The following morning, believing his friend dead, Hang Jebat's grief turned to anger, and he raced to the apartments of Pateh Karma Wijaya and stabbed the false noble through the eye as he rose from his bed.

Pateh Karma Wijaya's death scream roused the palace guards, who came to investigate, but Hang Jebat cut them down as he fought his way towards the sultan's chamber. The sultan and Bendahara Sri Nara fled to a place of safety, leaving the sultan's wives and concubines huddled in fear in a far corner of the palace. Sultan Mansur Shah sent forth his best warriors against Hang Jebat, but all were defeated, and eventually none of them would challenge Hang Jebat the usurper, for they knew it meant certain death. Then Hang Jebat sat upon the sultan's throne and ruled over his wives and concubines, who brought him rich food and drink and betel nut. He fell in love with one of the sultan's wives, who soon found herself with child.

Months passed. The sultan surrounded the palace with his army, but none of his soldiers would attempt to enter therein. He began to wonder if he had been cursed, and stunned by the ferocity of Hang Jebat's retribution, admitted that he might have made a fateful mistake in condemning Hang Tuah to an unjust death. When Bendahara Sri Nara heard this, he confessed to the sultan:

'Forgive me, highness, but when you bade me put him to death, I did not think the sentence fitting for his alleged crime, so I held him chained in a safe prison. For he is no ordinary man, and I believed that one day you might have great need of him. I believe that day has come.'

Bendahara Sri Nana expected to be executed himself for his disobedience, but the sultan replied:

'It is as you say, Bendahara Sri Nana – you are a true servant of mine. Bring Hang Tuah to me and I will bestow upon him a full pardon.'

Then Hang Tuah was brought before the sultan. He could barely stand, so long had his feet been shackled, but he stood straight-backed before his royal master.

'I grant you a full pardon, Hang Tuah, and restitution of your former positions. Your first task is to defeat the rebel Hang Jebat, who has killed my people and defiled my palace. I want you to strike him down with my own royal kris, forged by my ancestors, who founded the great Sultanate of Malacca.'

Sultan Mansur Shah drew his jewel-encrusted kris from his yellow sash, and handed it to Hang Tuah, who received it and said:

'I have always been loyal to you, Highness. I am yours to command as you will.'

Later that same day, Hang Tuah set out for the sultan's palace, where Hang Jebat now ruled over the sultan's women. His heart was heavy, for Hang Jebat was a warrior brother and an old and trusted friend. Yet Hang Jebat had challenged the authority of the sultan, which was the basis of law and order and justice, and he knew where his duty lay.

As Hang Tuah passed through the palace gate, Hang Jebat rushed down the stairs to meet the intruder, the kris called Taming Sari flashing silver-grey in his right hand. He stopped halfway down when he recognized who approached him, and exclaimed:

'Hang Tuah! You are still alive! I thought that you were dead – otherwise I never would have done what I have done! I swear it to you in the name of God, the lord of all worlds. Now here we are, you and I, kris to kris, in the sultan's chamber.'

'Do you repent what you have done, Hang Jebat?' Hang Tuah cried out.

'I do not repent, Hang Tuah, for the sultan was wrong to condemn you to death on the false word of Pateh Karma Wijaya. I do not fear death. I know I am destined to die at your hands and I cannot avoid my fate. But I will not sell my life easily, and before I die you will see how well the rebel Hang Jebat fights!'

So saying, he rushed down the stairs and Hang Tuah rushed up to meet him. The blades of their krisses crashed together, causing great sparks of red and silver to flash in the air. For over an hour they drove each other up and down the palace stairs, until Hang Tuah managed to reach the pillared entrance to the sultan's inner chambers. Hang Jebat fought like a demon, and many times he got the better of his old friend, but just as he was about to strike a fatal blow, it seemed as if the Taming Sari kris refused to kill its former master. Summoning all his force, Hang Jebat overcame the resistance of the blade and drove it straight towards Hang Tuah's throat. But Hang Tuah managed to duck and slide around behind Hang Jebat, who drove the magic kris into a stone pillar, where it stuck fast. As Hang Jebat desperately tried to withdraw his weapon, Hang Tuah stabbed the sultan's kris deep into his back.

Hang Jebat gasped and stumbled to his knees, his hand slipping from the handle of Taming Sari, which remained embedded in the stone pillar.

'You have killed me, Hang Tuah,' Hang Jebat whispered in his pain. 'Grant me one last favour, for the sake of our old friendship. Dang Baharu, one of the sultan's wives, bears my child – she is four months pregnant. If the child is born, please save it from the wrath of the sultan. Promise me this only.'

'I promise you, Hang Jebat, with God's will your child will become my own, and I will honour it as my own.'

They heard a great clamour as the sultan's palace guard, hearing that the battle between Hang Tuah and Hang Jebat was over, rushed in to investigate. They saw that the usurper was mortally wounded and rushed forward to finish him off.

Then Hang Jebat said to his old friend: 'Master, quickly kill your slave! I would rather die by your hand than any other man!'

'Farewell, true friend,' Hang Tuah whispered in his ear, as he drove the sultan's kris into the heart of Hang Jebat, who died instantly. Then he held his friend in his arms, as tears streamed down his face and splashed into the pools of blood that had formed around Hang Jebat's lifeless body. The sultan's guards gathered round, but none would intervene, for now the kris named Taming Sari had withdrawn itself from the stone pillar and hovered in the air above Hang Tuah and Hang Jebat, protecting them against all danger.'

* * *

After Adil finished, Aswad sat in silence for a few moments, and then said:

'Thank you for relating the story, sahib Adil, it is one of my favourites. But who do you think did the right thing?'

'It is not for me to say, Aswad, but I think that they both did the right thing, in their own way.'

'What happened to Hang Tuah afterwards?' Aswad asked.

'No one is sure, little man, but that is a story for another time – we have had more than enough story telling for one evening. You have a big day ahead of you tomorrow, and you must get your rest. Selamat tinggal, lxxxix my little man.'

'Selamat jalan, xc sahib Adil,' Aswan replied. 'Go with God, and may He watch over you.'

'And you too, little man.'

---

lxxxix Goodbye, stay safe.
xc Goodbye, safe journey.

17

Madam Ang picked up the baby girl and held her close to her bosom, rocking the baby back and forth in her arms.

'Hush, little one,' she said, 'don't you know how lucky you are? When I took you in, you were all skin and bone. You almost died, you know, but now you are plump and happy, like any good man's baby, aren't you? You have your Auntie Ang to thank for your good fortune,' she continued, stroking the baby's head gently with her hand.

She felt tired and badly in need of a tonic. It was time again, she thought.

She carried the contented, half-sleeping child to the back of the room, and took down a large washtub from the shelf. She picked up an empty water pitcher and placed it inside the tub, and placed a full one beside it. Then she pulled the swaddling clothes from the baby, turning her over in her arm, until she held her poised naked over the empty pitcher. She bent over and kissed the baby on the head. The baby gurgled softly in response.

Then Madam Ang put her left hand over the baby's mouth and with her other hand took out a small knife from inside her shirt, which she drew sharply across the baby's throat. She held the baby before her as the blood ran down into the pitcher, and continued to hold her there until the flow slowed to a trickle. Then she wrapped the baby back in the swaddling clothes and placed her in an old sack behind the door, which she tied up tightly.

She took a long tall cup from the washstand. She poured the

blood from the pitcher into the cup and drank it down in a long, slow draught, all the while watching over the babies and young children sleeping blissfully in their cribs and on the floor – she had drugged them all by rubbing a sweet white paste on their lips at bedtime. She finished her drink and poured herself another, all the while watching her charges with her deep sad eyes. Then she rinsed out the cup and the pitcher with fresh water and threw the blood darkened water out into the darkness of the alley behind the shophouse. She picked up the sack and left the room, locking the door carefully behind her. She headed through the dark streets and alleys to the upper reaches of the river, with the sack under her arm. Then she went down to the edge of the river, where she looked around until she found a large stone, which she placed inside the sack. And then, checking to make sure nobody was around, she tossed the weighted bundle into the blackness of the river.

18

The Malay policeman took off his cap as he greeted Aswad, who was sitting up in bed trying to talk to the Sikh bodyguard. The bodyguard's English was poor and he was not a talkative type, although, like Captain Mehmood, he was genuinely fond of the boy.

'I've come to take you back to the police station,' the policeman said. 'I have an order from Superintendent Dunman, who asks after your health. My name is Constable Awang bin Bakar, but you can call me Awang.'

The Sikh bodyguard rose and held out his hand to receive the order, whereupon Constable Bakar drew out an envelope from his overalls and handed it to him. The Sikh in turn took it to the English medical officer, who confirmed that it was from Superintendent Dunman, and instructed him to release Aswad into the care of Constable Bakar. The letter was written in English by Superintendent Dunman and signed by him on police stationary.

'Everything seems to be in order,' said the medical officer, 'so let's get you dressed and out of here.'

'But where is sahib Adil?' asked Aswad, in a concerned voice. 'He has come most nights I have been in the hospital.'

'Don't worry, Aswad,' replied Constable Bakar. 'Captain Mehmood had to go with Superintendent Dunman to arrest a dangerous criminal, and they entrusted me with the task of seeing you safely back to the police station.'

'Will sahib Adil be there when we get to the police station?'

'He assured me he would meet you there, Aswad.'

'Well, then, let us go to him,' said Aswad, who dressed himself in the new Baju Melayu outfit that Captain Mehmood had brought him the previous day, a long sleeved dark blue cotton shirt with stiff raised collar and dark blue cotton trousers.

* * *

Outside the hospital a black gharry and driver were waiting for them. Aswad was excited to be travelling in such a grand means of transport and climbed eagerly into the carriage. Constable Bakar climbed in behind and called out to the driver to take them to the police station. Aswad thought himself very important and very brave – just like Hang Tuah.

They had not gone very far when the gharry slowed to a stop.

'Why have we stopped?'Aswad asked. 'Have we arrived at the police station?'

'I'm not sure, Aswad, I'll ask the driver,' Constable Bakar replied, opening the gharry door.

But Constable Bakar did not call out to the driver, and as Aswad leaned forward to see where they had stopped, Constable Bakar pulled him back sharply. He then pushed a gag into Aswad's mouth before he could scream – as Aswad was about to do when he saw two of Haji Safar Ali's cousins climb into the gharry, and force a dirty black sack over his head. The gharry turned around and headed north, away from the police station.

The Sikh bodyguard had watched the gharry depart with the policeman and the boy. The boy had seemed to trust him and the medical officer had said everything was in order. But he had a bad feeling about Awang bin Bakar who said he was a policeman and he had followed the gharry the short distance it had travelled. When the gharry stopped and turned around after the two men got in, he knew there was something wrong. He also turned around and followed the gharry as it headed north along River Valley Road.

An hour later Captain Mehmood arrived at the European Hospital to take Aswad to the police station.

* * *

Captain Mehmood was beside himself with grief, and Superintendent Dunman was furious when he heard what had happened to the boy.

'He stole my officer paper and forged my signature, God damn it! Safar Ali must have someone on the inside – someone sophisticated enough to forge a letter in English.'

'Wait, though,' he continued, suddenly having second thoughts. 'Someone might have got the paper at the printing press. Safar Ali was a star pupil of Reverend Keasberry, and he may know someone, or have influence over someone, at the Missionary Press. More than likely, I suppose.'

'What are we going to do about it?' asked Captain Mehmood.

'Nothing at the moment, Captain Mehmood, no point trying to close the stable door after the horse has bolted. We need to find that boy before the trial begins. I want every man on it until the court opens tomorrow. Don't blame yourself, son, there's nothing you could have done to prevent it. He took in my old Sikh bodyguard, and he's a suspicious fellow. Where is he, by the way?'

'I don't know. The medical officer said he left almost immediately after the boy, but he did not report back to the station.'

Dunman had every man on the force search the town and suburbs, but they found no trace of the boy. They found the old Sikh guard stabbed to death in a ditch at the two-mile marker on Thomson Road.

* * *

'But you can't just set him free,' Superintendent Dunman almost shouted at the recorder. [xci] 'He's kidnapped the boy and very likely murdered him, along with the old Sikh I sent to guard him.'

'It's a damnable situation, I admit,' replied Sir Christopher Rawlinson, 'although I always thought that Haji Safar Ali was a decent fellow. But without your boy to testify against him, there is no possibility of getting the grand jury to convict him.'

Dunman flushed red with anger, but Sir Christopher held up his hand to silence the outburst that he knew was coming.

'There is, however, something we can do. I discussed the matter with councillor Church before you came in. We can't convict him and we can't keep him in prison, but we're not going to let him and his cronies off scot-free. We are going to postpone their trial pending further investigation of the suspicious circumstances surrounding the disappearance of the witness and the death of the Sikh guard. Haji Safar Ali, his son, and his two associates will be released on bail until their new trial date, which I have set for January. You have until then to find the boy, or find evidence to implicate them in this act of skulduggery. God guide your hand. I don't suppose I need to tell you to keep these men under constant surveillance.'

'You do not, sir, and I thank you,' Dunman replied.

---

xci Professional part-time judge.

19

Dunman had all two hundred men on his force searching for the boy, in addition to their regular duties. They pressed their contacts in the Malay, Arab and Indian communities. They implored, cajoled and threatened; they watched, followed, and brought men in for questioning. They offered a reward for information about the boy, but all their efforts were in vain. There was a rumour that Aswad had been taken to Riau in a sampan the night of his capture, and another rumour that he had been taken back to Singapore again. Dunman took the matter personally, because Captain Mehmood took it personally, and for two weeks he scarcely returned to his plantation home. He remained on duty late at night and was up at the crack of dawn, grabbing a few hours' sleep on a cot in his office at the police station.

Two weeks passed, but the trail was dead, and Dunman was beginning to resign himself to the fact that the boy had been taken from Singapore, and either murdered or sold as a slave to some Malay pirate or sultan. Then there was a sudden break in the case. An Indian street sweeper, a former convict who slept in a room separated from his Malay landlord by only a thin partition, reported that he had heard the man crying out in his sleep that he had killed a boy, and begged God the merciful and compassionate for forgiveness.

The Malay landlord, Zedrin Osman, was arrested and charged with conspiracy to murder. He would not admit to the boy's murder, but said he had heard that the boy's body could be found in the upper reaches of the Singapore River, in the vicinity of Haji Safar Ali's home. For two days Captain Mehmood led a party of peons in longboats searching the area. They rowed up and down, dragging the river bottom with long poles to discover any submerged objects. As they were about to abandon their search on the evening of the second day, their trawling brought some bubbles to the surface, and the peons gagged at the putrid smell that issued forth as the bubbles broke upon the surface of the river. When Captain Mehmood was alerted, he dived into the river, and brought up Aswad's body, which had been weighed down by stones tied around his waist. The boy's wrists and feet were bound, and his neck was almost severed from his head. Captain Mehmood retched, but forced himself to hold down the rage that roared within him – he wanted to go directly to Haji Safar Ali's home and strike him down dead for this vicious act. But he knew his duty and ordered his men to search the boats moored along the edges of the river.

A short distance from Haji Safar Ali's house they found a boat with blood-stained timbers, and when they traced the owner and questioned him, he admitted that Haji Safar Ali had borrowed the boat. Haji Safar Ali had told him he needed it to transport some firewood and had paid him for it. Captain Mehmood sent two peons to arrest Haji Safar Ali, this time on a charge of murder. He did not trust himself to carry out the arrest; he thought he was likely to shoot the man dead on first sight.

Haji Safar Ali was taken to the new jail at the Sepoy Lines, while Aswad's body was taken to the European hospital, where Dr Oxley identified it as the body of Aswad by the distinguishing marks he had noted when the boy was first admitted.

* * *

'Good work,' Superintendent Dunman said when he congratulated

Captain Mehmood on finding Aswad's body. 'I'm sorry it ended like this. I just hope we can get a conviction.'

'Surely there is no doubt, sir. That man murdered the poor boy, I'm certain of it.'

'Not in my mind, nor many others, but I'm afraid the evidence is circumstantial. Safar Ali will maintain – indeed, he does maintain – that someone else used the boat to murder the boy. The man who owns the boat lets it out for hire, and it is moored at night by the river without a guard, so anybody could have taken it.'

'But surely everyone knows that it is much more likely that Safar Ali used it – he is the only one with the motive.'

'True enough, but motive does not prove the crime. We will need something better than that.'

'Then I will get something better than that,' replied Captain Mehmood, his brow furrowed in determination.

* * *

'What cell is Zedrin Osman in?' Captain Mehmood asked the duty officer.

'Last one on the left. Do you want me to bring him out?'

'Not necessary – I'll go to him,' Captain Mehmood replied.

The duty officer watched Captain Mehmood with a puzzled frown as he headed down the corridor to Zedrin Osman's cell. He was carrying a length of rope fashioned into a noose.

20

1848

On the day of the trial, which began at nine in the morning, a huge crowd of Malays gathered outside the courtroom, oblivious to the rain that fell in torrents all day. Many of them were relatives and supporters of Haji Safar Ali. At nine in the evening the verdict was declared, and a groan of despair ran through the crowd when the verdict was communicated to them. Haji Safar Ali was found guilty of the murder of the boy Aswad and sentenced to be hanged by the neck until dead one week later at the jail. He had been convicted on the testimony provided by Zedrin Osman, who had turned Queen's evidence, and received a lesser sentence of transportation.

* * *

'Seems too quick and easy a punishment,' Captain Mehmood complained, when Haji Safar Ali was cut down from the scaffold a week later, 'after what he did to that poor boy.'

'In one sense yes, but in another no,' Superintendent Dunman replied. 'His punishment will pursue him beyond the grave, if you'll excuse my bad pun. His family and followers have made preparations for his funeral, which they intend to make into a great public commemoration. But I have instructed Mr Ganno not to release the body to them tomorrow. Haji Safar Ali will be buried in quicklime in an unmarked grave within the prison walls. That is probably the greatest punishment one can inflict upon a Malay, and

I hope the bastard rolls over in his grave. For all eternity!'

As a fellow Muslim, Captain Mehmood was moved to pity for Haji Safar Ali's soul. But he did not remonstrate with Superintendent Dunman over the funeral arrangement.

* * *

In March, George Bonham passed through Singapore on his way to take up his appointments as governor of Hong Kong and plenipotentiary and superintendent of trade in China. Given his generous budget and his years of Singapore experience in keeping costs down, he managed to restrain government expenditures while encouraging the real-estate market, ensuring that the fledgling colony was placed on a sound financial footing. His easygoing personality and his excellent dinners soon won him the respect and affection of the merchants and residents of Hong Kong, as it had formerly done for the residents of Singapore, where many Malays still called Government Hill Bukit Tuan Bonham, or Lord Bonham's Hill.

* * *

On April 1, a cruel April Fool's Day, Joseph Balestier was declared bankrupt, and his sugar plantation at Balestier Plain put up for auction to pay his debts. Many felt pity for the man whose fortune had deserted him so quickly, and when Balestier left Singapore later in the month his friend Governor Butterworth assured him that he took with him the greatest respect and highest esteem of the community. Balestier told his friends and the US State Department that he would return to Singapore as consul after a period of rest and mourning, but he never did. He returned to Washington and managed to persuade the State Department to send him on a roving diplomatic mission to China, Cochin China, Siam and Sumatra, but it was not a success. He was forced to return to Washington much earlier than planned, to answer questions that were raised about his mission by senators hostile to the very idea of negotiating with 'savages'.

Later that month, St Andrew's Church was struck by lightning a second time, since those responsible for the church's upkeep had not learned their lesson and had still neglected to install a lightning conductor. Fortunately, nobody was injured, but the lightning strike caused extensive damage to the church. It ripped mortar off the steeple, roof and walls, destroyed the punkah fans,[xcii] and set fire to the pews and doors. The church was declared unsafe shortly afterwards, and the parishioners removed themselves to the old Mission Chapel on Hospital Road for services, which had to be held twice on Sundays because of its small size. The Chinese and Malays remained clear in their minds about the cause of the lightning strike – the Christian God was angry because not enough heads had been offered in sacrifice. And they were sure of one thing – that more heads would roll!

---

xcii Large swinging fans, fixed to the ceiling, usually pulled by a young Chinese or Malay boy.

21

Abdul bin Suleiman admired police captain Adil bin Mehmood. Abdul had only just joined the police force and was a mere peon. In fact, he was not even an official peon, but was working as an unpaid volunteer in the hope that he would eventually earn himself an official position. One day he hoped to be able to make his mark the way that Captain Mehmood had. The captain was a brave man – he had proved his bravery on numerous occasions – and was very clever, but he also treated his men with dignity and respect, and was modest about his own achievements. Captain Mehmood tried to get the best out of his men and had words of encouragement for Abdul, who strove to do his best for his mentor. When the opportunity arose, Abdul would show Captain Mehmood what he was made of.

One day his opportunity arose. He was on patrol along the upper reaches of Boat Quay when an Indian lighterman called him from his tongkang [xciii] and asked him to come aboard. He went down the steps and strode nimbly across three lighters that were tightly moored together before he reached the lighterman, who was leaning over the edge of his boat with a long pole in his hand. It had a curved hook at the end, which he had used to snag a small bundle floating in the river. As the man pulled it in, Abdul gagged when he realized what it was. It was the remains of a baby, badly decomposed, hanging part way out of a sack. The Indian lighterman was reluctant to bring the ragged bundle on board, but Abdul gently but firmly took the boathook from him, and manoeuvred the child's

---

xciii Light wooden boat used to transport goods on rivers.

remains onto the prow of the tongkang. He bound them up in another sack that the lighterman gladly provided, then carried the sad and foul-smelling bundle to the edge of the Muslim cemetery, where he buried it in a shallow grave. There was no way to know the religion of the child, or whether it had any religion at all, but Abdul knew that God reserved a special place in Heaven for babies and young children.

As Abdul made his way back to the police station he began to think. He had been moved to tears by the discovery of the dead baby, but it had also brought to mind the incident some weeks before when he had helped Captain Mehmood calm a hysterical Chinese woman who had accused an older Chinese woman of murdering her baby. Could this dead child have anything to do with that incident? Might he be able to trace this dead child to the old woman, as his hero Captain Mehmood had traced the remains of poor Aswad's body to the murderous Haji Safar Ali?

He had no illusions. Newborn babies, especially baby girls, were discovered with depressing regularity in the river, along with other human and animal remains. The tiny body was so badly decomposed that he could not tell how it had died, whether from foul play or natural causes – he could not even tell if it was a boy or a girl. It was most likely born to one of the prostitutes in Chinatown or abandoned by some distraught or impoverished mother. Yet he wondered about the old woman who had been accused. She seemed harmless enough, but he had heard of a recent case in which a seemingly harmless old grandmother had poisoned her whole family. And everyone had said that Haji Safar Ali was an upstanding citizen.

* * *

Abdul planned to report the discovery of the dead baby to Captain

Mehmood when he returned to the police station, but the captain had gone off-duty an hour before. Abdul was due to go off-duty himself, but his curiosity was aroused, so he looked up the woman's name in the recorder's book. Her name was Madam Ang, and he remembered where she lived. He decided to take the initiative himself, as he was sure Captain Mehmood would have done in his position. He signed himself out and left the police station, then headed off towards Chinatown.

Dusk was falling as he reached the shophouse where Madam Ang lived with her children. Abdul climbed up the dark stairwell and knocked on the door. The old lady opened the door cautiously. She held a baby in her arms, and said to him in a sharp voice: 'Who are you? Why you come here? Why you disturb my children?'

Abdul explained that he was a policeman, and that he simply wanted to ask her some questions. When he said this, her tone softened, and she invited him into the room. Most of the babies were asleep, although a couple of older children crawled around on the floor. She asked Abdul to take a seat, and to hold the baby for a moment while she fetched them some tea. Abdul was embarrassed, since he had never before held a living baby in his arms, and he did not quite know what to do, except to make sure that he did not drop it. Yet the child seemed happy enough to be held – she gurgled in his arms and looked up at him with her big brown eyes. Abdul began to wonder whether he had made a mistake in investigating Madam Ang – everything seemed normal, and Madam Ang treated the children as if they were her own. The old lady returned with a small tray which she placed on a low table before him. She poured out two bowls of green tea, then took the baby from his arms and sat down opposite him.

'Now, young man,' she said, in a soft voice, so as not to disturb the children, 'what was it you wanted to ask me?'

Now Abdul felt very nervous, and his mouth was dry. He took a sip from his bowl of tea. It was wonderfully refreshing and fragrant and seemed to revive his sense of purpose. He fortified himself with more of the delicious tea before proceeding.

Taking care not to offend Madam Ang, or suggest that she was in way under suspicion, he reminded her of the incident in which the overwrought young woman had accused Madam Ang of murdering her baby, then told her that he had found a dead baby in the river that afternoon. He assured Madam Ang that he did not suspect her of having anything to do with the death of the baby, and that he understood why she could not tell the young woman the name of the family with whom she had placed the baby. But she could tell him, Abdul said, for he was a police officer. He would make sure that the family to whom she had entrusted the baby had not caused it any harm – he would make sure, he finally confided, that they had not mistreated the baby and drowned it in the river.

Madam Ang smiled at him across the table, and nodded her head sadly, as if in wonder at the cruelty of the world. Of course, she could do that she said, for she kept a written record of the names and addresses of her adoptive parents. When Madam Ang said that Abdul was greatly relieved. He felt relaxed, and suddenly, very, very tired. Madam Ang continued to smile and assure him that she had the names and addresses in her book, but she did not get up from her seat to get them. Abdul tried to ask her to do so, but found that his mouth was so dry that he could not speak, and he reached out for his bowl of tea. His arm felt like lead and began to tremble, and then his whole body was torn with convulsions. He tried to rise, but he could not. Madam Ang continued to smile at him, her soft voice murmuring meaninglessly at the edge of his consciousness. Then the poison reached his heart and Abdul died.

* * *

Madam Ang sat watching Abdul for a few moments, until she was convinced he was properly dead. Then she rose from her chair and began to make preparations, after she had put the children to sleep. The dead policeman was small and skinny, but he was too big for her to risk moving, even at night. She lit a fire under her stove and placed two large pots upon it. She pulled out her tin bath and lifted Abdul's body into it. She sat him up in the bath and stripped off his clothes, as if preparing to wash him, but then proceeded to cut his flesh from his bones with a meat cleaver and a sharp knife, and dropped the bloody chunks into the two pots, including the organs and the viscera. She was left with the head and the bones and a bath full of blood. But she did not drink it – she had no taste for the blood of grown men. She ladled it carefully into the pots, making a thick stock for the already browning human stew. She added chillies and some vegetables and rice, then left the pots to simmer. She bundled the head and bones into a sack, and then lay down and slept for a few hours. She woke up, as if by instinct, just after midnight. She left the house and carried the sack to the edge of the mangrove swamp. She added some bricks and stones that she had picked up along the way, to give it extra weight. Then she threw it out as far as she could into the stinking mud and smiled in satisfaction as she heard the ghastly parcel slurp down into the swamp.

When she returned home, she built up the fire once more, and added more herbs to her simmering pots. She washed out the bath and drained her washcloths into the stew. Then she lay down on her own cot and slept like a baby. The following evening, after she had put the children to sleep, she went out into the street and offered plates of her spicy stew to the many starving Chinese paupers and unemployed coolies walking the streets or lying in the five-foot ways. This gained Madam Ang a reputation as a kind and charitable woman as well as a great lover of children.

A few days later the desk sergeant queried Captain Mehmood as he entered the police station.

'Have you seen Abdul bin Suleiman recently, captain?'

'I have not,' Adil replied. 'Why, is something wrong?'

'Signed himself out a few days ago, but not been back since,' said the sergeant.

'I hope he's not given up on us – he seemed such an enthusiastic young man,' said Adil.

'They all are at first,' the sergeant opined, 'until they find something safer and better paid.'

'That doesn't sound like Abdul, but I suppose you never know. Keep your eye out for him, will you, and let me know if he returns.'

A week later Adil asked the sergeant if there was any news of Abdul.

'None, I'm afraid, captain,' replied the sergeant, 'and I doubt any foul play. We've had no reports of bodies or missing persons this last week – almost a record in fact! I suspect he's just found more gainful employment. Like all the others.'

'I suspect you're right,' Adil replied, and thought no more of it.

22

Duncan had become a regular visitor at the d'Almeidas' home, and Marie had become a regular visitor to the Simpsons' home, at first accompanied by one of Jose d'Almeida's daughters as chaperone, but eventually on her own as everyone came to accept the foregone conclusion – that they were deeply in love and would soon be married. Yet Rosalia d'Almeida insisted on a long courtship, so Duncan spent almost a year attending musical evenings at the d'Almeidas', accompanying Marie to operas and theatrical productions at the Theatre Royal in Dutronquoy's London Hotel, and by word and deed doing his best to persuade Dr d'Almeida that he was a man of upright moral character and good financial prospects. On February 14, the anniversary of their first meeting during the fire at Kampong Glam, Duncan proposed to Marie and she accepted. Dr d'Almeida gave his blessing after Duncan, an unenthusiastic Protestant, promised that their children would be brought up in the Catholic faith. Both families were delighted at their engagement and began to make plans for the wedding.

The only person left unhappy at the culmination of the affair was Joaquim d'Almeida. Although Duncan had spent many hours coaching him out in the woods past Mount Sophia, Joaquim had not improved his marksmanship by 'one jot or one tittle', as he put it, quoting Matthew, Chapter 5, verse 18.

* * *

Duncan Simpson and Marie Abreu Melo were married in the Cathedral of the Good Shepherd in June. Father Beurel presided over the ceremony and Dr d'Almeida gave away the bride. The reception was held at Dr d'Almeida's mansion on Beach Road, with Ronnie Simpson providing the refreshments: fresh fruit juices, beer, champagne, wine, brandy and the best malt whisky in the Straits Settlements. As Sarah's sharp eyes roved over the dancing couples, she noticed that Annie, now eighteen years of age and a 'right bonnie lass', as Ronnie put it, was giving most of her dances to Charlie Singer, now an under-manager at Boustead, Schwabe and Co. There was also no mistaking the stolen glances between them.

'Looks like we'll be attending another wedding soon,' she remarked to her husband.

'The mair the merrier,' he replied.

* * *

They fought like cat and dog, over matters great and small. Marie had a fiery temper and Duncan had a strong stubborn streak, and the servants trembled when they screamed and shouted at each other with a ferocity that they feared would lead to murder. Yet their love for each other was so intense that it consumed everything, including their quarrels, and they always ended each fight by drowning themselves in passion in each other's arms. Nevertheless, Ronnie and Sarah heaved a sigh of relief when Duncan announced that they had bought Mr Purvis's old house on Beach Road. They would be close at hand, but out of earshot!

23

On May 25 HMS *Meander* anchored in Singapore, and Captain Keppel and James Brooke were welcomed ashore by Governor Butterworth and the leading officials and merchants, including Ronnie and Duncan Simpson. On June 12 Keppel and Brooke received the mysteries and privileges of the Fraternal Order of Freemasons at 'Lodge Zetland [xciv] in the East' on North Bridge Road, and on August 12 they attended the wedding of Mr Hugh Low and Miss Napier in St Andrew's Church. Keppel called it a 'cheery wedding,' but Miss Napier, having recently survived the rigours of the voyage from Southampton aboard the *Meander*, complained that the motion of the punkah fans in the church made her seasick. On August 15, a supper and ball were held at Government House to celebrate James' appointment as Governor of Labuan, with over one hundred and fifty guests in attendance. The ball went on until after midnight and ended with a spectacular display of fireworks.

Then on August 20 there came the crowning glory. Mr Napier, the lieutenant-governor of Labuan, received the news by royal warrant from Prince Albert that James Brooke was to be created Knight Commander of the Order of the Bath. He was to be Sir James at last! His service and sacrifice had at last been recognized and rewarded.

The ceremony took place in the Assembly Rooms at the foot of Government Hill, which had recently been completed by Mr McSwiney the architect, after funds for their construction had been

---

xciv Shetland (Scotland).

raised by public subscription. They were decorated for the occasion with flags and bunting. The marines of HMS *Meander* formed an honour guard and the ship's band played 'God Save the Queen'. Mr Napier presided over the ceremony, while Mr Hugh Low, secretary to the government of Labuan, read out the royal warrant for the investiture. After a prayer by Reverend H. Moule, the residency chaplain, Mr Napier gave a speech that extolled James' many merits and achievements, and then invested him with the order. Sir James Brooke then gave a short speech in response, in which he expressed his gratitude and pride at being so honoured. Mr Napier hosted a ball in the evening following the investiture, which was well attended. The dancing went on into the small hours, and the ball was considered memorable by many of the attendees. The ball certainly lived on in the memory of Governor Butterworth and his wife. The governor lost his watch at the ball, and Mrs Butterworth had her jewellery stolen while she was absent from Government House.

The following morning Sir James Brooke and his party left for Labuan aboard HMS *Meander*.

* * *

Captain Robert 'Bully Bob' Waterman came out of the London Hotel at three o'clock in the afternoon and decided to take a walk along the Esplanade to clear his head. He had been drinking with the other captains since ten in the morning, and wanted to be back on board his ship and ready to sail with the evening tide. Waterman was a New York opium trader, who ran his light Baltimore clipper ships up and down the coast of China, easily outrunning any armoured junks he came across. Waterman was of slim build, but had a barrel chest and muscular arms, dark hair and eyes, flashing white teeth, and a hawk-like nose. He was a real dandy strutting down

High Street and along the Esplanade in his beaver-skin top hat and Canton silk frock coat, raising his hat to the ladies as he went along – as if he was a Wall Street banker strolling down Broadway. When he reached Scandal Point, he stopped for a moment and looked out at the shipping and native craft in the roads. He watched as a Malay sailing prow skimmed across the water, weaving in between the square-riggers and junks.

'My, but she's a grand wee flier,' he said to himself, rubbing his chin, and admiring the line of her hull as it cut through the water. The next moment he was down on the beach, and wading out to an Indian lighter, his frock coat streaming behind him in the light surf. He asked the lighterman to take him out to the Malay prow, and managed to persuade the crew in his broken Malay to show him over the boat and demonstrate her sail and steerage. He then persuaded them to take him out to his own ship, which was anchored in the roads, and invited them on board. After some delicate negotiations and avowals of sincerity, he arranged to buy the prow for a generous sum in silver bullion. He left three of his crew to take possession of the prow, and when he returned from China with a shipment of tea, he brought it back with him around Cape Horn to Boston.

24

In July, Dr Clark the coroner went out with the police to inspect the body of a dead Chinese man who had been found close to the mouth of the Jurong River. A hard time they had of it, since a group of young Chinese men, who were likely members of one of the secret societies, did their best to prevent them. The police finally drove them away so that Dr Clark could make his inspection, but there was little point to their trouble, for the body was so badly decomposed that Dr Clark could make no determination of the cause of death. He instructed the police to take the body back to the pauper's graveyard, and did not bother to hold a formal inquest.

For some reason this outraged Robert Carr Woods, the editor of the *Straits Times*, who demanded to know why an inquest had not been held and called for an inquiry into the matter. An inquiry was duly held, and in October Governor Butterworth dismissed Dr Clark as coroner and appointed Dr Little in his place. Dr Clark was not sorry to be done with the thankless position he had held for nearly twenty years, on and off. He was ready for retirement and wished Dr Little the best of it. Unfortunately, Dr Little did not have the best of it.

* * *

Dr Little was a popular choice as coroner and did his best to live up to expectations. But he very quickly found himself in conflict with Mr Jackson, the deputy superintendent of police, and Governor

Butterworth. Originally the conflict arose over Dr Little's request – they called it his demand – that court interpreters be made available at coroner's inquests. But the real trouble started when Dr Little refused to allow a jury to hold an inquest into the death of a Chinese man whose body had been taken to Tan Tock Seng hospital at Pearl's Hill, because of the prevalence of smallpox in the hospital. Dr Little advised the deputy superintendent of police – in no uncertain terms – that he would not hold an inquest until the body had been removed to a more suitable place. Mr Jackson responded that it was not any part of his duty to arrange for the transportation of, or suitable accommodation for, dead bodies. Some months later, when Dr Little ordered that the body of a Malay who he suspected of having been poisoned by his wife be taken to the police stables for dissection, Mr Jackson had the body removed and taken to Tan Tock Seng hospital. Dr Little wrote a letter of complaint to Governor Butterworth, stating that he would not tolerate undue interference with his duties. Although the governor had agreed to the creation of a dead house with a separate entrance in the police compound, he wrote a bitter response to Dr Little in which he deplored the unbecoming critical stance that Dr Little had adopted, which was unsuited to the honourable service of his public duty. The governor intimated that he would be obliged to make other arrangements if Dr Little did not adopt a more cooperative attitude.

'Colonel Butterworth! The stuffed-up Colonel Bampot, more like!' was all that Dr Little had to say when he read the letter, although he said it only to himself. But he resigned his position as coroner the very next day.

* * *

W.H. Read continued to complain about the Temenggong's

monopoly of the gutta percha trade. In August he managed to persuade the Chamber of Commerce to send a letter to the governor protesting that Ibrahim's actions constituted a threat to the freedom of the port. Colonel Butterworth doubted that they did, and most of the merchants were won over to Daing Ibrahim's cause when he hosted an extravagant St Andrew's Day dinner at his Telok Blangah compound in November, complete with haggis, pipers and rivers of the best malt whisky – even W.H. was grudgingly appreciative. Most who attended the dinner, including the governor, were impressed with the changes that Daing Ibrahim had brought to the Telok Blangah community. Where once there had only been mean plank and attap huts, there were now neat rows of wooden and brick houses with verandahs, painted white, with green Venetian shuttered windows and red tiled roofs. They generally concurred that at least the Temenggong had spent his profits wisely in improving the lot of his people, in sad contrast with Tengku Ali, whose impoverished and run-down compound at Kampong Glam was a disgrace even to his devotees.

25

Ronnie sat in the waiting room of Dr Little's surgery at the rear of the Singapore Dispensary in Commercial Square. He was very uncomfortable, both from the pain in his groin and his embarrassment at having to bring his case to the doctor. He had managed without doctors most of his life – save for the ship's surgeon who had saved him from bleeding to death from a leg wound at Trafalgar – and thought most of them were quacks.

He had come to Dr Little because the doctor had a reputation for being up to date with the latest advances in medicine and treatment, and, if he was honest about it, to avoid the embarrassment of bringing his case to his friend Dr Oxley. For the past few months he had noticed some discomfort in his lower regions, and then a nagging pain. When the pain had increased he had explored his scrotum with his fingers and discovered the hard mass that seemed to be causing the pain. At first, he dismissed it as some form of internal swelling due to overexertion. He was in the habit of riding his Sydney pony hard in the early morning, but had been forced to give this up because of the pain, and had supposed that the grinding of the saddle must have been the cause. But it was weeks since he had ridden Lucky Lad, and the lump had expanded and was causing him increasing pain – nowadays he was even finding it difficult to walk. Once the size of a walnut, the lump had now grown to the size of an orange and caused him so much pain that there were days when he had to take to his bed. So, eventually, and after much pressure from Sarah, he had decided to visit Dr Little.

He travelled to the Singapore Dispensary in their carriage, supported by cushions, one of which Ronnie carried in with him.

'Good morning, Mr Simpson,' said Dr Little, as he invited him into the surgery. 'What ails you this day – you look fit as a fiddle to me!' Then he noticed the cushion that Ronnie was carrying. He asked Ronnie to describe his problem, and then asked him to drop his breeks [xcv] so he could conduct an examination. As he did so, he appealed to Ronnie as a fellow Presbyterian to support him in his attempt to organize a Presbyterian congregation. Dr Little thought it disgraceful that the many Scots in Singapore were forced to worship in an Episcopalian Church – named after St Andrew, the patron saint of Scotland, for goodness sake! Ronnie did not much care where he worshipped since he was not much of a churchgoer – and it was the same God they worshipped after all – but he humoured the doctor, and said that he would be happy to make a contribution.

'I don't just mean money, Mr Simpson, although of course I'd be grateful for that,' Dr Little responded. 'We'll need church elders and Sunday school teachers and the like.'

Ronnie grunted non-committally as Dr Little told him he could pull up his breeks and take a seat. As he eased himself onto the cushion he had placed on Dr Little's offered chair, he noted the concern on the doctor's face.

'What is it, Dr Little? Can ye get rid of it?'

Dr Little paused a moment and stapled his fingers under his chin, like a man praying.

'Bad news, I'm afraid, Mr Simpson,' he eventually replied. 'You have a growth, very likely a black cancer, in your scrotum. It will continue to grow and cause you increasing pain, and produce ulcers on your groin and rectum. These are not in themselves life-threatening, but eventually the growth will cause internal haemorrhaging, which will kill you.'

---

xcv Trousers (Scots).

'Can't you cut it out?' Ronnie replied, 'I don't mind how much pain it causes – I just want to be rid of it, and be able to ride my pony again in the mornin'. Nae tae mention ...'

'I understand,' Dr Little replied, looking grave. 'I could do the operation, but it would likely kill you quicker than the growth itself. The surgery is excruciatingly painful and impossible to do unless the patient is thoroughly sedated; otherwise the movement would result in fatal wounding.'

'Can't you use opium? Or a lot of whisky,' Ronnie asked, forcing a grin.

'The amount you would need to render you insensitive to the pain would likely kill you, or more likely give me a dangerously drunken patient. I'd be afraid to operate on a man like yourself in an inebriated condition,' Dr Little confessed, as he took in Ronnie's heavy build and flint blue eyes.

'In any case,' he continued, 'even if you could stand the pain, and even if I could sedate you or have men secure you to complete the operation, the shock to your physical system would likely prove fatal – as it has in all the past cases I have known.'

Ronnie sat stony-faced for a few moments, taking it all in. Then he said: 'So, the choice I hae – as I see it and as ye have described it to me – is as follows. Either I choose a lingering and painful death as thon black cancer grows, or choose a quick and painful death if I ask you to cut it out.'

'I'm afraid that about sums it up,' Dr Little replied, 'although the choice is not quite as stark as you describe it. You could live on, perhaps for a year or more, and I could give you laudanum to ease the pain.'

'Some life,' Ronnie grunted in disgust. 'Hardly worth the livin' o'.'

'Indeed,' Dr Little acknowledged, 'and you have some chance of a better life with the operation, albeit a very slim one. However, there is no need to decide today. Go home to your family and talk to them about it, then return to me in a week or two and tell me what you have decided.'

Ronnie thanked Dr Little for his frankness, and said he would think on it. Then he picked up his cushion and returned to his carriage, to make the painful journey home.

26

They were all for him bearing with it and living longer. Sarah assured him she would love him for as long as he lived, whatever affliction he suffered. His father told him jokingly that he would be happy to spend his days pushing him along the Esplanade in a bath chair, and then sharing a glass or two with him at the London Hotel, although he secretly confided to his good friend Captain Scott his awful fear that his son would die before him. But they both knew that Ronnie's mind was already set on the operation, however dangerous it might be. He was not afraid of pain or death, but was horrified at the prospect of gradual debilitation and a lingering death. They knew that he was only humouring them by discussing the options, while he arranged for the transfer of his business interests and revised his last will and testament.

* * *

Ronnie was sitting in his study enjoying the view from his window – bright white clouds floated high in a clear blue sky, as the waves broke softly on the silver beach. How sharp and clear are your senses as you contemplate death, he thought to himself; how fierce the beauty that you ordinarily take for granted. He noted his reaction, but did not dwell on it, as he tried not to dwell upon the increasing pain and discomfort between his legs. He just got on with it, as he always had.

The Malay houseboy knocked softly on the door and Ronnie

gave him permission to enter.

'A message from Dr Little,' the boy proclaimed, in his rapidly improving English (he was being well-taught by Annie's English governess). 'He wishes you to call on him again at your earliest convenience.'

Ronnie was annoyed. Couldn't the man wait until he had made up his mind? Well, he had made up his mind, although it was still a bit of a liberty to be pressing him on it. But he decided he would go that afternoon to see what Dr Little had to say for himself before he passed judgment on his apparent rudeness.

* * *

When Ronnie arrived at the Singapore Dispensary, Dr Little greeted him heartily and shook his hand vigorously. Ronnie remained cautious and sceptical, but took a seat in the surgery and waited to see what Dr Little had to say for himself.

The doctor did not sit down opposite him as before, but paced back and forth behind his desk. Eventually he started talking, but never stopped pacing all the time he talked.

'A rather remarkable thing happened to me the other day, Mr Simpson. Our industrious Mr Dutronquoy, of the London Hotel, asked me to have tiffin with him at his restaurant, where he told me about his new plan to open a hotel for invalids and convalescents, when he has secured a suitable property. He clearly wanted to impress me sufficiently that I would send some of my invalids and convalescents to him, and I told him that I probably would. Then he started talking about one of the Indian doctors he had recruited, who had just arrived in Singapore, and was staying in a room at his hotel. The man had told him about an extraordinary Scottish doctor, James Esdaile – from Perth originally, I believe – who has been working for the East India Company these past years in Hooghly, outside Calcutta. Apparently, he's been using mesmeric techniques to induce insensibility in his patients, both native and European, with remarkable results.'

'You mean that animal magnetism stuff, Dr. Little?' Ronnie interjected, annoyed that his time was being wasted. 'Alignments of the planets and magnetic fluids, and a' that mumbo jumbo. Stuff and nonsense, if you ask me.' Ronnie had taken Sarah and his father to a lecture and performance by a travelling mesmerist and phrenologist – Professor Browning, as he called himself – at the Assembly Rooms, and had not been impressed. 'I hope you're nae recommendin' that we use Indian fakirs to put me into some sort o' a trance. I'm nae havin' that.'

'Wait up, Mr Simpson,' said Dr Little, 'and hear me out. I'm not recommending that, although as it turns out it might not be such a bad idea.'

Seeing Ronnie glower back at him, he continued quickly.

'First off, this Esdaile is a Scots doctor in the India service, not an Indian fakir. Second, he has a consistent record of success, validated by independent surgeons and government officials – he has written a number of papers on the technique, and a book apparently. He's conducted literally hundreds of successful operations on mesmerized patients, including over a dozen with scrotal tumours. Dr Leslie assured me of this personally, since he attended one of the operations.'

'Ah, I see I have your interest, Mr Simpson!' Dr Little declared, now standing facing him from behind his desk, his hands grasping the back of his chair. 'Oh, I have to admit I was as sceptical as you were at first, but I should have known better. It's not only Esdaile who has been using mesmerism to induce anaesthesia. Professor John Elliotson of University College, London and my own Professor Gregory at Edinburgh University are both champions of the technique, although I'm afraid it cost Elliotson his job at the

University Hospital – many of my colleagues are even more sceptical about it than you or I. But I've been looking into the matter, and rereading the reports and critiques, with more care than I did before. What seems very clear is that the phenomenon is real. The techniques employed do seem to put people into a painless dream or trance state, enabling the surgeon to operate without danger. There is plenty of evidence for this – the fraud comes from inflated explanations about the transfer of magnetic fluids, clairvoyance, and communication with the dead. Forget all that claptrap and you have a well-established natural phenomenon that does a power of medical good, whatever its natural explanation. I suspect my colleague James Braid may have the best explanation for it. He thinks it's a form of deep nervous sleep induced through suggestion, so long as the patient is willing to temporarily abandon his will to the surgeon. He calls the state hypnosis, after the Greek for 'sleep', and says it has nothing to do with magnetism, animal or otherwise. And getting back to fakirs, that's probably how they manage to walk on fire and pierce themselves with needles and hooks, apparently without pain. They must put themselves into a deep sleep or trance.'

'Well, I don't know about that,' Ronnie replied cautiously, 'but I'm a practical man, Dr Little, and if a thing has been shown to work, I'm willing to give it a try.'

'Spoken like a true empiric!' said Dr Little, finally taking his seat, and grinning from ear to ear. He had not known how Simpson would take his news and was relieved to find him finally agreeable.

'Of course, we would have to test the procedure on you to see if you are a suitable candidate.'

'How would you do that?' Ronnie asked.

'Och, man, that's easy,' Dr Little replied. 'We just apply the techniques and then see if you respond to pain. We pinch you hard, stick pins into you, put a few drops of sulphuric acid on your toes, that sort of thing. If you don't yell and protest, we've succeeded; if you do, we've failed!'

'Doesn't seem too dangerous,' Ronnie said. 'All right, Dr Little, I'm game whenever you are.'

'You're right about that, Mr Simpson,' Dr Little replied, 'but I'm duty-bound to tell you about another means of inducing painless sleep that my colleagues back home claim is more medically reliable than mesmerism. Some have been using the inhalation of ether vapours to bring about the same result, and they predict that such treatments – which have recently been sanctioned by the Royal College of Surgeons – will quickly displace mesmeric techniques, at least among properly qualified physicians.'

'But is it as safe as mesmerism?' Ronnie asked, noting the hesitation in the doctor's voice.

'Aye, weel, there's the rub,' Dr Little responded. 'The correct dose is difficult to estimate, and it takes special training to get it right.'

'Well, answer me this,' said Ronnie, 'has anybody been harmed by ether inhalation?'

'I'm afraid so,' Dr Little replied. 'Some were brain damaged, and a few are reported to have died, although the physicians employing the method were not properly trained.'

'And how many have died as a result of being put into nervous sleep, as you call it?' Ronnie asked him.

'None I know of, Mr Simpson, and James Braid says it is perfectly harmless,' Dr Little replied. 'He used it on all his family, including his children, who all reported a very refreshing sleep.'

'That's decided then, Dr Little, let's try the mesmerism first. Just dinna tell anybody else aboot it, at least nae until we see if it's successful or no.'

'As you wish, Mr Simpson. I will arrange for an experimental session with Doctor Leslie. I am sure Mr Dutronquoy will oblige us with a private room, so we will have no need to worry about prying eyes. I must confess I'm eager to observe the procedure myself, and see what all the hullabaloo is all about!'

27

Later that week Ronnie travelled to Dutronquoy's hotel. Dr Leslie, who met him in the lobby, told him that Dr Little and Dr Innis, who was also interested in observing the procedure, had already arrived, and were waiting in the private consulting room that Dutronquoy had provided. Ronnie noticed that Dr Leslie had beautiful hands, with long, slender fingers.

'I've ordered some refreshments for them, since the procedure may take a bit of time. It depends on you really, Mr Simpson.'

'What do you mean by that?' Ronnie asked, as Dr Leslie led him to the consulting room.

'Well, the most important thing for you is to relax, and not to fight me,' Dr Leslie replied. 'To put it plainly, Mr Simpson, for the purpose of this experiment, you must abandon your consciousness and will to my own.'

When they entered the consulting room, Ronnie greeted Drs Little and Innis. Dr Leslie asked his colleagues to darken the room by closing the shutters, and then asked Ronnie to take off his coat and shirt and lie down on the camp bed that had been set up in the middle of the room.

'As you wish,' said Ronnie, as he lay down on the camp bed, 'but what do you want me to do?'

'Just close your eyes, and breathe easily, while I pass my hands over you. Don't be concerned – I will not touch you, at least not until the time comes when we are ready to test you.'

'Go ahead, then,' Ronnie said, leaning back and closing his eyes.

Dr Leslie leaned forward and with palms open, passed his hands over Ronnie's head and face, down his chest to the pit of his stomach, and then back to his face and head, always keeping his hands about half an inch from Ronnie's body, and breathing gently on his head and eyes. As first Ronnie could feel them close to his face and the faint breath of air on his eyes, but eventually he ceased to notice as Dr Leslie repeated the procedure over and over, occasionally whispering in Ronnie's ear, while Drs Little and Innis stood by, both with puzzled looks upon their faces.

* * *

Ronnie woke to the snap of Dr Leslie's fingers and his command: 'Awake, Mr Simpson!' He opened his eyes, but could see nothing but darkness all around.

'I'm blind, Dr Leslie!' he exclaimed, with panic in his voice. 'I can't see a damn thing! What have you done to me?'

'Don't worry, Mr Simpson, just rub your eyes gently, and be patient – your sight will soon return. You have just been in a very deep sleep, and it will take a moment to come out of it.'

Ronnie did as he was told and within a minute his sight had returned to normal, to his great relief. He sat up and saw Drs Little and Innis standing before him, both grinning sheepishly like conspiratorial schoolboys.

'Well, did it work?' Ronnie asked them.

'Unless you're the hardiest trickster Scot I know, I'd say it worked, Mr Simpson,' Dr Leslie assured him. 'We stuck pins in your hands and put a knife under your nails. We slapped your face and gave you a glass of vinegar to drink, which you happily quaffed. Then to be absolutely sure, we put a little sulphuric acid on your pinkie, but not even a flutter of your eyebrows did we get in response. What do you remember?'

Ronnie looked down at the blackened tip of his pinkie, which was now beginning to nip vigorously.

'Nothing at all,' Ronnie replied, 'except for laying back on this bed a few moments ago.'

'About an hour ago, Mr Simpson,' said Dr Leslie, triumphantly. 'I'd say you were an excellent subject, and so long as you bear with me, I'm sure we can get you through your operation safely without pain.'

'I'm amazed, truly amazed,' said Dr Little, and Dr Innis nodded in agreement.

'No near as amazed as me,' Ronnie responded, rising from the bed and shaking Dr Leslie's hand in gratitude. Then he stretched like a contented cat.

'Strike me down if I lie, but I dinna think I've slept so well in years. I feel like I've been floatin' on a bed of feathers. I think it has also eased the pain in my groin. Could that be true, Doctor Leslie?'

'Undoubtedly so, although I'm afraid the effect will wear off now you're back in the land of sensibilia, as I'm sure you've noticed with respect to your pinkie.'

'Aye, indeed,' Ronnie replied, 'but I can bear that little tickle any day. So when can we schedule the operation? I'm rarin' to go!'

Dr Little frowned and cautioned him not to be so headstrong.

'There is still reason for concern, Mr Simpson. You may lose a lot of blood and there is always the danger of putrefaction. So, you should still take care to put your affairs in order before we go ahead. If you don't mind, I suggest we do the surgery in your own house, sir. It saves us having to move you after the operation, and you have some fine airy rooms facing the sea, I believe. But we could do it here or at the Dispensary if you like.'

'No, I think I would prefer to have it done at home, Dr Little, just in case something does go wrong. If I'm going to die, I'd prefer to die in my ain hame. But let's nae be so gloomy, and let's get the thing done as soon as we can – sometime next week, if possible. God, it does me good just to think I hae a chance to be rid of it.'

'Aye, hope is sometimes as good a tonic as anything,' concurred Dr Little. 'But now I'm beginning to sound too much like a true mesmerist for my own liking, even though I'm sure there's some sort of truth in it.'

Ronnie thanked them all again, and they arranged to do the operation at Ronnie's house the following Friday, with Dr Leslie in attendance to induce the nervous sleep. As he left to depart, Ronnie had a final question for Dr Leslie: 'One last question, Dr Leslie. If you were able to bend my will to yours when I was in deep sleep, couldn't someone use this mesmerism or hypnoses to evil ends? Couldn't they use it to seduce women, or make someone steal or murder for their own purpose?'

'Undoubtedly so, Mr Simpson,' Dr Leslie granted, 'for like every great power, it can be used or abused. But beyond its medical uses, it can also be used to help people overcome their greatest fears and rid them of addictions, or so Professor Elliotson has claimed.'

'No doubt the sort of claim that lost him his job,' Dr Little interjected, 'but we can debate the merits and demerits of the technique after we have seen Mr Simpson safely through his operation. He might even invite us to his lovely home for a regular discussion after he has made a complete recovery, as we sincerely hope he will.'

'Ye can depend on it,' said Ronnie, 'and I'll supply the grog in case the debate slackens! Good day to you all, gentlemen.'

He pulled on his shirt and coat and despite the pain between his legs, positively strode out of Dutronquoy's hotel.

28

The family wanted him to wait until after Christmas and New Year to have the operation, but Ronnie would have none of it. As he told them, he did not wish to spend what might be his last Christmas and Hogmanay [xcvi] on this earth in miserable pain, and he was confident that Dr Little and Dr Leslie would bring him through. Drs Innis and Oxley were also going to be in attendance as observers, so he felt he was in good hands. His affairs were in order, and he was anxious to proceed as soon as possible.

It was agreed that Dr Little would perform the operation at eleven o'clock on December 15, giving Dr Leslie a few hours to put him in a deep sleep. Dr Leslie arrived in Ronnie's home at nine in the morning, as arranged, where he received the well wishes of his family.

'And how are we feeling this morning, Mr Simpson?' said Dr Leslie, with a cheerful grin, as he entered the sea-facing room that had been prepared for the operation. The window shutters were closed to darken the room, but a gentle breeze drifted in between the partially opened slats. Drs Little, Innis and Oxley followed close behind, accompanied by a hospital orderly that Dr Oxley had brought along to assist in the operation. They all knew there was going to be a lot of blood, but they were all hoping that with Dr Leslie's help there would be little or no pain.

'Ready and rarin' to go,' said Ronnie, sitting up in bed to greet them but grimacing at the pain of it. 'I didna get much sleep last

---

xcvi Scots for the last day of the year.

night, so I'm hoping tae do better today.'

'I hope so too,' replied Dr Leslie, as he eased Ronnie back on the bed, and helped to remove his nightclothes. Then he began to pass his hands over his head, face and upper body, moving his long fingers to within a half inch of Ronnie's frame, while blowing gently on Ronnie's face and eyes. Now and again he would whisper words close to Ronnie's ear, but none of the other doctors could hear what he was saying, and they wondered whether Ronnie could. Eventually Dr Leslie seemed satisfied that his patient was deep in nervous sleep, but he was taking no chances, and proceeded to pierce Ronnie's naked body with long sharp pins, which he also stuck beneath his fingernails and toenails. When these elicited no response, he told Dr Little he could proceed, and they turned Ronnie over on the bed.

* * *

The operation took two hours, but went well, at least to the satisfaction of Dr Little. He had little difficulty in removing the tumour from Ronnie's scrotum, since he did not flinch or fight, and responded to what they knew would be excruciating pain to a conscious man with barely a sleepy murmur. Ronnie lost a lot of blood, and his pulse was weaker, but he remained stable as they bandaged him and gently turned him over on the bed, with cushions beneath him for support. Sarah had engaged a nurse, who Dr Little instructed on how the bandages were to be changed. He told her that he would visit his patient every day until he was satisfied that Ronnie had made a full recovery.

They were all feeling very pleased with themselves, and amazed by the fact that Dr Little had been able to perform this difficult and dangerous operation without interference from the patient. The doctors began to imagine other forms of surgery in which this mesmeric technique might prove useful, including the possibility of relieving the pain of childbirth. Dr Little then advised Dr Leslie to revive Mr Simpson, so that he could give him some laudanum to deaden the residual pain.

* * *

Dr Leslie went to the head of the bed and snapped his fingers over Ronnie's face.

'Awake, Mr Simpson!' he cried out.

Ronnie did not open his eyes. He did not say a word. He did not move a muscle.

'Awake, Mr Simpson! Awake! Awake!' Dr Leslie cried louder, clapping his hands together above Ronnie's head, and then next to his ears.

But Ronnie lay motionless and unresponsive upon the bed.

Dr Leslie then tried working backwards, passing his hands over Ronnie's body from his stomach to his head, blowing softly on his face, and whispering in his ear. To no avail.

'What have you done to him?' cried Sarah, who had come into the room upon learning that the operation had been a success. 'What have you done to my husband? Will he ever wake again?'

She looked at Dr Leslie and saw the anxiety in his face.

'I don't know, ma'am,' he replied. 'I don't know for sure. Most people come out of a nervous sleep pretty quickly, but an extended dormant period is not unknown. But please do not worry, the sleep can do him no harm.'

Yet Dr Leslie was worried, and she could tell it from his face. Dr Little intervened to try to provide some reassurance.

'Let's not be unduly concerned at the moment, Mrs Simpson. First, let's look on the bright side. Your husband has survived the operation, and admirably well. He's lost a lot of blood, but we've staunched the bleeding, and his pulse is stable, if somewhat weaker than normal. That is only to be expected of any man whose body has gone through the strain of such an operation, even if he did not experience the pain of a normal man – and it's a blessing that he did not. But his body is in traumatic shock, and it's not surprising that he remains unconscious. This form of deep sleep is the body's natural way of healing, I believe, so I don't think we should be so surprised that Dr Leslie can't wake him yet. Give him some time to recover, and make up a room for Dr Leslie, so he can be on hand when Mr Simpson shows signs of waking. And you can send a message for me at any time if things take a turn for the worse. I suggest we just let him sleep for the moment and see how things work out. Just make sure you give him some water now and again – you shouldn't have any trouble, since he will retain the swallowing reflex, and you might try a little thin soup.'

They all agreed that this was the sensible course of action, but they all had their doubts and questions, including Dr Little and Dr Leslie. For they all knew that they had entered uncharted territory, and could only wait and pray that their patient would return safely to them.

29

The passage out had been a smooth one so far. They had left the harbour and picked up fair winds that had borne them northeast into the South China Sea. The schooner skimmed across the ocean like a heron skimming across a lake, and he felt calm and contentment in his heart.

Yet now he could see the storm approaching. Heavy cumulonimbus clouds were forming up ahead, and slowly rotating, like some giant Catherine wheel bearing steadily down upon the ship. The wind howled at gale force and blew out the mainmast sails and the mizzenmast rigging. The schooner rose and dived as the sea reared high on either side, like great black mountains of water rising to hide him from the wrath of God. Lightning forked upon the water, flashing silver white over the monstrous black waves. It was what the Chinese called a tai fong, or great storm. A typhoon.

He was heading straight into it, and there was nothing he could do. If he tried to turn the schooner she would be swept over, and even if he succeeded, he knew he could not outrun the storm. He ordered the men to cut away the sails and the rigging, but as he watched them moving like condemned souls in the darkness, the gale took the masts and rigging overboard, and swept the men from the deck into the pitiless sea.

Now he was alone at the tiller, as the banks of spindrift whipped over the tops of the waves and blasted the deserted deck. He stood alone as the lightning crackled, the wind howled and the spray whip-lashed his eyes and face, and he knew that he was heading to his doom. Then suddenly the winds that had been driving before him leapt behind and drove the ship with the force of a cannon blast deep into the black wall of death.

A great whooshing sound – and then silent darkness as he drifted down deeper, deeper, ever deeper into the everlasting night.

* * *

Dr Leslie tried to wake him again in the evening after the operation. He snapped his fingers, he clapped his hands and he stuck pins into Ronnie's hands and feet. In his desperation he lit a match under his right hand, but it had no effect. Ronnie was gone from the conscious world of sensation.

When Dr Little returned the next day and there was no change, he began to worry. He suggested that Sarah sit by his bed and talk to him, perhaps read him some of his favourite poems by Robert Burns, in the hope that the familiarity of her voice might rouse his memory. She did as he requested, but Ronnie did not stir to the sound of her voice, or to the voice of his father, or Duncan, or Marie, or Annie or any of the servants. John Simpson asked Dr Innis to play 'Scotland the Brave' on his bagpipes, which he did, very loudly and very badly. John Simpson had thought that it was surely enough to waken the dead, but it did not waken Ronnie.

* * *

Slowly, very slowly, the darkness receded and he floated through an ocean of white light, borne by a gentle wind. Then the light faded and he slipped back into the black depths. He thought he heard the murmuring of voices, the whispering of leaves in the breeze, the lake waters gently lapping on the shore. Then the empty silence engulfed him again. He felt his nerve endings tingling like tiny bells, as if swept gently by rushes or feathers. Then he felt nothing at all, like a hollow man floating in empty space.

* * *

Seven days passed, and they were at their wits' end. Dr Leslie had searched the medical reports of Dr Esdaile and Dr Elliotson, but there was no mention of anyone placed in a hypnotic trance who had not recovered from it. Except, Dr Little pointed out, intending to comfort Dr Leslie, who was clearly blaming himself for the outcome, when the patient did not recover from the operation at all. But that did not comfort any of them as they watched over Ronnie Simpson. They all suspected that his brain could have been damaged by the trauma of the surgery, and that he might remain a sleeping vegetable for the rest of his days on the earth.

Oh Ronnie, Sarah thought to herself, this is the last outcome you would have wanted – you would rather have died!

John Simpson poured himself another large shot of whisky, and as he raised his glass to his lips, he said absent-mindedly: 'Perhaps we could try givin' the boy a wee dram?'

They all looked at him with mild reproof.

'I thocht ye'd never ask,' said a hoarse voice from the bed, as Ronnie raised himself up and rubbed his eyes. 'I need something strong – my arse hurts like hell!'

The doctors were so dumbfounded that they did not consider whether it was a good idea to give whisky to a man who had been unconscious for nine days, and Sarah ran to him and flung her arms about his neck.

'Welcome back, my darling. And Merry Christmas!'

'That means it will soon be Hogmanay,' Ronnie grinned at her. 'Now where's that dram!'

30

1849

James Brooke received news that his old enemy Mahkota was agitating in Brunei and that Sherip Muller had returned from Dutch Borneo and was rousing the Saribus Dayaks to rebellion once again. They had been raiding up and down the coast and had killed scores of peaceful Malays, including some who lived close to Sarawak. James wrote to Duncan saying he believed that he had cornered the evil Prince Mahkota at last and urged him to join Captain Wallage on the company steamer *Nemesis* when it left Singapore in July, bringing reinforcements to join him in Sarawak. Duncan wrote a quick reply assuring him that he would. He had no particular desire to join yet another expedition against Dayak pirates, but Mahkota was a different matter altogether. As he explained to his wife, Mahkota was a matter of honour and revenge, and she understood when he told her why.

* * *

After the New Year celebrations, Hong Xiuquan and Feng Yunshan returned to Guanlubu, because Hong's earthly father was close to death. When his father died, Hong was gratified to learn that his earthly father requested to be buried not in accordance with traditional Confucian or Buddhist rites, but in accordance with the rites of the God-followers. The traditional Confucian rites required that Hong refrain from cutting his hair and shaving his head during his three years of mourning. Hong did not feel bound by this requirement, but now he viewed the prohibition in a different light. Since the Qing dynasty had displaced the Ming dynasty two centuries ago, they had mandated that all men follow the Manchu practice of shaving their forehead and braiding their remaining hair in a long queue reaching down their back. Those who refused to comply were branded as rebels, a crime against the kingdom that was punishable by death.

Hong did not shave his head, and let his hair grow long and unbraided, so that it flowed down his neck and over his shoulders. One day when Feng Yunshan saw him he declared: 'Hong Xiuquan! You look like the pictures of your brother Jesus, the ones circulated by the foreign missionaries, who are now free to evangelize in all the regions of China. You are truly the son of God.'

Feng Yunshan let his own hair grow long and unbraided and did not shave his forehead. After bidding farewell to their families, Hong Xiuquan and Feng Yunshan set off once again for Thistle Mountain. But this time they went not only as redeemers and devil-slayers, but also as rebels against the Manchu.

31

Much to James' delight, Captain Wallage arrived with the *Nemesis* in July, with Duncan on board, as part of an armoured squadron commanded by Captain Farquhar, which included HMS *Albatross* and *Royalist*, James' old schooner. James met him in the *Rajah Singh*, accompanied by eighteen Sarawak war canoes and fifty more Dayak and Malay war prahus. James had heard that the Saribus pirates were raiding the northern coastline, and decided to spring a trap at Batang Marau, at the mouth of the Saribus River. There he hoped to capture Prince Mahkota, who was reported to be with Sherip Muller. With the native prahus positioned to the south, the *Albatross*, *Royalist*, *Rajah Singh* and *Nemesis* blocked the mouth of the river and waited for the pirates' return.

* * *

One week later, the large Saribus pirate fleet passed Batang Marau as dusk was falling. It was a bright moonlit evening, and the leading Saribus prahus spotted the blockade at exactly the moment that Duncan spotted them entering the river and sounded the alarm. Captain Farquhar gave the order to alert the Sarawak prahus by firing off rockets and flares, which cast an eerie blue light over the waters as the pirate prahus tried to force entry into the river. The battle raged for five hours, and the Saribus pirates fought with great courage, but were driven back by the superior firepower of the British gunships. When they turned around to make a dash for the open sea, they were blocked by the Sarawak prahus, which had come up and encircled the mouth of the river. As the pirates foundered in the trap, the *Nemesis* drove among them, her paddles thrashing and heavy guns blazing, like some dreadful monster of the night, spitting red death in the pale blue moonlight. As the pirates leapt overboard to try to save themselves, they were shot at close range by the marines or cut down in the water by the Sarawak Dayaks and Malays. Captain Farquhar's force destroyed over one hundred prahus and killed over five hundred pirates, with only a handful of European and Sarawak casualties. Captain Farquhar proclaimed a great victory over the enemy, but Duncan was appalled by the wholesale slaughter. This was not a noble engagement of arms, or the fierce hand-to-hand fighting of the Skrang River, but an obscene massacre by a technologically overwhelming force. He did not fire off his rifle or his pistol, and as he watched the broken bodies of the pirates floating in the ghastly moonlit sheen of human blood on the water, he vomited over the side of the *Nemesis*.

James Brooke had taken no part in the battle, having been confined to his cabin with a recurrence of malarial fever. Flushed with their victory, Captains Farquhar and Wallage conferred with him over the fate of the hundreds of pirates who had run their prahus ashore and escaped into the jungle. Captain Farquhar was eager to pursue them and send Captain Wallage and the *Nemesis* up the river to cut them off – they were worth a potential fortune in prize money for their capture or death. But Rajah Brooke would have none of it. The Saribus had learned their lesson, he assured Farquhar, and they should be left to spread the word of their own annihilation in battle. Besides, he pointed out to them, the jungle was deep and dense, and only the Saribus knew the pathways. They were likely to get lost or ambushed if they tried to pursue the pirates, and it would be a great shame for the expedition if they were to snatch defeat from the jaws of victory.

James asked Duncan if they had captured or killed Prince Mahkota and Sherip Muller. Duncan told him that he did not know, but knew in his heart that he no longer cared. He would not take part in such wholesale slaughter again, not even if there was a certain chance of finally running Mahkota to ground. He told James as much, before boarding a supply ship that was returning to Singapore.

* * *

Munshi Abdullah never returned to Malacca to join his wife, but stayed on in Singapore with his four sons, his only and beloved daughter having died in 1836 at the age of eight. He continued to serve as a private Malay tutor to European businessmen, but devoted most of his time to teaching in the Reverend Keasberry's Malay School, and working with him for the Mission Press. Aside from merchant bills of lading and government proclamations, they published Malay folk tales and legends, and Abdullah helped Keasberry produce Malay translations of the Bible. On Keasberry's suggestion and with his help, Abdullah had begun to write out his own life story, based upon diaries he had kept from the age of fourteen. Towards the end of the year the Mission Press published his memoirs, the *Hikayat Abdullah*, the Autobiography of Abdullah. Reverend Keasberry set the elaborate lithography for the work, which described Abdullah's early days in Malacca with Tuan Farquhar, with Tuan Raffles on the Java expedition, the founding of Singapore, the discovery of the Singapore stone, the departure of Raffles and Farquhar, and the residency of John Crawfurd.

32

By late summer, there were different groups of God-worshippers spread out across the hills and valleys of Thistle Mountain. These were hectic times for Hong Xiuquan. In addition to preaching and writing, he oversaw the printing of religious tracts, the assembly of arms for local defence, and the stockpiling of grain and other food supplies. He also travelled frequently between the different groups, to maintain authority and moral discipline, and to adjudicate the claims of those who claimed to be possessed by the spirit of the Heavenly father or Jesus. He deemed the claims of some to be genuine, and those he welcomed into his family, but in other cases he had to exorcise the devil spirits that had been sent by the demon-king through public beatings and occasional executions.

Up until this time, Hong Xiuquan had always been vague about the nature of the demon-devils he condemned. Sometimes he directed his ire against the slaves of the devil King Yan Luo; sometimes against the Confucian ancestor-worshippers; sometimes against the Taoist and Buddhist priests; and sometimes against any non-believers in God and Jesus. Now he proclaimed loudly and often that the demon-devils were the Manchu rulers and the officials and nobles who supported them, and that it was the duty of the God-followers to destroy them forever.

As a result, Hong Xiuquan aligned himself with and attracted many members of the Heaven and Earth Society, who were also devoted to the overthrow of the Manchu. Hong likened himself to the founders of the Han and Ming dynasties, who had risen from humble beginnings to overthrow great tyrannies. Hong was committed to the overthrow of the Qing, but unlike the Heaven and Earth Society, he had no intention of restoring the Ming, but instead aimed to create a new world order of Heavenly Peace on earth. Yet from this point onwards, Hong Xiuquan was on a collision course with the man who considered himself the son of heaven, the Emperor Tao Kwang.

In November, Hong Xiuquan learned that his earthly wife had given birth to a son. Hong named him Tiangui Fu, the Precious One of Heaven. He sent word to Hong Rengan to arrange for his family to join him on Thistle Mountain, since their lives were now in increasing danger. Hong Rengan sent them off at dead of night with an armed escort – and in the nick of time, for Qing troops were raiding the villages searching for the family and followers of Hong Xiuquan. After he had seen them safely on their journey, Hong Rengan bade farewell to his own family, and set off to join Hong Xiuquan on Thistle Mountain, but found he could not penetrate the Qing lines. It would be eight years before he would see his cousin Hong Xiuquan again.

* * *

In November, news of the Battle of Batang Marau, as Captain Farquhar's expedition against the Saribus pirates came to be called, reached the British press. At first there was celebration of Rajah Brooke's great victory, but then doubts began to be raised about whether the Saribus really were pirates, and questions asked about what the overpaid governor of Labuan was doing taking part in an engagement three hundred miles from his constituency.

Robert Carr Woods published an editorial in the *Straits Times* on September 10 about the Battle of Batang Marau that was highly critical of Sir James, and which questioned the legality of the whole campaign:

'The Rajah believes, or professes to believe, that a horde of irreclaimable pirates have established themselves on a river in the vicinity of his territories at Sarawak. He is too well acquainted with human nature to know that the Borneans will, to gratify him, relinquish at one and the same time the indulgence of piratical and all other wicked propensities. He therefore offers a compromise – "Some of you," we fancy we hear him exclaim, "have a fancy for plundering vessels; others prefer burning villages, and cutting off human heads to be smoke dried and hung up as ornaments in their houses. Now piracy is really intolerable; nor can I say much in favour of the house-burning and head-smoking; but all of you who give up piracy may cut off and smoke as many heads and burn as many villages as you please."

'Our Singapore correspondent expresses just indignation at the thought of the India Company's steamer *Nemesis*, at present hired for the Queen's service, having taken part in the decapitating and head smoking expedition of Rajah Brooke and his allies.'

Copies of Wood's editorial were widely circulated among the liberal critics of colonialism in parliament. The Peace Society and the Aborigines' Protection Society campaigned against the 'fiendish atrocities' committed by British force of arms. Captain Mundy, an enthusiastic supporter of James Brooke, incautiously published an unexpurgated edition of James' journal that included horrific passages in which he seemed to positively gloat over the destruction of his enemies. Lord John Russell, the Prime Minister, who had always been a supporter of Rajah Brooke, began to have his own doubts. The slaughter at Batang Marau was beginning to weigh heavily upon the public conscience, and even Lord Russell had to admit that for an enlightened patriarch Sir James Brooke had killed an awful lot of Borneans.

* * *

By the end of the year patients had finally begun to be admitted to Tan Tock Seng Hospital and Poor House for the Relief of All, which had been completed three years previously. During the interim the diseased paupers, beggars and vagrants for whom the hospital was intended had been housed in a series of attap sheds at the foot of Pearl's Hill. Their condition was only marginally improved with the opening of Tan Tock Seng Hospital, since the engineer had neglected to install a water supply. The patients had to perform their ablutions in the puddles in the grounds behind, or in the swamp facing the hospital, which also served as the town's rubbish dump. From its inception the hospital was overcrowded, the population in need being far greater than the accommodation provided for them, and conditions deteriorated further as more and more patients were admitted. Although Tan Tock Seng had transferred ownership of the hospital to the East India Company, the Company did not provide the anticipated funds for its maintenance, whose cost continued to be borne by public donations. Tan Tock Seng's eldest son, Tan Kim Ching, donated two thousand dollars for additional buildings and additional money for regular maintenance. The small Parsee community donated one thousand dollars, and Syed Omar Bin Ali Al-junied, the Arab merchant, donated the annual rents from his properties in Victoria Street and Arab Street. While some gave money, others donated in kind. Thomas Dunman, the superintendent of police, donated the fighting cocks that he confiscated from illegal gambling dens, so that the poor and sick of all nations could have a chicken dinner every now and then.

33

1850

As a Justice of the Peace and respected member of the Chinese merchant community, Tan Tock Seng had hoped to play a major role in the celebrations welcoming James Andrew Broun-Ramsay, the Marquis Dalhousie and the Governor-General of India, on his official visit to Singapore in February. The governor-general had come to acquaint himself first hand with the economic prospects of the port, and it was important to ensure that he heard the Chinese side of the story, and particularly the need for government support for the poor and the sick. Unfortunately, Tan Tock Seng himself became ill and was too incapacitated to play any role in the ceremonies, although the governor-general did visit Tan Tock Seng hospital and donated a thousand rupees for its upkeep.

The Singapore merchants raised a subscription to finance the erection of a white marble obelisk commemorating the visit of the Marquis Dalhousie, which was designed by John Turnbull Thomson, and erected at the mouth of the river at Dalhousie Ghaut, which was the name given to the pier at which he came ashore. Marquis Dalhousie was so impressed by the commercial success of Singapore and the expressions of civic loyalty he received that on his return to India he removed the administration of the Straits Settlements from the Bengal Presidency, and brought it under his own direct control as governor-general of India.

About a week after Marquis Dalhousie departed, Tan Tock Seng died. Taoist priests from the Thian Hock Keng Temple led the funeral procession through the streets, where people of all races and stations in life came to pay their last respects to one of the richest Chinese merchants in Singapore who had devoted himself to the welfare of the least of his countrymen. Tan Tong Seng Hospital at the foot of Pearl's Hill remained the living memorial to the life of this good man.

Tan Tong Seng was survived by his wife, Lee Seo Neo, a wealthy landowner whose extensive land holding included the Sri Geylang Ayer Molek coconut plantation at Geylang, and by his three sons and three daughters. Tan Tock Seng left his wife and three daughters thirty-six thousand dollars each, and his landed properties to his sons. His eldest son Tan Kim Ching took over his father's business, which he renamed Kim Ching and Co, and also his father's offices as head of the Hokkien clan association and chairman of the management committee of the Thian Hock Keng Temple. In the years that followed, Kim Ching donated additional sums of money to Tan Tock Seng Hospital, both for new buildings and general assistance, and continued his father's tradition of providing proper burial and funeral ceremonies for the poor and the sick.

* * *

In March Mr Joseph Hume, the Liberal member of parliament from Montrose, and Richard Cobden, the Radical member from West Riding, raised questions in the House of Commons about the morality and legality of Sir James Brooke's actions in Borneo, and the authority by which he had used the ships of the British Navy against vastly inferior native forces. Matters came to a head over the thirty thousand pounds of bounty money that Captain Farquhar had claimed as reward for the Saribus pirates killed or captured during the battle of Batang Marau, which the House had to approve. Many considered this to be obscene, given the gross imbalance between the naval strength of the combatants – a fact that Hume exploited to the full.

James Brooke did not stand to profit by the bounty money, since he had no official naval appointment, but Cobden managed to assign him guilt by association and innuendo. He questioned the actions of the gentleman called Brooke – the 'sometimes styled' Rajah Brooke of Sarawak – against those disputative neighbours who he had decided to call pirates. He had waited for his declared enemies in the darkness at the mouth of the Saribus River with ships of Her Majesty's Navy, and when the native boats had come into view he had not called for them to surrender or communicated his own intentions to them. Instead, Cobden proclaimed, Sir James had fired a broadside of shot, canister and rockets into them, so that they were unable to resist or defend themselves:

'The English steam-vessels of war were then driven among the boats, and the miserable creatures were crushed under the paddle wheels and annihilated by hundreds in the most inhumane manner.'

Cobden concluded his attack on James Brooke with biting scorn for the hypocrisy of those who claimed to bring the blessings of Christian civilization to the native peoples:

'After this mighty feat of valour had been performed, they came to a Christian assembly and demanded twenty pounds a head for slaughtering the unhappy wretches.'

Some government supporters responded that there was plenty of evidence that the Saribus who had died in the battle had been pirates, and were cheered by some of their colleagues, but this only provided further fuel for Cobden's fire. Where was the evidence?

– and more to the point – where was the evidence that they had ever molested an Englishman or a single English ship? There was none, Cobden declared. These were innocent men who had been murdered for bounty money.

The navy bounty funds were finally approved. Yet the damage had been done, and there were further questions in the House, public meetings, and calls for an inquiry into the Batang Marau affair – even demands for the trial of Sir James Brooke, the 'sometimes-styled' Rajah Brooke of Sarawak.

* * *

In April, the old Emperor Tao Kwang died and his fourth son Hsien Feng became the Son of Heaven, the new Emperor of China and All Under Heaven. Hsien Feng was only nineteen years old when he ascended the Dragon Throne, but his pasty face and emaciated body already displayed the symptoms of debauchery and perversion, to which he had been introduced at an early age by the palace eunuchs, who managed his life in the inner sanctum of the Forbidden City in Peking. They had carefully nurtured his promiscuity and bisexuality, which had matured into a sexual obsession with a young actor who impersonated female characters. Hsien Feng had married as soon as he came of age, but his first wife, the Empress Xiao De Xian, had died childless, and he was obliged to honour the twenty-seven months of official mourning for his father before selecting a new bride.

* * *

Charlie Singer and Annie Simpson were married on Sunday, April 16, in the Assembly Rooms, since the old Mission Chapel on Hospital Road was too small to hold the invited guests. The reception was held in Dutronquoy's London Hotel, after which close friends and family returned to Ronnie and Sarah's home on Beach Road. Ronnie had made a complete recovery and was hugely enjoying himself – he was gratified to have survived and seen his two children married. As they looked on with approval at the recently married couples, Sarah turned to Ronnie and said:

'Well, that's them both married. What next?'

'Bairns, I hope,' Ronnie replied, 'bairns!'

* * *

After Charlie and Annie Singer returned from their honeymoon in Siam, Ronnie, with his father and son's agreement, invited Charlie to join Simpson and Co as a junior partner. Charlie was delighted to accept their offer and gave his notice to Boustead, Schwabe and Co the next day. Edward Boustead, who had indulged himself mightily at Charlie's wedding reception and was still recovering from it, was sorry to see him go, but he wished Charlie well and waived the customary period of notice. Later in the year Edward Boustead retired to England, where he set up a new company, Edward Boustead and Co, to oversee his offices in Hong Kong, Manila, Shanghai and Singapore.

34

Father Beurel was gratified by the completion of the beautiful Cathedral of the Good Shepherd, which he hoped would lend respectability to his mission in Singapore and make his superiors at the Society of Foreign Missions in Paris take his efforts more seriously. He had great plans for the expansion of the Catholic mission on the island, and the personal resolve to see them to fruition. As he wrote to one of his former teachers in Paris, he considered the conversion of the Chinese of critical importance, since he believed that they would eventually become the dominant population in Singapore – they were already the most numerous race, comprising just over fifty percent of the population. Father Beurel raised funds and contributed a considerable amount of his own private means to establish community churches throughout the island, such as Father Maudit's St Joseph's Church at Kranji.

Father Beurel's new goal was to establish Catholic schools in Singapore. He thought that it would be a good idea to convert the old chapel on Hospital Road into a Catholic school for boys. He contacted the Superior General of the Institute of the Brothers of the Christian Schools in Paris,[20] asking for four brothers to come out to Singapore to establish a school in the converted chapel.

Father Beurel also wrote to Reverend Mother de Faudoeas, Superior General of the Institute of the Charitable Schools of the Holy Infant Jesus, at Saint Maur in Paris.[21]

In his letter to the Reverend Mother, Father Beurel extolled the virtues of a Christian education for young women and the desperate lack of teachers in the Far East. Father Beurel, who had a reputation in Singapore and with his superiors in Paris as a direct and forceful advocate, ended his letter with the blunt request:

'We want nuns. Will you give me some?'

* * *

As the port continued to prosper, the waterfront and Singapore River became increasingly congested, as cargo was carried to and from the merchant godowns by fleets of lighters. The congestion was exacerbated with the arrival of steamers, including the regular Peninsular and Oriental (P & O) Steamship service, which required the transportation of coal from storage bunkers on shore. To relieve the congestion, a number of companies started building shipping wharfs, docks and coal bunkers at New Harbour, the deep-water anchorage between the mainland and Pulau Belakang Mati [xcvii] and Pulau Brani, [xcviii] which had been recommended by Captain Keppel – and earlier by Captain Ross and Colonel Farquhar – as the safest and most secure anchorage close to the town. Jardine Matheson and Co had built their own private wharf at New Harbour in the early 1840s, which they used to transfer the Royal Mail to Shanghai in their own faster vessels. In 1850 they built a coaling station at their wharf to accommodate their new steamers – they had been one of the first companies to employ steamers in the Far East, having commissioned the *Jardine* as early as 1835. Other firms quickly followed suit. The P & O Steamship Company built a coal store and depot at Tebing Tinggi [xcix] in 1852. The British Navy built their own store on Pulau Brani in 1853, and that same year the Patent Slip and

xcvii The Back and Beyond of Death. Present day Sentosa Island.
xcviii Island of the Brave.
xcix Outcrop of land at the edge of New Harbour.

Dock Company opened the first dry dock at Pantai Chermin.[c] Other companies such as John Purvis and Son and the Borneo Company quickly followed Jardine Matheson in establishing private docks, wharfs and godowns, as the steamship traffic moved westward from the river mouth towards Tanjong Pagar and Telok Blangah.

35

Father Beurel's prayers were answered. The superior general of the Institute of the Brothers of the Christian Schools agreed to send four brothers to set up the school for boys, and the Reverend Mother de Faudoeas of the Institute of the Charitable Schools of the Holy Infant Jesus agreed to send some nuns. On October 28, Father Beurel left Singapore for France, to organize the travel arrangements for the brothers and sisters, and to accompany the sisters on their journey to Singapore.

* * *

Duncan and Marie were as happy in their love for each other as they were on the day they had first met, save for one sad lack in their otherwise satisfied lives. They had been married for over two years, and notwithstanding their two years of passion, Marie had failed to conceive a child. She prayed every night to God to forgive her sins and bless her with a child. She went to Mass every Sunday at the Cathedral of the Good Shepherd and repeated her prayer. Yet she remained barren. Sometimes it nearly broke her heart, and it broke Duncan's heart to see her so. Yet she was a strong woman, and strong in her faith: she was still young, and told herself she must be patient. But both of them found it hard to hide their own private sorrow when they heard that Annie Singer was pregnant.

* * *

Marie-Justine Raclot was born on February 9, 1814, in Suriauville, a village in the Vosges département of northeastern France. Her parents, Francois and Charlotte Raclot, were farmers, and Marie-Justine lived with her brother Joseph and her grandfather in their modest stone house looking out over rolling green hills and meadows. She loved going to the local church on Sundays, and dreamed of giving her life to God. When she played with her dolls in the garden, she would dress them in nun's habits made from pieces of black and white cloth she had sewn together, and led her imaginary sisters in songs of praise that she composed herself. She was careful to hide her dolls from her mother, who had made it very clear that she did not want Marie-Justine to become a nun. Charlotte Raclot wanted her daughter to marry into a good family, who would help to support their farm, and give her grandchildren to comfort her in her old age. One day when she found Marie-Justine singing to her dolls, she asked her what she was doing. Marie-Justine replied that she was singing to the Chinese people she had made, who grandfather had told her always dressed in black and white.

When she turned twelve, Marie-Justine was sent to a boarding school run by the Sisters of the Holy Infant Jesus in Langres, a town a few miles from her home. The disciplined life of the convent school suited her nature, and she became even more attracted to the religious life. She felt her vocation lay as a missionary in the Far East, but although she desperately wanted to become a sister in the order, she did not dare tell her parents out of fear of their response.

On her return from boarding school, she worked on the farm and did some charitable work with the poor and sick of Suriauville, and eventually summoned up enough courage to tell her parents that she wanted to become a sister in the Order of the Holy Infant Jesus. Yet at the last moment her courage failed her, and she persuaded her cousin Victor to tell them instead, while she waited beneath the pear tree at the bottom of the garden. A few minutes later, her father found her in the garden and embraced her. With tears in his eyes, he said to her:

'My beloved daughter, if this is what your heart desires, you must follow the path to which God calls you. Go with him, my precious one.'

Yet her mother never accepted nor forgave her decision. She refused to talk to her daughter ever again, and would not even bid farewell to Marie-Justine when she left to become a postulant at the convent school in Langres. After two years in the novitiate in Paris, Marie-Justine consecrated herself to God as Sister St Mathilde in March 1835.

For the next seventeen years she taught in a variety of convent boarding schools, where she demonstrated her ability to manage even the most unruly charges, and gained a reputation as a dedicated and successful teacher. Yet deep in her heart she still yearned to be a missionary in the Far East. When she heard that the congregation was planning to set up a convent school in Malaya, she prayed to the Virgin Mary to intercede on her behalf, and began to prepare herself by sleeping with the windows closed on summer evenings, buried under heavy woollen blankets. She was deeply disappointed when she was not included in the Malayan mission, but she continued to serve her students and her mother superior with the same dedication as before.

* * *

When James Brooke first heard about the attacks by Hume and Cobden in parliament, he was amazed. He thought he had finally achieved what he had set out to achieve – a peaceful and prosperous Sarawak, where former pirates now swore honest allegiance to their Rajah and to Her Majesty the Queen. Yet now they were questioning his judgment! Then he dismissed the complaints against him as a joke, so mean-spirited that it was beneath his dignity to concern himself with them. In the end he felt betrayed, as his hero Raffles had been betrayed by the board of directors of the East India Company.

James determined to return to England to answer the charges against him, and left his nephew John Brooke Johnson Brooke, also known as Brooke Brooke,[22] in charge of Sarawak. On route he stopped off in Singapore, where he complained to Governor Butterworth about the behaviour of Robert Carr Woods, the editor of the *Straits Times* who had written those scathing articles about the battle of Batang Marau. He was not pleased to learn that Woods had recently been appointed Deputy Sheriff in Singapore. James demanded that the governor fire Woods, which he politely declined to do.

'Damn the man!' James exclaimed. 'I'll see him in court!'

'You may get your chance, Sir James,' the governor replied. 'I believe Mr Woods is organizing a petition demanding a parliamentary inquiry.'

James arrived back in England in May, where he immediately set about defending his reputation.

36

1851

In early December the previous year, a Qing expeditionary force had advanced upon Thistle Mountain from the northwest, having heard reports of armed military training from their spies and from some of the local gentry. Hong Xiuquan had sent out his best-trained troops to circle around the Qing force and attack them in the rear, killing about fifty Qing soldiers and wounding many others. The battle had finally been joined with the demon-devils, and the 'Old One' – the folk-name that the God-worshippers had given to their God – had granted them their first victory.

In January Hong Xiuquan destroyed a much larger Qing force that had been sent to revenge the defeat of the expeditionary force. Hong Xiuquan now knew that his time had come and that there was no turning back. Shortly after the Chinese New Year, he publicly donned robes of Imperial yellow and announced to his followers the beginning of the first year of the Taiping Heavenly Kingdom.

* * *

Then one day in February, Marie's prayers were answered. She discovered she was pregnant, and her discovery was happily confirmed when she visited Dr Little in Commercial Square.

'You're very definitely pregnant, Mrs Simpson,' he advised her. 'You are also young and in very good health, so I don't anticipate any problems with the birth. Nevertheless, you ought to take care of your health for the sake of the baby. No food or drink in excess, a little exercise but nothing too strenuous.'

'I will be a paradigm of moderation and will confine my exercise to shopping in your brother's department store,' she laughed in reply.

That night there was a celebration at Duncan's home on Beach Road. Marie was a paradigm of moderation, but except for Annie Singer, who was also pregnant, the others were not. Old John Simpson had to be put to bed in their spare room, suffering from a surfeit of champagne and whisky.

37

Father Maudit was at his morning prayers at St Joseph's Church in Kranji village when the Chinese boy came running in, sweating from head to toe and breathless from his exertions. He was a servant of Fang Ah Chon, a wealthy Hakka with a number of pepper and gambier plantations not far from the village. Fang was a recent convert who had made a generous donation to the church.

'Tuan Maudit – they are killing the children of God, and destroying the plantations! You must flee for your life, my master says, or they will kill you too!'

Father Maudit gave the boy some water to drink, and tried to calm his fear.

'A shepherd of the Lord does not abandon his flock, and must die for them if it is God's will,' he assured the boy gently.

'But how is Ah Chon? Is he safe? How are the others of my flock?'

The boy told him what he knew, which was but little, since his master had sent him to warn Father Maudit as soon as the gangs of armed men had come out of the jungle and begun to attack his workers – the boy did not know if Fang Ah Chon had survived or not. When the boy mentioned the armed gangs, Father Maudit asked him if they were secret society members, but the boy only trembled in response.

'Then let us go and see,' he told the boy, taking him by the hand and leading him out of the cool darkness of the church into the bright sunlight and humid heat of the morning.

They did not have to go far. On the path leading to Fang's plantations they came upon a dozen or so Chinese men armed with swords, spears and knives, who blocked their way. The leader of the group, the smallest in size but a hard-looking man with knotted muscles and scars on his arms and face, told them they were holding Fang Ah Chon as a hostage. They would kill him if they did not pay his ransom of one hundred dollars.

Father Maudit told the man that he did not have such an amount, but said he would do his best to gather what he could from among his parishioners. The man told him to send the boy with the money at sunset. If the ransom was paid in full, the boy could return to the church with Fang Ah Chon; if it was not, both of them would be killed and he would return with his men to burn Father Maudit's church to the ground. With that, the men turned around and made their way back the way they had come. Father Maudit had no doubt they were society men.

Father Maudit went back to the church to see what money he had. When he counted it he found that he had just over forty dollars – more than he thought he had, but much less than the robbers had demanded. He knew he had to act quickly. He travelled west to the estates of Tseng Pin Shung, an hour's trek through the jungle, but when he arrived there he came upon a scene of horror and devastation. Tseng Pin Shung had been brutally murdered – he had been hacked to pieces outside his bungalow, as had most of his plantation workers, save for one man who had been badly wounded but was still alive. Father Maudit recognized the man as one of his poor parishioners. They tended to him as best they could – the boy brought him some water and Father Maudit gave him the last rites.

Father Maudit knew that he ought to stay and arrange a Christian burial for these men, but the needs of the living were more pressing – he had only a few more hours to raise the money for Ah Chon's ransom. He continued inland, only to find the same scenes of death and devastation at the other plantations he visited, and his heart sank in his breast. The society men seemed intent on massacring all his Christian brothers. Then, as he circled back towards Kranji village and his church, he came upon Chang Jun Mun, another plantation owner who was fleeing through the jungle towards the Bukit Timah Road, accompanied by some of his workers carrying bags of gambier and pepper. The man was too frightened to stop and talk for long, but agreed to give Father Maudit thirty of the eighty dollars he had managed to carry away in his cash-box. He was ruined, Chang Jun Mun said, and he would need the rest of his money to survive.

Father Maudit thanked him gratefully, then headed back towards his church. The sun was sinking low in the sky, and he knew he was running out of time; he had no hope of raising any more money today. So, when he returned to the church, he gave the boy the seventy dollars he had and added the only item of value he possessed – a small silver candlestick that he kept buried in waxed wrapping paper in the corner of his bedroom, which he kept for special ceremonies. He said a quick prayer and asked the Lord's forgiveness, and then sent the boy on his way with the money and the candlestick.

* * *

The sun had long set and the boy had still not returned. Father Maudit was not unduly concerned at first, for the plantation was about half an hour distant and Fang Ah Chon was probably traumatized by his ordeal, so he did not expect them to return quickly. When another hour passed, he became concerned; when yet another hour passed, he became alarmed. He decided to wait one more hour before investigating himself; it was a clear night, with a shimmering silver moon against a blue-black canopy of stars.

He was deeply troubled about another matter. Normally his parishioners would visit the church in the evening. Some would come to pray, some to beg for a little rice, some to ask his advice, and some occasionally to make a donation. But tonight, nobody had come. Were they killing all the Christian farmers and workers? Were they killing all the Christians on the island? What was happening in the town, and to Father Beurel and his flock?

When another hour passed without any sign of Fang Ah Chon and the boy, Father Maudit, anxious and impatient, set off to investigate. He armed himself with a stout stick that he used to protect himself against snakes, although he knew it would be of little use against the society men. He reached Fang Ah Chon's plantations around midnight. They were silent and deserted. Father Maudit expected the worst, and his worst expectations were soon realized. The plantations had been destroyed – the gambier and pepper plants had been cut to pieces and their roots torn out. The bodies of the coolies lay in little ragged and bloody patches among the ruined plants. As he approached Fang Ah Chon's bungalow, he blinked his eyes in horrified disbelief. But his eyes were not deceiving him, for in the ghostly blue moonlight the three severed heads impaled upon stakes greeted him with their hideously contorted grins and lifeless staring eyes. They were the heads of Ah Chon, his mistress and their servant boy. Their dismembered body parts lay scattered all around, save for the woman's breasts and their sexual organs, which were displayed in a grotesque and obscene combination. Father Maudit fell down on his knees and retched the watery contents of his stomach – he had eaten nothing all day save for a little rice for his early breakfast.

There was nothing he could do, and nobody to help him. He decided to return to his church for the rest of the night, then try to catch a fishing boat in the morning to take him round the island to the town. He did not know if the government or townspeople knew what was happening in the north of the island, or whether the massacre had extended to them. If they did not, he ought to warn them, and he certainly needed their help. When he arrived back at his church, he knelt before the simple bamboo altar and prayed for the many souls who had died that day. He was dog-tired, and when he finished praying he lay down in front of the altar and fell fast asleep.

* * *

He woke suddenly in the pale hour before the dawn. He heard the harsh voices outside and the tramping of many feet. He crawled away from the altar and hid between two plank pews. They offered little protection, but he was less exposed than before. He strained his ears to hear what they were saying. He thought he heard them saying that they should leave some men at the church to catch the Christians when they returned, although he also thought he heard them talking about killing the Hakkas. He knew it was no use trying to reason with them now and wondered if they would dare to kill him also – he supposed that would depend upon the extent of the rebellion. He knew that if any of his parishioners did return to seek shelter in the church he would have to try to save them, although he also knew that his efforts would be futile. He decided to remain hidden and bide his time – if he revealed himself now, they would probably kill him and he would be of no use to anyone.

38

The thin light of dawn crept in through the open windows and gently flooded the dirt floor of the church with golden dust. Father Maudit inwardly marvelled at the simple beauty of the morning amid such horror. He stretched his limbs gently to avoid them cramping and kept a wary eye out for scorpions and snakes, which seemed to love the dark warm places of his church. He could still hear the society men chattering and moving about outside, but could not make any sense of what they were saying. He was surprised that they had not entered the church and wondered why. Maybe these superstitious society men were afraid to enter or to interfere with a holy man – if so, he might be able to use their fear to his advantage.

Suddenly a shot rang out, followed by another. Both came from close by, so the society men must have fired them. Father Maudit rose quickly and dusted himself down. They must be firing at some of the farmers or workers and he must go and try to save them. He must be the good shepherd as best he could. But then he heard more shots coming from the south, in repeated volleys. He ran to the door and saw the society men fleeing into the jungle, only occasionally turning to fire off their muskets. He stepped out of the church and into the sunlight, oblivious to the danger of the balls whistling by, and was overjoyed to see about fifty sepoys and smaller groups of Europeans and police peons firing at the society men, and pursuing them to the edge of the jungle. He thanked God and went forward to meet them.

'Good morning, Father,' said Lieutenant Jenkins, who was the officer in charge of the sepoys. 'Sorry to wake you so early, but I trust you're grateful for our company! We've been chasing these fellows all over the island – Superintendent Dunman and Sergeant Hale have arrest warrants they're hoping to serve on some of them. Are you all right? Have you been injured or threatened?'

'I'm all right, although I have been threatened,' Father Maudit replied. 'But far worse, these society men have been killing all the Chinese Christians who live and work at Kranji. I paid a ransom to try to save Mr Fang Ah Chon, but they killed him and his mistress and workers, and all the plantations around here seem to have been destroyed. What is going on? Has the trouble spread to the town? Is it just the society men, or is there a general Chinese rebellion?'

'Fortunately not,' said Thomas Dunman, who had come up with Captain Kraal. Captain Kraal was the captain of the steam gunboat *Charlotte*, which had landed armed men at Kranji to provide support for Dunman and his police peons.

'We had a bit of trouble last night when they attacked Sergeant Hale at the Bukit Timah police station, when we were out serving warrants and trying to retrieve property, which is why we brought along Lieutenant Jenkins and the sepoys. We also have about fifty convicts searching the jungle for them. You're right – they're mainly society men. I've talked to the governor and Mr Read to see if we can't get some of the leading Chinese merchants to help put a stop to it.'

'In the meantime, I think you should come back to town with us, Father,' said Lieutenant Jenkins. 'It's too dangerous to stay here, and we have many more warrants to serve. We'll be a day or two searching the jungle and expect we'll be in for a few more scrapes before we're finished. We were attacked a couple of times on the road, although they break off pretty quick once they've tasted our hot lead. But they're still on the rampage, and we think it likely they'll have killed a few hundred coolies before we can put a stop to them.'

'I will remain here, and you need not fear for me,' said Father Maudit. 'My fate is in God's hands. But why are they doing this? Are they only killing Christians? Or only Chinese Christians?'

'Looks like it,' said Thomas Dunman. 'I'm not exactly sure why, but I suppose your conversions pose a threat to the societies. They lose their membership and dues, and they cannot count on your converted Chinese to lie for them as witnesses in court.'

This was partly true, but in a sense almost incidental. Dunman knew that the real problem was much deeper and long standing, although it had only recently come to a head. The original pepper and gambier farmers, including those who had farmed the interior of the island before Raffles and Farquhar had landed and those who had expanded the trade in the two decades following, were Teochews, either plantation managers or town financiers. Things had worked out well for them in the early decades because the system of informal short leases had suited their particular form of cultivation – the pepper and gambier exhausted the soil within ten years, and they had to keep moving further and further inland to clear new patches. Yet because of the much-vaunted promise of other forms of agriculture, such as cotton, coffee, sugar, nutmeg, coconut and pineapple, which the European merchants were particularly enthusiastic about, in the late 1830s the government had introduced a system of land registry with longer leases, including a new system of land taxation. This had driven many Teochews out of business, because they could not afford the new leases or the new taxes, for the profit margin on pepper and gambier was very slim. This had bred considerable resentment, but the real poison in the mix was the development of new pepper and gambier plantations that had been made possible by the extension of the roads from the town to the north of the island – the Bukit Timah Road had been extended all the way to Kranji, in sight of Johor, and a new road had been built to Seletar in the north-east. Close by these new roads were new plantations that had sprung up on land that had practically been gifted to Hakka Christians by Governor Butterworth, who was impressed by their religious fervour as well as their enterprise. These new plantations had been financed by Hokkien merchants who controlled the agricultural export trade.

The root cause of the rioting was the threat to the Teochew managers and financiers, and they were using the Ghee Hin kongsi to combat the threat in the only way they knew, by destroying the new plantations and killing the workers. That was why all the trouble erupted on plantations recently developed by Hakka Christians, close by the new roads – at Serangoon, Bukit Timah, Bookah Khan, Lauw Choo-Khan, Nam To Kang, Chan Chwee Kang, Kranji, Propo and Benoi.

Yet he knew it was pointless to explain this to those around him, or to the governor and the chamber of commerce when he returned to town. The Hokkien merchants would of course do their best to calm the situation, since it was in their interest to do so – but it was the pursuit of their own interest that was largely to blame for the trouble. And now they had a ready-made justification to petition the government for the protection of their property and the suppression of the Ghee Hin. They knew they would win in the end – they had the money, the support of the European merchants and consequently the government, and they had their own membership in the Ghee Hok society. The prevalent rumour that the Teochews and the Ghee Hin were indiscriminately slaughtering Christian converts because of a supposed threat to their criminal activities played directly into the hands of the Hokkien merchants – it would bring the righteous vengeance of the government down upon their enemies.

Dunman and Lieutenant Jenkins took their leave of Father Maudit and returned to town with their prisoners, and those farmers and their property they had managed to save. As they made their way back down the Bukit Timah Road, the society men, who suddenly emerged from the jungle making a great din by beating their gongs and drums, attacked them from the front and the rear. But they quickly dispersed when the sepoys fired into their massed ranks, and in the immediate confusion that followed Dunman sent his best officers to rush out and seize the society leaders just before the sepoys gave them a second volley, after which they usually fled back into the jungle. Only once did the society men make a concerted stand, when an older man, with white hair but with the muscular frame and vigour of a young man, forced them to stand and fight. But they fled once again after a musket ball took him in the head.

When they reached the Bukit Timah police station, they handed over their prisoners, and then spread out across the island to serve their search warrants and rescue those beleaguered managers and workers who had managed to escape the Ghee Hin. Within a week they had brought the situation under control, with the help of Teochew merchants from Malacca such as Seah Eu Chin and Wee Ah Hood, who had some influence with the Ghee Hin. The ringleaders were tried and those found guilty were either executed or exiled. But the society men had inflicted a heavy price – they had destroyed twenty-seven plantations and killed nearly five hundred men, most of whom were Christian converts. And the tensions between the factions remained.

Father Maudit saw to the burial and prayers for the dead, but did not continue with his mission at Kranji. Many of the plantation managers and workers were dead, and those who had survived told him that they did not wish to remain in such a dangerously isolated location, where most of the workable land had already been exhausted. They were going to start new plantations in Johor, or closer to town, near the police station at Bukit Timah. So Father

Maudit also moved inland, and rebuilt the Church of St Joseph's at Bukit Timah the following year.

39

In May, Annie Singer gave birth to a healthy baby girl, whom Charlie and Annie named Sarah Jane, after their own mothers. Marie was due in another three-month's time. She looked the picture of health, but Duncan fussed over her like a clucking hen. He was filled with joy at the prospect of his own child, whether it be a boy or a girl, he did not care. There was plenty time to make up the difference.

One morning in early June, as he went to kiss his wife goodbye before heading to the office, a small frown crossed his brow when he saw that Marie was also preparing to go into town.

'Is everything all right?' he asked her. 'Are you sure you ought to be going into town, rather than resting here at home? Or are you going to see Dr Little again?'

'Don't fuss, my darling,' she replied. 'I went to see Dr Little last week, and he assured me I was perfectly fine. But I want to get out – I'm going to be cooped up at home soon enough. I'm going into town with Marianne d'Almeida to buy some things for the baby – do you want to meet us for tiffin?'

'I'm afraid I can't, Marie,' Duncan replied. 'I have a business meeting with the local manager of Jardine Matheson – I want to pick his brains about the merits of opening a branch of Simpson and Co in Hong Kong, something my father has been thinking about for some time. But are you sure you should be buying baby things before the baby is born?'

'Bah!' she exclaimed, 'that's just an old Scots superstition!' Which it was, albeit one that reflected the grim reality of the dangers of childbirth in Scotland and Singapore.

'Off to work with you, before I lose my temper!' she cried. And then she kissed him hard on the lips before he left.

* * *

A few minutes later Marianne d'Almeida arrived in her carriage. As the two women headed towards town, Marianne happened to comment on the simple beauty of the Armenian Church and wondered if Marie had seen inside it. When Marie answered that she had not, Marianne insisted that they visit on their way to John Little and Co, and instructed the syce to stop on Hill Street opposite the church.

'It's not as grand as the cathedral, but it has its own modest charm,' Marianne assured Marie.

* * *

When Duncan returned from tiffin with Mr Levinson, the Singapore manager of Jardine, Matheson and Co, he was surprised to see Dr Little and his father waiting outside his office. When they came forward to meet him, he could see from their faces that something was dreadfully wrong.

'Dr Little, what has happened!' he cried out. 'Has something happened to the child? To Marie? For God's sake man, what is wrong!'

'I'm very sorry, Duncan,' Dr Little replied, 'so dreadfully sorry, but I'm afraid your wife has met with a horrific accident. She ... and your child ... are both dead.'

Duncan howled like a wounded animal, a man cut to the very depths of his soul. He fell down on his knees and began to cry in great gulping sobs, as Dr Little explained to him the circumstances of the accident. Marie and Marianne d'Almeida had stopped off to visit the Armenian church, but as they were crossing Hill Street, a buffalo pulling a Kling cart had broken free of its traces and had charged towards them. Marianne had tried to pull Marie to safety, but the buffalo had gored her in the stomach, and she and her baby had died from loss of blood before Dr Little could reach them. Thomas Dunman had arrived and shot the buffalo dead, but not before it had gored Mr Catchick, the Armenian priest, who had come out of the church to try to help Marie. But they were all too late to save her.

Duncan suddenly roared and leapt up from the ground and swore that he would kill the Kling whose buffalo had killed his wife. But Ronnie held him fast. Although he was much older than his son, he was still much stronger, and he held him tight until Duncan admitted that killing an innocent Kling would not bring her back. He agreed to return to his house with his father to wait for the undertaker.

* * *

That night, as he stood before her coffin, and saw the colour gone from her beautiful face and the light gone from her loving eyes, he felt that his life had come to an end. He had never known such happiness as he had known with her, and knew he would never find that happiness again. She was gone from his world forever, along with his unborn child. In his sorrow he thought of killing himself, but could not move himself towards it. For what was the point? he thought to himself. I am already dead.

40

In August, Hong Xiuquan announced to his ten thousand followers that they had to leave Thistle Mountain. He told them to cast aside their doubts and fears and follow him to the earthly paradise. Catching the Qing forces unawares, the God-followers broke through their lines and headed northeast toward the walled city of Yongan, which they reached before the pursuing Qing columns could catch up with them. The God-followers scaled the walls of the city carrying coffins over their heads to protect them from the enemy fire, and captured the city after a fierce fight in which they slaughtered the eight hundred troops of the Qing garrison. Hong Xiuquan immediately issued a declaration to his followers prohibiting them from looting.

A few days later Hong Xiuquan announced the inauguration of a new calendar, the traditional mark of legitimacy for a new regime, to mark the beginning of Taiping time. The new calendar, which had been drawn up by Feng Yunshan, was based upon ancient Chinese cosmology, but also included Sabbath days of prayer and rest. Hong declared himself the Sovereign and Heavenly King of the Taiping, and named his five most trusted generals as subordinate kings: Yang Xiuqing, the voice of God, was named the East King; Xiao Chaogui, the voice of elder brother Jesus, was named the West King; Feng Yunshan, who had first assembled the God-followers on Thistle Mountain, was named the South King; Wei Changhui, whose family had devoted their fortune to the Taiping cause, was named North King; and the nineteen year old Shi Dakai, who had already proven his military worth, was named Wing King. Together they would exterminate the demon-devils in great battles, and crush their leader, the Manchu devil Hsien Feng.

The capture of Yongan gave the Taiping army time to reorganize their military units, and for Hong Xiuquan to prepare them spiritually for the fight ahead, through a series of specially printed moral and religious texts. Yet the Qing would give them no respite. Although the ranks of the victorious Taiping army had grown to twenty thousand God-followers, they found themselves under siege by over forty thousand regular Qing troops and local militia. By the spring of the following year the Qing had built a fortified wall that completely encircled the city, cutting off all food, supplies and reinforcements.

* * *

In December Captain Robert 'Bully Bob' Waterman arrived in Singapore on the *Staghound*. Waterman had taken the Malay prow he had purchased in Singapore back to Boston, and shown it to Donald McKay, the Boston shipbuilder. McKay incorporated the design in his new fleet of 750- to 1,500-ton clipper ships, with their long low hulls and massive amount of sail, which cut the sailing time from New York to San Francisco round Cape Horn from one hundred and fifty-nine to ninety-seven days. The year after he had watched the Malay prow skimming across the water in Singapore, Captain Waterman had taken the *Sea Witch*, with her main, fore and mizzen-masts carrying five tiers of sail, from Boston to Hong Kong in seventy-four days, a new record.

The *Staghound* was another extreme clipper that had been built by McKay the previous year. She was at that time the largest ship in the American merchant marine, and her design had also been based upon the Malay craft that Bully Bob had transported back to Boston. He celebrated by drinking a bottle of champagne on the verandah of the London Hotel, and watching the graceful prows cut across the harbour.

41

Ronnie and Sarah were worried about their son. Duncan carried himself through the funeral with stoic dignity, and did not shed a tear as his wife and unborn child were laid to rest in the Christian cemetery on Government Hill. He returned to work a few days later and carried on his business as usual. But he no longer laughed. He no longer joked. And he no longer smiled. He dutifully visited his parents and grandfather, he paid his respects to the d'Almeidas, he dined with his sister and brother-in-law, and agreed to be godfather to their daughter Sarah Jane. But they could see that the spirit had gone out of him, and that he went through life like a somnambulist, attending to his business without caring for anything at all. While others walked in bright sunlight, he walked in shadows. While others lifted their hearts to the sweet song of the mata puteh [ci] bird, his heart sank like a stone in his deep, dark pool of despair. Ronnie tried to talk him into meeting with Dr Leslie, who had hypnotized him during his surgery. Leslie and Dr Little had heard that some physicians in Europe had used the same technique to relieve the pain of deep psychological trauma, from which Duncan was clearly suffering. But Duncan refused to see him, saying that there was no cure on earth for the pain he suffered.

They worried because he sat night after night alone on his verandah, staring out over the ocean, as the rays of the setting sun splashed golden streamers over the rolling surf, until the darkness fell and the silver moon and stars sparkled overhead. He must feel

---

ci White eye in Malay.

so terribly alone, they thought to themselves. They did not know that on these nights he did not feel so alone, for each night as he sat on the rattan sofa on the verandah, Marie came and sat with him as he stared out over the ocean, her hair still raven black against her white skin, her pale lips drawn into a thin sad smile. Duncan knew his pallid vision was not real, but it gave him an ounce of comfort in his otherwise empty world. Yet his heart broke all over again when her image faded and the hard darkness of the night embraced him.

PART FOUR

A CRAZE FOR NUTMEGS

1852 – 1854

1

1852

Reverend Mother Lucile de Faudoas selected Reverend Mother St Paulin to head the group of Sisters of the Holy Infant Jesus who would travel with Father Beurel to Singapore. She accompanied them from Paris to Antwerp, where they set sail for Singapore on *La Julie* on December 6. The voyage did not go well. A great storm arose in the English Channel the day after they left and they came close to shipwreck, despite their fervent prayers. They met rough seas once again as they rounded the Cape of Good Hope, and the following month all five sisters were confined to their cabin with fever.

Mother St Paulin never recovered. Near the end of their gruelling five-month journey, she died on March 29, as *La Julie* passed by the south coast of Java en route to Singapore. Just before she died, she prayed for the Malayan mission, but her prayers were not answered. When they finally arrived in Singapore, one of the sisters developed brain fever, from which she never recovered. One of the novices disappeared and was afterwards discovered to have married the *La Julie's* Irish captain; she had originally come from Drishane Parish in County Cork. Father Beurel knew that he could not hope to found a convent school with the single remaining novice and lay teacher, so he sent them to live with a Catholic family and wrote once again to Reverend Mother de Faudoas.

'Please send more nuns!'

* * *

In April the Taiping army abandoned Yongan and fought its way through the besieging Qing lines. They headed north through the mountains, and left their trail littered with homemade mines and booby traps. Then, after a surprise rearguard action, they left over five thousand enemy dead in the narrow mountain passes. On the march north their ranks increased to over forty thousand, and they accumulated valuable arms and gunpowder abandoned by the Qing. They travelled by land and by river, using fleets of barges to transport their ammunition and food supplies, their treasury, and their women and children, until they came before Quanzhou, which they found heavily fortified. Hong Xiuquan decided to bypass the city and continue on to Changsha, the provincial capital.

Hong Xiuquan and Feng Yunshan rode together in their ornate sedan chairs as the Taiping army marched past the walls of Quanzhou.

'We could capture this city,' said Hong to Feng Yunshan, 'even though the devil-dogs are nipping at our tails, but it would serve no useful purpose. If my Heavenly father had wanted the city to be taken, he would have given me a sign.'

'You are wise to leave them be,' Feng replied. 'Let them tremble behind their walls while we seek the Heavenly City.'

'We have not far to go, old friend. Do you remember when we first set out on our travels to share the doctrine of repentance? It now seems so long ago.'

'I remember it as if it were yesterday, although it was eight years ago,' Feng replied. 'We have faced many trials together, you and I, but I know we will triumph over the demon-devils, with the Great father and your elder brother watching over us.'

Hong raised his hand to his friend in acknowledgement of his true and lasting faith and looked into his eyes. Hong Xiuquan could look deep into a man's heart, to the very depths of his soul. Yet today Hong could see nothing in Feng's eyes. No expression of faith, no recognition, no sign of life at all. He stared in puzzlement for a frozen moment, then his mouth opened in horror as Feng pitched forward, and Hong saw the bloody mess where the lucky Qing sniper had sent a musket ball into the back of Feng's head.

Hong leapt down from his sedan chair, screaming for the column to halt. But he did not have to issue any commands, exhortations or admonishments. As word of Feng Yunshan's death spread among the soldiers, the Taiping army turned like a great angry beast from its path and flung itself at the city of Quanzhou. The city was heavily fortified and well-garrisoned, but the Taiping launched wave upon wave of wild-eyed, long-haired warriors at the city walls. The Qing forces that had been in pursuit caught up with them and threatened their rear, but their officers declined to engage the rebels once they saw the naked ferocity of the Taiping assault. One week later, the God-followers breached the city walls and massacred every living creature in Quanzhou.

2

Reverend Mother Mathilde thanked God once again that Reverend Mother de Faudoas had selected her to head the second Malayan mission. This was her greatest wish come true, and she knew that God had answered her prayers. She travelled with the Reverend Mother de Faudoas to Southampton, where she boarded the SS *Bentick* bound for Alexandria, with Sisters St Apollinaire and St Damien from France, Sister St Gregory Connelly from Ireland, and Sister St Margarite from the Isle of South Uist on the west coast of Scotland, one of the few Catholic enclaves in Scotland to have survived the Reformation. As the SS *Bentick* moved out into the English Channel, Mother Mathilde thought of the rolling green hills and meadows beyond her parent's home in Suriauville, while Sisters St Apollinaire and St Damien thought of the woods of Lorraine and the tree-lined Rue de l'Abbé Grégoire in Paris. Sister Connolly thought of the rushing streams and lush green fields of County Cork, and Sister Margarite thought of the hundreds of wild mute swans on Loch Druidibeag. They all wondered if they would ever see the places of their birth again, but they were strong in their faith and their mission.

When the sisters reached Alexandria, they disembarked and boarded a smaller boat that took them down the Nile to Cairo. After a few hours rest, they travelled overnight in a camel caravan to Suez, where they boarded the *Indostan*, bound for Penang. The first night out, the sisters had trouble sleeping in their stuffy cabin, since they were not used to the tropical heat, except for Mother

Mathilde, who had been training for this eventuality for years. Yet even Mother Mathilde's sleep was disturbed by Sister St Gregory, who was leaping about in their small cabin, her wide eyes darting back and forth across the floor.

The other sisters thought she had been out in the sun too long, but Mother Mathilde tried to comfort her.

'What ails you, sister?' she said in a soothing voice.

'Oh, dear Reverend Mother,' Sister St Connolly answered in her broken French, 'I saw a great black monster running around on the floor!'

Before Mother Mathilde could reply, Sister St Connolly's eyes were on the floor again, and she fell down upon her knees and began to beat the floor with her slipper.

'There!' she declared triumphantly. 'I've killed the black beast!'

Mother Mathilde told her to calm herself, and said that it was only a giant cockroach, which was not dangerous, which pleased Sister St Connolly greatly, and that there were many more of them aboard the ship, which pleased Sister St Connolly not at all.

They arrived in Penang on October 28 after six gruelling months at sea, but immediately set to work establishing a school and orphanage. They founded the Convent of the Holy Infant Jesus in Penang, or Convent Light Street, as it came to be known.

3

Lee Yip Lee walked across Thomson's Bridge towards Boat Quay. There were many slats missing from the rickety wooden bridge, through which a man could easily fall if he were not careful. Yip Lee was not afraid of falling, but the fragility of the bridge's supports added to his feelings of unease, for he felt as if he was poised above a great void. He was now nearly fifty years old, though still in good physical health and with a lean strong body. He had made a good living for himself as a Tiger general in the Ghee Hin and had a decent amount of money saved. But he was a troubled man. He had killed many men over the years. Many had deserved their deaths, and he had relished the thrill of taking their lives at the time. But now he no longer relished such deaths. Now he felt as if their ghosts followed him like pale shadows all the livelong day, even in the bright silver light of the noonday sun, eager to drag him down to hell on the day of his own demise.

In recent years he had taken to smoking a pipe or two of opium in the evening, although of late his once soothing dreams had turned to nightmares, and he had found himself sobbing in the arms of his mistress Leong Hon Ming. She was the owner of an opium den and brothel on Nankin Street in Chinatown; she had been the concubine of the former owner, who had left it to her when he died of cholera two years before. Yip Lee was on his way to visit her, but he decided to stop to listen to the storyteller who was setting himself up on a mat in the middle of Boat Quay, and around whom a crowd of coolies was gathering. Yip Lee was glad to leave Thomson's Bridge and feel the solid ground beneath his feet again. The sun was setting as he walked along the quay, flashing golden shadows across the dark waters of the river and the merchant godowns. A sizeable crowd had now gathered around the storyteller, and torches had been lit in a small circle surrounding him. Yip Lee went forward and dropped a copper coin into the man's cup, and then went and lay with his back against the low wall that ran along the edge of the quay.

The storyteller began with reports of what was happening in the world. The former British prime minister Robert Peel had died in a riding accident; gold had been discovered in Australia, and the first gold field had been opened. Yet the most important news, and the news that had the assembled coolies hanging on his every word, was from their homeland China. The storyteller recounted how the God-worshippers, founded by the Hakka Hong Xiuquan, aimed to bring about the downfall of the Manchu and to establish the Taiping, the Kingdom of Heavenly Peace on Earth. Hong Xiuquan claimed to be the younger brother of Jesus, the son of the Christian God. His religious movement had already attracted many devoted followers and was causing the Manchu rulers to tremble in their boots.

Yip Lee had heard about this man. Some of the missionaries in Singapore were singing his praises, and urging his countrymen to join their Christian religion, and many of the blind fools were embracing it. Yip Lee could not understand it. He had seen the images and statues of the naked man on the wooden cross. What kind of God was that, and who could worship such a thing? And if this man's father really was God, who had created the world and mankind, why could he not have saved his son? It was a mad religion, and a dangerous one too. Already many had been converted, especially the Hakka gambier and pepper farmers, who were easy targets for the missionaries, living out alone on their plantations. This was of great concern to his masters, who saw them as a threat to their brotherhood. It had led to the recent massacres on the plantations that had been executed by the tiger soldiers of the Ghee Hin. But even that blood-letting had not staunched the spread of this mystical poison. Something more would need to be done, and he felt sure he would have a bloody hand in it. But tonight he would not think on it. He would lose himself in the storyteller's song, and then find opium oblivion in the arms of his mistress.

The storyteller then began the tale of Chang-e:

During the time of Emperor Yeo, many, many years ago, there were ten suns, who took turns to bring light and heat to the earth. Then one day, the suns thought they would play a great game and all shine together in unison. This was a disaster for the earth and the poor people who dwelt upon it. The rivers dried up, the crops were parched, and the people could scarcely breath the hot air. The Jade Emperor sent an order to Hou Yi, one of the immortals and a legendary archer, to control the suns, and return them to their natural order. When Hou Yi set off on his mission, his wife Chang-e begged to go with him, since she did not want to be parted from her husband for even a moment. When Hou Yi came down to earth and saw the plight of the people, he was greatly angered. He drew his great bow and began to shoot the suns down one by one. Chang-e begged him to stop, for Hou Yi had only been ordered to control the suns and not to destroy them. She warned him that he would be punished if he disobeyed the Jade Emperor's instructions.

But Hou Yi exalted in his victory over the suns and cried out in triumph as they crashed to the ground one by one. As he was about to fire an arrow at the last remaining sun, Chang-e stood in front of him and pleaded with Hou Yi to save it, so that it could continue to light and heat the earth. Hou Yi agreed to do this, and with the other suns gone, the rain began to fall again and replenish the rivers, the grass and trees turned green and lush, and the people breathed the sweet air in relief and gratitude.

Yet the Jade Emperor was not grateful. He was furious that Hou Yi had disobeyed his orders, for the ten suns were the ten sons of the Jade Emperor, and Hou Yi had killed nine of them. The Jade Emperor banished Hou Yi to live on earth as an ordinary mortal, as punishment for his disobedience. Because she loved him so, Chang-e chose to live on earth as a mortal herself, taking only her jade rabbit as her companion. When he saw how beautiful the human world was, Hou Yi told Chang-e that they would be happy there, and Chang-e replied that she would be happy anywhere so long as she was with Hou Yi.

They walked along the edge of a river, marvelling at the sparkling waters, and wandered through a forest, listening to the sweet music of the birds singing in the trees. They came upon a small village, which was in a great panic, because a giant bear was rampaging through the streets, causing death and destruction. Hou Yi shot the bear dead with a single arrow through its throat. The villagers were overjoyed and celebrated Hou Yi as a hero. One of them, named Feng Meng, begged Hou Yi to teach him archery so that he too could be a great warrior. Hou Yi agreed to teach the young man, and soon Feng Meng became almost as proficient as his master, who appointed Feng Meng as his bodyguard. Hou Yi wandered the earth, performing great feats of bravery and archery, and became famous throughout the earth as the man who had destroyed the errant suns. He became a great king, and boasted to Chang-e that being a king on earth was better than being a servant in Heaven.

Yet he was not satisfied with his great power and the riches and glory it brought him, for he knew that he was mortal, and that one day he must die. He set off on a dangerous journey across land and sea until he came to the jade palace of the Queen Mother of the West. The Queen Mother owned a peach tree, which produced one peach every three thousand years, whose juice bestowed immortality upon those who drank it. The Queen Mother took pity on Hou Yi and gave him a bottle containing enough elixir of immortality for two persons, himself and Chang-e. But she warned him that if any one of them drank the entire potion, that person would be returned to Heaven. 'Have no fear of that, good mother,' Hou Yi cried out as he was leaving, 'I'd sooner be immortal on earth any day!' When he returned to his kingdom, he went straight to Chang-e's chamber and told her the wonderful news about the elixir. 'We can both rule as immortals on earth!' he exclaimed. But as he handed her the elixir, he warned her: 'Be careful to drink only half, for if you drink it all you will return to Heaven.'

Chang-e looked Hou Yi in the eye. She had once loved him more than life itself, but he had become vain and proud, obsessed with power and his own self-gratification. Her heart was now cold towards him, and she had no wish to spend eternity with him on earth. As he watched her eyes, Hou Yi suddenly realized what she was thinking, but it was too late, for in a swift movement she drank down all the elixir in a single swallow. As Hou Yi screamed and cursed, Chang-e retreated backwards from him. Hou Yi fitted an arrow into his bow and fired it at Chang-e, but for the first time in his life his arrow missed its target. Chang-e then turned and leapt out of the open window. She did not fall to the ground, but instead drifted up into the sky. Hou Yi ran to the window, and drew back another arrow in his bow, but before he could release it, Feng Meng, who had been standing watching in the doorway, released an arrow from his own bow, which pierced Hou Yi through the neck. Hou Yi fell to the ground, and his life bled away from him.

Feng Meng ran to his master's side. 'Forgive me, great king,' he cried, 'but I could not let you kill a defenceless woman.'

But Hou Yi was already dead. Chang-e continued to drift higher and higher into the sky until she disappeared from view. In her grief over what had happened to their love after she and Hou Yi had descended to earth, she was determined to go to a cold and desolate place, and chose to live on the moon. On the moon her only companion was her jade rabbit, and a woodcutter who spent his days cutting the limbs from a cassia tree, the giver of life, which grew new limbs every time they were chopped away. Chang-e became a goddess, and now looks down upon the earth through the silver light on the moon.

Yip Lee looked up at the moon, which now shone pale and white above the dark buildings along the riverside. A cold shiver ran through him despite the humid night, and he rose and stretched his limbs. He needed a pipe. He needed it badly. He left the storyteller and made his way towards the house of Leong Hon Ming.

* * *

When he arrived at Hon Ming's house, Yip Lee went up the back stairs to her room, past the guards at the bottom and the top of the stairs. They knew him well and nodded to him as he passed by. The room was empty, so he went and lay down upon her bed. A few moments later she appeared in the doorway, having been alerted of his arrival. Hon Ming stood before him in a magnificent red silk robe, covered with golden phoenixes, perched upon her bound feet, encased in golden slippers. She was only about five feet tall, but her presence dominated the room. She was beautiful, her powdered face as white as alabaster, with full red lips and high cheekbones, and long black hair and deep black eyes. She smiled at him and bent forward to prepare his pipe, her plump white breasts pressing forward under her robe. He felt strained and exhausted, but the sight of her aroused him. Her fine features were outlined sharply in the flickering light, like the lines of a statue. And, he thought with a momentary shudder, as cold as a statue.

He drew upon the pipe and the opium eased his aches and pains and calmed his restless spirit, at least for the moment. He lay back on the bed, feeling the power returning to his body, staring into the deep blackness of her eyes, and savouring the sensuality of her sweet red smile. Then he reached out with his right hand and fondled her left breast under her robe, and with his left hand grabbed her black hair and pulled her down upon him. White and silver lights exploded like firecrackers in his head as they rolled over and over upon each other on the bed. When their lovemaking was done, Yip Lee drew on the pipe once again, and passed into a blissful sleep in a wind-whispering bamboo grove beside a shimmering lake. Hon Ming rearranged her robe and went downstairs to attend to business.

4

A change had come over him. It was as if in some dark place in his soul his spirit had suddenly stirred from a deep slumber and decided that it must live or die. And it had decided to live. Duncan came to realize with sudden clarity that this was what Marie would have wanted him to do, not waste away like the lovers in the old song 'Barbara Allen'. When it was his time he would be with her, but until then he must get on with his life. She still came and sat with him each night, and she still brought him her cool comfort, but now he could bear the fading of her vision with a stronger heart. He knew it was time to get up and move on.

* * *

Ronnie was greatly relieved when Duncan told him that it was high time they opened an office in Hong Kong, so they could take advantage of the expanding China trade. Ronnie was not relieved to see his son go, but by the fact that Duncan had finally taken his life into his own hands again. He arranged for start-up capital to be transferred to the Oriental Bank in Hong Kong, and persuaded Ian Fraser, one of the senior clerks, to accompany Duncan. Ronnie and Sarah gave him a subdued going away party, but in their hearts, they rejoiced. Although they could tell that Duncan had not yet returned to his old self, they could also tell that he was heading purposively toward a new life.

5

Liu Ah Chew dismissed the gang of coolies who worked on his gambier and pepper plantations at Bukit Timah at the end of the working day. Before returning to his own quarters for the meal that his servant was preparing for him, he made his way to the makeshift wooden chapel at the edge of the jungle. It was no more than a shed constructed from planks and attap, but two planks were angled at the entrance to form a miniature steeple, in imitation of the Church of St Joseph at Bukit Timah. On the short table inside that served as an altar was a wooden image of the crucified Jesus Christ, the saviour of the world. Liu Ah Chew had paid a Chinese carpenter to make this wooden copy of the statuette in the Church of St Joseph. It was not an exact copy, for the face of the saviour had distinctive Chinese features, but Ah Chew did not think it mattered, since Father Maudit assured him that Jesus Christ had died for all men, including his Chinese brothers. He lit the joss sticks surrounding the statuette and knelt down to pray. He knew they were not quite right, but they were the closest thing to incense, and they gave Ah Chew a sense of continuity. His makeshift chapel was a building that formerly served as a joss house, where he had once paid homage to Tian Zu, the god of the farmlands. He had converted to Catholicism through the teachings of Father Maudit, whose piety and humanity made such a strong impression on him. This was a man who was willing to share his rice with others even when he had not enough to feed himself. Ah Chew thanked the Lord for his good health and the prosperity of his plantations, and began to recite the prayer that

Father Maudit had taught him.

The tiger's claw caught him on the right side of his head, ripping out his right eye and gouging his nose from his face. He opened his mouth to scream as his head spun round under the force of the blow, but the second strike tore across his throat and ripped open his jugular vein. As the blood and life gushed out of him, he felt his flesh being ripped by the great cat's claws, and his body being dragged out of the chapel and into the jungle. He gurgled a silent prayer to his Christian God as the great darkness and silence engulfed him. When his servant came to investigate his master's delay, he found tiger tracks around the chapel, and signs of a struggle inside. With some of the coolies armed with parangs, he followed the bloody trail into the jungle until he came across Liu Ah Chew's butchered body.

* * *

Superintendent Thomas Dunman marched into Captain Adil bin Mehmood's office, strapping on his revolver.

'Come with me, Adil,' he said, 'we've got a little investigating to do. Bring constable Saiful with you. We'll take the buggy – it's sitting outside. I don't want to waste time saddling horses.'

The three men left the police station and climbed into the rig; Dunman took the reins and set the Sydney pony off at a smart trot down towards the Bukit Timah Road.

'What's up, sir?' asked Adil, turning to his commanding officer.

'The strangest thing, Captain. Last week a tiger killed the gambier farmer Liu Ah Chew on his plantation. Just this morning, another tiger – or perhaps the same tiger – killed his cousin Liu Fan Chung on his plantation, when he returned from his morning inspection.'

'Most unusual,' Adil responded, 'and an unlucky coincidence, if coincidence it be. The Chinese say that when a man is killed by a tiger his ghost becomes the slave of the tiger, and leads the beast to where his relatives are living, so that he can kill them too.'

'Humph!' Dunman exclaimed. 'I don't believe in coincidences, and I certainly don't believe in ghosts. But there is a connection – both men were recently baptised as Catholics, and actively proselytized their faith among their workers. The first was killed in his own chapel, although I believe his brother was killed in his lodgings. But I want to take a look around as soon as we can. There's something not right about this.'

About twenty minutes later they arrived at the plantation. The coroner had already been and gone, declaring Liu Fan Chung dead by misadventure. The undertaker had also arrived, but they told him to hold off until they had inspected the body and the scene of the tiger attack. They entered the planter's lodgings, which were in a state of great disarray – clearly there had been a vigorous and mortal struggle. Fan Chung lay on the earthen floor, his throat torn out and his body ripped to shreds. His cheap plaster cast statue of the Virgin Mary lay smashed on the ground, which was dark and sticky with his congealed blood. As Superintendent Dunman inspected the body, Captain Adil inspected the tiger tracks in the red dirt outside his lodgings. When Dunman came outside again, brushing aside the flies that were beginning to swarm over the corpse, he declared:

'Well, there's little doubt about it. He was got by a tiger all right, although one with a peculiar appetite for Christians.'

'I wonder,' Adil replied softly, putting on his spectacles and peering closely at the tiger tracks.

'Got anything?' said Dunman. 'Anything unusual?'

'With your permission, sir, I'd like to leave Constable Saiful here to take down statements – although I'm sure they'll declare to the last man that they saw and heard nothing – and go and take a look at the site where his cousin was killed. It may be too disturbed by now to be of any use, but there may be enough to answer my question.'

'You mean whether they were killed by the same tiger?' said Dunman.

'Perhaps,' Adil replied, 'but what I meant was the question of how they were killed. I doubt that a tiger killed them, and if it did, it was a very odd sort of beast. Look closely at these tracks, sir, very closely. Look at this one. There's an impression on the inside of the paw, almost crescent in shape, probably a cut or tear of some sort.'

'Yes, I see it,' Dunman replied, 'but so what? I'm not surprised by a tiger with a cut or tear on its paw, especially after what it did to Fan Chung.'

'But all four paws?' asked Adil, grinning. 'Look at these others – they all show the same impression. Either another great coincidence, or a one-legged hopping tiger!'

'By Jove, you're right man!' exclaimed Dunman, going down on his knees and inspecting the tracks more closely. 'No doubt about it. Curiouser and curiouser! I think you're right – we ought to go and look at the place where his cousin was killed.'

They left constable Saiful to take down statements from the workers, and told the undertaker he could continue with his work. Then they headed off to the plantation where Liu Ah Chew had been killed. When they arrived, they found that the tracks outside the makeshift chapel had been washed away by the rain that fell almost daily in Singapore, and that the chapel itself had been destroyed. The planks and attap lay in a heap upon the ground. Dunman and Adil began to carefully clear the site, laying the planks and palm leaves to one side. The earth underneath was disturbed by the destruction of the chapel, but they managed to make out two tiger tracks that had been preserved beneath the debris. And sure enough, both had the same telltale impression as the others.

'Well, I'll be damned,' said Dunman. 'What do you think,

Captain Mehmood? Same tiger, or same murderer?'

'Same murderer, I think,' Adil replied. 'I don't think it was an accident that both men were Christians. I think the murders were designed to frighten Christian converts, and discourage those thinking of converting. Father Maudit has gained quite a following among the Chinese plantation owners and their workers, and someone doesn't like it. Pretending they are killed by tigers is especially effective, given the Chinese belief that a tiger can enslave its victim's ghost.'

'Exactly my thought,' said Dunman, 'and we know who doesn't like it, don't we?'

'The Ghee Hin,' Adil answered, without a moment's hesitation.

'Yes, the Ghee Hin. Not tigers, but tiger soldiers. I'm sure this is their way of getting around their agreement to stop persecuting Christians after the riots in February. We should warn the farmers, especially those who have converted, and we ought to warn Father Maudit. But I expect we'll have more tiger attacks, real and feigned. See if you can find out anything from your men in the Ghee Hin. I'd like to try and head this off, because there's going to be serious trouble if we don't.'

6

Their revenge satiated by the sack of Quanzhou but with their blood lust running high, the Taiping army drove on north like a wild animal released, and drove straight into a careful river ambush laid by the Qing. Over ten thousand Taiping soldiers died in the battle that followed, including some veterans of Thistle Mountain.

The remains of the Taiping army managed to fight their way through to the city of Daozhou in Hunan province by the end of June, where they recruited vigorously. They not only shared their message of hope and salvation with the poor and oppressed, but also condemned the Manchu demon-devils in the hope of attracting members of the secret societies and political sects dedicated to the overthrow of the Qing. Hong Xiuquan represented the Manchu Emperor Hsien Feng and his consorts as descendants of a race whose first ancestors were a white fox and a red dog, whose inhuman offspring had established their demon throne over the greatest kingdom under Heaven.

With new recruits, the Taiping army numbered over fifty thousand by the time they abandoned Daozhou. Hong Xiuquan led his army northward along the Xiang River to the Yangtze River. Gathering new recruits along the way, they began the six-hundred-mile march along the banks of the river to the great city of Nanking, the former capital of China during the ancient and early Ming dynasties, now known as the Southern capital. Nanking was the centre of Chinese scholarship, and the capital of China's richest province; after Peking, it was the second greatest gem in the

Imperial crown.

* * *

While the sisters of the Order of the Holy Infant Jesus were on their way to Malaya, Father Beurel had written to Governor Butterworth asking for land next to the Cathedral of the Holy Shepherd in Victoria Street to establish a charitable institution for girls. The La Salle brothers had arrived safely and set up a school for boys in the old chapel on Bras Basah Road, which was originally called Saint John's. Father Beurel suggested to the governor that it might be a good idea to set up a similar school for girls. When Governor Butterworth refused to provide the land requested, Father Beurel bought the house on the corner of Victoria Street and Bras Basah Road that was formerly owned by H. C. Caldwell, senior clerk to the magistrates, to provide a base for the Sisters of the Holy Infant Jesus when they came down to Singapore. He paid for the house with four thousand dollars of his own money, which he had already spent liberally on the Catholic mission in Singapore. Caldwell's house was a beautiful neoclassical structure, which had been built by George Coleman between 1840 and 1841. The house had Doric pilasters surmounted by a perfectly executed architrave, frieze and cornice, with a jack roof and semicircular projection facing Victoria Street. The building had been neglected in recent years, and was now in a rather dilapidated state, but Father Beurel wrote to the Bishop and Mother Mathilde in Penang and told them he was now able to provide accommodation for the Sisters of the Holy Infant Jesus and looked forward to receiving them in Singapore.

7

1853

By the time the Taiping army approached the giant walls of the great city of Nanking in March, their number had swelled to hundreds of thousands – a great multitude of long-haired soldiers, male and female, devotees of the new religion, secret society men, pirates and bandits. They surrounded the city, set their mines and one week later breached the walls at their weakest northeastern point. The fifty thousand Qing troops retreated to the inner Tartar city, which was quickly surrounded by the Taiping forces. As the long-haired warriors scaled the walls and fought their way into the inner city, the Manchu Bannermen burned their homes, killed their wives and children, and committed suicide over their charred remains. The Taiping slaughtered every last demon-devil until the inner city flowed red with their blood. Then Hong Xiuquan entered the city in his yellow dragon robes, borne upon a golden palanquin, while his God-followers and the city residents prostrated themselves at his feet. To the sound of celestial music, the Heavenly King entered his Heavenly City.

* * *

Hong Xiuquan had completed one journey, but now embarked on another. He had established a Heavenly capital for his followers, in a strongly walled and fortified city, with well-stocked granaries, set in a strategic location on the Yangtze River, amid fertile farmland and prosperous market towns. Now he had to establish the Kingdom of Peace and extend it over the whole of the Middle Kingdom.

Hong Xiuquan had great plans for the organization of his new kingdom, in which combinations of families would form integrated social units as combinations of army units formed integrated chains of command. All would labour on the land, in addition to their individual occupations such as masons, carpenters or silk-weavers, donating their surplus to the public treasuries, giving these things to God for all to use in common.

Yet this great social system could only be for the future. At the present moment, too many of his followers were engaged full-time in the Taiping army, defending the city and carrying Hong Xiuquan's message of redemption throughout the land. The city was divided into guan, social groups organized by occupation and gender, with sexual separation of men and women rigidly enforced – a prohibition that Hong Xiuquan declared would have to remain in force until the day when the Taiping victory was complete.

For Hong Xiuquan, there were two immediate tasks at hand. The first, over which he took direct and personal control, was the translation and mass printing of the books of the Old and New Testament, and the Taiping proclamations and prayers. Over four hundred scholars and printers were set to work on this task in the former Temple of the God of Literature, now designated as the Taiping Printing Office.

The second was the extension of Taiping rule throughout the Middle Kingdom. Hong Xiuquan conferred with his three remaining kings [cii], Yang Xiuqing, the East King, Wei Changhui, the North King, and Shi Dakai, the Wing King. They agreed that Shi Dakai should consolidate their position in the west, by establishing dominion over the towns and villages that they had captured – or

cii Xiao Chaogui, the West King, and the voice of Jesus, had died in battle the previous year, as had Feng Yunshan, the South King.

bypassed – on their long march from Thistle Mountain. This would enable them to establish a strong Taiping base in the south and the Yangtze valley, from which they could extend their campaign throughout the north and east. The critical question before them, given their limited resources, was whether they should first strike east towards the prosperous port city of Shanghai, which might enable them to form an alliance with the foreign barbarians against the Manchu, or whether they should strike directly at the dragon's head, by sending an army north to Peking to drive the Emperor Hsien Feng from his throne.

The three kings all supported an eastern expedition first. They were optimistic that they could form an alliance with their fellow Christians in the foreign factories, or at least be able to purchase modern munitions from them. This would enable them to strengthen their hold over the city of Zhenjiang, from which they could control the approaches to the Grand Canal and Peking, which would be their final goal.

Hong Xiuquan listened to them patiently and then declared:

'What you say is surely wise and worthy of consideration. We should entreat with our foreign brothers, who worship the same God, and work with them to further our great mission. But we cannot delay – the demon-devils are trapped like rats in their northern refuge. They must be immediately driven from Peking!'

Hong Xiuquan divided the Taiping army into three smaller armies. The first would remain to protect the city, and be commanded by Wei Changhui, the North King, who would also be in charge of coordinating food supplies. The second would secure the west, and be commanded by Shi Dakai, the Wing King, while the third, commanded by General Lin Fengxiang, would drive north across the Yellow River to capture Peking. Yang Xiuqing, the East King, was given charge of the overall military campaign and general administration, while Hong Xiuquan supervised the printing of the holy books and the construction of the new Palace of the Heavenly King. Ten thousand craftsmen and labourers worked to erect this sumptuous dwelling for Hong Xiuquan, his family, and his concubines – for the Taiping prohibition governing sexual separation did not apply to Hong Xiuquan or his subordinate kings.

8

By March, Sir James Brooke was ready to return to Sarawak. He had been in England two years, defending his reputation, and marshalling his supporters to help defeat three parliamentary proposals for a public inquiry into his actions in Borneo. His bags were packed, and he only waited in London until they were sent to Southampton. Although Lord John Russell's Whig government had been defeated in the recent election, and had been replaced by Lord Aberdeen's coalition government, he remained optimistic that the storm had blown over. Lord Clarendon, the new foreign secretary, had recently assured James that the government's position towards him had not materially changed. As he reflected on the two years he had spent in England, James felt satisfied if not entirely vindicated, and looked forward to celebrating his return to Sarawak. Consequently, he felt cruelly betrayed when he received an urgent dispatch from Lord Clarendon's secretary, informing him that the government intended to institute a Commission of Inquiry in Singapore, under the direction of the Governor-General of India.

* * *

While Hong Xiuquan and his three remaining kings were considering whether to send an army east to Shanghai to form an alliance with the foreign barbarians, one of the foreign barbarians, Sir George Bonham, former resident councillor and governor of Singapore, now governor of Hong Kong, superintendent of trade and British plenipotentiary to China, was enjoying dinner with Captain Fishbourne and Mr T. T. Meadows, the British consul's Chinese interpreter, in Captain Fishbourne's cabin aboard the armoured steamer *Hermes* in Shanghai harbour. Governor Bonham, like many of the Shanghai merchants, was concerned with the potential threat to trade posed by the Taiping rebellion.

'What do you think of their prospects of success?' Bonham asked Meadows, after they had finished the excellent meal prepared by Captain Fishbourne's cook. 'And would they prove any more reliable than the Manchu?'

'From what I have heard, I believe they have a very good chance of establishing an independent state in the south, and moreover, one that would be ruled by a Chinese dynasty committed to the Christian religion. Surely that would be in our interest?' Meadows offered.

'But is it real Christianity that they are committed to?' Bonham questioned him. 'Or is it Hong Xiuquan worship? What do you make of this story about him being Jesus's younger brother, eh? Sounds like superstitious nonsense to me.'

'Maybe, your honour, but it may just be their peculiar way of expressing themselves – and they do have a peculiar way of expressing themselves,' Meadows replied. 'Issachar Roberts, the Baptist missionary in Canton, knows Hong Xiuquan personally, and speaks very highly of him. Says he is just seeking religious liberty for his people.'

'I heard that too,' Bonham acknowledged, 'but how strong are they? Will the Manchu crush them? My superiors – and the merchants of this city – are wondering whether we should support the Imperial government, as we have been asked to do. In fact, God damn 'em, some of the local mandarins are already claiming that we've agreed to help them crush the Taiping!'

'I think that would be most unwise, your honour,' Meadows

cautioned. 'The Taiping are a highly disciplined force. They punish rape, adultery and opium smoking by death, and they have some very capable generals, whereas the Manchu are weak and corrupt. And many other dissatisfied groups, such as the secret societies in the primary cities and the countryside are liable to unite with the Taiping in their opposition to the Manchu – in point of fact, a good many already have. The Manchu are still hated by many as foreign usurpers, and many long for the return of the Ming – but they will also settle for the ouster of the Qing. If we come in on the Manchu side, we may only prolong what is likely to prove to be a bloody civil war, which – if the Taiping win – would be very bad for our future hopes for expanded trade.'

'I agree with you about that,' Bonham replied. 'At the very least we need to maintain strict neutrality at the moment, until we find out more. I've already advised the foreign office that this should be our present position. But we need more information. We need to find out their attitude towards us, and – but please keep this between the three of us – we need to determine whether it might be in the interests of Her Majesty's government to negotiate some sort of memorandum of understanding with the Taiping, so long as we have assurances that they will respect the treaty rights we secured from the Emperor.'

'And how will we do that?' Meadows asked.

'We will go to Nanking and see and hear for ourselves, Mr Meadows. Always the best policy, I say. Captain Fishbourne, please weigh anchor tomorrow and set a course for what they call the Heavenly Capital. Mr Meadows, please send some of your Chinese messengers upriver and let them know we are coming! Captain Fishbourne, more port, if you please!'

* * *

They arrived in Nanking three days later, on April 25. As they approached the city from the river, some of the surprised Taiping gunners fired upon the *Hermes*, mistaking her for a Qing vessel. George Bonham remained calm, cool and collected, and ordered Captain Fishbourne not to respond, but to send messengers to assure the Taiping of their peaceful intent. Mr Meadows and Captain Fishbourne went ashore, where they were met by Yang Xiuqing, the East King, and Wei Changhui, the North King, while Sir George waited for a response to his formal request for an audience with Hong Xiuquan. Meadows and Fishbourne had what they thought was a friendly and fruitful exchange of views with the Taiping leaders, who assured them that they hoped for peaceful relations with their British friends. The Taiping leaders appealed for their aid in helping them exterminate the demon-devils, but said that if this was not possible, for their part they had no objection to the British continuing their trade. Yet although negotiations appeared to be going well, and the junior officials of both parties enjoyed a lively trade of jade and silver for swords and music boxes, Sir George Bonham was not granted an audience with the Heavenly King, but entered into a laborious written correspondence with Hong Xiuquan's brother-in-law, Lai, over the proper rules of ceremony for a meeting between such high-ranking persons. Then negotiations came to an abrupt end when Bonham received an insulting decree that was hand delivered by Lai aboard the *Hermes*:

'Now that you distant English have come to acknowledge our sovereignty, not only are the soldiers and officers of our Celestial dynasty delighted and gratified thereby, but even in High Heaven itself our Celestial Father and Elder Brother will also admire this manifestation of your fidelity and truth. We therefore issue this special decree, permitting you, the English Chief, to lead your brethren out or in, backwards or forwards, in full accordance with your own will or wish, whether to aid us in exterminating our impish foes, or to carry on your commercial operations as usual; and it is our earnest hope that you will, with us, earn the merit of diligently serving our royal master, and, with us, recompense the goodness of the Father of Spirits.'

'Acknowledge your sovereignty be damned!' Sir George exploded, beating his fist upon his desk, his normal calm and composure blown to the winds. He instructed Meadows to send a brief note to Hong Xiuquan advising him that Her Majesty's representative did not recognize his sovereignty, and warning him of the dire consequences if any injury were to be inflicted upon British subjects or British interests by the Taiping. Then he ordered Captain Fishbourne to weigh anchor and return full steam to Shanghai.

9

In June Sir James Brooke arrived in Singapore to find himself the unwelcome centre of attention. Joseph Hume had written to Robert Carr Woods advising him of the Commission of Inquiry before James had left Southampton, and the papers were full of the subject. The *Singapore Free Press* celebrated Rajah Brooke as the scourge of the Borneo pirates while the *Straits Times* condemned his massacre of innocents.

James set sail for Sarawak as quickly as he could, hoping that the sight of his beloved Kuching and Santubong mountain would prove a salve for his troubled soul, but within a few days of his arrival he fell victim to smallpox. While his loyal Malays nursed him, the holy men of many religions offered prayers, to their Muslim and Christian God, and to the gods and spirits of the forests and rivers. Although Sherif Moksain, who was in charge of his care, declared that the Rajah was dying, James eventually recovered, but he was a much-changed man. The cherub bloom of his youth was gone, and his body was ravished by the disease. He suddenly looked like an old man. His face was severely pitted, scarred, and deeply lined, and his hair had turned white.

* * *

Lee Yip Lee climbed up the back stairs to Hon Ming's house. He shivered in the dark shadows of the stairwell, even though the heat of the day made it difficult to breathe in the enclosed space. He held his right hand in his left to stop it shaking – he did not want her to see how badly he wanted opium. He felt as if he walked all the day in shadows, even in the bright light of the noonday sun. The grey ghosts of those he had murdered clung to him like the dank mist along the riverbank in the early morning. So many men he had killed, and women and children too. He took a deep breath, and after steadying himself for a moment, entered her private room.

Normally Hon Ming would be in the brothel below, and would only come up when her servant announced his arrival. However, this night she was standing waiting for him, his pipe already prepared beside the bed. She smiled at him in her usual sensual way, but also held his eyes with a strange and penetrating gaze. She waited until he had lain down on the bed, his back propped up against the cushions, and taken a deep draw on the opium pipe.

'I have something to tell you,' she said, in her businesslike way. 'I take every precaution, and given my occupation, I know the best and most effective ways. But none are foolproof, and sometimes nature takes its course. I am with child. What do you wish me to do?'

It took a long moment for Yip Lee to grasp what she had said. As Hon Ming watched his face, expressionless as stone, she was afraid he was going to fly into a rage – he had done so over much less in the past. Yet as it dawned on him, his face broke into a slow smile, and a great peace came over his body and soul. Perhaps the gods were merciful after all. Perhaps they would reward a strong man who always followed his masters' orders with a strong male child, a son who would honour him and pay filial respect to his memory, a son who would pray for his soul and burn offerings of food and money to relieve his suffering in hell.

'No matter,' he said, 'in fact I am glad to hear it. Assuming it is a boy, you have made me very happy. I will make you my wife, and surrender my society rank. And we shall live together in a house and watch him grow.'

Hon Ming was greatly relieved to hear him say that, but hesitated before she responded.

'And if it is a girl?' she asked him.

'You can sell it, give it away, or drown it – I don't much care,' he replied, taking another deep draw on his pipe and sinking back into the cushions.

10

1853

In May, the Taiping northern expedition, commanded by General Lin Fengxiang and comprised of some seventy thousand Thistle Mountain veterans and new recruits, set off on the long road to Peking, nearly two thousand miles to the north. The going was very hard. They were constantly harried by Qing forces, and they were totally unprepared for the northern winter that eventually set in. Without winter clothes or footwear, many were crippled by frostbite, crawling through the snow and ice until they froze to death while lying exhausted on the ground. Some thirty thousand managed to fight their way to within three miles of Tianjin, less than seventy miles from their ultimate goal – the Imperial city of Peking, the lair of the demon-devil Manchu – but there they were halted by fresh and numerically superior Qing battalions, reinforced by Mongol cavalry. Exhausted, the remnants of the northern expedition threw up defensive earthworks and dug in for the winter, while the Qing forces, commanded by the Mongol General Senggelinqin, employed thousands of labourers to build a ring of siege trenches that completely encircled the beleaguered Taiping army.

* * *

In July, members of the Short Daggers Society,[ciii] a branch of the Ghe

---

ciii So-called because of the short-knives the members used in close combat.

Hok kongsi, rebelled against their Qing masters and seized control of the port city of Amoy. They had been encouraged by the Taiping capture of Nanking, which they knew would weaken the hated Manchu, and were supported financially by some of the Hokkien merchants in Singapore. In September members of the Short Daggers society captured Shanghai and drove the Qing forces from the city. They were careful not to invade the British, French, American and other foreign concessions, which were established in independent factory compounds, and assured the foreigners that they could continue their business as usual, including their trade in opium. In November the Qing forces managed to retake Amoy – some of the society members fled north and continued their resistance in the country, while others fled south on coolie junks bound for Singapore – but the Qing failed to recapture Shanghai. The Short Daggers had secured what was now the Celestial Kingdom's most prosperous trading port, and they sent representatives to Hong Xiuquan asking for his support in holding the city against the Qing. For the Taiping, this was a golden opportunity handed to them on a plate – access to a major trading port, and control of the Grand Canal and approaches to Peking.

Yet they were not in any position to seize it. The negotiations with the Short Daggers were first delayed when Hong Xiuquan demanded that they recognize his supreme authority over them. They were then suspended for weeks while Hong anguished over the spiritual significance of the fire that had recently destroyed his newly constructed Heavenly Palace, and then became completely absorbed in making even more complicated plans for its immediate rebuilding. Yang Xiuqing, the East King in charge of overall military operations, who had originally championed an immediate advance on Shanghai, desperately wished that he could exploit the situation, but could not spare any soldiers for an eastern campaign. Shi Dakai's western campaign was drawing heavily on his reserves, and he had recently sent massive reinforcements to support General Lin Fengxiang's beleaguered army in the north. He was hard-pressed by strong Qing armies that had encircled Nanking, and his remaining reserves were insufficient to break out and fight their way through to Shanghai. Shanghai would have to wait until victory was attained in the north and west.

11

Lee Yip Lee looked around to make sure that no one was watching him, then quietly opened the door of the plantation owner's bungalow and slipped inside. There were only two rooms in the bungalow. One long room was sparsely furnished with a table and chairs, a lounger and a bookcase, with a black lacquered screen standing before the door that led out to the washhouse at the back; the other room was a small single bedroom with a plank bed and rough mattress. At the far end of the long room was an altar, which had formerly supported representations of the household gods, but which now displayed one of those carved images of the man nailed to the cross. Yip Lee glanced at the figure in disgust, then crept behind the screen and waited for the plantation owner to return. The plantation owner was Lim Chuan Neo, a prosperous Teochew businessman who owned a number of plantations, and was an assistant chief in the Ghee Hok. Yet, just like the Hakkas, he had been converted by the priest – by a man who was almost as poor as the coolies who worked the plantations. Yip Lee snorted in contempt, and gripped his weapon in his hand. The sinking evening sun cast a shimmering golden light on the trailing specks of dust that had followed his movement across the room, and cast dark shadows behind the furniture.

Yip Lee did not see the snake. The king cobra had slipped in through the back door and lay in the dark shadows behind the screen. The cobra raised its hooded head and struck Yip Lee on the left shoulder just as he heard the deadly growling hiss in the darkness. He swung round wildly with his weapon, but he missed the snake, which had withdrawn itself and already raised its hooded head for a second strike. Again, the soul-chilling growling hiss, before it sank its fangs deep into his right arm. Now Yip Lee did not even bother trying to defend himself, for he knew he was beyond hope. He sat on the floor helpless, waiting for the snake to strike again, staring into its cold black eyes. He saw nothing in those cold black eyes, except his own death.

Yet the snake was done, and after watching Yip Lee for a few moments, turned away and slithered across the floor and out the back door. Yip Lee pushed himself back from the screen until he could brace his body against the wall, and sat motionless gazing out towards the dark trees beyond the open window, waiting for the venom to take effect. He could feel the puncture holes in his shoulder, and could see them on his arm, but to his surprise he felt no pain. He expected to die in excruciating pain, but as the venom took effect he felt nothing but a deep relaxation and release passing through his body, as deep a relaxation and release as he had ever experienced with an opium pipe. He knew he was dying, but he did not care about that, or about anything else in the world. He no longer feared the cruel punishments and tortures of hell, the metal spikes hammered into his head or the skin stripped from his body. He did not fear the revenge of the ghosts of the souls he had murdered. He did not care whether the child that Hon Ming carried was a boy or a girl. Nothing had any meaning beyond the cool calmness that enveloped him like a silken sheet, which seemed to bring the greatest peace that he had ever known.

Some time later he heard the plantation owner come in, but made no attempt to move, and knew he could not even if he tried. He watched the man light the candles on the altar, then kneel down before the crucified man. He heard him uttering prayers to the father, the son and the holy ghost. Yip Lee thought about the holy ghost –

perhaps this strange religion was not so different after all. But what did it matter, anyway? What did anything matter? The man's voice began to fade in the distance, as the dim light faded before his eyes. He vaguely heard the man walking back across the room towards the back door, and then his footsteps stopping before him. But Lee Yip Lee did not hear the man shouting for his servant when he saw the figure on the floor, for Lee Yip Lee was already dead.

12

Superintendent Dunman and Captain Adil bin Mehmood bent over to inspect the body, as the peon held the lantern over it.

'Died of snakebite all right,' said Dunman, checking the wounds, 'but I never saw a man looking so happy about it.' They were both amazed by the beatific smile on Lee Yip Lee's face.

'And I think we've solved our tiger mystery,' said Captain Mehmood, prising the wooden club from the dead man's right hand. It was no ordinary club, but a stout wooden stake with a tiger's paw and bared claws bound to it.

'Bring the lantern closer, Jamal,' Captain Mehmood said to the peon, as he turned the club round to get a better look at the tiger paw, which displayed the telltale crescent marking.

'Well, I'll be damned!' Dunman exclaimed. 'Looks like we got our man-tiger at last. Hopefully this means we can stop worrying about losing any more of Father Maudit's converts.'

Yet his hope was to prove empty.

* * *

When Leong Hon Ming heard the news a few days later she did not cry. She had left her tears behind long years before, for she had not survived by allowing herself to be stricken by bad news. She would miss Lee Yip Lee and his hard lovemaking, but there were plenty of hard lovemakers in Chinatown. She did not love him, but she had thought he would protect her if she ever needed protection and had hoped that if she produced a son she could count on him for that. Yet she knew she had some good years left. She went to the Thian Hock Keng Temple and burned some offerings for her former lover, and gave some money to the Ghee Hin so that he would receive a proper funeral service. Then she continued with her life. She would decide what to do with the child when it was born – it was too late and too dangerous to try and lose it.

* * *

About four months after the death of Yip Lee, Hon Ming gave birth to a baby girl after a long and difficult labour, during which she had screamed and cursed and smoked a lot of opium. She remembered what he had said, but she had no wish to drown the baby. She was tempted to keep the child, but knew it would be difficult, and she did not want her daughter to grow up to the life into which she had been forced. She wanted more for her than that. She wanted a home with a good family for the beautiful ruby-lipped baby girl with the plump cheeks and dimpled nose that sucked at her breast. She wanted something better for her daughter than she could ever hope to give her. She suddenly remembered that there was an old woman known for her love of children and her generosity to the poor, who devoted her life to finding good homes for abandoned children. If only she could remember her name! And then she remembered. Madam Ang. Yes, Madam Ang. She would go and visit her before the week was out, before she got too attached to the beautiful little thing at her breast.

13

'There is no justice on earth,' Poh Neo said to her father in frustration. 'Why is it that a vicious man is not punished for his evil deeds, and thrives more than the virtuous man, the man of ren.[civ] I swear Gan Eng Seng must have paid some demon to protect him in this life, for nothing seems to touch him. He prospers, while we are burdened with bad debts because you have been generous in support of your Hokkien brothers, too many of whom have absconded with our loans when their businesses have faltered. We will need to be tighter with our credit in the future, Father, but for now we must sell some of our holdings to cover our losses. And, I hate to say it, we will probably have to sell to Gan Eng Seng.'

'And it would not hurt if some of the husbands in this family put a bit more work into the business that supports their extravagant lifestyles,' she continued. Poh Neo's husband still had his job with Boustead, Schwabe and Co, but he took no interest in her father's business, and now spent money lavishly to maintain what he thought was an appropriate European lifestyle, as did her older brother-in-law, who was a clerk with Guthrie and Co. Poh Neo saw the point in maintaining a social network with the dominant Europeans, but they did not really need to host croquet matches and fancy-dress parties, even if they had been fun at the time. They were also very expensive.

'Oh, you are worth the two of them, Poh Neo,' her father responded, with a wry smile. 'Now I am glad I insisted on your

---

civ One who possesses the inner Confucian values.

proper schooling, although this was never my intention,' he said, pointing to the account books on which Poh Neo was working. 'I don't know what I would do without you, Poh Neo, I really don't.'

'But we cannot sell to that evil man,' Tan Swee Yan said, turning serious. 'I would rather sell my soul to the King of Hell than sell to Gan Eng Seng. And I would sell my soul if I thought it would help me find a way to punish him.'

'I know, Father,' Poh Neo replied, 'I feel the same way. But it makes poor business sense. If we don't sell to him, we might not be able to sell at all; and if we sell to someone else, we may have to accept a lower price, and he may still get them in the end.'

Swee Yan looked at his daughter with admiration, and sighed. 'You are right, Poh Neo, and you are so wise for your age, my daughter. I wish you had been my son,' he smiled at her.

Poh Neo smiled back. She supposed it was a compliment of sorts, and was no doubt meant as one.

'What do you think we should sell?' he asked her.

'We should sell our nutmeg plantations,' she replied. 'We could use part of the money to cover our losses, and the rest to buy some land west of New Harbour. As the steamship traffic increases, so will the need for additional space for landing goods and cargoes, as well as port facilities and warehouses. It would be a sound investment, and likely to bring a greater return in the long run than the plantations.'

'But I thought the plantations were doing well at the moment?' her father responded. 'Are you sure it is wise to sell them at this time?'

'Oh, I think this is probably the best time, Father,' she replied. 'There is a positive craze for nutmegs at the moment – they're all the rage among the European and Chinese merchants. And we will get the best price from Gan Eng Seng – he is buying up plantations all over the island. They call him the Nutmeg King.'

'The Nutmeg King?' Swee Yan turned over the words in his mouth with distaste. 'But you are probably right, so do what you think is best. But as you say, where is the justice on this earth?'

* * *

Hon Ming bit her lip to hold back her tears. She was a hard woman, but she did not realize how difficult it would be to give up her daughter. But she knew it must be done – the child had no future as the bastard of a brothel madam. She wrapped the baby she had not named – had dared not name, in case she grew to love it more than she already did – in a red silk scarf and picked up a bag of silver dollars with which to pay the old lady for her services. Then she left the brothel in the early afternoon and made her way to the shophouse where Madam Ang lived with her charges.

The sun beat down mercilessly and she was glad of the shelter of the five-foot way, although she was often forced onto the street because the shop displays and hawkers blocked her passage. Then, just as she was about to step into the shadowed stairwell that led up to Madam Ang's room, she saw him standing there, white as a ghost but his black eyes shining like burning coals. Then she realized it was a ghost – the ghost of Lee Yip Lee – who stood before her, his right hand raised to block her passage, his head nodding from side to side, warning her not to enter. He did not speak, but he did not need to, for she could feel the oppressive force that emanated from the upstairs room, as if a chill stream of evil flowed down the stairs through the dusty heat and humidity and encircled her wildly beating heart.

She dragged herself away from the stairwell and stepped back into the sunlight of the street. As Hon Ming turned to leave, she looked back quickly over her shoulder, but the ghost of Lee Yip Lee had already returned to hell.

14

1854

On January 30, three more sisters arrived in Penang, with letters from Mother de Faudoas. Sister St Damien was appointed Mother Superior in Penang, and Mother Mathilde was instructed to found a new convent school in Singapore. She set off with Sisters St Apollinaire, St Gregory Connolly, St Margarite and St Gaeten Gervias, who was newly arrived from France, on the steamship *Hoogly*. They arrived in Singapore at noon on Sunday February 5. There were cheering crowds on the dock to greet them, and Father Beurel met them at the end of the gangplank. Once their luggage had been unloaded, they were taken by carriage to the Cathedral of the Good Shepherd, which was decked out with flowers. The air was heavy with incense and the organ boomed out in celebration of their arrival. The nuns were given seats of honour close to the altar during the special Mass that followed.

Later that afternoon they were taken to Caldwell House, and they were grateful to have some peace and quiet to adjust to their new environment – if one could find peace and quiet amid the cries of the hawkers, the lowing of the bullocks, the hammering of the carpenters and the many other discordant sounds that cacophoned from Victoria Street. As she turned the key in the door, Mother Mathilde turned to her sisters and gave them a thin smile.

'Hymns, flowers and glowing speeches are all very fine, I'm sure, but I fear they are not very filling!'

They had received nothing to eat or drink since their light

breakfast of water and biscuits aboard the *Hoogly* earlier that morning.

While Caldwell House was elegant on the outside, it was almost devoid of furniture and furnishings within. There was one bed, two mats, two chairs and two stools, and the place was overrun with rats and cockroaches. There was rubble and plaster on the kitchen floor, where part of the ceiling had caved in, and only one saucepan on the tiny stove. Most of the tiles on the bathroom floor were broken, and all the doors had fallen from their rusted hinges, so when the sisters needed to answer the call of nature, they had to use their big black umbrellas for privacy. Undeterred, they straight away set out to clean the house from top to bottom, and in the early evening, one of the Catholic parishioners brought them a meal of curried mutton and rice.

Despite their difficulties and poverty, they opened the convent school within ten days of their arrival. They started two classes for girls, one for fee-paying students, and another for the poor and orphans. The sisters did sewing for the ladies of the town to raise money to support themselves and their charges, and spent many a night huddled around a single candle in their quarters on the upper story of the house. In their black gowns and veils, they looked like hooded crows gathered together in a circle.

Two weeks after they moved in, Sister St Margarite woke suddenly to a wailing noise in the courtyard. She knew immediately what it was. She rose quickly and descended the stairs to the ground floor. She opened the front door and found a Chinese baby wrapped in red silk lying on the doorstep, with a leather pouch tied around its waist, which she found contained silver dollars. As she tried to comfort the child she peered out into the darkness, but Hon Ming was already streets away, racing home through the empty night.

15

Father Maudit thanked Goh Hua Chew for his generous donation and walked him to the door of the Church of St Joseph. He was about to re-enter the church when he suddenly noticed a European man, about six foot tall and with a bushy black beard, waving to him as he approached from the Bukit Timah Road. The man was dressed in white flannel trousers, shirt and waistcoat, with a black frock coat and a wide brimmed hat, which he kept pressed to his head with his left hand, while his right continued to wave. He marched up the road in great strides, like the giant in the fairy tale, thought Father Maudit, who was a small man who took very short steps.

As the man drew closer, Father Maudit noticed that his face was bright red, and that his cheeks were puffed out – he wondered if the poor fellow was about to have an attack of apoplexy. The man reached out and shook his hand vigorously, and then made rapid signs with his right hand, pointing to his mouth, and indicating that he was about to retch. Father Maudit raised his hand to indicate that the man should wait, then rushed by him and picked up a bucket that lay beside one of the outbuildings. The man's eyes lit up with gratitude and pleasure. Then to Father Maudit's amazement and horror, the man opened his mouth and spewed out a stream of black and brown beetles, strange shades of blue, green and indigo reflecting from their hard shells in the morning sunshine. Father Maudit crossed himself. What was this? Had the man come to church to exorcize his demons?

'What ails you, my son?' Father Maudit asked, his voice trembling with fear. Society men he could handle, but this was something strange and unknown.

'Sorry to bother you, Father,' the man replied, 'but could I trouble you for a glass of water? I'm a bit dry after carrying around those fellows.'

Then he removed his hat and poured out another load of beetles into the bucket, which he promptly covered with his hat.

Father Maudit fetched him a glass of water, which he drained in a single gulp. Then he took off his glasses and cleaned them with his handkerchief.

'Thank you very much, Father – I believe it is Father Maudit? My name is Alfred Russel Wallace, [23] and I'm a naturalist from London. Mr Napier suggested I come up here – he said it's a great place for specimens, and he was surely right about that. I think I've seen more species of beetle in the last hour than I've seen in the past year! I'm sorry to surprise you like this – I see I gave you a bit of a shock. My assistant Mr Grant has all my sample boxes, but he was delayed in town, and I came on ahead. But when I saw those marvellous creatures at the side of the road, I could not wait for him, and filled my hat with them, and when my hat was full, I had to store them in my mouth!'

Alfred Wallace grinned from ear to ear and shook Father Maudit's hand again energetically.

Father Maudit quickly recovered from his shock and chuckled at Wallace's explanation.

'You must be very fond of these marvels of God's creation – there's not many men have such a passion for these lowly creatures.'

'Lowly they may be, but they can tell us a great deal about the development – the transmutation – of species. At least, that is what I have come out to explore.'

'But my good man,' Father Maudit replied, 'you are wasting

your time! God created the animals in their glorious forms on the sixth day.' And he quoted from the Book of Genesis: 'God said, let the earth bring forth the living creature after his kind, cattle, and creeping thing, and beast of the earth after his kind: and it was so. And God made the beast of the earth after his kind, and cattle after their kind, and everything that creeps upon the earth after his kind: and God saw that it was good.'

'Oh, I don't deny he had a hand in it, Father,' Wallace replied, 'but the forms have changed over time. And I'm sure there's an ultimate reason for it, perhaps beyond our ken. I just want to discover the means by which species change over time. Or at least test some of my hypotheses.'

'Well, I've not seen any of them change,' replied Father Maudit, 'although I could do with someone changing my lazy old donkey. But I'm not going to argue with you, Mr Wallace. I have a spare room with two beds and a washhouse that you are welcome to share with your assistant when he arrives, and you may stay as long as you like. You are also most welcome to attend our services, including the one tonight.'

'I'm very grateful to you, Father,' Wallace replied, 'and I will of course contribute to the church as a mark of our gratitude. And Charles and I will attend the service tonight – assuming he arrives on time.'

* * *

During the previous year in London, Wallace had made the acquaintance of many of the leading naturalists of the day, including Charles Darwin, whose *Voyages of the Beagle* he greatly admired. Wallace had travelled to the Far East in the hope of finding evidence for the transmutation of species in the forests and jungles of the Malayan Peninsula, with the intent of developing a theory to explain what he now took to be the incontrovertible fact of species change. Yet he did not try to impress this incontrovertible fact on Father Maudit, for whose simple faith and humility he had nothing but respect and admiration. Father Maudit shared his modest meal of dried fish, rice and fruit with Wallace and his assistant Charles Grant, who had eventually arrived laden with nets and boxes, and out of courtesy the two men attended evening service in the Church of St Joseph. Although he was a dedicated scientist and naturalist, Alfred Russel Wallace was also a deeply spiritual man, and was greatly moved by the service that evening, conducted in Chinese before a large Chinese congregation. He did not know the words of the catechism, but he understood the expressions on the faces of the parishioners. They listened in rapt attention, as the smoke from the incense mingled with the motes of dust dancing in the fading light, which streamed in through the shuttered windows and spaces in the attap roof. The choir sang, and the birds of the forest joined in the chorus.

Wallace and Charles Grant spent many happy weeks with Father Maudit, collecting specimens by day and joining the father for his simple meal in the evening, which was usually provided by one of his parishioners. Wallace made a contribution to the church for their board and lodging and Charles sometimes supplemented their table with snipe or wild boar, which he shot with his rifle. Their conversations regularly ranged over the beauty and diversity of God's creation, but never again touched on the question of the transmutation of species. Wallace thought it would be uncivil, to say the least, given their host's generosity.

Charles was a little concerned about the presence of tigers in the jungle, but Father Maudit told him not to be bothered by them. They were cowardly creatures, he said, that only attacked men from behind – usually poor Chinese coolies, when they were bent over harvesting pepper or gambier. They would not enter the church or the outbuildings, he assured them, for they were afraid to encounter a man face to face. He himself had met one in the middle of the Bukit Timah Road some months ago. He admitted that he had been afraid at first, but when he opened up his black umbrella to protect himself, the great beast had dashed off back into the jungle.

16

Thomas Dunman was expecting trouble, at least as much trouble as there had been during the riots of '51. There was still bad blood between the Teochews and Hokkiens over the gambier and pepper trade, although there had been relative peace on the plantations following the death of the 'tiger-man'. But now the rivalry had extended to the more lucrative rice and coolie remittance trade, as the Ghee Hin and the Ghee Hok strove to gain control over the increasing numbers of sinkeh that flooded the settlement, refugees from the poverty, famine and civil war on the Chinese mainland.

Until recently the Teochew financiers in town had dominated the Siamese rice trade, given their control of shipping and their contacts in Siam and China, which also enabled them to dominate the market in remittances. When the trading junks from China returned home, they carried money, goods and letters sent by the local coolies to their families in their home villages in China. Most of the coolies were sojourners, who intended to return home when they had saved enough money. Some eventually did, although many others succumbed to arrack or opium, and then to disease and death.

The Hokkien merchants also imported rice, mainly from Java, but were now trying to capture a share of the Siam trade after Java decreased its rice exports. Since 1852, British merchants had made significant inroads to the Siamese trade, and now much of the rice exported from Siam to Singapore was carried on British square-rigged vessels rather than Siamese junks owned or partnered by

Teochew traders. This created an opportunity for the Malaccan Hokkiens in particular, since the British treated them with special favour because they believed them to be more industrious and honest than the other Chinese dialect groups. One of the most successful was Tan Kim Ching, the son of Tan Tock Seng, who had taken over his father's businesses after his death, and had become leader of the Hokkien clan in Singapore. Tan Kim Ching now owned a number of rice mills in Siam and Cochin China.

Dunman mentioned his concerns to John Purvis when they had tiffin at Dutronquoy's new dining room in the London Hotel. Purvis had served on the grand juries in 1851 and 1853 that had petitioned the governor to take steps to curtail the activities of the secret societies, especially those allied to the dominant Teochew and Hokkien groups. The grand juries had complained about their inability to find reliable witnesses among the Chinese in cases involving Chinese defendants, and of the nightly gang attacks; although Dunman's revitalized police force had recently had considerable success in suppressing these attacks, at least within the outskirts of the town. Purvis was sympathetic, but thought Dunman was probably exaggerating the danger.

'We certainly need to do something about the courts, Tom – it's a bloody disgrace, that it is – but this competition over rice and remittances is just the cut and thrust of business. The Hokkiens make inroads into Teochew businesses, while the Teochews drive the Kling lightermen from the river. They all know public feuding is bad for business all round, so I don't think we have much to worry about.'

He paused to serve himself some mutton curry and then continued:

'Or at least not yet we don't. But one day – and I suspect that day is not so very far away – these Celestials will forget their dialect and clan differences and organize themselves into a Chinese merchant community, and form their own Chinese Chamber of Commerce.'[24]

'I think you're right about that,' Dunman replied, 'but we have a more immediate problem. We have a lot more sinkeh these days – we had around thirteen thousand last year alone – and with a shortage of rice from Java, which the Hokkien used to import, prices are high and tempers are frayed. And there is a much more specific cause of tension between the Teochew and Hokkien, and consequently an increased danger of serious violence. A lot of the new arrivals are refugees from the Short Daggers rebellion in Amoy last year – a bunch of armed rebels and society men with grudges to bear.'

'You don't mean we're going to have trouble with Taiping rebels here – all that mad stuff about Jesus' brother and suchlike!' Purvis exclaimed, leaning back in his chair with a look of surprise.

'Different bunch of characters altogether,' Dunman assured him. 'The Taiping are fundamentally a Hakka operation, although they've united with many other factions in their opposition to the Manchu. You won't find our local Hokkien rushing out to cut off their queues and accept women as equals, or our local Teochew for that matter. But our Hokkien merchants did support the Short Daggers rebellion – they sent them men, money, arms and supplies, and appealed to the Teochew for their support, which was not forthcoming. So, there's a lot of bitterness between the societies over that, and the ranks of the Ghee Hok are swollen with gangs of cut-throats bent on revenge and recompense. I've managed to have a few of the leaders deported, but they're just the tip of the iceberg.'

'I trust you've warned the governor, Tom. What did he have to say?' Purvis inquired.

'Oh, he thinks there is little cause for alarm,' Dunman replied, with a disapproving grunt. 'He still maintains that the Chinese are the most peaceful colonists in the world – despite the trouble on the plantations three years ago. He assures me that the leading Chinese merchants will keep their people under control, at least in the town. I talked to him about increasing the size of the police force, and the particular need for Chinese recruits, but he dismissed the idea. He said that he had no money for it, and that the local merchants would not pay for such an increase, even if it was in their interest to do so.'

'I'm afraid he's right about that Tom,' Purvis said, waving to their server to clear their table. 'So, let's hope for the best.'

'Let's do so, and it's not all bad news, John. The same junks that brought these troublemakers from Amoy also brought the wives and families of some of our most respectable Chinese merchants. The government has also agreed to the naturalization of Chinese immigrants – if we can persuade some of these immigrants to stay and bring their wives and families, we'll have a more effective weapon against opium and prostitution than any increase in our police force.'

'But if they keep coming in their present numbers and stay permanently, then Singapore will eventually become a Chinese city,' Purvis opined.

'That day will come, I'm sure, and we're close enough to it already,' Dunman replied. 'Last count they represented more than half of the population. However, they don't appear to have much interest in taking over the government. They're quite content to get on with the business of making money, so long as they're left alone to do so. But if there is serious trouble between the societies and heavy government interference, then things may change. So, let's hope for the best, as you say.'

Dunman and Purvis went on to discuss the recent declaration of war on Russia by Britain and France, and the dispatch of allied troops to the Crimean peninsula. Negotiations were still continuing in the hope that all-out war could be avoided, but both men knew that there was little chance of that. They also knew that Singapore would be helpless in the face of an attack by warships from the Russian Asiatic fleet, since the Royal Navy had established its eastern base in Hong Kong.

17

Hoo Ah Kay's businesses continued to prosper. Not content to rest on his laurels, he donated his sixty-acre nutmeg plantation at Tanglin to the government for the relocation of the Botanical Gardens from Government Hill, in exchange for a plot of land next to Coleman Bridge on Boat Quay. There he and his business partner Gilbert Angus built a warehouse, which they used to store ice that was cut in New England and transported to Singapore in insulated ships. Frederic Tudor, the 'Ice King' of Boston, had perfected the method of storing and shipping ice in the early nineteenth century, and had made huge profits shipping ice to his warehouses in the American south, in India and the East Indies – including a number of ship's worth of ice to Hong Kong each year. Given the prodigious thirst of the European merchants and the tropical heat of Singapore, Whampoa and Angus thought they were on to a sure thing. Unfortunately, they overestimated the demand, and much as the passers-by admired their splendid factory building, with its magnificent wrought-iron balustrades, their business lost money from the beginning.

Whampoa had more luck when he went into the bakery business on Pulau Saigon, [cv] which he quickly developed to capture a majority share of the market in butter bread, until he later came to face stiff competition from Boey Ah Foo.

---

cv Island that used to sit in the upper reaches of the Singapore River, now merged with the mainland.

On Friday, May 5, just after noon, Tang Ying Chow, a Teochew provisions merchant who ran a shop on Market Street, weighed out five catties [cvi] of rice for Kim Gang Guo, a Hokkien stevedore. Guang Guo watched the scales carefully, then took the bag of rice from Ying Chow, who held out his hand for payment. Guang Guo was about to hand over his money, but then he paused. He lifted the bag up and down in his right hand, and then transferred it to his left. It seemed lighter than he remembered, having purchased the same amount of rice in the past. He asked Ying Chow to weigh it once more, to be sure he had the right amount.

'Why you want to do that?' Ying Chow replied. 'You already watched me weigh out five catties.'

'That is true, but I don't believe there are five catties in this bag. I am no fool, and I know the weight of rice.'

Ying Chow shrugged his shoulders and took back the bag of rice and replaced it on the scales. The scales indicated five catties.

'There you are, take it or leave it,' he said.

Gang Guo saw it with his own eyes, but when he lifted up the bag again he did not believe it.

'There must be something wrong with your scales. Let us take the bag to Tan Sock Hen's shop, so we can check its weight.' Tan Sock Hen was a Hokkien shopkeeper whose store was a few streets away.

'You accuse me of cheating you! Pay for your rice or take your Hokkien shit-face out of my store!'

Gang Guo took this as proof that Ying Chow was trying to cheat him. He dropped his bag of rice and drew out a knife from under his shirt. But Ying Chow was too quick for him, and struck

---

cvi A cattie is an Asian unit of measurement equivalent to 1.33 pounds or .45 kilograms.

him on his left shoulder with a small axe that he pulled out from beneath the counter.

'Death to Ghee Hok scum,' he cried, as he ran out from behind the counter and pursued the wounded and bleeding Gang Guo into the street. Gang Guo saw two of his friends on the other side of the street and called out for help. One of them picked up a big stick from a nearby pile of firewood and went to his aid, while the other ran off to get help from the Ghee Hok. Ying Chow, recognizing the danger, called out to his servant to summon help from the Ghee Hin.

Within a few minutes their argument over rice had expanded into a street brawl between members of the two societies. Within half an hour it had developed into a full-blown riot, as more and more members of the Ghee Hok and Ghee Hin joined the fight, with swords, knives, sticks, stones and bricks. As the conflict between the two societies spread into Telok Ayer Street, those society members who had temporarily gained the upper hand looted the stores of their rivals, until their rivals gained the upper hand and fought to retrieve their stolen goods.

When Superintendent Dunman arrived on the scene, he knew right away that the riot was beyond anything the town police could control by themselves. Dunman ordered Captain Mehmood to send for reinforcements from the outlying police stations and to try to contain the riot as best he could, while he went off to press the governor to call out the troops. When Dunman arrived at his office at the courthouse, he found Governor Butterworth reluctant to do so.

'Are you sure that is necessary, superintendent? I'm sure the leaders of the kongsi will soon put a stop to it themselves, even if you can't. I don't want the merchants panicked for no good reason.'

Dunman ignored the implied criticism in the governor's remark.

'I hope you're right, sir, but tensions are running very high between the Hokkiens and Teochews – partly over the Amoy rebellion, partly over rice and remittances. I'm sure both are looking to damage each other as much as they can before we intervene.'

'I want to avoid bloodshed if I can, superintendent,' Butterworth replied, 'and if I call out the troops we'll have bloodshed for sure.'

'With respect, sir,' Dunman replied, 'we already have bloodshed. Some men are dead and some severely wounded.'

'I mean the European community, superintendent,' Butterworth responded. 'Once we have troops firing upon the Chinese, we'll have all-out war, and the fighting will spread to the town proper.'

'It will do so in any case if we do not contain the riot now,' Dunman insisted, 'and we need the troops to contain it now.'

Colonel Butterworth raised his hand to signal the end of their debate.

'All right, superintendent. I'll come with you and take a look for myself. I need to see the field of battle before I call out the troops!'

Superintendent Dunman and Governor Butterworth set off with a party of police peons and the governor's staff. When they reached Coleman Bridge, they found that the riot had already spread beyond the Chinese town. A group of society men were fighting on the corner of Hill Street and River Valley Road, and one man stumbled towards them, blood streaming from both sides of his head, where his ears had been cut off. Mr Frank, a member of the governor's staff, rushed forward to help him, but was knocked to the ground by the man's pursuers, who dragged their victim back into the melee and cut off his head with a butcher's knife. As the governor watched aghast, a brick flew through the air and knocked off his top hat. Dunman dashed forward with a police peon and pulled Mr Frank to safety, and then returned to the governor.

'All right, Dunman, I'm convinced!' Governor Butterworth exclaimed. He scribbled a note on a pad he took from his frockcoat, and handed it to his adjutant. 'Captain Greenway, take this to the day officer and have him call out the sepoys. Half are to be deployed on guard duty, the other half as Superintendent Dunman commands.'

'God speed, superintendent,' he said to Dunman. 'Get this thing under control as soon as you can – I don't want this trouble spreading across the river!'

Then without another word, he turned and headed back to the safety of his office.

* * *

With police and sepoy reinforcements, Dunman managed to quell the rioting near Coleman Bridge and around Market Street. But he found that as soon as he controlled the fighting in one part of town, it would break out in another part, and he spent most of the afternoon and evening moving his police peons and soldiers around town. The society men did not put up much resistance when challenged by the police and sepoys, and were quickly dispersed, but only to resume their fight in another part of town, where they plundered the shops and attacked their rivals' businesses. By late afternoon all the Chinese shops and businesses were closed, and as darkness fell, the street fighting died out. Dunman reported to the governor that the European town was secured but that he expected more trouble the following day. The governor told him to deal with it.

18

Dunman had police patrols stationed at strategic points around town, but knew there was going to be trouble when none of the Chinese merchants showed any sign of opening their shops and businesses. The fighting and plundering erupted shortly after dawn, and Dunman had to request that the troops be retained to help control the situation. However, they were no longer enough, and the governor was obliged to request the aid of the marines from HMS *Sybille, Lily* and *Rapid,* which were anchored in the roads.

The marines helped to quell the violence, and the riot settled into the familiar pattern of the previous day. As the authorities approached the scene of a conflict, the society men melted away, only to resume their fighting and plundering in another place. By early morning the European merchants were deeply alarmed by the sight of men and women lying dead in the street with their genitals and breasts savaged. They closed their own businesses and godowns; they armed themselves and sent their wives and families out to the merchant ships in the harbour. At ten o' clock they held an emergency meeting in the Assembly Rooms, after which they sent a deputation to the governor urging upon him the serious nature of the situation, and offering their services to help suppress the rioting.

* * *

The Ghee Hin poured down Hokkien Street like a human wave. They dragged the traders and craftsmen from their shophouses and hacked them to pieces in the five-foot ways and out in the main street. When Madam Ang came down to investigate, they pulled her screaming from the doorway, and flung her into the street. Madam Ang was Cantonese, but Tan Keong Lan, who owned the silversmith shop below her, was Hokkien, and in their frenzy they assumed that she was too. Madam Ang cried out to them, but they quickly stifled her cries by stuffing Tan's severed genitals into her gaping mouth. Then they proceeded to slice off her breasts and vagina with their axes and knives, and then her hands and feet. When they were done with their mutilation they cut off her head, but by that time Madam Ang had already died of suffocation.

Upstairs, the babies began to cry, but no one paid them any mind.

* * *

Governor Butterworth thanked the merchant deputation for their concern, but assured them that the authorities were doing everything in their power to bring the situation under control, and that he had every confidence they would be successful. He advised them that the situation was not as serious as they made it out to be, and that he could deal with it quite adequately without their help.

When W.H. Read reported the governor's response, there was uproar among the merchants.

James Spottiswoode was the first to speak: 'I for one have no confidence that they will be successful – the thing is way out of control already. And if the society men perceive that we cannot control them, we'll be in for real trouble – it'll be our godowns that'll be plundered next.'

'I agree,' W.H. replied. 'The governor said he was going to use the Kling convicts to help out, but they're just as likely to join the looting as the Chinese and Malays.'

'I don't think so,' said Ronnie Simpson. 'They've too much to lose, and I hear that the Malays have shown no sign of joining the fighting – and they've not been attacked so far. But the answer is surely obvious. We should press the governor to let Tom Dunman swear us in as special constables – most of us are handy enough with a rifle or pistol.' And some of our wives too, he thought to himself, recalling his wife's refusal to seek the safety of the merchant ships in the harbour.

'Grand idea, Simpson,' said W.H., and they all agreed that they would request a meeting with the governor, resident councillor Church, and superintendent Dunman at the central police station at noon, during which they would offer their services as special constables. With Dunman and Church's support, the governor reluctantly agreed and thanked them for their support and cooperation. W.H. Read was the first to be sworn in.

The merchants quickly organized themselves into squads of about a dozen men, headed by magistrates or police officers. Ronnie sought out Seah Eu Chin and Tan Kim Ching, and together they quickly organized a meeting of thirty of the leading Chinese merchants, both Teochew and Hokkien, in the Reading Rooms in Commercial Square, where resident councillor Church urged them to help restore order. They agreed to bring in the heads of the secret societies, and persuaded them to sign a document agreeing to order their members to refrain from fighting and looting. Yet the fighting and looting continued throughout the afternoon and evening and resumed the following day at dawn. Meanwhile, the commerce of the port ground to a complete halt, with every shop, business and godown closed and barricaded.

The following day the governor ordered all Chinese boats to remain in the centre of the river, to prevent them from being used as a means of escape from one side of the river to the other. Armed longboats from the men-of-war in the harbour patrolled the river to ensure compliance. In the morning serious rioting broke out on Telok Ayer Street, and on South Bridge Road and Circular Road; in the afternoon the fighting shifted to Philip Street and Amoy Street. By evening Dunman and the army and navy officers finally had the situation under control, with armed patrols posted at critical points throughout the town, and about fifty society men taken into custody.

Yet their control of the town only drove the society men to the suburbs and the countryside, where they resumed their looting and slaughter the following day. They burned Chinese houses and bangsals [cvii] at Tanglin, and now seemed intent on taking the battle to the authorities, whereas previously they had restricted their attacks to their society enemies. By midday on Monday a large body of fighting men surrounded the police station at Bukit Timah, clashing their gongs and demanding the release of society prisoners. Fierce fighting broke out at Payah Lebar, [cviii] along the banks of the Kallang River, where the Teochews heavily outnumbered the Hokkiens, and where the river ran red with the blood of decapitated bodies. Captain Samad, in command of the police station at Bukit Timah, issued his men with rifles and ordered them to fire into the ranks of the rioters, who quickly dispersed and headed north after a few of their men were wounded. Mr Cluff, the deputy superintendent of police, led a party of peons out to put an end to the wanton destruction at Payah Lebar, where they found scenes of horrible mutilation – of men, women, children and livestock.

---

cvii Barns or storage houses.
cviii Wide swamp in Malay.

19

Alfred Russel Wallace had spent the past few weeks with Father Maudit at Bukit Timah, where he and his assistant Charles Grant had settled into a routine. They rose at five thirty, before sunrise. They bathed by dousing themselves with water ladled from a jug that was replenished daily by a Chinese boy who attended the mission school, then brewed up a pot of coffee to prepare them for their early morning work. Alfred organized the beetles and butterflies that they had collected the previous day, and set them out to dry, while Charles mended the nets and refilled the pincushions they used for fixing captured insects. They breakfasted with Father Maudit at eight if he was not occupied with his flock, and set out for the jungle at around nine.

They hiked for half a mile along a steep path until they reached their favourite spot near the summit of one of the adjacent hills, by which time they were drenched with perspiration. But here they enjoyed the delightfully cool shade afforded by the giant trees, while they caught their breath and admired the luxuriant vegetation – ferns, caladiums and climbing rattan palms formed a dense undergrowth beneath the high canopy of trees. They spent many happy hours wandering the winding paths left by the Chinese woodcutters, who came to cut down the trees and saw them into planks, but took special care to avoid the tiger traps when they ventured off the path in pursuit of butterflies or other insects. They tended to restrict their search to a single square mile of forest, which was particularly rich in varieties of beetles. Alfred had already identified more than six hundred species, including over a hundred different kinds of longicorns.[cix] They would return to the Church of St Joseph at about three in the afternoon, where they would prepare the specimens they had collected during the day, which usually amounted to around fifty beetles, and an assortment of butterflies, bugs and other insects. Charles worked on the butterflies and bugs while Alfred worked on the beetles – he did not trust his assistant with these treasures. They would take their dinner at four and work again until six, after which they would read or converse with Father Maudit, or continue with work until eight if their day had been more productive than usual. Then to their beds, where they had no difficulty sleeping, despite the loud whir of the crickets and the occasional sharp shrieking of owls in the jungle.

* * *

It was almost noon, and the sun was high in the sky, but it was cool in the green shade of the forest. Alfred marvelled once again at the diversity of species in this small section of jungle. He knew the reason for it – the soil was fertile, and the vegetation thrived in the filtered sunlight and regular refreshing showers. The Chinese woodcutters also played a major role. They left a carpet of dead and decaying leaves and bark, and a rich supply of wood shavings in the saw-pits, ideal for the nourishment of insect larvae. Yet he could not help but marvel at the sheer productivity and diversity he saw before him, and exclaimed to his assistant: 'Incredible, quite incredible! You know what this reminds me of, Charles? Milton's mazes of the tangled wood! Here is a tangled bank, full and overflowing with the rich diversity of life – a marvel to behold and ponder!'

'Yes, indeed, sir,' replied Charles Grant, who did not share his employer's enthusiasm. He had agreed to be Wallace's assistant so

---

cix Longhorned beetles, with long antennae.

he could have his passage paid to the Far East, but he really wanted to be a schoolteacher, and was hoping to leave his master's employ at the earliest opportunity.

A crashing through the undergrowth rudely interrupted Alfred's reverie, as a young Chinese man came running up crying out to them in Malay.

'What's he saying, sir? Is there some trouble?' Charles called out, not yet having mastered the language.

'Indeed there is, Charles, although I'm not quite sure what the trouble is. But he says that Father Maudit wants us to return to the church as soon as possible.'

The two men gathered up their nets and specimens as quickly as they could and ran back with the messenger to the church, where they found Father Maudit in a state of high agitation. He was issuing commands to his parishioners, urging them to hide themselves and their families in the jungle. They noticed he had an old flintlock pistol stuffed into his belt.

'Ah! Mr Wallace and Mr Grant! I'm so glad Jin Bee found you! There have been riots in the town, with the Ghee Hin and the Ghee Hok fighting in the streets, looting shops and murdering merchants and their families. We must get you back to the safety of the town as soon as possible – I will send some men to lead you there, so please gather up your necessities and prepare to depart.'

'But I thought you said there was fighting in the town?' Wallace questioned him. 'What's the point of us returning to town? – we'd surely be safer staying here.'

'The man who came from town to warn me says that the authorities now have the town under control,' Father Maudit replied. 'The governor has called out the sepoys and the marines, and has deputized the European merchants as special constables – even roped in the Kling convicts, he said. Now the fighting and looting has spread to the countryside, and they're bound to show up here soon. I've sent most of my congregation away to safe hiding places, which I'm glad we had the foresight to construct after the troubles of '51, but I have a few trusted men who can lead you safely back to town.'

Wallace did not move or reply, and Charles looked at him quizzingly.

'I think it's bit late for that,' Wallace said quietly and calmly, as he pointed down the Bukit Timah Road towards town, where in the dusty distance they saw a mob of over fifty men racing towards them. Wallace took out the telescope he carried with him – he often liked to survey the surrounding countryside from the top of Bukit Timah Hill – and gasped aloud at what he saw. Some of the men were displaying the severed heads of their victims on wooden stakes, shaking them up and down in the air like gory battle flags.

'I'm afraid we're in for some trouble, gentlemen, and we're not going anywhere until it's over.' He told Charles to follow him back to their room, where they picked up their rifles and ammunition.

Wallace was surprised by his own calm and control, which seemed to help steady Charles' nerves – although he noticed the young man's hands were trembling as he loaded his rifle. It had been the same when the *Helen* had gone down, when he had been sure there could be no escape from a watery grave – what had concerned him most at the time was that he might lose his pocket watch. But now his concern was for poor Charles, who had hardly lived his life, and Father Maudit, who had led such a good life – neither deserved to die at the hands of a Chinese mob. He had no concern about his own life – if he were destined to die in this hilly tropical glade, then so be it. He would die here and be buried amongst his beloved beetles.

He noticed that Father Maudit was praying silently to himself, while cocking his ancient flintlock.

'Hold your fire until they get closer, and aim low,' Wallace told them. 'We want to make every shot count. If we can drop some of their leaders, we might give them pause – and might even scare them off.'

Some hope, he thought to himself. Now they were getting closer, like some great wave of murderous humanity threatening to overwhelm them.

Then all of a sudden, another great human wave came crashing out of the jungle from the east, and broke over the mass of men coming up the Bukit Timah Road. The approaching mob ground to a halt, as they turned to face their attackers. The human waves swayed back and forth as the Ghee Hin and the Ghee Hok fought for supremacy, and then the mob on the road gained the upper hand and drove their enemies back into the jungle, where they pursued them with screams and yells and crashing gongs.

The Bukit Timah Road now lay deserted before them, save for the dead and wounded, and all three men wiped the perspiration from their brows as they listened to the sounds of fighting fading deeper into the jungle.

'Well, that was a close-run thing, as the Duke of Wellington would have said,' Wallace remarked, putting his hand on Charles' shoulder. He then turned to Father Maudit. 'Father, I don't suppose you'd have a spot of brandy back there, do you? I think we all deserve a nip.'

'I'm afraid not, Mr Wallace, but I do have some Chinese plum wine that might do the trick.'

Which they all agreed it did when he produced three overflowing wooden beakers.

'Now you must make your way back to town as soon as possible,' said Father Maudit. Charles Grant nodded vigorously.

'I think not,' Wallace replied. 'We've as much chance meeting them on the road or in the jungle, so I think we'll just take our chances here, if you don't mind, Father. In any case we have work to do. I don't think it prudent to return to the jungle at present, but we have this morning's specimens to work on, after we have helped you attend to the wounded men, of course.'

'Very well,' Father Maudit replied, 'and I'm obliged for your help. I'll get my bag and we'll go at once to see what we can do for these poor fellows. But at least let Mr Grant seek the safety of the police station at Bukit Timah, and warn them of our close shave – perhaps they will be able to spare some men to protect us.'

Wallace agreed to this, since Charles was clearly enthusiastic about the idea, although he questioned the wisdom of it – it was a bit like hiding from the bees in the honey pot.

Most of the men on the road were dead or dying because they had been horribly mutilated. They brought some comfort to a dying man by answering his desperate call for water; although they could not understand his dialect, they understood well enough what he wanted. The man's lips were the only recognizable part of his face; his ears and nose had been sliced off, and his eyes gouged out. Father Maudit knelt and said a prayer for his heathen soul as the man expired before them.

20

Back in town W.H. Read led a party of armed volunteers and police peons through the streets, accompanied by a Chinese convict called Mo Choon, who could speak Teochew, Hokkien, Hakka and Cantonese. They stopped every hundred yards while Mo Choon proclaimed peace throughout the town, and told any assembled men to return to their homes, businesses, and trades, on pain of imprisonment and deportation.

'But how do you know he's not urging them to riot rather than return peacefully to their homes?' asked Thomas White, a clerk with Dyce and Co who had volunteered as a special constable, when they found themselves surrounded by about a hundred men. 'Do you understand what he's saying to them?'

'Haven't the foggiest idea,' W.H. replied cheerfully.

'But the first sign of trouble, Mo Choon gets one in the head,' he continued, as he levelled his Navy colt revolver in the convict's direction. 'I think he understands that well enough.'

Fortunately, there was no trouble, and the party managed to arrest some ringleaders and deposit them in the now heavily overcrowded jailhouse.

* * *

Yet the fighting continued throughout the day in the country, and continued on Tuesday, when more houses were burned at Tanglin. At noon Governor Butterworth issued a proclamation declaring that 'all persons found fighting with sticks or throwing stones will be apprehended and punished according to law, and all householders giving shelter to such persons either directly or indirectly, shall be forthwith apprehended and prosecuted.'

The governor and resident councillor Church also led a party of European, Arab, Parsee and Armenian merchants to meet with Seah Eu Chin and Tan Kim Ching and pressed upon them the need to bring their clansmen under control. They replied that they appreciated the need – it was bad for business for everyone – but that it was proving more difficult than they had originally supposed, with the fighting having spread to the countryside. Seah Eu Chin and Tan Kim Ching assured them they were doing their utmost to bring the disturbances to an end. They hoped that they could rein in the troublemakers in town within the next day or two, and the country leaders by the end of the week.

On Wednesday Superintendent Dunman landed parties of special constables and sepoys from the steamer *Hooghly* at strategic points on the north of the island – at Changi, Serangoon and Upper Thomson Road. As they fanned out across the roads and jungle paths, they surprised the society gangs and captured many of their leaders. As they marched down from Changi to Bukit Timah, Father Maudit and Alfred Wallace greeted them with gratitude and great relief, and by the following day Charles Grant felt safe enough to return to his work.

On Thursday, Superintendent Dunman, who had been up all night directing the police and the squads of sepoys and marines, stood in the darkness on the corner of Telok Ayer Street, as the golden sunlight spread across the waters of the bay and touched the gilded dragons on the tiled roofs of the Thian Hock Seng temple. He breathed a sigh of relief at what he saw. Shopkeepers were removing the shutters from their windows and the barricades from their doors; the hawkers were already out in the street cooking up their noodles; and even the barbers were setting up for business. Peace had come at last to the town, and news of it quickly spread to the Europeans, who reopened their shops and godowns with sighs of relief and much self-congratulation – although how much the peaceful conclusion was due to the actions of the special constables, nobody could tell.

* * *

Seah Eu Chin and Tan Kim Ching took responsibility for the children that had been found in the upstairs room on Hokkien Street, where Madam Ang had once lived. The boys and a few of the girls were placed with Chinese families, and the remaining girls put in the care of the Sisters of the Holy Infant Jesus. Seah Eu Chin paid for the funeral services for Madam Ang, who everyone said had been a kind old lady who had loved the children that she cared for.

21

The violence continued sporadically in the country for a few more days. On Thursday the governor issued another declaration, directed at those society men who continued to fight on, warning that 'all persons found committing acts of violence on their neighbours or their neighbour's property, or assembling with arms in their hands, will be hunted from place to place, until they are taken or destroyed.'

Eventually Superintendent Dunman managed to bring the situation under control in the country as well as the town, using a tactic that he developed in the early days of the riots. Under cover of fire directed over the heads of the rioters, he sent his best men rushing forward to seize the leaders and drag them from the crowd. When the ten days of rioting finally ended, Dunman had over five hundred society men held as prisoners in the police and army cells. He estimated that about four or five hundred society men and their families had been killed, and many others seriously wounded or maimed for life. And all as the result of a quarrel over five catties of rice – although he knew the root of the trouble went much deeper than that.

* * *

At a meeting with the leading merchants, Governor Butterworth and Resident Councillor Church thanked them for their efforts in bringing the violence to an end. The question then arose as to how to deal with the five hundred prisoners in the cells. W.H. Read and

William Napier were determined that the society men should be taught a very severe lesson, but Seah Eu Chin and Tan Kim Ching cautioned that a public display of judicial severity would do more harm than good, both for business and future security, although they agreed that the worse cases should receive full punishment under the law. They pointed out that although there been great loss of life and damage to property, most of it had been Chinese lives and Chinese property. Although the occasional attacks against the police or Europeans were to be deeply regretted, they were incidental to the struggle between the Ghee Hin and the Ghee Hok.

'What were your casualties, Superintendent Dunman?' Tan Kim Ching asked him.

'Practically none – quite surprising really. Mr Frank got knocked about a bit on the first day, but he's fine now. Charlie Cashin lost the end of one of his fingers, but he'll live. The only fatality was Mr Rohde, an assistant with Apel and Co, who was one of the special constables – but he died from sunstroke, the doctor said.'

'The governor was also assaulted, and had his hat knocked from his head,' said Governor Butterworth gravely.

'But I'm sure that was an accident,' Dunman assured the governor. 'I don't think they were aiming at you in particular.'

'A great comfort, I'm sure, Superintendent Dunman,' Butterworth replied tartly. 'But Mr Tan's point is well taken – I will communicate it to Sir William, who will preside over the grand jury.'

* * *

A special grand jury was convened on June 6, before Governor Butterworth, Sir William Jeffcott, the recorder, and Mr Church, the resident councillor. The jurors included Jose D'Almeida, Dunjeebhoy Hormusjee, Catchick Moses, John Purvis, James Spottiswoode and

George Schmidt. No Chinese were represented on the grand jury. Of the five hundred society men arrested, two hundred and fifty were brought to trial, which lasted seventeen days. Sixty were sentenced to hard labour, eight were transported for fourteen years, and six were sentenced to death, although only two were executed, by hanging in the prison yard.

On the grand jury's recommendation, Governor Butterworth presented Superintendent Dunman with a sword of honour at a special ceremony at Government House, for his service to the community during the riots. W.H. Read, who had scoffed when the governor had presented a similar sword to Temenggong Daing Ibrahim for his service in the suppression of piracy, whispered under his breath: 'At least Dunman deserved it, notwithstanding the little help from his friends.'

22

Riots or no riots, the Nutmeg King continued to prosper. Gan Eng Seng built himself a larger house out towards Tanglin and took himself a new wife; none of the Tans were invited to the very elaborate and expensive wedding that he held at his new house. Gan Eng Seng had become one of the richest men in Singapore, largely on account of his nutmeg plantations, which were now the most extensive on the island. His happiness was complete when his new wife became pregnant, and all the signs indicated it would be a boy. Surely, I deserve a son at last, he thought to himself, after all I have been through, and after all the offerings I have made to the gods and my ancestors. He stood looking out the window of his bedroom on the top story of his new house, which was built in the southern Chinese style, with elaborate dragons and phoenixes decorating the red tiled roof, and carved marble pillars adorning the cornices and courtyard. He looked down into the courtyard below, and admired the very expensive blue stone tiles that he had imported from Liverpool. He truly considered himself a fortunate man. Those spiteful Tans had failed to sweep his luck away.

* * *

Concerns about a possible recurrence of rioting among the Chinese, and the possibility of a Russian naval attack as an extension of the war in the Crimea, prompted the European merchants to call a meeting in the Reading Rooms on July 8. John Purvis chaired the meeting, and asked the merchants to consider a motion calling for the formation of a Volunteer Rifle Corps.

While most present thought they had conducted themselves well during the recent disturbances, they all recognized that their efforts would have been more effective had they been properly drilled and trained to act together as functioning units. The motion was approved unanimously, and thirty-two men signed the Volunteer Roll, the first being Mr W.H. Read. In the following days another twenty-nine men signed on, bringing the total to sixty-one. Governor Butterworth accepted their motion, and became the first colonel of the Corps, with Captain Ronald Macpherson of the Madras Artillery as its first commandant.

Before the meeting adjourned, the participants made a generous contribution to the Patriotic Fund for the widows and orphans of soldiers and sailors engaged in the Crimean War, which was collected by the Reverend C. Gladwin, the chaplain of Singapore.

23

One evening in July, Gan Eng Seng received a message from the manager of his nutmeg plantation on Orchard Road, advising him to visit immediately. Gan Eng Seng had been annoyed with the man, because he made regular inspections of his plantations according to his own schedule, but the following morning he called for his carriage and set off to visit him. As they pulled in off the main road and travelled down the path that led to the plantation offices and quarters, he understood why the manager had sent for him. Although they passed by row upon row of healthy trees, displaying their white and yellow blossoms and peach coloured flowers in the early morning sunlight, every now and then he saw a tree that stood pale and ghostlike amid the pastel colours, stripped of its flowers and foliage. His jaw dropped in horror, and he ordered his driver to stop. He climbed down from his carriage, and walked through the rows to inspect the nearest diseased tree. Tiny beetles crawled across the bleached and bark-less branches, like flies over a corpse. Eng Seng shuddered in disgust, and returned to his carriage.

His manager confirmed what he had already seen with his own eyes, that the plantation had been afflicted by a mysterious blight. The manager told him that the blight had spread to other plantations, including those of Mr Cuppage at Emerald Hill and Mr Carnie at Cairn Hill, but that fortunately the disease seemed to be isolated to a few trees spread out at some distance from each other throughout the plantations, and did not appear to afflict adjacent trees. He recommended that the diseased trees be uprooted and burned, including any tree that displayed early signs of disease, to which Gan Eng Seng readily agreed. Then Gan Eng Seng set off to inspect his other plantations. All were affected, but in each only relatively few isolated trees had succumbed to the blight. He met with other Chinese and European plantation owners, and although they had many theories and many suggestions – including destroying all the trees and planting anew – none had succeeded in eradicating the tiny beetle that they all believed to be the root of the problem. Gan Eng Seng instructed his managers to uproot and burn any afflicted trees. Then the Nutmeg King returned to town, where he made a very large donation to the Thian Hock Keng Temple.

* * *

When James Brooke recovered from his smallpox attack, Brooke Brooke built him a hilltop retreat on Santubong Mountain, where he recovered some of his strength, and for a few months James left the day-to-day administration of Sarawak to Brooke Brooke, his younger nephew Charles Johnson,[25] who had joined James' service two years previous, and their junior colleagues. But one matter demanded his attention, and he cursed the British government as he felt the supreme irony of it. News of the Commission of Inquiry had spread from Singapore to Sarawak and from Sarawak to Brunei. Now everyone knew that Rajah Brooke was out of favour with the Great White Queen and the British government, and that no British ships would come to support him against his enemies.

When the steamer *Lily* docked outside his residence, bearing a summons to appear before the Commission of Inquiry in Singapore, it was almost more than he could bear.

24

Gan Eng Seng looked out over his nutmeg plantation on Orchard Road. He could scarcely believe it. Where once there had been a delight of pastel colours, the trees now stood like rows of spectral skeletons, their bleached branches reaching out like pale ghosts in the moonlight, even though it was early morning. It was the same on all his plantations – acre upon acre of bone-white trees, around which black creepers were beginning to entwine themselves. He was not the only one to suffer – all the other nutmeg planters had seen their estates eventually succumb to the blight – but none had suffered as much as he, for he had the most extensive holdings. He was no longer the Nutmeg King.

* * *

Gan Eng Seng returned home dejected but not disconsolate. He had experienced ups and downs in the past, but he was a fighter, and he would survive this latest setback. He had the sudden thought that the Tans had brought this upon him, when they had swept the luck from his house after the death of his former wife. But he quickly dismissed it, for the other plantation owners had all been afflicted by the blight, and none had quarrelled with her family. He would be forced to sell some of his land, it was true, and perhaps at a loss, but he had other investments, and remained confident about the future. His new wife was close to her time, and all the indications were that she would be delivered of a healthy son, who would honour his father and perform the ancestral rites for him after his death.

* * *

One week later his wife was delivered of a male child, but the baby was stillborn. His wife died from a fever a few days later. On the day after the funeral, in the late evening, Gan Eng Seng sat alone on a chair in his ornate bedroom, crying like a child. He moaned and sobbed for nearly an hour and then, exhausted by his grief, he lay down on the bed and waited for sleep to overcome him. But as he did so, he seemed to hear the faint sound of a baby crying, coming from some distant place within the house. He tried to ignore it and fall asleep, but he could not – the persistent crying kept him wide awake. He called for his servant, and demanded that the man go and stop the baby crying. The servant looked at Gan Eng Seng in horror and fear, and in a faltering voice told his master that there was no baby in the house.

'But do you not hear it crying?' Eng Seng demanded.

'No, master,' the servant responded. 'I hear nothing but the wind whispering through the willow trees.'

Eng Seng leapt up from his bed and dragged the man through the house to where he heard the sound of the baby crying. But when Eng Seng reached the room where he thought the sound was coming from, it seemed to have moved to another part of the house, and when he went there, it seemed to have moved on again. Gan Eng Seng beat his servant severely, and returned to his bedroom in anger and disgust. As he entered the room and closed the door behind him, he heard the baby's cries echoing around him. Then in his heart he knew the origin of the crying. It was Poh Ling's baby, whose orphan ghost had come to haunt him from its lonely grave. He lay down on the bed trembling, and pressed his hands hard against his ears to block out the sound. But it was no use, for the baby's cries reached into his brain and pierced the very depths of his soul. Although he had his eyes tightly shut and his head covered with a pillow, he could see the image of the baby before him, its ugly harelip twisted in an evil grimace.

And then he heard another sound, a soft creaking. He knew that noise. It was the noise of a light female body dangling from a silken noose. He screamed and leapt out of bed, his eyes darting all around, wide in horror. He heard his name being called out from the courtyard below, in a voice shrill and piercing. He rushed to the window and flung the shutters wide, but could see nothing in the cool moonlight that bathed the blue tiles in the courtyard. His mind racing, he suddenly remembered the passage in the Jade Chronicle, which told of how the demons Life-is-Short and Death-has-Graduations sometimes took pity on women who had committed suicide because of mistreatment by their husbands, and who had suffered the trials of the ten levels of hell. Sometimes the demons allowed them to return as ghosts to revenge themselves upon their oppressors, before they drank the goddess Meng's wine of forgetfulness and returned to earth in their animal reincarnations. The thought made him angry, for it was not he who had mistreated her, but she who had mistreated him! She had brought the hare-lipped monster into the world, and then shamed him with her suicide. His anger helped him control his fear, and he remembered how he could rid himself of her ghost. He must sacrifice to Lord Zhuan Lun, the king of the tenth court of hell.

The beginnings of a grim smile formed upon his lips as he made his plan, but then vanished when he turned back from the window and saw her standing before him, pale and white as the branches of his dead nutmeg trees, and carrying her dead baby in her arms. She fixed his eyes with her deathly gaze and moved slowly towards him. Gan Eng Seng stepped back in fear, and toppled over the low window edge, his arms flailing as he fell to the courtyard below.

His skull exploded like a ripe watermelon as it struck the ground, spilling his red brains over the elegant blue tiles.

25

1854

In May, General Senggelinqin ordered that the waters of the Grand Canal be diverted to flood the fortified position of the remnants of the northern expedition. As the exhausted Taiping soldiers tried to escape, they were picked off or captured and executed by the Qing battalions. Although it would be another year before they finally surrendered, they were spent as a fighting force.

Despite the failure of the northern expedition, the Taiping continued to wage war on many fronts. Shi Dakai, the Wing King, had more success in the western campaign, although he was harried by Zeng Guofan, the scholar-gentleman who had founded the Hunan army [26] to help the regular Qing forces defeat the Taiping. As the campaigns in the west and south raged on, and cities and towns changed hands and changed hands again, many fled to the eastern ports, and many found their way to Singapore.

Hong Xiuquan remained as determined and confident of success as ever, and the Taiping still controlled major centres and three hundred miles of the southern Yangtze valley. Hong now returned his attention to the east, to the Yangtze delta and the port-city of Shanghai, as an economic base for a renewed assault on the 'demon-devils' of Peking.

* * *

Duncan was preparing to leave Singapore, having returned for a spell to visit his family. They were relieved to see that the darkness seemed to have lifted from him. He was enthusiastic about the prospects for their business in Hong King, but despite the display of his old fire and energy, there was still a sense of melancholy about him. He did not mention his late wife and seemed to take only a polite interest in his sister's children. He still seemed a lonely character, never talking of his old or any new friends, except insofar as it related to business. Yet still he was not alone. Marie's ghost had followed him to Hong Kong and back to Singapore, and now sat with him in his cabin as his ship made its way back to Hong Kong.

* * *

Little did either of these men know that their paths were soon to cross.

26

After seeing his son off on his steamer, Ronnie Simpson walked back to his office. He was in a reflective mood, and as he passed Johnston and Co, he paused a moment and sat at the edge of Boat Quay, looking upriver towards Government Hill, or Forbidden Hill as he still thought of it. He thought about the men he had known when the settlement was first founded, and who had since passed. Stamford Raffles, William Farquhar, Alexander Laurie Johnston and George Coleman, to name but a few – all good men in their own ways, and he was proud to have known them. Others not so much, Captain Methven and Captain Flint, for example, but he would not think ill of them. They had all played their parts and contributed in their own ways. He hoped that his family and friends would think as well of him when he was gone.

* * *

After he returned home from the office, Tan Kim Ching said a prayer before the ancestral tablet of his late father, Tan Tock Seng, and made offerings to the household gods. He knew his father had been a good man and a devout Taoist, a man of great generosity of spirit who did not squander his wealth but used it for the good of the poor and sick of all nations. He hoped that he and his brothers could live up to the example set by their father, so that their own children would come to recognize their humble merits.

* * *

Captain Adil bin Mehmood visited his father's grave in the old Muslim cemetery at Jalan Kubor. He had been very young when his father had been murdered by Syed Yassim, but he remembered well the man who had inspired him to become a policeman. He hoped that his father would have been proud of his police work, and that God would forgive him for failing to save the life of the boy Aswad.

* * *

Sadad bin Badang watched over his wife Nadu and his son Adi and reflected on his good fortune. He had survived the evil magic of the bomoh and had managed to make a decent living for his family. He wondered what his ancestor Badang, the great warrior, would have thought of him. Not much perhaps, but he hoped that in his own way he served God and his community with the humble talents he had. He said a prayer for his ancestor, who had not known the true religion, and hoped that one day they would all be united in Heaven.

* * *

Abdullah bin Abdul Kadir, Munshi Abdullah, having completed his Holy Haj to Mecca, died in Jeddah in October, as he was preparing to return to Singapore. One of his friends brought back the diary he had kept of his journey, which the Reverend Keasberry published posthumously. Abdullah was remembered well by all the races in Singapore, among whom he had gained an honourable reputation in the thirty-five years he had dwelt there. As he himself had reflected in his autobiographical *Hikayat Abdullah*, when commenting on the lives of Raffles and Farquhar, reputation was all that endured in the end:

'More especially is it with us human beings, whose nature is weak, whose life is uncertain, and who are perishable creatures, which state is not to be avoided, from one age to another; for the greatness and mightiness of this world flits – they are not guaranteed to one for any length of time, but only the name of being good or bad. This people speak of after they are gone.'

NOTES

1 Peranakan or Straits Chinese were descendants of Chinese merchants who came to Malacca and married Malay women, in the absence of suitable Chinese brides. The female children of their unions were not allowed to marry Malay men, and became available as brides for future generations of Chinese men. The male Peranakans called themselves Babas and the women Nonyas. The Peranakans maintained the dress and beliefs of traditional Chinese, but absorbed many aspects of Malay culture. They spoke a distinctive Peranakan patois, which was a mixture of Hokkien, Malay, and a smattering of English words drawn from business and commerce. They also developed a distinctive cuisine, which combined Chinese ingredients such as rice, noodles and stir-fried dishes with Malay staples such as coconut milk, green chillies, lime and lemongrass. Given their established links with the Malay community and the good relations they had developed with the British in Penang and Malacca, they were ideally situated to mediate commercial relations between the Chinese, British and Malay communities in Singapore.

2 William Jardine was born near Lochmaden, Dumfriesshire, Scotland on February 24, 1784. He was the son of a farmer, but excelled at school, and was admitted to the University of Edinburgh to study medicine in 1800 at the age of 16. With support for his tuition from his elder brother, and an apprenticeship with an Edinburgh surgeon, who provided board and lodgings, he was able to graduate in 1802, when he became a member of the Royal

College of Surgeons of Edinburgh. That same year he joined the East India Company as surgeon's mate aboard the *Brunswick*, en route to India and China. Employees in the Company's maritime service were allowed to trade in goods for their own profit and were assigned cargo space aboard Company ships. Jardine exploited this opportunity by not only trading on his own behalf, but by leasing the assigned space of other employees to expand upon it. Through such enterprise he had accumulated a sizeable sum of money by the time he left the Company in 1817, to serve as commercial agent and junior partner in the trading house of Cowasjee, Weeding and Jardine of Bombay. In 1823 Jardine travelled to Canton to become a junior partner in the firm of Charles Magniac and Co, one of the oldest British firms trading in China. When Charles Magniac died in Paris the following year, his son Hollingworth, who was intent on returning to England, appointed Jardine as senior managing partner in the firm, while he remained a silent partner. When Hollingworth's younger brother Daniel was forced to resign from the firm in 1824 because it was discovered that he had married his Chinese mistress, Jardine found himself in control of the largest trading house in Canton.

3   James Matheson was born in the village of Lairg, in the northern county of Sunderland, Scotland, on October 17, 1796. His father was a successful merchant who traded with India, and after attending Edinburgh University, James followed him into the family business. When his father died, James sold the business and sailed with his nephew Alexander Matheson for China, where both men thought the future lay. William Jardine invited James and his nephew to join Magniac and Co in 1827.

4   Thomas Oxley was born in Dublin in 1805. After his medical training at Marischal College, Aberdeen, he joined the

administration of the Straits Settlements in Penang in 1825 and was appointed assistant surgeon to the Penang Residency in 1830. That same year he was transferred to Singapore as assistant surgeon to Dr Montgomerie, then the senior surgeon. Oxley married Lucy Caroline Garling in 1833, and the couple had three children. He became senior surgeon in 1844 after Dr Montgomerie went on furlough. He purchased 173 acres of jungle which he formed into the Killiney Estates plantation, devoted to the cultivation of nutmeg.

5 Seah Eu Chin was born in 1805 in Guangdong province in China. He came from a wealthy Teochew family and was educated in the Chinese classics. He immigrated to Singapore in 1823, originally working as a clerk and accountant. One of the few literate migrants of his day, he quickly established himself in the local merchant community, founding his own company in 1830. He established his first gambier plantation in 1835 and consolidated his many business enterprises into Eu Chin and Co that year. One of the wealthiest Chinese merchants, he was one of the few admitted to the (European dominated) Singapore Chamber of Commerce. A founder of the Ngee Ann kongsi, he contributed much to the Chinese community and played a mediating role between the Chinese community and the British administration. In recognition of his regular work as a grand juror, he was appointed as a justice of the peace, and became a naturalized British subject in 1853. He published the first accounts by a Chinese author of the living and working conditions of Chinese immigrants in Singapore.

6 After John Crawford, the third resident of Singapore, retired in August, 1826, the East India Company united Singapore with Penang and Malacca to form the Presidency of the Straits Settlements. Penang became the official seat of the governor of the Settlements, until George Bonham transferred it to Singapore

in 1837, with resident councillors appointed to each of the three settlements. From 1833 onwards, the governor of the Settlements no longer communicated directly with the Court of Directors of the East India Company in London, but with the Governor-General in India, who provided quarterly reports to the East India Company. The Indian government managed the Settlements for the next thirty-four years (until Singapore became a Crown Colony in 1867), during which time the governor-general in India appointed the governors and resident councillors of the Straits Settlements.

7   The main Chinese dialect groups in Singapore, most of whom came from the provinces of Kwangtung and Fukien in south east China, were Hokkien, Teochew, Cantonese and Hakka. The Hokkiens were the largest group, and dominated commercial life in Singapore from the early days, both as businessmen and shopkeepers. The Teochews were the second largest group, comprising farmers, shopkeepers and business rivals of the Hokkiens. The third largest group were the Cantonese, employed mainly as agricultural labourers and artisans. The Hakkas, the fourth largest group, generally worked as labourers and farmers.

8   James Brooke was born on April 29, 1803 and raised in the European quarter of the city of Benares in India. James' father Thomas Brooke was a High Court judge and an official of the East India Company. His mother, Anne Marie, was the illegitimate daughter of the Scottish peer Colonel William Stuart, the ninth Lord Blantyre. James had two elder brothers, Henry and Charles William, and four sisters. When James was twelve, he was sent as a boarder to King Edward VI Grammar School in Norwich, and then privately tutored in Bath when his parents returned from India for their retirement.

His brothers Henry and Charles William joined the Bengal

army in the service of the East India Company, and James followed them by joining the 6th Bengal Native Infantry in 1819 at the age of sixteen. In 1825, he was wounded in action in Burma, and was invalided home, where he spent five years of convalescence. When he returned to India in 1830, he was delayed at sea, and arrived too late to join his regiment. His five years approved leave having expired en route, he resigned his commission before he was dismissed.

When he returned to England, James begged his father to buy him a vessel, so he could start his own trading business in the Far East. His father bought him both a ship, the *Findley*, and a cargo of goods. James set off for China and Japan, but the trip was a disaster. James discovered he had no aptitude for trade and was forced to sell his cargo at a great loss before returning to England. That might have put an end to his dreams of foreign adventure, but shortly before he returned home his father died, leaving each of his children thirty thousand pounds sterling.

Three months later James bought himself a schooner, the *Royalist*, and spent the next two years getting to know his vessel and training his crew while sailing in and around the Mediterranean. He set off for Singapore and Borneo in December 1838.

9 Father Jean-Marie Beurel was born on February 5, 1813, in Plouguenast, Lower Brittany. He was ordained as a Catholic priest at the age of twenty-five and joined the Society of Foreign Missions in Paris in 1838. Father Beurel was originally sent to Singapore as part of the Mission of Siam, but the following year Bishop Courvezy of Penang appointed him priest of the Good Shepherd parish in Singapore.

10 Dr Martin was the brother of Alexander Martin, who had come to Singapore with Raffles and set up a dispensary in 1826,

but who had died in 1831. For the first three years Dr Little lived in the dispensary, while Dr Martin lived in the house next door. Then Dr Martin moved out to Annanbank on River Valley Road and Dr Little bought Bonnygrass House from Adam Sykes of Robert Wise and Co, where he lived for the next twenty years.

11 Alexander Laurie Johnston died nine years later at his home in Bluehill, Kirckudbright, on February 19, 1850.

12 James Matheson was elected to William Jardine's vacant parliamentary seat in 1843 and served as member of parliament for Ashburton until 1852, when he became member of parliament for Ross and Cromarty from 1852-1868. He became a baronet in 1851 and died peacefully in 1878 at the age of 82 in Mentone, France.

13 Now the National Museum of Singapore, where the 'Singapore Stone' can be seen today.

14 Two other uses of gutta percha were developed that created a substantial demand for the product, and eventually led to the foundation of the Gutta Percha Company in London by Henry Bewley, Charles Hancock and Charles Goodyear in 1845.

1n 1843 Thomas Morse used rubber to insulate his wire cable in a lead pipe that he ran across New York harbour. Although he found that the rubber worked well enough as an insulator, he also found that it quickly deteriorated underwater. Shortly after the British scientist Michael Faraday suggested that gutta percha could serve the same insulative function as rubber and would not suffer from water exposure. On his suggestion, gutta percha was used to insulate the telegraph cables laid in the English Channel to connect Dover and Calais, and throughout the nineteenth century the primary use of the substance was for the insulation of telegraph and submarine cables. Reflecting this trend, the Gutta Percha Company eventually became the Telegraph Construction and Maintenance Company.

In 1845 the Reverend Dr Robert Adams Patterson created the first 'gutta' golf ball at Carnoustie in Scotland, by hand rolling balls from lumps of gutta percha latex that had been softened in boiling water. These quickly replaced the older wooden balls and the more expensive leather balls stuffed with chicken and goose feathers. The introduction of 'gutta' balls transformed the game, since they dramatically reduced the price of golf balls, which made the game more affordable to the general population. When it was accidentally discovered that nicked balls flew truer than smooth balls, manufacturers cast gutta balls in metal moulds that produced markings on the balls, which soon replaced the older smoother balls.

15 Charles Andrew Dyce (1816 – 1853) was born in Aberdeen and came to Singapore in 1842. During his time in South East Asia he produced sepia and watercolour paintings of Singapore and Malaysia. *The Charles Dyce Collection* is now housed in the National University of Singapore Museum.

16 Henry Keppel was born on June 14, 1809, the son of William Charles Keppel, the Fourth Earl of Albemarle and his wife Elizabeth, the daughter of Edward Southwell, the 20th Baron de Clifford.

Keppel entered the Royal Naval Academy at Portsmouth in 1822 at the age of thirteen, and after graduation his promotion was swift in the Royal Navy. His first command was off the coast of Spain during the First Carlist war, after which he spent some time engaged in the suppression of the slave trade on the West Coast of Africa.

17 Benjamin Peach Keasberry was born in Hyderabad, India in 1811. His father, who was a colonel in the Indian Army, died when he was three years old. His mother married a local merchant, Mr Davidson, and Keasberry spent his early years at boarding schools in Mauritius and Madras. He started a business in Singapore in the late 1820s, but it failed, and he worked for a while as a clerk in Batavia. There he met Dr Medhurst of the London Missionary Society, when he applied to become an assistant missionary. Dr Medhurst had founded the London Missionary Society Press in Shanghai some years earlier, and during the years he lived with Dr Medhurst in Batavia, Keasberry learned the skills of printing, bookbinding and lithography.

In 1834, at the age of 23, Keasberry received some money from his stepfather's estate, which enabled him to complete three years of college in the United States. There he met Miss Charlotte Parker, the daughter of a Boston vicar, and they were married the following year. The couple left Boston in 1837 as Missionaries to the Malays, under the auspices of the American Board of Commissions for Foreign Missionaries.

18 James Legge was the youngest of seven children of an Aberdeen merchant. Born in Huntly on December 20, 1815, he was educated at Aberdeen Grammar School and Kings College Aberdeen. After theological study in London, where he was ordained as a Congregationalist Minister, Legge set off for China as a missionary in 1839. But he stayed over in Malacca for four years, where he served as principal of the Anglo-Chinese College. In 1843 he was appointed principal of the Protestant Theological Seminary in Hong Kong.

Some of Legge's former students followed him to Hong Kong. Song Hoot Kiam, the second son of Song Eng Chong of Malacca, had been a boarder at the Anglo-Chinese College from age eleven to thirteen. When the family moved to Singapore, the Reverend Alexander Stronach came to learn that Hoot Kiam and another former boarder, Lee Kim Yin, were anxious to continue their studies with Dr Legge, and arranged for them to travel to Hong Kong at Dr Legge's expense. When Dr Legge returned to Scotland on furlough from 1845-1846, he took Hoot Kiam and and Lee Kim Yim with him. During these years the boys were educated at the Duchess of Gordon's School in Huntly (some twenty-eight miles from the author's home town).

In later years Song Hoot Kiam returned to Singapore, first as a teacher and then as a cashier for the P & O Steam Navigation Company. One of his sons was Song Ong Siang, a Cambridge trained lawyer, who made significant contributions to the Chinese community in Singapore. The author of *One Hundred Years' History of the Chinese in Singapore (1923)*, Song Ong Siang served as a member of Singapore's legislative council and was knighted by George V in 1936.

19 Father Imbert had been appointed bishop in Korea, where the local Catholic converts were threatened with execution. He wrote to the missionary fathers Chasten and Maubant asking them to surrender themselves in the hope that their action might placate the authorities and save their converts. He reminded them that 'in desperate circumstances the Good Shepherd is the one who lays down his life for his sheep.' But all three men had been tortured and beheaded along with their converts.

20 The Institute of the Brothers of the Christian Schools was founded by Father John Baptist de la Salle in the seventeenth century. He renounced his wealth and position as canon of the cathedral at Rheims to form a community of lay teachers dedicated to bringing religious and vocational instruction to the children of the poor,

which came to be known as the De La Salle Brothers. Throughout the eighteenth century their mission was confined to France, but in the nineteenth century the brothers began to expand overseas, and Father Beurel hoped that they would be willing to establish a school in Singapore.

21 The order was created by Father Nicolas Barré, a Minim priest, in 1662. He recruited educated young women to run a school for the poor in Rouen, which was so successful that he established other schools throughout France, which eventually combined to form a religious congregation devoted to the education of the poor. The Congregation of the Sisters of the Holy Infant Jesus was formally established in 1666, with each school within the congregation headed by a Mother Superior. The order continued to expand after Father Barré's death in 1686, and eventually achieved full pontifical approval in 1866. During the office of the Reverend Mother de Faudoas (1837-1877), the order expanded its mission to America, the Mediterranean and the Far East.

22 John Brooke Johnson was born in South Stoke, near Bath in 1823, the son of James Brooke's elder sister, Emma Frances Brooke. He served in the British army from 1839 to 1848, rising to the rank of captain. After he left the army, he changed his surname to Brooke before joining his uncle in Sarawak. Since he was known as Brooke Johnson before the change, he came to be known as Brooke Brooke.

23 Alfred Russel Wallace was born in the village of Llanbadoc in Wales on January 8, 1823. At the age of fourteen he moved to London to work with his older brother William as an apprentice surveyor, where he also attended the London Mechanics Institute. When his brother's business declined in 1843, Wallace left and secured employment as a master at the Collegiate School in Leicester.

There he met Henry Bates, a taxonomist who got him interested in collecting insects; Bates had already published a paper on beetles in the journal *Zoologist*. After a failed attempt to revive his brother's business after his death in 1845, and a few years working for an architectural firm, in 1848 Wallace agreed to join Henry Bates on an expedition to the Amazon rainforest.

Initially Bates and Wallace worked together, but eventually they went their separate ways. Wallace spent most of his time exploring Rio Negro, the largest black water tributary of the Amazon. He spent six years collecting a mass of specimens, making notes and sketches of the local flora and fauna, and recording information about the local tribes and their languages. In July 1852 he set off for home with his collection aboard the *Helen*, eager to establish his reputation as a naturalist when he displayed his specimens and published his findings. He hoped that his work would be sufficiently worthy to justify his election as a Fellow of the Royal Society, or at least the Geographical Society.

His hopes were dashed when the *Helen* caught fire three weeks out, and Wallace lost all of his collection save for a few notebooks and sketches. He almost lost his life as well, for he and the surviving crew members drifted in an open longboat for ten days in shark-infested waters, until the *Jordeson* rescued them. Fortunately, Wallace had the foresight to insure his cargo, and for the next year and a half he lived off his insurance settlement in London. During this period, he managed to write six academic papers, which were favourably received, and two books documenting his travels in South America.

24 The Chinese Chamber of Commerce was finally founded in 1906.

25 Charles Johnson, born in Somerset on June 3, 1829, was

a younger son of James' older sister, Emma Frances Brooke. After serving in the Royal Navy, during which time he was transferred to support Brooke and Keppel's expedition against the Skrang pirates, he joined his uncle's service in 1852.

26   Army founded by Zeng Guofan from local militias and financed by local nobles and gentry.

Other books in the Singapore Saga

Forbidden Hill (Vol. 1)

On 6 February 1819, Stamford Raffles, William Farquhar, Temenggong Abdul Rahman and Sultan Hussein sign a treaty that grants the British East India Company the right to establish a trading settlement on the sparsely populated island of Singapore. While Raffles and Farquhar clash over the administration of the settlement, the Scottish merchant adventurer Ronnie Simpson and Englishwoman Sarah Hemmings find love and redemption as they battle an American duellist and Illanun pirates.

Hungry Ghosts (Vol. 3)

Hungry Ghosts continues the vivid portrayal of the lives of the early pioneers of Singapore, set against the backdrop of the Indian Mutiny, the Second Opium War and the last years of the Taiping rebellion. A female refugee from the Taiping rebellion is kidnapped in Amoy and sold as a concubine in Singapore; an enterprising Indian convict converts his training as a metalworker into the more lucrative business of counterfeiting; an English wife escapes a loveless marriage with a Confederate lieutenant when the 'ghost-ship' CSS *Alabama* puts into Singapore; a secret-society soldier spends a terror-filled night in the ten courts of hell; Duncan Simpson meets with the Taiping Heavenly King, Hong Xiuquin, in Nanking, and discovers his destiny when he joins Lord Elgin's expeditionary force on its final assault on the Chinese capital Peking. As the fates and fortunes of its protagonists play themselves out, Singapore celebrates the fiftieth anniversary of its founding.